OLD DREAD RETURNS

A shadow fell across the circle. A creature of nightmare loomed. It wore the shape of a man and a man might have lurked within that chitinous armor. Or might have not.

"Ma!" Lang shrieked. With club foot and half an arm he wasn't hard to catch.

Four more giants entered the clearing. They bore naked, long black swords with razor edges and tips that glowed red hot.

"Oh Gods," the woman moaned. "They've found me."

Berkley books by Glen Cook

DREAD EMPIRE SERIES

A SHADOW OF ALL NIGHT FALLING
OCTOBER'S BABY
ALL DARKNESS MET

All Darkness Met

Third in the haunting Dread Empire series by
GLEN COOK

BERKLEY BOOKS, NEW YORK

ALL DARKNESS MET

A Berkley Book / published by arrangement with
the author

PRINTING HISTORY
Berkley edition / June 1980
Second printing / February 1984

ISBN: 0-425-06541-3

A BERKLEY BOOK® TM 757,375
The name "BERKLEY" and the stylized "B" with design
are trademarks belonging to Berkley Publishing Corporation.
PRINTED IN THE UNITED STATES OF AMERICA

All Darkness Met

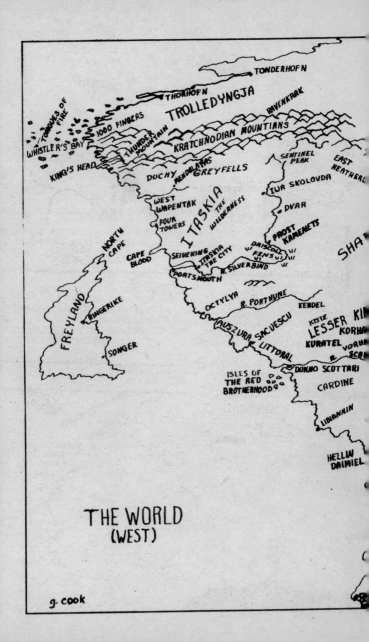

THE WORLD
(WEST)

g. cook

MOUNTAINS OF M'HAND

HIGH GALMICHE

LONCARIC

LOW GALMICHE

•Timpe

WERNECKE

BREITENBACH

SAVERNAKE

Baronodale

Maisak

ROHRWASTE

ECHTENACHE

MOERSCHEL

VORDREBERG
Gudbrandsdal
Forest

FAHRIG

FORBECK

UHLMANSIEK

TRAUTWEIN

ORTHWEIN

KAPENRUNG MOUNTAINS

KAVELIN
and neighboring
Kingdoms

HAMMAD AL NAKIR

g. COOK

CONTENTS

CHAPTER ONE: The Years 980—989 After
the Founding of the Empire of Ilkazar;
O Shing, Ehelebe   1
CHAPTER TWO: Spring, 1010 AFE; Mocker   13
CHAPTER THREE: Spring, 1010 AFE;
Old Friends   24
CHAPTER FOUR: Spring, 1011 AFE;
Intimations   36
CHAPTER FIVE: Spring, 1011 AFE;
A Traveler in Black   45
CHAPTER SIX: Spring, 1011 AFE;
The Attack   51
CHAPTER SEVEN: Spring, 1011 AFE;
The Old Dread Returns   61
CHAPTER EIGHT: Winter—Spring, 1011
AFE; The Prisoner   70
CHAPTER NINE: Spring, 1011 AFE;
A Short Journey   79
CHAPTER TEN: The Years 989—1004 AFE;
Lord of Lords   87
CHAPTER ELEVEN: Spring, 1011 AFE;
Marshall and Queen   100
CHAPTER TWELVE: Spring, 1011 AFE;
The Stranger in Hammerfest   109
CHAPTER THIRTEEN: Spring, 1011 AFE;
Regency   115
CHAPTER FOURTEEN: Spring, 1011 AFE;
Lady of Mystery   123
CHAPTER FIFTEEN: Spring, 1011 AFE; The
Stranger's Appointment   133
CHAPTER SIXTEEN: Spring, 1011 AFE;
Deaths and Disappearances   138
CHAPTER SEVENTEEN: Spring—Summer,
1011 AFE; Michael's Adventure   148
CHAPTER EIGHTEEN: Spring, 1011 AFE;
The Unborn   161

CHAPTER NINETEEN: Summer, 1011 AFE;
  Funerals and Assassins   169
CHAPTER TWENTY: The Years 1004—1011
  AFE; The Dragon Emperor   177
CHAPTER TWENTY-ONE: Summer, 1011
  AFE; The King Is Dead. Long Live the King   189
CHAPTER TWENTY-TWO: Summer, 1011
  AFE; Eye of the Storm   195
CHAPTER TWENTY-THREE: Summer, 1011
  AFE; The Hidden Kingdom   204
CHAPTER TWENTY-FOUR: Summer, 1011
  AFE; Kavelin A-March   211
CHAPTER TWENTY-FIVE: Summer, 1011
  AFE; The Assault on Argon   221
CHAPTER TWENTY-SIX: Summer, 1011
  AFE; Battle for the Fadem   229
CHAPTER TWENTY-SEVEN: Summer, 1011
  AFE; Mocker Returns   238
CHAPTER TWENTY-EIGHT: Summer, 1011
  AFE; A Friendly Assassin   249
CHAPTER TWENTY-NINE: Winter,
  1011—1012 AFE; A Dark Stranger
  in the Kingdom of Dread   261
CHAPTER THIRTY: Summer, 1011—Winter,
  1012 AFE; The Other Side   267
CHAPTER THIRTY-ONE: Spring, 1012
  AFE; Baxendala Redux   271
CHAPTER THIRTY-TWO: Spring—Summer—
  Autumn, 1012 AFE; Defeat.
  Defeat. Defeat.   284
CHAPTER THIRTY-THREE: Winter, 1012—
  Spring, 1013 AFE; Itaskia   291
CHAPTER THIRTY-FOUR: Spring, 1013
  AFE; The Road to Palmisano   301
CHAPTER THIRTY-FIVE: Spring, 1013
  AFE; Palmisano: The Guttering Flame   312
CHAPTER THIRTY-SIX: Spring, 1013
  AFE; Home   318

ONE: O Shing, Ehelebe

The woman screamed with every contraction. The demon outside howled and clawed at the walls. It roared like a wounded elephant, smashed against the door. The timbers groaned.

The physician, soaked with perspiration, shook like a trapped rabbit. His skin was the hue of death.

"Get on with it!" snarled the baby's father.

"Lord! . . ."

"Do it!" Nu Li Hsi appeared undisturbed by the siege. He refused even to acknowledge the *possibility* of fear, in himself or those who served him. Would-be Lord of All Shinsan, he dared reveal nothing the Tervola could call weakness.

Still the physician delayed. He was hopelessly trapped. He couldn't win. A demon was trying to shatter the sorceries shielding his surgery. Inside, his master was in a rage because the mother couldn't deliver normally. The child was just too huge. The woman was a friend, and the surgeon doubted she could survive the operation. The only assistant permitted him was his daughter. No fourteen-year-old was ready to face this.

Worse, there were witnesses. Two Tervola leaned against one wall. These sorcerer-generals, who managed Shinsan's armies and made up her nobility, were waiting to see the product of the Dragon Prince's experiments.

The goal was a child who could develop into a superstrong, supercompetent soldier, thinking, yet with little ability to become a personality in his own right, and immune to the magicks by which foes seized control of enemy soldiers.

"Start cutting," Nu Li Hsi said softly, with the "or else" transmitted by intonation, "before my brother's attacks become more imaginative."

For a millennium Nu Li Hsi and his twin, Yo Hsi, had battled

1

for mastery of Shinsan, virtually from the moment they had murdered Tuan Hoa, their father, who had been Shinsan's founder.

"Scalpel," said the surgeon. He could scarcely be heard. He glanced around the cramped surgery. The Tervola, with their masks and robes, could have been statues. Nu Li Hsi himself moved nothing but his eyes. His face, though, was naked. The Princes Thaumaturge felt no need to hide behind masks. The surgeon could read the continuing anger there.

The Dragon Prince, he realized, expected failure.

This was the Prince's eleventh try using his own seed. Ten failures had preceded it. They had become reflections on his virility....

The surgeon opened the woman's belly.

A half hour later he held up the child. This one, at least, was a son, and alive.

Nu Li Hsi stepped closer. "The arm. It didn't develop. And the foot...." A quieter, more dangerous anger possessed him now, an anger brought on by repeated failure. What use was a superhuman soldier with a clubfoot and no shield arm?

That wounded elephant roar sounded again. Masonry shifted. Dust fell. Torches and candles wavered. The walls threatened to burst inward. The door groaned again and again. Splinters flew.

Nu Li Hsi showed concern for the first time. "He *is* persistent, isn't he?" He asked the Tervola, "Feed it?"

They nodded.

The Tervola, second only to the Princes Thaumaturge themselves, seldom became involved in the skirmishes of Shinsan's co-rulers. If the *thing* broke the barriers contiguous with the room's boundaries, though, it would respect neither allegiances, nor their lack. Yo Hsi would make restitution to the surviving Tervola, expressing regrets that their fellows had been caught in the cross fire.

The Dragon Prince produced a golden dagger. Jet enamel characters ran its length. The Tervola seized the woman's hands and feet. Nu Li Hsi drove the blade into her breast, slashing, sawing, ripping. He plunged a hand into the wound, grabbed, pulled with the skill of long practice. In a moment he held up the still throbbing heart. Blood ran up his arm and spattered his clothing.

The screams of the doctor's daughter replaced those of the sacrifice.

From outside, suddenly, absolute silence. The thing, for the moment, was mollified.

No one who hadn't been in the room would know that it had been there. The spells shielding the walls weren't barriers against things of this world, but of worlds beyond, Outside.

Nu Li Hsi sighed resignedly. "So.... I have to try again. I know I can do it. It works on paper." He started to leave.

"Lord!" the surgeon cried.

"What?"

The doctor indicated woman and child. "What should I do?" The child lived. It was the first of the experimental infants to survive birth.

"Dispose of them."

"He's your son...." His words tapered into inaudibility before his master's rage. Nu Li Hsi had serpent eyes. There was no mercy in them. "I'll take care of it, Lord."

"See that you do."

As soon as the Dragon Prince vanished, the surgeon's daughter whispered, "Father, you can't."

"I must. You heard him."

"But...."

"You know the alternative."

She knew. She was a child of the Dread Empire.

But she was barely fourteen, with the folly of youth everywhere. In fact, she was doubly foolish.

She had already made the worst mistake girls her age could make. She had become pregnant.

That night she made a second mistake. It would be more dire. It would echo through generations.

She fled with the newborn infant.

One by one, over an hour, six men drifted into the room hidden beneath The Yellow-Eyed Dragon restaurant. No one upstairs knew who they were, for they had arrived in ordinary dress, faces bare, and had donned black robes and jeweled beast masks only after being out of sight in a room at the head of the basement stair.

Even Lin Feng, The Dragon's manager, didn't know who was meeting. He *did* know that he had been paid well. In response he made sure each guest had his full ten minutes alone, to dress, before the next was admitted to the intervening room.

Feng supposed them conspirators of some sort.

Had he known they were Tervola he would have fainted. Barring the Princes Thaumaturge themselves, the Tervola were the most powerful, most cruel men in all Shinsan, with Hell's mightiest devils running at their heels....

Waking, following his faint, Feng probably would have taken his own life. These Tervola could be conspiring against no one but the Princes Thaumaturge themselves. Which made him a rat in the jaws of the cruelest fate of all.

But Feng suspected nothing. He performed his part without trepidation.

The first to arrive was a man who wore a golden mask resembling both cat and gargoyle, chased with fine black lines, with rubies for eyes and fangs. He went over the chamber carefully, making sure there would be no unauthorized witnesses. While the others arrived and waited in silence, he worked a thaumaturgy that would protect the meeting from the most skilled sorcerous eavesdroppers. When he finished, the room was invisible even to the all-seeing eyes of the Princes Thaumaturge themselves.

The sixth arrived. The man in the gargoyle mask said, "The others won't be with us tonight."

His fellows didn't respond. They simply waited to learn why they had been summoned.

The Nine seldom met. The eyes and spies of the Princes and uninitiated Tervola were everywhere.

"We have to make a decision." The speaker called himself Chin, though his listeners weren't sure he was the Chin they knew outside. Only he knew their identities. They overlooked no precaution in their efforts to protect themselves.

Again the five did not respond. If they didn't speak they couldn't recognize one another by voice.

It was a dangerous game they played, for imperial stakes.

"I have located the woman. The child's still with her. The question: Do we proceed as planned? I know the minds of those who can't be with us. Two were for, one was against. Show hands if you still agree."

Four hands rose.

"Seven for. We proceed, then." Behind ruby eyepieces Chin's

eyes sparkled like ice under an angry sun. They fixed on the sole dissenter present.

A link in the circle was weakening. Chin had misjudged the man behind the boar mask. The absentee negative vote he understood, accepted, and dismissed. Fear hadn't motivated it. But the Boar.... The man was terrified. He might break.

The stakes were too high to take unnecessary chances.

Chin made a tiny sign. It would be recognized by only one man.

He had convened the Nine not for the vote but to test the Boar. He had learned enough. His decision was made.

"Disperse. The usual rules."

They didn't question, though meeting for so little seemed tempting Fate too much. They departed one by one, reversing the process of entry, till only Chin and the man who had been signaled remained.

"Ko Feng, our friend the Boar grows dangerous," Chin said. "His nerve is failing. He'll run to one of the Princes soon."

Ko Feng, behind a bear mask, had presented the argument before. "The cure?" he asked.

"Go ahead. What must be, must be."

Behind the metal Bear, cruel lips stretched in a thin smile.

"He's Shan, of the Twelfth Legion. Go now. Do it quickly. He could spill his terror any time."

The Bear bowed slightly, almost mockingly, and departed.

Chin paused thoughtfully, staring after him. The Bear, too, was dangerous. He was another mistake. Ko Feng was too narrow, too hasty. He might need removing, too. He was the most ambitious, most deadly, most coldhearted and cruel, not just of the Nine, but of the Tervola. He was a long-run liability, though useful now.

Chin began to consider possible replacements for the Boar.

The Nine were old in their conspiracy. Long had they awaited their moment. For centuries each had been selecting eight subordinates carefully, choosing only men who could remain loyal to the ultimate extremity and who would, themselves, build their own Nines with equal care.

Chin's First Nine had existed for three hundred years. In all that time the organization had grown downward only to the fourth level.

Which was, in truth, a fifth level. There was a higher Nine

than Chin's, though only he knew. Similar ignorance persisted in each subsidiary Nine.

Soon after the Bear's departure Chin faced another door. It was so well concealed that it had evaded the notice of the others.

It opened. A man stepped through. He was small and old and bent, but his eyes were young, mischievous, and merry. He was in his element here, conspiring in the grand manner. "Perfect, my friend. Absolutely perfect. It proceeds. It won't be long now. A few decades. But be careful with Nu Li Hsi. He should be given information that will help us, yet not so much that he suspects he's being used. It's not yet time for the Nines to become visible."

Chin knew this man only as the master of his own Nine, the world-spanning Master Nine, the Pracchia. Chin, perhaps, should have paid more attention to the old man and less to his problems with his own Nine. Evidence of the man's true identity was available, had he but looked for it.

"And the child?" Chin asked.

"It's not yet his time. He'll be protected by The Hidden Kingdom."

That name was a mystery of the Circle of which Chin was junior member. Ehelebe. The Hidden Kingdom. The Power behind all Powers. Already the Pracchia secretly ruled a tenth of the world. Someday, once the might of Shinsan became its tool, Ehelebe would control the entire world.

"He'll be prepared for the day."

"It is well."

Chin kept his eyes downcast, though the ruby eyepieces of his mask concealed them. Like the Bear, he had his reservations and ambitions. He hoped he hid them better than did Ko Feng.

"Farewell, then." The bent old man returned to his hiding place wearing an amused smile.

Moments later a winged horse took flight from behind The Yellow-Eyed Dragon, coursed across the moon into the mysteries of the night.

"Lang! Tam!" she called. "Come eat."

The boys glanced from their clay marbles to the crude hut, crossed gazes. Lang bent to shoot again.

"Lang! Tam! You come here right now!"

The boys sighed, shrugged, gathered their marbles. It was a

conundrum. Mothers, from the dawn of time, never had understood the importance of finishing the game.

There in the Yan-lin Kuo Forest, astride Shinsan's nebulous eastern border, they called her The Hag of The Wood even though she hadn't yet reached her twentieth birthday. With woodcutters and charcoal-burners she plied the ancient trade, and for their wives and daughters she crafted petty charms and wove weak spells. She was sufficiently tainted by the Power to perform simple magicks. Those and her sex were all she had.

Her sons entered the hut, Tam limping on his club foot.

The meal wasn't much. Boiled cabbage. No meat. But it was as good as the best forest people had. In Yan-lin Kuo the well-to-do looked at poverty from the belly side.

"Anybody home?"

"Tran!" Happiness illuminated the woman's face.

A youth of seventeen pushed inside, a rabbit dangling from his left hand. A tall man, he swept her into the bow of his right arm, planted a kiss on her cheek. "And how are you boys?"

Lang and Tam grinned.

Tran wasn't of the majority race of Shinsan. The forest people, who had been under Dread Empire suzerainty for a historically brief time, had a more mahogany cast of skin, yet racially were akin to the whites of the west. Culturally they were ages behind either, having entered the Iron Age solely by virtue of trade. In their crude way they were as cruel as their rulers.

Of his people Tran was the sole person for whom the woman felt anything. And her feelings were reciprocated. There was an unspoken understanding: they would eventually marry.

Tran was a woodsman and trapper. He always provided for the Hag, asking nothing in return. And consequently received more than any who paid.

The boys were young, but they knew about men and women. They gobbled cabbage, then abandoned the hut.

They resumed their game. Neither gained much advantage.

A shadow fell across the circle. Tam looked up.

A creature of nightmare loomed over Lang. It wore the shape of a man, and a man might have lurked within that chitinous black armor. Or a devil. There was no visible evidence either way.

He was huge, six inches taller than Tran, the tallest man Tam knew. He was heavier of build.

He stared at Tam for several seconds, then gestured.

"Lang," Tam said softly.

Four more giants entered the clearing, silently as death by night. Were they human? Even their faces were concealed behind masks showing crystal squares where eyeholes should be.

Lang stared.

These four bore naked, long black swords with razor edges and tips that glowed red hot.

"Ma!" Lang shrieked, scampering toward the hut.

Tam shrieked, "Monsters!" and pursued Lang.

With club foot and half an arm he wasn't much of a runner. The first giant caught him easily.

The Hag and Tran burst from the hut. Lang scooted round and clung to Tran's leg, head leaning against his mother's thigh.

Tam squirmed and squealed. The giant restrained him, and otherwise ignored him.

"Oh, Gods," the woman moaned. "They've found me." Tran seemed to know what she meant.

He selected a heavy stick from her woodpile.

Tam's captor passed him to one of his cohorts, drew his blade. Indigo-purple oil seemed to run its length. It swayed like a cobra about to strike.

"Tran, no. You can't stop them. Save yourself."

Tran moved toward the giant.

"Tran, please. Look at their badges. They're from the Imperial Standard. The Dragon sent them."

Sense gradually penetrated Tran's brain. He stood no chance against the least of Shinsan's soldiers. No one alive had much chance against men of the Imperial Standard Legion. That was no legion brag. These men had trained since their third birthdays. Fighting was their way of life, their religion. They had been chosen from Shinsan's healthiest, stoutest children. They were smart, and utterly without fear. Their confidence in their invincibility was absolute.

Tran could only get himself killed.

"Please, Tran. It's over. There's nothing you can do. I'm dead."

The hunter reflected. His thoughts were shaped by forest life. He decided.

Some might have called him coward. But Tran's people were realists. He would be useless to anyone hanging from a spike which had been driven into the base of his skull, while his entrails hung out and his hands and feet lay on the ground before him.

He grabbed Lang and ran.

No one pursued him.

He stopped running once he reached cover.

He watched.

The soldiers shed their armor.

They had to be following orders. They didn't rape and plunder like foreign barbarians. They did what they were told, and only what they were told, and their service was reward enough.

The woman's screams ripped the afternoon air.

They didn't kill Tam, just made him watch.

In all things there are imponderables, intangibles, and unpredictables. The most careful plan cannot account for every minuscule factor. The greatest necromancer cannot divine precisely enough to define the future till it becomes predestined. In every human enterprise the planners and seers deal with and interpret only the things they know. Then they usually interpret incorrectly.

But, then, even the gods are fallible. For who created Man?

Some men call the finagle factor Fate.

The five who had gone to the Hag's hut became victims of the unpredictable.

Tam whimpered in their grasp, remembering the security of his mother's arms when wolf calls tormented the night and chill north winds whipped their little fire's flames. He remembered and wept. And he remembered the name Nu Li Hsi.

The forest straddled Shinsan's frontier with Han Chin, which was more a tribal territory than established state. The Han Chin generally tried not to attract attention, but sometimes lacked restraint.

There were a hundred raiders in the party which attacked the five. Forty-three didn't live to see home again. *That* was why the world so feared the soldiers of Shinsan.

The survivors took Tam with them believing anyone important to the legionnaires must be worth a ransom.

Nobody made an offer.

The Han Chin taught the boy fear. They made of him a slave and toy, and when it was their mood to amuse themselves with howls, they tortured him.

They didn't know who he was, but he was of Shinsan and helpless. That was enough.

There was a new man among those who met, though only he, Chin, and Ko Feng knew. It was ever thus with the Nines. Some came, some went. Few recognized the changes.

The conspiracy was immortal.

"There's a problem," Chin told his audience. "The Han Chin have captured our candidate. The western situation being tense, this places a question before the Nine."

Chin had had his instructions. "The Princes Thaumaturge have chivvied Varthlokkur till his only escape can be to set the west aflame. I suggest we suborn the scheme and assume it for our own, nudging at the right moment, till *it* can rid us of the Princes. Come. Gather round. I want to repeat a divination."

He worked with the deftness of centuries of experience, nursing clouds from a tiny brazier. They boiled up and turned in upon themsleves, not a wisp escaping. Tiny lightning bolts ripped through....

"Trela stri! Sen me stri!" Chin commanded. "Azzari an walla in walli stri!"

The cloud whispered in the same tongue. Chin gave instructions in his own language. "The fate, again, of the boy...."

That which lived beyond the cloud muttered something impatient.

It flicked over the past, showing them the familiar tale of Varthlokkur, and showed them that wizard's future, and the future of the boy who dwelt with the Han Chin. Nebulously. The thing behind the cloud could not, or would not, define the parameters.

There were those imponderables, intangibles, and unpredict-ables.

As one, Chin's associates sighed.

"The proposal before us is this: Do we concentrate on shaping these destinies to our advantage? For a time the west would demand our complete attention. The yield? Our goals achieved at a tenth the price anticipated."

The vote was unanimous.

Chin made a sign before the Nine departed.

The one who remained was different. Chin said, "Lord Wu,

you're our brother in the east. The boy will be your concern. Prepare him to assume his father's throne."

Wu bowed.

Once Wu departed, that secret door opened. "Excellent," said the bent old man. "Everything is going perfectly. I congratulate you. You're invaluable to the Pracchia. We'll call you to meet the others soon."

Chin's hidden eyes narrowed. His Nine-mask, arrogantly, merely reversed his Tervola mask. The others wore masks meant to conceal identities. Chin was mocking everyone....

Again the old man departed wearing a small, secretive smile.

Tam was nine when Shinsan invaded Han Chin. It was a brief little war, though bloody. A handful of sorcerer's apprentices guided legionnaires to the hiding places of the natives, who quickly died.

The man in the woods didn't understand.

For four years Tran had watched and waited. Now he moved. He seized Tam and fled to the cave where he lived with Lang.

The soldiers came next morning.

Tran wept. "It isn't fair," he whispered. "It just isn't fair." He prepared to die fighting.

A thin man in black, wearing a golden locust mask, entered the circle of soldiers. "This one?" He indicated Tam.

"Yes, Lord Wu."

Wu faced Tam, knelt. "Greetings, Lord." He used words meaning Lord of Lords. O Shing. It would become a title. "My Prince."

Tran, Lang, Tam stared. What insanity was this?

"Who are the others?" Wu asked, rising.

"The child of the woman, Lord. They believe themselves brothers. The other calls himself Tran. One of the forest people. The woman's lover. He protected the boy the best he could the past four years. A good and faithful man."

"Do him honor, then. Place him at O Shing's side." Again that Lord of Lords, so sudden and confusing.

Tran didn't relax.

Wu asked him, "You know me?"

"No."

"I am Wu, of the Tervola. Lord of Liaontung and Yan-lin Kuo, and now of Han Chin. My legion is the Seventeenth. The

Council has directed me to recover the son of the Dragon Prince."

Tran remained silent. He didn't trust himself. Tam looked from one man to the other.

"The boy with the handicaps. He's the child of Nu Li Hsi. The woman kidnapped him the day of his birth. Those who came before. . . . They were emissaries of his father."

Tran said nothing, though he knew the woman's tale.

Wu was impatient with resistance. "Disarm him," he ordered. "Bring him along."

The soldiers did it in an instant, then took the three to Wu's citadel at Liaontung.

TWO: Mocker

These things sometimes begin subtly. For Mocker it started when a dream came true.

Dream would become nightmare before week's end.

He had an invitation to Castle Krief. He. Mocker. The fat little brown man whose family lived in abject poverty in a Vorgreberg slum, who, himself, scrabbled for pennies on the fringes of the law. The invitation had so delighted him that he actually had swallowed his pride and allowed his friend the Marshall to loan him money.

He arrived at the Palace gate grinning from one plump brown ear to the other, his invitation clutched in one hand, his wife in the other.

"Self, am convinced old friend Bear gone soft behind eyes, absolute," he told Nepanthe. "Inviting worst of worse, self. Not so, wife of same, certitude. Hai! Maybeso, high places lonely. Pacificity like cancer, eating silent, sapping manhood. Calls in old friend of former time, hoping rejuvenation of spirit."

He had been all mouth since the invitation had come, though, briefly, he had been suicidally down. The Marshall of all Kavelin inviting somebody like him to the Victory Day celebrations? A mockery. It was some cruel joke....

"Quit bubbling and bouncing," his wife murmured. "Want them to think you're some drunken street rowdy?"

"Heart's Desire. Doe's Eyes. Is truth, absolute. Am same. Have wounds to prove same. Scars. Count them...."

She laughed. And thought, I'll give Bragi a hug that'll break his ribs.

It seemed ages since they had been this happy, an eon since laughter had tickled her tonsils and burst past her lips against any ability to control.

Fate hadn't been kind to them. Nothing Mocker tried

worked. Or, if it did, he would suffer paraxysms of optimism, begin gambling, *sure* he'd make a killing, and would lose everything.

Yet they had their love. They never lost that, even when luck turned its worst. Inside the tiny, triangular cosmos described by them and their son, an approach to perfection remained.

Physically, the years had treated Nepanthe well. Though forty-one, she still looked to be in her early thirties. The terrible cruelty of her poverty had ravaged her spirit more than her flesh.

Mocker was another tale. Most of his scars had been laid on by the fists and knives of enemies. He was indomitable, forever certain of his high destiny.

The guard at the Palace gate was a soldier of the new national army. The Marshall had been building it since his victory at Baxendala. The sentry was a polite young man of Wesson ancestry who needed convincing that at least one of them wasn't a party crasher.

"Where's your carriage?" he asked. "Everyone comes in a carriage."

"Not all of us can afford them. But my husband was one of the heroes of the war." Nepanthe did Mocker's talking when clarity was essential. "Isn't the invitation valid?"

"Yes. All right. He can go in. But who are you?" The woman before him as tall and pale and cool. Almost regal.

Nepanthe had, for this evening, summoned all the aristocratic bearing that had been hers before she had been stricken by love for the madman she had married. . . . Oh, it seemed ages ago, now.

"His wife. I said he was my husband."

The soldier had all a Kaveliner's ethnic consciousness. His surprise showed.

"Should we produce marriage papers? Or would you rather he went and brought the Marshall to vouch for me?" Her voice was edged with sarcasm that cut like razors. She could make of words lethal weapons.

Mocker just stood there grinning, shuffling restlessly.

The Marshall did have strange friends. The soldier had been with the Guard long enough to have seen several stranger than these. He capitulated. He was only a trooper. He didn't get paid to think. Somebody would throw them out if they didn't belong.

And, in the opinion locked behind his teeth, they pleased him

more than some of the carriage riders he had admitted earlier.
Some of those were men whose throats he would have cut gladly.
Those two from Hammad al Nakir. . . . They were ambassadors
of a nation which cheerfully would have devoured his little
homeland.

They had more trouble at the citadel door, but the Marshall
had foreseen it. His aide appeared, vouchsafed their entry.

It grated a little, but Nepanthe held her tongue.

Once, if briefly, she had been mistress of a kingdom where
Kavelin would have made but a modest province.

Mocker didn't notice. "Dove's Breast. Behold. Inside of
Royal Palace. And am invited. Self. Asked in. In time past, have
been to several, dragged in bechained, or breaked—broked—
whatever word is for self-instigated entry for purpose of
burgurgalry, or even invited round to back-alley door to discuss
deed of dastardness desired done by denizen of same. Invited?
As honored guest? Never."

The Marshall's aide, Gjerdrum Eanredson, laughed, slapped
the fat man's shoulder. "You just don't change, do you? Six,
seven years it's been. You've got a little grey there, and maybe
more tummy, but I don't see a whit's difference in the man
inside." He eyed Nepanthe. There was, briefly, that in his eye
which said he appreciated what he saw.

"But you've changed, Gjerdrum," she said, and the lilt of her
voice told him his thoughts had been divined. "What happened
to that shy boy of eighteen?"

Gjerdrum's gaze flicked to Mocker, who was bemused by the
opulence of his surroundings, to the deep plunge of her bodice,
to her eyes. Without thinking he wet his lips with his tongue and,
red-faced, stammered, "I guess he growed up. . . ."

She couldn't resist teasing him, flirting. As he guided them to
the great hall she asked leading questions about his marital
status and which of the court ladies were his mistresses. She had
him thoroughly flustered when they arrived.

Nepanthe held this moment in deep dread. She had even tried
to beg off. But now a thrill coursed through her. She was glad
she had come. She pulled a handful of long straight black hair
forward so it tumbled down her bare skin, drawing the eye and
accenting her cleavage.

For a while she felt nineteen again.

The next person she recognized was the Marshall's wife,

Elana, who was waiting near the door. For an instant Nepanthe
was afraid. This woman, who once had been her best friend,
might not be pleased to see her.

But, "Nepanthe!" The red-haired woman engulfed her in an
embrace that banished all misgivings.

Elana loosed her and repeated the display with Mocker.
"God, Nepanthe, you look good. How do you do it? You haven't
aged a second."

"Skilled artificer, self, magician of renown, having at hand
secret of beauty of women of fallen Escalon, most beautiful of all
time before fall, retaining light of teenage years into fifth decade,
provide potations supreme against ravishes—ravages?—of
Time," Mocker announced solemnly—then burst into laughter.
He hugged Elana back, cunningly grasping a handful of
derriere, then skipped round her in a mad, whirling little dance.

"It's him," Elana remarked. "For a minute I didn't recognize
him. He had his mouth shut. Come on. Come on. Bragi will be so
glad to see you again."

Time hadn't used Elana cruelly either. Only a few grey wisps
threaded her coppery hair, and, despite having borne many
children, her figure remained reasonably trim. Nepanthe
remarked on it.

"True artifice, that," Elana confessed. "None of your
hedge-wizard mumbo jumbo. These clothes—they come all the
way from Sacuescu. The Queen's father sends them with hers.
He has hopes for his next visit." She winked. "They push me up
here, flatten me here, firm me up back there. I'm a mess
undressed." Though she tried valiantly to conceal it, Elana's
words expressed a faint bitterness.

"Time is great enemy of all," Mocker observed. "Greatest evil
of all. Devours all beauty. Destroys all hope." In his words, too,
there was attar of wormwood. "Is Eater, Beast That Lies
Waiting. Ultimate Destroyer." He told the famous riddle.

There were people all around them now, nobles of Kavelin,
Colonels of the Army and Mercenaries' Guild, and representa-
tives from the diplomatic community. Merriment infested the
hall. Men who were deadly enemies the rest of the year shared in
the celebration as though they were dear friends—because they
had shared hardship under the shadow of the wings of Death
that day long ago when they had set aside their contentiousness
and presented a common front to the Dread Empire—and had
defeated the invincible.

There were beautiful women there, too, women the like of which Mocker knew only in dreams. Of all the evidences of wealth and power they impressed him most.

"Scandalous" he declared. "Absolute. Desolution overtakes. Decadence descends. Sybariticism succeeds. O Sin, thy Name is Woman. . . . Self, will strive bravely, but fear containment of opinion will be impossible of provision. May rise to speechify same, castrating—no, castigating—assembly for wicked life. Shame!" He leered at a sleek, long-haired blonde who, simply by existing, turned his spine to jelly. Then he faced his wife, grinning. "Remember passage in *Wizards of Ilkazar*, in list of sins of same? Be great fundament for speech, eh? No?"

Nepanthe smiled and shook her head. "I don't think this's the place. Or the time. They might think you're serious."

"Money here. Look. Self, being talker of first water, spins web of words. In this assemblage famous law of averages declares must exist one case of foolheadedness. Probably twenty-three. Hai! More. Why not? Think big. Self, being student primus of way of spider, pounce. Ensnare very gently, unlike spider, and, also unlike same, drain very slow."

Elana, too, shook her head. "Hasn't changed a bit. Not at all. Nepanthe, you've got to tell me all about it. What have you been doing? How's Ethrian? Do you know how much trouble it was to find you? Valther used half his spies. Had them looking everywhere. And there you were in the Siluro quarter all the time. Why didn't you keep in touch?"

At that moment the Marshall, Bragi Ragnarson, spied them. He spared Nepanthe an answer.

"Mocker!" he thundered, startling half the hall into silence. He abandoned the lords he had been attending. "Yah! Lard Bottom!" He threw a haymaker. The fat man ducked and responded with a blur of a kick that swept the big man's feet from beneath him.

Absolute silence gripped the hall. Nearly three hundred men, plus servants and women, stared.

Mocker extended a hand. And shook his head as he helped the Marshall rise. "Self, must confess to one puzzlement. One only, and small. But is persistent as buzzing of mosquito."

"What's that?" Ragnarson, standing six-five, towered over the fat man.

"This one tiny quandary. Friend Bear, ever clumsy, unable to defend self from one-armed child of three, is ever chosen by great ones to defend same from foes of mighty competence. Is poser. Sorcery? Emboggles mind of self."

"Could be. But you've got to admit I'm lucky."

"Truth told." He said it sourly, and didn't expand. Luck, Mocker believed, was his nemesis. The spiteful hag had taken a dislike to him the moment of his birth.... But his day was coming. The good fortune was piling up. When it broke loose....

In truth, luck had less to do with his misfortunes than did compulsive gambling and an ironhard refusal to make his way up any socially acceptable means.

This crude little brown man, from the worst slum of the Siluro ghetto, had had more fortunes rush through his fingers than most of the lords present. Once he had actually laid hands on the fabled treasure of Ilkazar. \

He wouldn't invest. He refused. Someday, he knew, the dice would fall his way.

The fat man's old friend, with whom, in younger days, he had enjoyed adventures that would've frightened their present companions bald, guided him onto the raised platform from which his approach had been spotted. Mocker began shaking. A moment's clowning, down there, was embarrassing enough. But to be dragged before the multitudes....

He barely noticed the half dozen men who shared the dais with the Marshall. One eyed him as would a man who spotted someone he thinks he recognizes after decades.

"Quiet!" Ragnarson called. "A little quiet here!"

While the amused-to-disgusted chatter died, Mocker considered his friend's apparel. So rich. Fur-edged cape. Blouse of silk. Hose that must cost more than *he* scrounged in a month.... He remembered when this man had worn bearskins.

Once silence gained a hold, Ragnarson announced, "Ladies and gentlemen, I want to introduce somebody. A man I tracked down at considerable inconvenience and expense because he's the critical element that has been missing from our Victory Day celebrations. He was one of the unspoken heroes who guided us up the road to Baxendala, one of the men whose quiet pain and sacrifice made victory possible." Ragnarson held Mocker's hand high. "Ladies and gentlemen, I give you the world's foremost authority."

Puzzled, the ambassador from Altea asked, "Authority on what?"

Ragnarson grinned, punched Mocker's arm. "Everything."

Mocker had never been one to remain embarrassed long. Especially by public acclaim. He had forever been his own greatest booster. But here, because he had a predisposition to expect it, he suspected he was being mocked. He flashed his friend a look of appeal.

Which, despite years of separation, Ragnarson read. Softly, he replied, "No. I didn't bring you here for that. This's a homecoming. A debut. Here's an audience. Take them."

The wicked old grin seared the fat man's face. He turned to the crowd, fearing them no more. They would be his toys. Boldly, insolently, he examined the people nearest the dais. The merry mayhem in his eyes sparkled so that each of them recognized it. Most perked to a higher level of gaiety ere he spoke a word.

He founded the speech on the passage from the epic, and spoke with such joy, such laughter edging his voice, that hardly anyone resented being roasted.

The years had taught him something. He was no longer indiscreet. Though his tongue rolled inspiredly, in a high, mad babble that made the chandeliers rattle with the responding laughter, he retained sufficient command of his inspiration that, while he accused men of every dark deed under the sun, he never indicted anyone for something whispered to be true.

In the Siluro quarter, where dwelt the quiet little men who performed the drudgework of civil service and the mercantile establishments, there were a few secrets about the mighty.

He finished with a prophecy not unlike that of the poet. Punctuation, hellfire and brimstone.

And envoi, "Choice is clear. Recant. Renounce high living. Shed sybaritic ways. Place all burden of sin on one able to bear up under curse of same." He paused to meet eyes, including those of the sleek blonde twice. Then, softly, seriously, "Self, would volunteer for job."

Bragi slapped his back. People who remembered Mocker now, from the war, came to greet him and, if possible, swap a few lies about the old days. Others, including that svelte blonde, came to praise his performance.

Mocker was disappointed by the blonde. There was a message in her eyes, and nothing he could do.

"Oh, my," he muttered. "That this obesity should live to see day. . . ." But he wasn't distraught. This was his happiest evening in a decade. He wallowed in it, savoring every instant.

But he didn't stop observing. He soon concluded that there were skunks in paradise. The millennium hadn't arrived.

Three hard men in fighting leathers stood in the shadows behind the dais. He knew them as well as he knew Ragnarson. Haaken Blackfang, Bragi's foster brother, a bear of a man, a deadly fighter, bigger than his brother. Reskird Kildragon, another relic of the old days, and another grim fighter, who sprang like a wolf when Bragi commanded. And Rolf Preshka, that steel-eyed Iwa Skolovdan whose enmity meant certain death, whose devotion to Bragi's wife bordered on the morbid, and should have been a danger to her husband—except that Preshka was almost as devoted to him.

And, yes, there were more of the old comrades, in the out-of-the-ways, the shadows and alcoves of balconies and doors. Turran of Ravenkrak, Nepanthe's brother, white of hair now but none the less deadly. And their brother Valther, impetuous with blade and heart, possessed of a mind as convolute as that of a god. Jarl Ahring. Dahl Haas. Thom Altenkirk. They were all there, the old, cold ones who had survived, who had been the real heroes of the civil war. And among them were a few new faces, men he knew would be as devoted to their commander—otherwise they would be on the dance floor with the peacocks.

All was not well.

He had known that since climbing to the dais. Two of the occupants of seats of honor were envoys from Hammad al Nakir. From their oldest enemy, El Murid. From that hungry giant of a nation directly south of Kavelin, behind the Kapenrung Mountains. It had taken the combined might of a dozen kingdoms to contain that fanatic religious state in the two-decades-gone, half-forgotten dust-up remembered as the El Murid Wars.

These two had survived that harrowing passage-at-arms, as had Mocker and Bragi and most of those iron-eyed men in the shadows. They remembered. And knew that that argument wasn't settled.

One, in fact, remembered more than any other guest. More, especially, than this happily self-intoxicated little brown man.

He remembered a distant day when they had last met.

He remembered whom it was who had come out of the north into the Desert of Death, using cheap mummer's tricks to establish a reputation as a wizard, to strike to the heart the hope of his master, El Murid, the Disciple. The envoy had been a young trooper then, wild, untameable, in the rear echelon of Lord Nassef's Invincibles. But he remembered.

A fat, young brown man had come to entertain the guardians of El Murid's family with tales and tricks—and then, one night, had slain a half dozen sentries and fled with the Disciple's treasure, his Priceless, the one thing he valued more than the mission given by God.

The fat man had kidnapped El Murid's virgin daughter.

And she had never been seen again.

It had broken El Murid—at least for the time the infidels needed to turn the tide of desert horsemen sweeping the works of the Evil One from their lands.

And he, Habibullah, who slew like a devil when his enemies came to him face to face—he had lain there, belly opened by a blow struck in darkness, and he had wept. Not for his pain, or for the death he expected, and demanded when the Disciple questioned him, but for the agony and shame he would cause his master.

Now he sat in the palace of the infidel, and was silent, watching with hooded eyes. When no one was listening, he told his companion, "Achmed, God is merciful. God is just. God delivers his enemies into the hands of the Faithful."

Achmed didn't know how, but recognized that this embassy to the heathen had borne fruit at last. Unexpected fruit, sweet and juicy, to judge by Habibullah's reaction.

"This charlatan, this talker," Habibullah whispered. "We'll see him again."

Their exchange passed unnoticed.

All eyes had turned to the shadows behind the dais. Mocker whirled in time for the advent of the Queen, Fiana Melicar Sardyga ip Krief. He hadn't seen her for years, despite her inexplicable habit of wandering the streets to poll Vorgreberg's commons. Time hadn't treated her kindly. Though still in her twenties, she looked old enough to be the blonde's mother.

It wasn't that beauty had deserted her. She retained that, though it was a more mature, promising beauty than Mocker remembered. But she looked exhausted. Utterly weary, and buoyed only by wholehearted devotion to her mission as mistress of the nation.

She seemed unexpected.

She came directly to Bragi, and there was that in her eyes, momentarily, which clarified Elana's bitter remark.

It was a rumor he had heard in the Siluro quarter.

Hardly anyone cared as long as her affairs of the heart didn't collide with affairs of state.

Mocker studied Rolf Preshka. The man's pained expression confirmed his surmise.

"Your Majesty," said Bragi, with such perfected courtliness that Mocker giggled, remembering the man's manners of old. "An unexpected honor."

The assembly knelt or bowed according to custom. Even the ambassadors from Hammad al Nakir accorded the lady deep nods. Only Mocker remained straight-necked, meeting her eyes across Bragi's back.

Amusement drained five years from her face. "So. Now I understand the hubbub. Where did they exhume you?"

"Your Majesty, we found him in the last place anybody would look," Ragnarson told her. "I should've remembered. That's the first place to go when you're hunting him. He was here in the city all the time."

"Welcome back, old friend." Fiana did one of those things which baffled and awed her nobles and endeared her to her commons. She grabbed Mocker in a big hug, then spun him round to face the gathering. She stood beside him, an arm thrown familiarly across his shoulders.

He glowed. He met Nepanthe's eyes and she glowed back. Behind the glow he felt her thinking *I told you*. Oh, his stubborn pride, his fear of appearing a beggar before more successful comrades. . . .

He grinned, laid a finger alongside his nose, did to the Queen what he had done to so many of his audience, roasting her good.

The lady laughed as hard as anyone.

Once, when she controlled herself long enough, she rose on tiptoes and whispered to Ragnarson. Bragi nodded. When Mocker finished, Fiana took her place in the seat that, hitherto, had been only symbolic of her presence. She bade the merriment continue.

Winded, Mocker sat cross-legged at Fiana's feet, joining her and the others there in observing the festivities. Once she whispered, "This's the best Victory Day we've had," and another time, "I'm considering appointing you my spokesman to the Thing. They could use loosening up."

Mocker nodded as if the proposition were serious, then amused her by alternately demanding outrageous terms of employment and describing the way he would bully the parliament.

Meanwhile, Bragi abandoned them to dance with his wife and visit with Nepanthe, whom he soon guided to the lurking place of her brothers. She hadn't seen them in years.

Mocker had a fine sense of the ridiculous. There was funny-ridiculous and pathetic-ridiculous. He, dancing with a wife inches taller, was the latter.

He had an image to maintain.

THREE: Old Friends

It was the day after, and Mocker had remained in Castle Krief. Merriment had abandoned everyone but himself. Business had resumed. Bragi took him to a meeting, he explained, so he would get an idea of what was happening nowadays, of why old friends lay back in shadows wearing fighting leather instead of enjoying a celebration of victories won.

"Self," Mocker said as they walked to the meeting, "am confessing overwhelming bambazoolment. Have known large friend, lo, many years. More than can count." He held up his fingers. On those rare occasions when he wasn't proclaiming himself the world's foremost authority, he pretended to be its most ignorant child.

Ragnarson hadn't brought him because he was ignorant or foolish. And Mocker had begun to suspect, after the Queen's entrance last night, that he hadn't been "exhumed" just because he was one of the old fighters and deserved his moment of glory. Nor even because Bragi wanted to give him a little roundabout charity by introducing him to potential suckers.

Bragi trusted his intuitions, his wisdom. Bragi wanted advice—if not his active participation in some fool scheme.

It was both.

Those the Marshall had gathered in the War Room were the same men Mocker had discovered in last night's shadows, plus Fiana and the ambassadors of Altea and Tamerice. Their countries were old allies, and the ambassadors Bragi's friends.

"Mocker," Ragnarson told him after the doors were locked and guards posted, "I wanted you here because you're the only other available expert on a matter of critical importance. An expert, that is, whose answers I trust."

"Then answer damned question."

"Huh? What question?"

"Started to ask same in hall. Bimbazolment? Fingers?"

"All right. Go ahead."

"Self, am knowing friend Bear long ages. Have, till last night, never seen same shaven. Explain."

The non sequitur took Ragnarson off stride. Then he grinned. Of that device Mocker was past master.

"Exactly what you're thinking. These effete southerners have turned me into a ball-less woman."

"Okay. On to question about Haroun."

Ragnarson's jaw dropped. His aide, Gjerdrum, demanded, "How did you...?"

"Am mighty sorcerer...."

The Queen interrupted, "He gave enough clues, Gjerdrum. Is there anybody else who calls both bin Yousif and the Marshall friend?"

Mocker grinned, winked. Fiana startled him by winking back.

"Too damned smart, this woman," he mock-whispered to Bragi.

"Damned right. She's spooky. But let's stick to the point."

"Delineate dilemma. Define horns of same." Mocker's ears were big. He lived in a neighborhood frequented by exiles who followed El Murid's nemesis, Haroun bin Yousif, The King Without a Throne. He knew as much of the man's doings as anyone not privy to his councils. And he knew the man himself, of old. For several years following the El Murid Wars, before he had grown obsessed with restoring Royalist rule to Hammad al Nakir, bin Yousif had adventured with Mocker and Ragnarson. "Old sand rat friend up to no goods again, eh? Is in nature of beast. Catch up little chipmunk. Does same growl and stalk gazelle like lion? Catch up lion. Does same lie down with lamb? With lamb in belly, maybeso. Mutton chops. Mutton chops! Hai! Has been age of earth since same have passed starved lips of impoverished ponderosity, self."

Bragi prodded Mocker's belly with a sheathed dagger. "If you'll spare us the gourmet commentary, I'll explain."

"Peace! Am tender of belly, same being..."

Bragi poked him again. "This's it in a nutshell. For years Haroun raided Hammad al Nakir from camps in the Kapenrungs. From Kavelin and Tamerice, using money and arms from Altea and Itaskia. I've always looked the other way when he smuggled recruits down from the northern refugee centers."

"Uhm. So?"

"Well, he became an embarrassment. Then, suddenly, he seemed to get slow and soft. Stopped pushing. Now he just sits in the hills with his feet up. He throws in a few guys now and then so's El Murid stays pissed, but don't do him no real harm."

"And El Murid just gets older and crankier. You saw his ambassadors?"

"Just so. Snakes in grass, or maybe sand, lying in wait with viper fangs ready. . . ."

"They're out in plain sight this time. They've delivered a dozen ultimatums. Either we close Haroun down or they'll do it for us. They haven't so far. But they're on safe ground. Attacking Haroun's camps would cause a stink, but nobody would go to war to save them. Not if El Murid doesn't try converting us to the one true faith again. It might even solve a few problems for cities with a lot of refugees. Without Haroun keeping them stirred up, they'd settle down and blend in. Distracting the troublemakers is the main reason Haroun gets help from Raithel."

Altea's ambassador nodded. Prince Raithel had died recently, but his policies continued.

"So. Old friend, in newfound, secure circumstance, is asking, should same be safeguarded by selling other old friend down river?"

"No. No. I want to know what he's up to. Why he hasn't done anything the past few years. Part I know. He's studying sorcery. Finishing what he started as a kid. If that's all, okay. But it's not his style to lay back in the weeds.

"El Murid is a sword hanging over Kavelin by a thread. Is Haroun going to cut the thread? You know him. What's he planning?"

Mocker's gaze drifted to his wife's brother Valther. Valther was the shadow man of Vorgreberg, rumored to manage Bragi's cloak and dagger people.

Valther shrugged, said, "That's all we know. We don't have anybody in there."

"Oho! Truth exposes bare naked, ugly fundament before eyes of virginal, foolish self. O Pervert, Truth! Begone!" And to Bragi, perhaps the simplest statement he had ever made: "No."

"I didn't make my proposition."

kn
Am

(

A
its ma
Kaveli
Nordm
jerked a

Bragi
spoke this
man's dist

He proc
shaft of lig
Ethrian?" he
the polished
produced ano

The fat man
alcoholics stare
were Kaveliner

Glen Cook "We kno

"Like the old joke," said Bragi. "We kno
We're dickering at the price...
Mocker pointed his way like t
room. Heads pointed
loosed. He didn't like it. Not one w
...do for his wife
He had aged, he ha
security. Having
He raised h
round again
had thin
audie

28

...way
...abstinence. They
...struck for the eastern
trade, beautiful ... twin-headed eagle and Fiana's
profile in high, fr... relief. They weren't intended for normal
commerce, but for transfers between commercial accounts in the
big mercantile banks in Vorgreberg. The gold in one piece
represented more than a laborer could earn in a year.

Mocker had seen hard times. He did mental sums,
calculating temptation's value in silver. The things he could do
for Ethrian and Nepanthe....

Ragnarson deposited the second coin atop the first, dropping
his eye to table level while aligning their rims. He produced
another.

Mocker changed subtly. Bragi sensed it. He stacked the third
coin, folded his arms.

"Woe!" Mocker cried suddenly, startling the group. "Am
poor old fat cretin of pusillaminity world-renowned, weak of
head and muscle. Self, ask nothings. Only to be left alone, to live
out few remaining years with devoted wife, in peace, raising
son."

"I saw the place where you're keeping my sister," Turran
observed, perhaps more harshly than intended.

Bragi waved a hand admonishingly.

"Hai! Self, am not..."

w what you are.

...s. He looked round the
...ose of hounds eager to be

...hit. But gold! So much gold. What
...nd son. . . .

...mellowed, he had grown concerned with
...care for others can do that to a man.
...s left hand, jerkily, started to speak. He looked
...So many narrowed eyes. Some he didn't know. He
...gs to say to Bragi, but not here, not now, not before an
...ce.

"Define task," he ordered. "Not that poor old fat mendicant, on brink of old age, near crippled, agrees to undertake same. Only purpose being to listen to same, same being reasonable request to allow before telling man to put same where moon don't glow."

"Simple. Just visit Haroun. Find out what he's up to. Bring me the news."

Mocker laughed his most sarcastic laugh. "Self, am famous dullard, admitted. Of brightness next to which cheapest tallow candle is like sun to dark of moon. Forget to come in from rain sometimes, maybeso. But am alive. See? Wound here, here, everywhere, from listening to friends in time past. But am favored of Gods. Was born under lucky star. Haven't passed yet. Also, am aware of ways men speak. Simple, says old friend? Then task is bloody perilous. . . ."

"Not so!" Ragnarson protested. "In fact, if I knew where Haroun was, I'd go myself. But you know him. He's here, he's there, and the rumors are always wrong. He might be at the other end of the world. I can't take the time."

"Crippled. Excuse limps like sixty-year-old arthritic."

Actually, it was unvarnished truth. And Mocker knew it. He rose. "Has been enjoyable matching wits with old half-wit friend. Father of self, longtime passing, said, 'Never fight unarmed man.' Must go. Peace." He did an amusing imitation of a priest giving a blessing.

The inner door guard might have been deaf and blind. Or a path-blocking statue.

"So! Now am prisoner. Woe! Heart of heart of fool, self, told same stay away from palaces, same being dens of iniquitous. . . ."

"Mocker, Mocker," said Bragi. "Come. Sit. I'm not as young as I used to be. I don't have the patience anymore. You think we could dispense with this bullshit and get down to cases?"

Mocker came and sat, but his expression said he was being pushed, that he was about to get stubborn. No force in Heaven or Hell could nudge a stubborn Mocker.

Ragnarson understood his reluctance. Nepanthe was absolutely dead set against allowing her husband to get involved in anything resembling an adventure. Hers was an extremely dependent personality. She couldn't endure separations.

"Turran, could you convince Nepanthe?"

"I'll do it," Valther said. He and Nepanthe had always been close. "She'll listen to me. But she won't like it."

Mocker grew agitated. His domestic problems were being aired. . . .

Bragi began massaging his own face. He wasn't getting enough sleep. The demands of his several posts were getting to him. He considered resigning as publican consul. The position made limited demands, yet did consume time he could use being Marshall and virtual king-surrogate.

"Why don't you list your objections—take them down, Derel—and we'll deal with them in an orderly fashion."

Mocker was appalled. "Is end. Is perished. Is dead, absolute, friend of youth, wrapping self in cocoon of time, coming forth from chrysalis as perfect bureaucrat, all impatient and indifferent. Or is imposter, taking place of true gentleman of former time? Rising from Sea of Perdition, snakes of rules and regulations for hair—not my department, go down hall to hear same—Bastard Beast-Child of order. . . . Enough. Self, am beloved get of Chaos. Am having business of own. Otherwheres. Open door."

He was irked. And Ragnarson *was* tempted to apologize, except he wasn't sure what to apologize for. "Let him go, Luther. Tell Malven to take him to his room." One by one, he palmed the double nobles.

Part of his failure came from inside, he reflected. He *had* changed. But as much blame lay with Mocker. Never had he been so touchy.

Michael Trebilcock, one of the faces Mocker didn't know, asked, "What now?"

Ragnarson gestured for silence.

Mocker didn't make it past Luther. As the guard stepped

aside, the fat man turned and asked musingly, "Double nobles five?" He grinned. "Hai! Might soothe conscience, same being sufficient to keep wife and son for year or two in eventuation of certain death of cretinic chaser-after-dreams of old friends." He then railed against the Fates for several minutes, damning them for driving him into a corner from which he had no exit but suicide.

It was all for show. The mission Bragi had shouldn't be dangerous.

They settled it then, with Mocker to leave Vorgreberg the following morning. The group gradually dissolved, till only Bragi and Fiana remained.

They stared at one another across a short space that, sometimes, seemed miles.

Finally, she asked, "Am I getting boring?"

He shook his head.

"What is it, then?"

He massaged his face again. "The pressure. More and more, I have trouble giving a damn. About anything."

"And Elana, a little? You think she knows?"

"She knows. Probably since the beginning."

Fiana nodded thoughtfully. "That would explain a lot."

Bragi frowned. "What?"

"Never mind. You have trouble with your conscience?"

"Maybe. Maybe."

She locked the door, eased into his lap. He didn't resist, but neither did he encourage her. She nuzzled his ear, whispered, "I've always had this fantasy about doing it here. On the table. Where all the important laws and treaties get signed."

There were some things Ragnarson just couldn't say, and first among them was "no" to a willing lady.

Later, he met with Colonel Balfour, who commanded the Guild regiment being maintained in Kavelin till the country produced competent soldiers of its own. High Crag was growing a little arrogant, a little testy, as the inevitable withdrawal of the regiment drew closer. Each year the Guild grew less subtle in its insistence that the regiment's commission be extended.

There were mercenaries and Mercenaries. The latter belonged to the Guild, headquartered at High Crag on the western coast just north of Dunno Scuttari. The Guild was a brotherhood of free soldiers, almost a monastic order, consisting of approximately ten thousand members scattered from Ipopotam to Iwa Skolovda, from the Mountains of M'Hand to Freyland. Ragnarson and many of his intimates had begun their adulthood in its ranks and, nominally, remained attached to the order. But the connection was tenuous, despite High Crag's having awarded regular promotions over the years. Because the Citadel recognized no divorce, it still claimed a right to demand obedience.

The soldiers of the Guild owned no other allegiance, to men, nations, or faith. And they were the best-schooled soldiers in the west. High Crag's decision to accept or reject a commission often made or broke the would-be employer's cause without blows being struck.

There were suspicions, among princes, that the Citadel—High Crag's heart, whence the retired generals ruled—was shaping destiny to its own dream.

Ragnarson entertained those suspicions himself—especially when he received pressure to extend the regiment posted to Kavelin.

Ragnarson had, on several occasions, tried to convince the Guild factors that his little state just couldn't afford the protection. Kavelin remained heavily indebted from the civil war. He argued that only low-interest loans and outright grants from Itaskia were keeping the kingdom above water. If El Murid died or were overthrown, that aid would end. Itaskia would lose its need for a buffer on the borders of Hammad al Nakir.

Following the inevitable bitter argument with Balfour, Bragi spoke to the Thing, doing his best to shuffle his three hats without favoring any one. Still, as chief of the armed forces, he concentrated on an appropriations measure.

The bill was for the maintenance of the Mercenary regiment. The parliament supported its hire even less enthusiastically than Ragnarson.

Such matters, and personal problems, distracted him so much during subsequent months that he took little notice of the enduring absence of his fat friend, whom he had instructed to disappear, so to speak, anyway.

His immediate goal, Mocker decided, had to be Sedlmayr. Kavelin's second largest city nestled between the breasts of the

Kapenrungs within days of Haroun's primary camps. He would make inquiries there, alerting Haroun's agents to his presence. Their response would dictate his latter activities.

There were a dozen moving camps within fifty miles. He might end up wandering from one to another till he located Haroun.

The rooftops of Vorgreberg had just dipped behind the horizon when he heard the clop-clop of a faster horse coming up behind him. He glanced back. Another lone rider.

He slowed, allowing the rider to catch up. "Hail, friend met upon trail."

The man smiled, replied in kind, and thereafter they rode together, chance-met companions sharing a day's conversation to ease the rigors of the journey. The traveler said he was Sir Keren of Sincic, a Nordmen knight southbound on personal business.

Mocker missed the signs. He had taken Bragi at his word. No danger in the mission. He didn't catch a whiff of peril.

Until the four ambushers sprang from the forest a half day further south.

The knight downed him with a blow from behind as he slew a second bushwhacker with a sword almost too swift to follow. Half conscious, he mumbled as they bound him, "Woe! Am getting old. Feeble in head. Trusting stranger. What kind fool you, idiot Mocker? Deserve whatever happens, absolute."

The survivors taunted him, and beat him mercilessly. Mocker marked the little one with the eye-patch. He would undergo the most exquisite tortures after the tables turned.

Mocker didn't doubt that they would. His past justified that optimism.

After dark, following back-ways and forest trails, his captors took him southeastward, into the province of Uhlmansiek. So confident were they that they didn't bother concealing anything from him.

"A friend of mine," said the knight, "Habibullah the ambassador, sent us."

"Is a puzzlement. Self, profess bambizoolment. Met same two nights passing, speaking once to same, maybeso. Self, am wondering why same wants inconsequential—though ponderous, admit—self snapped up like slave by second-class thugs pretending to entitlement?"

Sir Keren laughed. "But you've met before. A long time ago.

You gutted him and left him for dead the night you kidnapped El Murid's daughter."

That put a nasty complexion on the matter. Mocker felt a new, deeper fear. Now he knew his destination.

They would have a very special, very painful welcome for him at Al Rhemish.

But Fate was to deprive him of his visit to the Most Holy Mrazkim Shrines. They were somehwere in the Uhlmansiek Kapenrungs when it happened.

They rounded a bend. Two horsemen blocked their path. One was Guild Colonel Balfour, the second an equally hard and scarred Mercenary battalion chieftain. Mocker remembered both from the Victory Day celebration.

"Hai!" he cried, for, if Sir Keren had made any mistake at all, it had been leaving him ungagged. "Rescue on hand. Poor old fat fool not forgotten...." The little fellow with an eye missing belted him in the mouth.

Sir Keren's rogues were old hands. Despite his circumstances, Mocker found himself admiring their professionalism. They spread out, three against two. There was no question of a parley.

The currents of intrigue ran deep.

The one-eyed man moved suddenly, a split second after Sir Keren and his comrade launched their attack. His blade found a narrow gap below the rim of Sir Keren's helmet.

Balfour's companion died at the same moment, struck down by Sir Keren's companion. Balfour himself barely managed to survive till the one-eye skewered the remaining man from behind.

Mocker's glee soon became tempered by a suspicion that his rescue wasn't what it seemed. It might, in fact, be no rescue at all. He seized the best chance he saw.

Having long ago slipped his bonds, he wheeled his mount and took off.

They must be ignorant of his past, he reflected as forest flew past. Otherwise they would've taken precautions. Escape tricks were one way he had of making his meager living.

He managed two hundred yards before the survivors noticed. The chase was on.

It was brief.

Mocker rounded a turn. His mount stopped violently, reared, screamed.

A tall, slim man in black blocked the trail. He wore a golden cat-gargoyle mask finely chased in black, with jeweled eyes and fangs. And while words could describe that mask, they couldn't convey the dread and revulsion it inspired.

Mocker kicked his mount's flanks, intending to ride the man down.

The horse screamed and reared again. Mocker tumbled off. Stunned, he rolled in the deep pine needles, muttered, "Woe! Is story of life. Always one more evil, waiting round next bend." He lay there twitching, pretending injury, fingers probing the pine needles for something useful as a weapon.

Balfour and the one-eyed man arrived. The latter swung down and booted Mocker, then tied him again.

"You nearly failed," the stranger accused.

Balfour revealed neither fear nor contrition. "They were good. And you've got him. That's what matters. Pay Rico. He's served us well. He deserves well of us. I've got to get back to Vorgreberg."

"No."

Balfour slapped his hilt. "My weapon is faster than yours." He drew the blade a foot from its scabbard. "If we can't deal honorably amongst ourselves, then our failure is inevitable."

The man in black bowed slightly. "Well said. I simply meant that it wouldn't be wise for you to return. We've made too much commotion here. Eyes have seen. The men of the woods, the Marena Dimura, are watching. It would be impossible to track all the witnesses. It'll be simpler for you to disappear."

Balfour drew his blade another foot. Rico, unsure what was happening, moved to where he could attack from the side.

The thin man carefully raised his hands. "No. No. As you say, there must be trust. There must be a mutual concern. Else how can we convert others to our cause?"

Balfour nodded, but didn't relax.

Mocker listened, and through hooded eyes observed. His heart pounded. What dread had befallen him? And why?

"Rico," the stranger said, "Take this. It's gold." He offered a bag.

The one-eyed man glanced at Balfour, took the sack, looked inside. "He's right. Maybe thirty pieces. Itaskian. Iwa Skolovdan."

"That should suffice till the moves have begun and it's safe for you to return," said the masked man.

Balfour sheathed his weapon. "All right. I know a place

where no one could find us. Where they wouldn't think of looking. You need help with him?" He nudged Mocker with a toe.

The fat man could feel the wicked grin behind that hideous mask. "That one? That little toad? No. Go on, before his friends hear the news."

"Rico, come on."

After Balfour and Rico had departed, the tall man stood over Mocker, considering.

Mocker, being Mocker, had to try, even knowing it futile. He kicked.

The tall man hopped his leg with disdainful ease, reached, touched....

Mocker's universe shrank to a point of light which, after a momentary brightness, died. After that he was lost, and time ceased to have meaning.

FOUR: Intimations

Ragnarson dismounted, dropped his reins over a low branch. "Why don't you guys join me?" he asked as he seated himself against an oak. A cool breeze whispered through the Gudbrandsdal Forest, a Royal Preserve just over the western boundary of the Siege of Vorgreberg. "It's restful here."

He narrowed his eyes to slits, peered at the sun, which broke through momentary gaps in the foliage.

Turran, Valther, Blackfang, Kildragon, and Ragnarson's secretary, a scholar from Hellin Daimiel named Derel Prataxis, dismounted. Valther lay down on his belly in new grass, a strand of green trailing from between his teeth. Ragnarson's foster brother, Blackfang, began snoring in seconds.

This had begun as a boar hunt. Beaters were out trying to kick up game. Other parties were on either flank, several hundred yards away. But Bragi had left the capital only to escape its pressures. The others understood.

"Sometimes," Ragnarson mused, minutes later, "I think we were better off back when our only problem was our next meal."

Kildragon, a lean, hard brunet, nodded. "It had its good points. We didn't have to worry about anybody else."

Ragnarson waved a hand in an uncertain gesture, reflecting his inner turmoil. "It's peaceful out here. No distractions."

Kildragon stretched a leg, prodded Blackfang.

"Uhn? What's happening?"

"That's it," said Bragi. "Something." Peace had reigned so long that the first ripples, subtle though they were, had brought him worriedly alert. His companions, too, sensed it.

Valther grumbled, "I can't put my finger on it."

Everyday life in Vorgreberg had begun showing little

stutters, little stumbles. A general uneasiness haunted everyone, from the Palace to the slums.

There was just one identifiable cause. The Queen's indisposition. But Bragi wasn't telling anyone anything about that. Not even his brother.

"Something's happening," Ragnarson insisted. Prataxis glanced his way, shook his head gently, resumed scribbling.

The scholars of Hellin Daimiel took subservient posts as a means of obtaining primary source material for their great theses. Prataxis was a historian of the Lesser Kingdoms. He kept intimate accounts of the events surrounding the man he served. Someday, when he returned to the Rebsamen, he would write the definitive history of Kavelin during Ragnarson's tenure.

"Something is piling up," Bragi continued. "Quietly, out of sight. Wait!"

He gestured for silence. One by one, the others saw why. A bold chipmunk had come to look them over. As time passed and the little rascal saw no threat, he sneaked closer. Then closer still.

Those five hard men, those battered swords, veterans of some of the grimmest bloodlettings that world had ever seen, watched the animal bemusedly. And Prataxis watched them. His pen moved quietly as he noted that they could take pleasure in simple things, in the natural beauties of creation. It wasn't a facet of their characters they displayed in the theater of the Palace. The Palace was a cruel stage, never allowing its actors to shed their roles.

The chipmunk finally grew bored, scampered away.

"If there was anything to reincarnation, I wouldn't mind being a chipmunk next time around," Turran observed. "Except for owls, foxes, hawks, and like that."

"There's always predators," Blackfang replied. "Me, I'm satisfied here on top of the pile. Us two-leggers, we're Number One. Don't nothing chomp on us. Except us."

"Haaken, when did you take up philosophizing?" Bragi asked. His foster brother was a taciturn, stolid man whose outstanding characteristic was his absolute dependability.

"Philosophizing? Don't take no genius to tell that you're in the top spot being people. You can always yell and get a bunch of guys to gang up on any critter that's giving you trouble. How come there's no wolves or lions in these parts anymore? They all went to Ipopotam for the season?"

"My friend," said Prataxis, "you strip it to its bones, but it remains a philosophical point."

Blackfang regarded the scholar narrowly, not sure he hadn't been mocked. His old soldier's anti-intellectual stance was a point of pride.

"We can't get away from it," said Ragnarson. "But the quiet may help us think. The subject at hand, my friends. What's happening?"

Valther spat his blade of grass. While searching for another, he replied, "People are getting nervous. The only thing I know, that's concrete, is that they're worried because Fiana has locked herself up at Karak Strabger. If she dies..."

"I know. Another civil war."

"Can't you get her to come back?"

"Not till she's recovered." Bragi examined each face. Did they suspect?

He wished the damned baby would hurry up and the whole damned mess would get done with.

His thoughts slipped away to the night she had told him.

They had been lying on the couch in his office, on one of those rare occasions when they had the chance to be together. As he had let his hand drift lightly down her sleek stomach, he had asked, "You been eating too much of that baclava? You're putting on a little...."

He had never been a smooth talker, so he wasn't surprised by her tears. Then she whispered, "It's not fat. Darling.... I'm pregnant."

"Oh, shit." A swarm of panic-mice raged round inside him. What the hell would he do? What would Elana say? She was suspicious enough already....

"I thought.... Doctor Wachtel said you couldn't have any more. After Carolan you were supposed to be sterile."

"Wachtel was wrong. I'm sorry." She'd pulled herself against him as if trying to crawl inside.

"But.... Well.... Why didn't you tell me?" She had been well along. Only skilled dress had concealed it.

"At first, I didn't believe it. I thought it was something else. Then I didn't want you to worry."

Well, yes, she had saved him that, till then. Since, he'd done nothing *but* worry.

Too many people could get hurt: Elana, himself, his children, Fiana, and Kavelin—if the scandal became a cause célèbre. He spent a lot of time cursing himself for his own stupidity. And a little admitting that his major objection was having gotten caught. He'd probably go right on bedding her if he got through this on the cheap.

Before it showed enough to cause talk, Fiana had taken trusted servants and Gjerdrum and had moved to Karak Strabger, at Baxendala, where Ragnarson had won the battle Kavelin celebrated on Victory Day. Her plea of mental exhaustion wasn't that difficult to believe. Her reign had been hard, with seldom a moment's relief.

Horns alerted him to the present.

"Game's afoot," Kildragon observed, rising.

"Go ahead," Bragi said. "Think I'll just lay around here and loaf."

Haaken, Reskird, Turran, and Valther were habituated to action. They went. They would get more relaxation from the hunt.

"And you, Derel?"

"Are you joking? Fat, old, and lazy as I am? Besides, I never did see any point to hounding some animal through the woods, and maybe breaking my neck."

"Gives you a feeling of omnipotence. You're a god for a minute. 'Course, sometimes you get taken down a peg if the game gives you the slip or runs you up a tree." He chuckled. "Damned hard to be dignified when you're hanging on a branch with a mad boar trying to grab a bite of your ass. Makes you reflect. And you figure out that what Haaken said about us being top critter isn't always right."

"Can you manage this charade another two months?"

"Eh?"

"My calculations say the child will arrive next month. She'll need another month to make herself presentable...."

Ragnarson's eyes became hard and cold.

"Too," said Prataxis, who hadn't the sense to be intimidated, because in Hellin Daimiel scholars could make outrageous, libelous remarks without suffering reprisals, "there's the chance, however remote, that she'll die in childbirth. Have you considered possible political ramifications? Have you taken steps? Kavelin could lose everything you two have built."

"Derel, you walk a thin line. Take care."

"I know. But I know you, too. And I'm speaking now only because the matter needs to be addressed and every eventuality considered. The Lesser Kingdoms have been stricken by deaths lately. Prince Raithel last year. He was old. Everybody expected it. But King Shanight, in Anstokin, went during the winter, in circumstances still questionable. And now King Jostrand of Volstokin has gone, leaving no one but a doddering Queen Mother to pick up the reins."

"You saying there's something behind their deaths? That Fiana might be next? My God! Jostrand was dead drunk when he fell off his horse."

"Just trying to make a point. The Dark Lady stalks amongst the ruling houses of the Lesser Kingdoms. And Fiana will be vulnerable. This pregnancy shouldn't have happened. Bearing the Shinsan child ruined her insides. She's having trouble, isn't she?"

It took a special breed not to be offended by the forthrightness of the scholars of Hellin Daimiel. Ragnarson prided himself on his tolerance, his resilience. Yet he had trouble dealing with Prataxis now. The man was speaking of things never discussed openly.

"Yes. She is. We're worried." *We* meant himself, Gjerdrum, and Dr. Wachtel, the Royal Physician. Fiana was scared half out of her mind. She was convinced she was going to die.

But Bragi ignored that. Elana had had nine children now, two of whom hadn't lived, and she had gone through identical histrionics every time.

"To change the subject, have you thought about Colonel Oryon?"

"That arrogant little reptile? I'm half tempted to whip him. To send him home with his head under his arm."

He found Balfour's replacement insufferably abrasive. High Crag's recent threat to call in Kavelin's war debts had done nothing to make the man more palatable. And Bragi thought he was kicking up too much dust about Balfour's disappearance.

Ragnarson wondered if that were related to High Crag's threats. Though ranked General on its rosters, he had had little to do with the Mercenaries' Guild the past two decades. High Crag kept promoting him, he suspected, so a tenuous link would exist should the Citadel want to exploit it. He wasn't privy to the thinking there.

"Actually," he said, "you've conjured enough into the Treasury to pay them off. They don't know yet. My notion is, they want to do to us what they've done to some of the little states on the coast. To nail us for some property. Maybe a few titles with livings for their old men. That's their pattern."

"Possibly. They've been developing an economic base for a century."

"What?"

"A friend of mine did a study of Guild policies and practices. *Very* interesting when you trace their monies and patterns of commission acceptance. Trouble is, the pattern isn't complete enough to show their goals."

"What do you think? Would it be better to give them a barony or two? One of the nonhereditary titles we created after the war?"

"You could always nationalize later—when you think you can whip them heads up."

"If we pay there won't be much left for emergencies."

"Commission renewal is almost here. There won't be much favorable sentiment in the Thing."

"Ain't much in my heart, either." Ragnarson watched the sun play peekaboo through the leaves. "Hard to convince myself we need them when we haven't had any trouble for seven years. But the army isn't up to anything rough yet."

The real cost of the war had been the near-obliteration of Kavelin's traditional military leadership, the Nordmen nobility. Hundreds had fallen in the rebellion against Fiana. Hundreds had been exiled. Hundreds more had fled the kingdom. There was no lack of will in the men Bragi had recruited since, simply an absence of command tradition. He had made up somewhat by using veterans he had brought to Kavelin back then, forming several sound infantry regiments, but the diplomatically viable military strength of the state still hinged on the Guild presence. Their one regiment commanded more respect than his native seven.

Kavelin had greedy neighbors, and their intentions, what with three national leaderships having changed within the year, remained uncertain.

"If I could just get the Armaments Act through. . . ."

Soon after war's end Fiana had decreed that every free man should provide himself with a sword. Ragnarson's idea. But he had overlooked the cost. Even simple weapons were expensive. Few peasants had the money. Distributing captured arms had helped only a little.

So, for years, he had been pushing legislation which would

enable his War Ministry to provide weapons.

He wanted the act so he could dispense with the Mercenaries. The Thing wanted rid of the Mercenaries first. An impasse.

Bragi was finding politics a pain in the behind.

Reskird and Haaken returned, then Turran and Valther. Empty-handed. "That kid Trebilcock, and Rolf, got there first," Reskird explained. "Tough old sow anyway."

"Sour grapes?" Bragi chuckled. "Valther, you heard anything from Mocker yet? Or about him?"

Most of a year had passed since he had sent the fat man south. He hadn't heard a word since.

"It's got me worried," Valther admitted. "I made it top priority two months ago, when I heard that Haroun had left his camps. He's gone north. Nobody knows where or why."

"And Mocker?"

"Practically nothing. I've scoured the country clear to Sedlmayr. He never made it there. But one of my men picked up a rumor that he was seen in Uhlmansiek."

"That's a long way from Sedlmayr...."

"I know. And he wasn't alone."

"Who was he with?"

"We don't know. Nearest thing to a description I have is that one of them was a one-eyed man."

"That bothers you?"

"There's a one-eyed man named Wilis Northen, alias Rico, who's been on my list for years. We think he works for El Murid."

"And?"

"Northen disappeared about the right time."

"Oh-oh. You think El Murid's got him? What're the chances?"

"I don't know. It's more hunch than anything."

"So. Let's see. Mocker goes to see Haroun. El Murid's agents intercept him. Question. How did they know?"

"You've got me. That bothers me more than where Mocker is. It could cost us all. I've tried every angle I can think of. I can't find a leak. I put tagged information through everybody who was there when we conned Mocker into going. Result? Nothing."

Ragnarson shook his head. He knew those men. He had bet his life on their loyalties before.

But the word had leaked somehow.

Had Mocker told anybody?

Thus the spy mind works. There had to be a plot, a connection. Coincidence couldn't be accepted.

Habibullah hadn't had the slightest idea of Mocker's mission. He had simply set his agents to kidnap a man, acting on news, which was common talk in the Siluro quarter, that he was traveling to Sedlmayr. Mocker had spread that story himself. The man in black had other resources.

"Keep after it. In fact, get in touch with Haroun's people."

"Excuse me?"

"Haroun has people here. I know a little about your work. I've done some in my time. Admit it. You know them and they know you. Ask them to find out. Or you could go through our friends from Altea. They're in direct contact. Even if you find out they don't know anything, we're ahead. We'd know Mocker didn't reach the camps. Oh. Ask the Marena Dimura. They know what's happening in the hills."

"That's where I got my Uhlmansiek rumor."

The Marena Dimura were the original inhabitants of Kavelin, dwelling there before Ilkazar initiated the wave of migrations which had brought in the other three ethnic groups: the Siluro, Wessons, and Nordmen. The semi-nomadic Marena Dimura tribes kept to the forests and mountains. A fiercely independent people—though they had supported her during the civil war—they refused to recognize Fiana as legitimate monarch of Kavelin. Centuries after the Conquest they still viewed the others as occupying peoples. . . . They put little effort into altering the situation, though. They took their revenge by stealing chickens and sheep.

It was early spring. The sun rolled west. The afternoon breeze rose. The air grew cooler. Shivering, Bragi announced, "I'm heading back to town. Be damned cold by dark." It would take that long to get home.

Prataxis and Valther joined him. They had work to do.

"You ought to go see your wife sometime," Ragnarson told Valther. "I had a wife who looked like that, I wouldn't go out for groceries."

Valther gave him an odd look. "Elana isn't bad. And you leave her alone all the time."

Guilt ragged Ragnarson's conscience. It was true. His position was opening a gulf between him and Elana. And he hadn't only neglected her. The children, too, were growing up as strangers. He stopped chiding Valther. The man's marriage was even more successful than Mocker's.

"Yeah. Yeah. You're right. I'll take a couple days off soon as I get the new armaments thing lined up. Maybe dump the kids on Nepanthe and take Elana somewhere. There's some pretty country around Lake Turntine."

"Sounds perfect. And Nepanthe would love having them. She's going crazy, bottled up with Ethrian."

Nepanthe was staying at the Palace. There were no children her son's age at Castle Krief.

"Maybe she should move out to my place?" Ragnarson's family occupied the home of a former rebel, Lord Lindwedel, who had been beheaded during the war. It was so huge that his mob of kids, and servants, and Haaken when he stayed over, couldn't fill it.

"Maybe," Valther murmured. "My place would be better." His wasn't far from Ragnarson's.

The head of an intelligence service doesn't always tell his employer all he knows.

FIVE: A Traveler in Black

North of the Kratchnodians, at the Trolledyngjan mouth of the Middle Pass, stood the inn run by Frita Tolvarson. It had been in his family since the time of Jan Iron Hand. The main trade road from Tonderhofn and the Trolledyngjan interior passed nearby, spanned the mountains, formed a tenuous link with the south. For travelers it was either the first or last bit of comfort following or preceding a harrowing passage. There was no other hospice for days around.

Frita was an old man, and a kindly soul, with a child for almost every year of his marriage. He didn't demand much more of his customers than reasonable payment, moderate behavior, and news of the rest of the world.

There was a custom at the inn dating back centuries. Every guest was asked to contribute a story to the evening's entertainment.

Winding down from the high range, a path had been beaten in the previous night's snow. The first spring venturers were assaulting the pass from the south. The path made a meandering ribbon of shadow once it reached the drifted moor, its depths unplumbed by the light of a low-hanging, full Wolf Moon. A chill arctic wind moaned through the branches of a few skeletal trees. Those gnarled old oaks looked like squatting giants praising the sky with attenuated fingers and claws.

The wind had banked snow against the north wall of Frita's establishment. The place looked like a snowbound barrow from that direction. But on the south side a traveler could find a welcoming door.

One such was crossing the lonely moor, a shivering black silhouette against the moonlit Kratchnodians. He wore a dark great cloak wrapped tightly about him, its hood pulled far forward to protect his face. He stared down dully, eyes watery. His cheeks burned in the cold. He despaired of reaching the inn, though he saw and smelled the smoke ahead. His passage through the mountains had been terrible. He wasn't accustomed to wintery climes.

Frita looked up expectantly as a cold blast roared into the inn. He put on a smile of welcome.

"Hey!" a customer grumbled. "Close the goddamned door! We aren't frost giants."

The newcomer surveyed the common room. There were just three guests.

Frita's wife bade him quit gawking and offer the man something to drink. He nodded to his oldest daughter. Alowa slipped off her stool, quickly visited the kitchen for mulled wine. "No!" she told a customer as she passed him on her way to the newcomer. Frita chuckled. He knew a "yes" when he heard it.

The newcomer accepted the wine, went to crouch before the fire. "There'll be meat soon," Alowa told him. "Won't you let me take your cloak?" Her blonde hair danced alluringly as she shook it out of her face.

"No." He gave her a coin. She examined it, frowned, tossed it to her father. Frita studied it. It was strange. He seldom saw its like. It bore a crown instead of a bust, and intricate characters. But it was real silver.

Alowa again asked the stranger for his cloak.

"No." He moved to the table, leaned forward as if to sleep on his forearms.

There'll be trouble now, Frita thought. She won't rest till she unveils the mystery. He followed her to the kitchen. "Alowa, behave yourself. A man deserves his privacy."

"Could he be the one?"

"The one what?"

"The one the Watcher is waiting for?"

Frita shrugged. "I doubt it. Mark me, girl. Let him be. That's a hard man." He had caught a glimpse of the man's face as he had turned from the fire. Fortyish, weathered, thin, dark-eyed, dusky, with a cruel nose and crueler lines around his mouth. There was a metallic sound when he moved. The worn hilt of a sword protruded through the part in his cloak. "That's no merchant trying to be first to the prime furs."

Frita returned to the common room. It lay silent. The

handful of customers were waiting for the newcomer to reveal something of himself and his business. Frita's curiosity grew. The man wouldn't push back his hood. Was his face so terrible?

Time passed, mostly in silence. The newcomer had dampened the mood that had prevailed earlier, when there had been singing, joking, and good-natured competition for Alowa's favors. The stranger ate in silence, hidden in his hood. Alowa, gradually, moved from mystification to hurt. Never had she encountered a man so oblivious to her charms.

Frita decided the time for tales had come. His guests had begun drinking to fill the time. The mood was growing sour. Something was needed to lighten it before drink led to unpleasantness. "Brigetta, get the children." Nodding, his wife rose from her needlework, stirred the younger children from their evening naps and the older from the kitchen. Frita frowned at the youngsters when they began playing with one of the traveler's dogs.

"Time for tales," he announced. There were just seven people at the table, including himself. Two of the others were his wife and Alowa. "A rule of the house. Not required. But he who tells the best pays no keep." His eyes lingered on the one they called the Watcher, a small, nervous, one-eyed rogue. He had arrived nearly a year ago, in company with a gentleman of means, who had behaved like a fugitive. The gentleman had left the Watcher and had hurried northward as if his doom pursued him. Yet nothing had ever come of it.

Frita didn't like the Watcher. He was a sour, evil, small-minded little man. His only redeeming feature was a fat purse. Alowa made him pay for what she gave everyone else freely, and hinted that his tastes were cruel.

One guest said, "I'm from Itaskia, where I was once a merchant sailor." And he told of grim sea battles with corsairs out of the Isles, with no quarter given nor taken. Frita listened with half an ear. The feud of Itaskia's shipping magnates with the Red Brotherhood was a fixture of modern history.

The second visitor began his tale, "I once joined an expedition to the Black Forest, and there I heard this tale." And he spun an amusing yarn about a toothless dragon who had terrible problems finding sufficiently delicate meals. The smaller children loved it.

Frita had heard it before. He hated to declare an old story the winner.

But, to his surprise, the Watcher volunteered a tale. He hadn't bothered for months.

He stood, the better to fix his audience's attention, and used his hands freely while speaking. He had trouble moving his left arm. Frita had seen it bare. He had taken a deep wound in the past.

"Long ago and far away," the Watcher began, in the storyteller's fashion, "in a time when elves still walked the earth, there was a great elf-king. Mical-gilad was his name, and his passion, conquest. He was a mighty warrior, undefeated in battle or joust. He and his twelve paladins were champions of the world till the events whereof I speak."

Frita frowned, leaned back. A story new to him. A pity its teller had little feel for the art.

"One day a knight appeared at the gates of the elf-king's castle. His shield bore an unknown coat of arms. His horse was twice as big as life and black as coal. The gate guards refused him passage. He laughed at them. The gates collapsed."

Yes, Frita thought, it would make a tale in the mouth of a competent teller. The Watcher described the elf-king's encounter with He Who Laughs, after the stranger had slain his twelve champions. He then fought the king himself, who overcame him by trickery, but couldn't kill him because of the unbreachable spells on his armor.

Frita thought he saw where it was going. He had heard so many tales that even the best had become predictable. It was a moral tale about the futility of trying to evade the inevitable.

The elf-king had his opponent thrown on a dung heap outside his castle, whereupon He Who Laughs promised another, more terrible meeting. And, sure enough, the next time the elf-king went a-conquering, he found the knight in black and gold riding with his enemies.

As he talked, the Watcher nervously played with a small gold coin. It was a tick Frita no longer noticed. But the newcomer seemed mesmerized by the constant tumble of the gold piece.

In the end, He Who Laughs ran the elf-king down and slew him.

The ex-sailor from Itaskia said, "I don't understand. Why was the king afraid of him if he wasn't afraid of anybody else?"

For the first time the newcomer uttered more than a monosyllable. "The knight is a metaphor, my friend. He Who Laughs is one of the names of the male avatar, the hunter aspect, of Death. She sets that part of herself to stalk those who would evade her. The elves were supposed to have been immortal. The point of the story was that the king had grown so arrogant in his immortality that he dared challenge the Dark Lady, the Inevitable. Which is the grossest form of stupidity. Yet even today men persist in the folly of believing they can escape the inevitable."

"Oh."

All eyes were on the newcomer now. Especially that of the Watcher. The remark about the inevitable seemed to have touched his secret fears.

"Well then," said the innkeeper. "Which wins? The pirate? The dragon? Or the lesson of the elf-king?"

Half a dozen little ones clamored for the dragon.

"Wait," said the newcomer. His tone enforced instant silence. "I would like a turn."

"By all means," Frita nodded, eager to please. This man had begun to frighten him. Yet he was surprised. He hadn't expected this dour, spooky stranger to contribute.

"This is a true story. The most interesting usually are. It began just a year ago, and hasn't yet ended.

"There was a man, of no great stature or means, completely unimportant in the usual ways, who had the misfortune to be a friend of several powerful men. Now, it seems the enemies of those men thought they could attack them through him.

"They waylaid him one day as he was riding through the countryside...."

From beneath his hood the newcomer peered at the Watcher steadily. The one-eyed man tumbled his coin in a virtual blur.

"Just south of Vorgreberg...." the stranger said, almost too softly for any but the one-eyed man's ears.

The Watcher surged up, a whimper in his throat as he dragged out a dagger. He hurled himself at the stranger.

One finger protruded from the newcomer's sleeve. He said one word.

Smoke exploded from the Watcher's chest. He flew backward, slammed against a wall. Women and children screamed. Men ducked under the table.

The stranger rose calmly, bundled himself tightly, and vanished into the frigid night.

Frita peeked from beneath the table. "He's gone now." He joined his surviving guests beside the body.

"He was a sorcerer," the sailor muttered.

"Was that the man he was watching for?" Alowa asked. Her excitement was pure thrill.

"I think so. Yes. I think so." Frita opened the Watcher's shirt.

"Who was he?" the sailor asked.

"This here fellow's version of He Who Laughs, I reckon, the way he went on."

"Look at this," said the other man. He had recovered the coin the dead man had dropped when going for his knife. "You don't see many of these. From Hammad al Nakir."

"Uhm," Frita grunted. The silver coin the stranger had given him had been of the same source, but of an earlier mintage.

Bared, the dead man's chest appeared virtually uninjured. The only mark was a small crown branded over his heart.

"Hey," said the ex-sailor. "I've seen that mark before. It's got something to do with the refugees from Hammad al Nakir, doesn't it?"

"Yes," Frita replied. "We shared our meal with a celebrity. With a king."

"Really?" Alowa's eyes were large. "I touched him...."

The sailor shuddered. "I hope I never see him again. Not that one. If he's who I think you mean. He's accursed. Death and war follow him wherever he goes...."

"Yes," Frita agreed. "I wonder what evil brought him to Trolledyngja?"

SIX: The Attack

Three men lurked in the shadows of the park. They appeared to be devotees of the Harish Cult of Hammad al Nakir. Dusky, hawk-nosed men, they watched with merciless eyes. They had been there for hours, studying the mansion across the lane. Occasionally, one had gone to make a careful circuit of the house. They were old hunters. They had patience.

"It's time," the leader finally murmured. He tapped a man's shoulder, stabbed a finger at the house. The man crossed the lane with no more noise than the approach of midnight. A dog woofed questioningly behind the hedges.

The man returned five minutes later. He nodded.

All three crossed the lane.

They had been studying and rehearsing for days. No one was out this time of night. There was little chance anyone would interfere.

Four mastiffs lay rigid on the mansion's lawn. The three dragged them out of sight. Poisoned darts had silenced them.

The leader spent several minutes examining the door for protective spells. Then he tried the latch.

The door opened.

It was too easy. They feared a trap. A Marshall should have guards, enchantments, locks and bolts protecting him.

These men didn't know Kavelin. They couldn't have comprehended the little kingdom's politics had they been interested. Here political difficulties were no longer settled with blades in darkness.

They searched the first floor carefully, smothering a maid, butler, and their child. They had orders to leave no one alive.

The first bedroom on the second floor belonged to Inger,

51

Ragnarson's four-year-old daughter. They paused there, again using a pillow.

The leader considered the still little form without remorse. His fingers caressed a dagger within his blouse, itching to strike with it. But that blade dared be wielded against but one man.

To the Harish Cult the assassin's dagger was sacred. It was consecrated to the soul of the man chosen to die. To pollute the weapon with another's blood was abomination. Deaths incidental to a consecrated assassination had to be managed by other means. Preferably bloodless, by smothering, drowning, garroting, poisoning, or defenestration.

The three slew a boy child, then came to a door with light showing beneath it. A murmur came through. Adult voices. This should be the master bedroom. The three decided to save that room for last. They would make sure of the sleeper on the third floor, Ragnarson's brother, before taking the Marshall himself, three to one.

The plans of mice and men generally are laid without considering the foibles of fourteen-year-old boys who have been feuding with their brothers.

Every night Ragnar booby-trapped his door certain that some morning Gundar would again sneak in to steal his magic kit. . . .

Water fell. A bucket crashed and rattled over an oaken floor. From the master bedroom a woman's frightened voice called, "Ragnar, what the hell are you up to?" Low, urgent discussion accompanied the rustle of hasty movement.

A sleepy, "What?" came from behind the booby-trapped door, then a frightened, "Ma!"

Ragnar didn't recognize the man in his doorway.

The intruder pawed the water from his eyes. His followers threw themselves toward the master bedroom. The door was locked, but flimsy. They broke through.

Inside, a man desperately tried to get into his pants. A woman clutched furs to her nakedness.

"Who the hell . . . ?" the man demanded.

An assassin flicked a bit of silken handkerchief. It wrapped the man's throat. A second later his neck broke. The other intruder rushed the woman.

They were skilled, these men. Professionals. Murder, swift and silent, was their art.

Their teachers had for years tried to school them to react to the unexpected. But some things were beyond their teachers.

Like a woman fighting back.

Elana hurled herself toward the bodkin laying on a nearby wardrobe, swung it as the assassin rounded the bed.

He stopped, taken aback.

She moved deftly, distracting with her nakedness. Seeing him armed with nothing more dangerous than a scarf, she attacked.

He flicked that scarf. It encircled her throat. She drove the dagger in an upward thrust. He took it along his ribs.

Gagging, Elana stabbed again, opened his bowels.

Ragnar suddenly realized that death was upon him. He scrambled to the shadowed corner where he had hidden the weapons Haaken had been training him to use. They were there by sheer chance. He had been too lazy to return them to the family armory after practice, and Haaken had forgotten to check on him.

He went after the assassin in the wild-swinging northman fashion before the man recovered from the drenching. His blows were fierce but poorly struck. He was too frightened to fight with forethought or calculation.

The assassin wasn't armed for this. He retreated, skipping and weaving and picking up slash wounds. He watched the boy's mad eyes, called for help. But there would be none. Through the door of the master bedroom he saw one of his comrades down. The other wrestled with a woman. . . . And someone was stirring upstairs.

The man, though, was dead. He lay halfway between bed and door, silk knotted round his throat.

The night was almost a success. The primary mission had been accomplished.

The leader fled.

Ragnar chased him to the front door before he realized that his mother was fighting for her life. He charged back upstairs. "Ma! Ma!"

The house was all a-scream now. The little ones wailed in the hall. Haaken thundered from the third floor, "What's going on down there?"

Ragnar met the last assassin coming from the bedroom. His mouth and eyes were agape in incredulity.

Ragnar cut him down. For an instant he stared at the bodkin in the man's back. Then he whipped into his parents' bedroom. "Ma! Papa! Are you all right?"

No.

He saw the dead man first, his pants still around his knees.
It wasn't his father.

Then he saw his mother and the disemboweled assassin.

"Ma!"

It was the howl of a maddened wolf, all pain and rage....

Haaken found the boy hacking at the assassin Elana had
gutted. The corpse was chopped meat. He took in the scene,
understood, despite his own anger and agony did what he had to
do.

First he closed the door to shield the other children from their
mother's shame. Then he disarmed Ragnar.

It wasn't easy. The boy was ready to attack anything moving.
But Haaken was Ragnar's swordmaster. He knew the boy's
weaknesses. He struck Ragnar's blade aside, planted a fist.

The blow didn't faze Ragnar. "Like your grandfather, eh,
Red?" He threw another punch. Then another and another. The
boy finally collapsed. Ragnar's grandfather had, at will, been
capable of killing rages. Berserk, he had been invincible.

Shaking his head dolefully, Haaken covered Elana. "Poor
Bragi," he muttered. "He don't need this on top of everything
else."

He poked his head into the hall. The surviving children and
servants were in a panic. "Gundar!" he roared. "Come here. Pay
attention." The ten-year-old couldn't stop staring at the assassin
lying in the hall. "*Run* to the Queen's barracks. Tell Colonel
Ahring to get your father. Right now."

Haaken closed the door, stalked round the bedroom. "How
will I tell him?" he mumbled. He toyed with disposing of the
dead man. "No. Have to do it in one dose. He'll need all the
evidence.

"Somebody's gonna pay for this." He inspected the chopped
corpse carefully. "El Murid has got himself one big debt."

The hand of the Harish had reached into Vorgreberg before.

There was nothing he could do there. He slipped out, sat
down with his back against the door. He laid his sword across his
lap and waited for his brother.

One oil lamp flickered on Ragnarson's desk. He bent close to
read the latest protest from El Murid's embassy. They sure could
bitch about petty shit.

What the hell was Haroun up to?

Haroun was what he was, doing what he thought necessary. Even when he made life difficult, Bragi bore him no ill will. But when bin Yousif stopped conforming to his own nature. . . .

There hadn't been a serious protest in a year. And Valther said there had been no terrorist incursions for several. Nor had many bands of Royalist partisans passed through Kavelin bound for the camps. Nor had Customs reported the capture of any guerrilla contraband.

It was spooky.

Ragnarson wasn't pleased when people changed character inexplicably.

"Derel. Any word from Karak Strabger?"

"None, sir."

"Something's wrong up there. I'd better. . . ."

"Gjerdrum can handle it, sir."

Ragnarson's right hand fluttered about nervously. "I suppose. I wish he'd write more often."

"I used to hear the same from his mother when he was at the university."

"It'd risk letters falling into unfriendly hands anyway." The Queen's condition had to remain secret. For the good of the state, for his own good—if he didn't want his wife planning to cut his throat.

Bragi didn't know how to manage it, but the news absolutely had to be kept from Elana.

Rumors striking alarmingly near the truth ran the streets already.

He massaged his forehead, crushed his eyelids with the heels of his hands. "This last contribution from Breidenbach. You done the figures yet?"

"It looks good. There's enough, but it'll be risky."

"Damned. There's got to be an honest, legal way to increase revenues."

In the past, when he had been on the other end, Bragi's favorite gripes had been government and taxes. Taxes especially. He had seen them as a gigantic protection racket. Pay off or have soldiers on your front porch.

"By increasing the flow of trade."

Economics weren't his forte, but Ragnarson asked anyway. "How do we manage that?"

"Lower the transit tax." Prataxis grinned.

"Oh, go to hell. The more you talk, the more I get confused. If

I had the men I'd do it the Trolledyngjan way. Go steal it from the nearest foreigner who couldn't defend himself."

Prataxis's reply was forestalled by a knock.

"Enter," Ragnarson growled.

Jarl Ahring stepped in. His face was drawn.

Premonition gripped Ragnarson. "What is it? What's happened, Jarl?"

Ahring gulped several false starts before babbling, "At your house. Somebody.... Assassins."

"But.... What...?" He didn't understand. Assassins? Why would...? Maybe robbers? There was no reason for anyone to attack his home.

"Your son.... Gundar.... He came to the barracks. He was hysterical. He said everybody was dead. Then he said Haaken told him to have me find you. I sent twenty men over, then came here."

"You checked it out?"

"No. I came straight here."

"Let's go."

"I brought you a horse."

"Good." Ragnarson strapped on the sword that was never out of reach, followed Ahring at a run. And then at a wild gallop through deserted streets.

A quarter mile short of home Ragnarson shouted, "Hold up!" A patch of white in the park had caught his eye.

The man was on the verge of dying, but he recognized Ragnarson. Surprise shown through agony. He tried to use a dagger.

Bragi took it away, studied him. Soon he was dead. "Loss of blood," Ragnarson observed. "Somebody cut him bad." He handed the knife to Ahring.

"Harish kill-dagger."

"Yeah. Come on."

The news was spreading. Lean, sallow Michael Trebilcock had arrived already, and Valther and his wife, Mist, showed up as Bragi did. Their house stood just up the lane. Neighbors clogged the yard. Ahring's troops were keeping them out of the house.

Bragi took the dagger from Ahring, passed it to Valther's wife. "It is consecrated?"

That tall, incredibly beautiful woman closed her oval eyes.

She moaned suddenly, hurled the blade away. A soldier recovered it.

Mist took two deep breaths, said, "Yes. To your name. But not in Al Rhemish."

"Ah?" Ragnarson wasn't surprised. "Where, then?"

"It's genuine. A Harish knife. Under your name is another, without blood."

"Stolen blade. I thought so."

"What? How?" Ahring asked.

"There still some here?" Bragi asked. Harish assassins usually worked in teams. And they didn't leave their wounded behind.

"Yes sir," a soldier replied. "Upstairs."

"Come," Ragnarson told Ahring, Valther, and Mist. "You too, Michael."

Trebilcock was a strange young man. He had come from the Rebsamen with Gjerdrum when Ragnarson's aide had graduated from that university. His father, Wallice Trebilcock of the House of Braden in Czeschin of the Bedelian League, had died shortly before, leaving him an immense fortune.

He didn't care about money, or anything but getting near the makers and shakers of history.

Ragnarson had felt a paternal attraction from their first meeting, so the youth had slipped into his circle through the side door.

Ragnarson, though unaware of the extent of his losses, was already in a form of shock. It was a protective reaction against emotion, a response learned the hard way, at fifteen. It had been then that disaster and despair had first overtaken him, then that he had learned that swords don't exclusively bite the men on the other side.

He had learned the night he had watched his father die, belly opened by an axe....

Others had died since, good friends and brothers-in-arms. He had learned, and learned, and learned—to stifle emotions till the smoke had cleared, till the dust had settled, till the enemy had been put away.

He knelt by the dead man in the hallway, opening his clothing. "Here." He tapped the man over his heart.

"What?" Valther asked. "He has the tattoo. They always do."

"Look closer," Ragnarson growled.

Valther peered intently at a tricolor tattoo, three cursive

letters intertwined. They meant "Beloved of God." Their bearer was guaranteed entry into Paradise. "What?"

"You see it?"

"Of course."

"Why?"

Valther didn't reply.

"He's dead, Valther. They fade with the spirit."

"Oh. Yes."

So they did, with a genuine Harish assassin, supposedly to indicate that the soul had ascended. Some cynics, though, claimed they vanished to avoid an admission that a Cultist had failed.

"Somebody went to a lot of trouble here," Bragi observed. "But for that, the frame would've worked." It should have. Not many men outside the Harish knew that secret. Most of those were associates of Haroun bin Yousif.

Ragnarson's mysterious friend had researched the Cult thoroughly. He'd had to. He had been its top target for a generation.

And he was still alive.

"There's a trap here," said Bragi.

"What now?" Valther demanded.

"You've got the mind for this. Suppose these are part of the plan? If they failed, and we didn't jump to the conclusion that El Murid was responsible? Who would you suspect then?"

"Considering their apparent origins. . . ."

"Haroun. Of course. There're other folks like them, but who else would be interested?"

"A double frame?"

"Levels. Always there're these levels. Direct attack is too unsubtle. . . ."

"Is something beginning?"

"Something has begun. We've been into it for a long time. Too many impossible things have happened already."

Bragi rose, kicked the corpse, growled, "Get this out of my house." Then he dropped to a knee beside Haaken. He slid an arm around his brother's shoulders, crushed him to his chest. "Haaken, Haaken, it was an evil day when we came south."

Tears still rolled down into the wild dark tangle of Haaken's beard.

He sniffed. "We should've stood and died." He sniffed again, wrapped both arms around Bragi. "Bragi, let me get the kids and we just go home. Now, and the hell with everything. Forget it all. Just you and me and Reskird and the kids, and leave these damned southrons to their own mercies."

"Haaken...."

"Bragi, it's bad. It's cruel. Please. Let's just go. They can have everything I've got. Just take me home. I can't take it anymore."

"Haaken...." He rose.

"Don't go in. Bragi, please."

"Haaken, I have to." There were tears in his own eyes. He knew part of it now. Elana. She was a loss more dire than his father. Mad Ragnar had chosen his death. Elana.... She was a victim of his profession.

Blackfang wouldn't move. And now the younger children, Ainjar and Helga, clung to his legs, bawling, asking for Mama, and what was wrong with Inger and Soren?

Ragnarson asked a question with his eyes. Haaken nodded.

"My babies? No. Not them too?"

Haaken nodded again.

The tears faded. Ragnarson turned slowly, surveying the faces in the hall. Every eye turned from the flame raging in his. Hatred was too mild a word.

Blood would flow. Souls would spill shrieking into the outer darkness. And he wouldn't be gentle. He would be cruel.

"Move aside, Haaken."

"Bragi...."

"Move."

Haaken moved. "You lead, Bragi," he said. "I'll follow anywhere."

Ragnarson briefly rested a hand on his shoulder. "We're probably dead men, Haaken. But somebody will carry the torches to light our path into Hell." For an instant he was startled by his own words. Their father had said the same thing just before his death. "Valther! Find out who did this."

"Bragi...."

"Do it." He shoved into the bedroom.

Valther started to follow him. Mist seized his arm.

She had the Power. Once she had been a Princess of the Dread Empire. She knew what lay behind that door.

Ragnarson had his emotions under control again. He kept hand on sword hilt to remind himself. This was a battlefield. These had fallen in a war....

"Oh."

Haaken tried to pull him out.

"No. Valther. Come here."

The man with his pants half on was Valther's brother Turran. Their eyes met over the corpse, and much went unsaid—words which couldn't be spoken lest blood be their price.

"Take care of him." Ragnarson moved round the bed to his wife. First he dropped to one knee, then he sat. He held her hand and remembered. Twenty years. Sixteen of them married. Hard times and good, fighting and loving.

That was a long time. Nearly half his life. There were a lot of memories.

Behind him, Valther shed tears on his brother's chest.

An hour passed before Bragi looked up.

Rolf Preshka, Captain of the Palace Guards, sat on the edge of the bed. His grief mirrored Ragnarson's.

Bragi had never known for sure, but he had suspected. Rolf had joined him when Elana had. They had been partners before.... But there hadn't been a moment's dishonor since. He knew Preshka that well.

There was that, beneath the grief, which said that Rolf, too, meant to extract payment in blood and pain.

But Preshka was in no shape for it. He had lost a lung in the war. He refused to die, but he was never healthy either. That was why he held the unstrenuous Palace command.

Later still, Nepanthe came. She cried some. Then she and Mist calmed the children and moved them to Valther's house.

"You are my hand that reaches beyond the grave," Bragi told Ragnar before he left, and went on to explain what he knew and felt. Things Ragnar should know in case the next band of assassins succeeded.

The boy had to grow up fast.

Throughout the night Michael Trebilcock observed in silence. Trebilcock remained an enigma. He was a sponge, soaking up others' pain and joy and never revealing any emotion himself.

Once, though, he came and rested a comforting hand on Bragi's shoulder. For Trebilcock that was a lot.

Before sunrise all Bragi's old comrades had come, except Reskird, whose regiment was on exercise around Lake Turntine.

Shortly before dawn, thunder rolled over the mountains. Lightning walked the cloudless night.

It was an omen.

SEVEN: The Old Dread Returns

The wind never ceased its howl and moan through the wild, angry mountains called The Dragon's Teeth. It tore at Castle Fangdred with talons of ice and teeth of winter. The stronghold was the only evidence that Man had ever braved these savage mountains. The furious wind seemed bent on eradication.

It was a lonely castle, far from any human habitation. Only two men dwelt there now, and but one of those could be called alive.

He was old, that man, yet young. Four centuries had he lived, yet he looked not a tenth of that. He stalked Fangdred's empty, dusty halls, alone and lonely, waiting.

Varthlokkur.

His name. The west's dread.

Varthlokkur. The Silent One Who Walks With Grief. Also called The Empire Destroyer.

This man, this wizard, could erase kingdoms as a student wipes a slate.

Or such was his reputation. He was powerful, and *had* engineered the downfall of Ilkazar, yet he was a man. He had his limitations.

He was tall and thin, with earth-toned skin and haunted mahogany eyes.

He was waiting. For a woman.

He wanted nothing to do with the world.

But sometimes the world assailed him and he had to react, to protect his place in it, to secure his own tomorrows.

The other man sat on a stone throne, before a mirror, in a chamber high atop a tower. Its only door was sealed by spells which even Varthlokkur couldn't fathom. He wasn't dead, but neither was he alive. He, too, waited.

A malaise had descended on Varthlokkur. Evil stalked

61

abroad again. Not the usual evil, everyday evil, but the Evil that abided, awaiting its moment to engulf.

This evil had struck before, and had been driven home.

It waxed again, and its burning eyes sought a target for its wrath.

Varthlokkur performed his divinations. He conjured his familiar demons and sped them over the earth on wings of nightmare. He sang the dark songs of necromancy, calling up the dead. He wheedled from them secrets of tomorrow.

It was what they wouldn't, or couldn't, tell him that inspired dread.

Something was happening.

It had its foundation in Shinsan. Once again the Dread Empire was preparing to make its will its destiny. But there was more.

For a while Varthlokkur concentrated on the west and unearthed more evidence of sprouting evil. Down south, at Baxendala, where the Dread Empire had been turned before. . . .

If one word could describe Varthlokkur, it might be *doleful*. His mother had been burned by the Wizards of Ilkazar. His foster parents had passed away before he was ten. Obsessed with vengeance for his mother, he had made devil's bargains in Shinsan—and had rued his decision a thousand times. The Princes Thaumaturge had taught him, then used him to shatter forever the political cohesion of the Empire.

And then? Four centuries of loneliness in a world terrified of him, yet constantly conspiring to use him. Four centuries of misery, awaiting the one pleasant shadow falling across his destiny, the woman who could share his life and love.

And there had been pain and sadness in that, too. She had taken another husband—his own son, from a marriage of convenience, ignorant of his paternity, by then known under the name Mocker. . . .

Those blind hags, the Norns, snickered and wove the threads of destiny in an astounding, treacherous warp and woof.

But he had beaten them. He and Nepanthe had come to an understanding. He had the sorcery to enable it.

Upon her he had placed the same wizardries that had made him virtually immortal. In time Mocker would perish. Then she would share Varthlokkur's destiny.

So he waited, in his hidden stronghold, and was sad and

lonely, till the undertides of old evil washed against his consciousness and excited him.

He performed his divinations, and they were clouded, irresolute, shifting, revolving on but one absolute axis. Something wicked was afoot.

The first nibble of the beast would be at the underbelly of that little kingdom at the juncture of the Kapenrungs and Mountains of M'Hand. At Kavelin.

His final necromancy indicated that he had to get there quickly.

He prepared transfer spells that would shift him in seconds.

Thunder stalked the morning over the knife-edged ridges of the Kapenrungs. Lightning sabered the skies. A hard north wind gnawed at the people and houses of Vorgreberg.

In the house on Lieneke Lane, sad and angry men paused to glance outside and, shivering, ask one another what was happening.

Suddenly, in the bedroom where the lips of Death had sipped, a mote of darkness appeared. Preshka spied it first. "Bragi." He pointed.

It hung in the air heart high, halfway between bed and door.

Ragnarson eyed it. It began growing, a little black cloud taking birth, becoming more misted and tenuous as it expanded. Within, a left-handed mandala revolved slowly, remaining two-dimensional and face-on no matter from what angle Ragnarson studied it.

"Ahring! Get some men in here."

In seconds twenty men surrounded the growing shadow, shaking but ready. Their faces were pale, but they had faced sorcery before, at Baxendala.

The mandala spun faster. The cloud grew larger, forming a pillar. That pillar assumed the shape of a man. The mandala pulsed like a beating heart. For an instant, vaguely, Bragi thought he saw a tired face at the column's capital.

"Be ready," he snarled. "It's coming through."

A voice, like one come down a long, twisted, cold cavern, murmured, "Beware. Shield your eyes."

It was powerfully commanding. Ragnarson responded automatically.

Thunder shook the house. Lightning clawed the air. Blue

sparks crackled over the walls, ceilings, and carpets. Ozone stench filled the air.

"Varthlokkur!" Ragnarson gasped when he removed his palms from his eyes.

A mewl of fear ran through the room. Soldiers became rigid with terror. Two succumbed to the ultimate ignominy, fainting.

Ragnarson wasn't comfortable. They were old acquaintances, he and Varthlokkur, and they hadn't always been allies.

Michael Trebilcock showed less fright and more mental presence than anyone else. He calmly secured a crossbow, leveled it at the sorcerer.

The idea hadn't occurred to Bragi. He appraised the pale youth. Trebilcock seemed immune to fear, unaware of its meaning. That could be a liability, especially when dealing with wizards. One had to watch the subtleties, what the left hand was doing when the sorcerer was waving his right. To not fear him, to be overconfident, was to fall into the enemy's grasp.

Varthlokkur carefully raised his hands. "Peace," he pleaded. "Marshall, something is happening in Kavelin. Something wicked. I only came to see what, and stop it if I can."

Ragnarson relaxed. Varthlokkur, usually, was straightforward. He lied by ommission, not commission. "You're too late. It's struck already." The rage that had been driven down by fear returned. "They killed my wife. They murdered my children."

"And Turran too," Valther said from the doorway. "Bragi, have you been downstairs yet?"

"No. It's bad enough here. I don't want to see Dill and Molly and Tamra. Just take them out quietly. It's my fault they died."

"Not that. I meant they didn't just kill everybody. They searched every room. Lightly, like they'd come back again if they didn't find what they wanted the first time."

"That don't make sense. We know they weren't robbers."

"It wasn't for show. They weren't just here to kill. They were looking for something."

Varthlokkur's expression grew strained. He said nothing.

"There wasn't anything here. Not even much money."

"There was," Varthlokkur interjected. "Or should have been. Looks like the secret was kept better than I expected."

"Uhn? Going to start the mystery-mouthing already?" Bragi had always thought that wizards spoke in riddles so they couldn't be accused of error later.

"No. This is the story. Turran, Valther, and their brother

Brock served the Monitor of Escalon during his war with Shinsan. In the final extremity the Monitor, using Turran, smuggled a powerful token, the Tear of Mimizan, to the west. Turran sent it to Elana by trade post. She had it for almost fifteen years. I thought you knew."

Ragnarson sat on the edge of his bed. He was confused. "She kept a lot of secrets."

"Maybe one of the living can tell us something," Varthlokkur observed, searching faces with dreadful eyes.

"I saw it once," Preshka volunteered. "When we were on the Auszura Littoral, when I was wounded and we were hiding. It was like a ruby teardrop, so by so, that she kept in a little teak casket."

"Teak?" Bragi asked. "She didn't have any teak casket, Rolf. Wait. She had one made out of ebony. Runed with silver. It just laid around for years. I never looked inside. I don't even know if it was locked. It was always around, but I never paid any attention. I thought she kept jewelry in it."

"That's it," Preshka said. "Ebony is what I meant. The jewel, though.... It was spooky. Alive. Burning inside."

"That's it," said Varthlokkur. "One of its most interesting properties is its ability to escape notice. And memory. It's incredibly elusive."

"Hell, it ought to be around somewhere," Ragnarson said. "Seems like I saw it the other day. Either in that wardrobe there, or in the clothes chest. She never acted like it was anything important."

"A good method of concealment," Varthlokkur observed. "I don't think it's here. I don't feel it."

Ragnarson grumbled, "Michael, Jarl, look for it." He buried his head in his hands. Too much was happening. He was being hit from every direction, with worries enough for three men.

He had a premonition. He wasn't going to get time to lie back and absorb his grief, to settle his thoughts and redefine his goals.

The search revealed nothing. Yet the assassin in the park had carried nothing. And Ragnar had said the man hadn't gotten into the master bedroom. "Jarl, where's Ragnar?"

"Mist took him to her place."

"Send somebody. It's time he saw what grown-up life can be like." He might not be alive much longer. There would be more assassins. Ragnar would have to be his sword from beyond the grave.

"Jarl," he said when Ahring returned, "bring some more men over here tomorrow. Find this amulet or talisman or whatever. Valther. Do you think Mist would mind taking care of my kids for a while? I'll be damned busy till this blows away."

"With Nepanthe's help she can handle it."

Ragnarson eyed him. The strain remained. Valther must have known. . . . But that was spilled ale.

What would he have had Valther do? Rat on Turran?

Who else had known? Who had cooperated? Haaken? Haaken had been in the house. . . . No. He knew his brother. Haaken would have cut throats had he known.

He was starting to dwell on the event. He had to get involved in the mystery.

Varthlokkur beckoned him to an empty corner. "I appeared at an emotional moment," the sorcerer whispered. "But this wasn't what brought me. That hasn't yet happened. And it might, if we're swift, be averted."

"Eh? What else can happen? What else can they do to me?"

"Not to you. To Kavelin. These things aren't personal. Though you could suffer from this too."

"I don't understand."

"Your other woman."

Ragnarson's stomach tightened. "Fiana? Uh, the Queen?"

"The child is what caught my attention."

"But it's not due. . . ."

"It's coming. In two or three days. The divinations, though obscure, are clear on one point. This child, touched by the old evil in Fiana's womb, can shake the roots of the earth—if it lives. It may not. There're forces at work. . . ."

"Forces. I'd rid the world of your kind if I could. . . ."

"That would leave you a dull world, sir. But the matter at hand is your Queen. And child."

"Gods, I'm tired. Tired of everything. Ten years ago, when we had the land grant in Itaskia, I griped about life getting dull. I'd give anything to be back there now. My wife would be alive. So would my kids. . . ."

"You're wrong. I know."

Ragnarson met his gaze. And yes, Varthlokkur knew. He had lived with the same despair for an age.

"Karak Strabger. . . . Baxendala. That's almost fifty miles. Can we make it?"

"I don't know. Fast horses. . . ."

"We'll rob the post riders." One of Ragnarson's innovations, which Derel had proposed, was a fast postal system which permitted rapid warning in case of trouble. Its way stations were the major inns of the countryside. Each was given a subsidy to maintain post riders' horses.

The system was more expensive than the traditional, which amounted to giving mail to a traveler bound in the right direction, to pass hand to hand to others till it reached its destination. The new system was more reliable. Ragnarson hoped, someday, to convince the mercantile class to rely on it exclusively, making his system a money-earner for the Crown.

"Jarl. Have some horses saddled and brought round front. Make it...three. Myself, the wizard, and Ragnar. Haaken's in charge till I get back. His word to be law. Understand?"

Ahring nodded.

"Valther?"

"I've got it." He eyed Bragi, expression unreadable.

Bragi realized that his going to the Queen would support the rumors. But he didn't comment. His associates could decide for themselves if they should keep their mouths shut.

He studied faces. His gaze settled on Michael Trebilcock. The pallid youth still held his aim on Varthlokkur. A machine, that man.

"Excuse me," Ragnarson told the wizard. "Michael, come with me a minute."

He took Michael downstairs, outside, round to the garden. Dawn had begun painting the horizon toward the Kapenrungs. Somewhere there Fiana lay in pain, this child of theirs struggling to rip itself from her womb before its time.

"Michael."

"Sir?"

"I don't know you very well yet. You're still a stranger, even after several years."

"Sir?"

"I've got a feeling about you. I like you. I trust you. But am I right?"

The garden was peaceful. From the rear Ragnarson's house looked as innocent of terror as were its neighbors.

"I'm not sure I follow you, sir."

"I don't know who you are, Michael. I don't know *what*. You stay locked up inside. I only know what Gjerdrum says. You don't give away a thing about yourself. You're an enigma.

Which is your right. But you've become part of the gang. I hardly noticed you doing it. You're unobtrusive.

"You hear things. You see things. You know everybody. I've got a feeling you've got the kind of mind that leaps to conclusions past missing data, and you're usually right. Am I wrong?"

Trebilcock shook his head. In the dawnlight he appeared spectral, like a mummy returned to life.

"The question, again. Can you be trusted?" Bragi waited half a minute. Trebilcock didn't respond. "Are you really with me? Or will I have to kill you someday?"

Trebilcock didn't react in the slightest. Again Ragnarson had the feeling that fear, to this young man, was meaningless.

"You won't need to kill me," Michael finally replied. "I've been here since graduation. This's my country now. You're my people. I am what I am. I'm sorry you don't see it. And you can't help thinking whatever you do. But I'm home, sir."

Ragnarson peered into Trebilcock's pale, pale eyes and believed. "Good. Then I've got a job for you."

"Sir?" For the first time since he had met Michael, Bragi saw emotion. And thought he understood. Michael was a rich man's son. What had he ever been able to do for himself or others?

"It's simple. Do what you do. Eyes and ears. Hanging around. Only more of it. Gjerdrum says you're always prowling anyway." Ragnarson stared toward the sunrise. "Michael, I can't trust anybody anymore. I hate it...."

Ahring came out. "The horses are ready. I had some things thrown together for you."

"Thank you, Jarl. Michael?"

"Sir?"

"Good luck."

Ragnarson left the pale young man in deep thought. "Jarl, I've changed my mind. You know what's happening with me and the Queen?"

"I've heard enough."

"Yeah. Well. There's not much point my hiding it now. But don't quote me. Understand?"

"Of course."

"Does it suggest any problems?"

"A thousand. What scares me is what might happen if she doesn't make it. Your witch-man friend sounded.... They say she had trouble with the first one."

"Yeah. Here's what I want. All capital troops but the Vorgrebergers and Queen's Own confined to barracks starting tomorrow, before what's happening leaks. And right now have Colonel Oryon report to me ready to travel. I'll keep one serpent in my pocket by taking him along. Oh. Put the provinces on alert. Militia on standby. Border guards to maximum readiness. Valther can drop hints about an intelligence coup. It'll distract questions about the confinement to barracks. Got it?"

"It's done."

It was well past dawn before three men and a boy rode eastward.

EIGHT: The Prisoner

The pain never ended.

The whispers, the gentle evils in his ears, went on and on and on.

He was stubborn. So damned stubborn that yielding in order to gain surcease never occurred to him.

He didn't know where he was. He didn't know who had captured him. He didn't know why. Pain was the extent of his knowledge. The man in black, the man in the mask, was his only clue. They wouldn't tell him a thing. They just asked. If they spoke at all.

At first they had questioned him about Bragi and Haroun. He had told them nothing. He couldn't have. He didn't know anything. They had been separated too long.

He wakened. Sounds....

The Man in the Mask had returned.

"Woe!" Mocker muttered, slumping lower against floor and wall. It would be rough this time. They hadn't visited for weeks.

But there were just four of them this round. He was thankful for little favors.

Each bore a torch. Mocker watched with hooded eyes as the assistants placed theirs in sconces beyond his reach, one on each wall. The Man in the Mask fixed his above the door.

Mask closed the door. Of course. Not because Mocker might escape. He didn't order it locked from without. He simply closed it so his prisoner wouldn't get the idea there was a world beyond that slab of iron.

Mocker's world was twelve by twelve by twelve, black stone, without windows. Furniture? Chains.

There were no sanitary facilities.

Having to endure his own wastes was good—for his captors' designs.

The most distressing thing was the Mask's silence. Invariably he just stood before the door, statuelike, while his assistants demonstrated their pain-mastery.

This time they had given him too long to recover, and hadn't brought enough muscle.

He exploded.

He tripped the nearest, drove stiffened fingers into the man's throat. He screamed, "Hai!" in bloodthirsty exultation. Cartilage gave way. He made a claw, yanked with all his remaining strength.

One was dead. But three were left.

He hoped they would get mad enough to kill him.

Death was all he had to live for.

He scrambled away, bounced up, threw a foot at the crotch of the Man in the Mask.

The others stopped him. They were no off-the-street amateurs. They put him down and took him apart.

There had been so much pain, so often, that he didn't care. It had gone on so long that he no longer feared it. Only two things mattered anymore. Hurting back, and getting them to kill him.

They didn't get mad. They never did, though this was the worst he had done them. They remained pure business.

Once they had beaten him, they rolled him onto his belly and bound his wrists behind him. Then they pulled his elbows together. He groaned, writhed, sank his teeth into a bare ankle.

The blood taste was pure pleasure.

He tasted his own when a boot smashed into his mouth. He wouldn't learn. Resistance just meant more pain.

They attached a rope at his elbows and hoisted him.

It was an old torture, primitive and passive. When first Mocker had arrived he had been fifty pounds overweight. His weight had yanked his shoulder bones from their sockets.

After he had screamed awhile, and had lost consciousness, someone would doctor him so they could hoist him up again.

Back then there had been no night whispers, just the pain, and the unending effort to break him.

Why?

For whose benefit?

What would the program be this time? Five or ten days on the hook? Or straight to the point for once?

One thing was certain. There would be nothing to eat for a while. Food was strictly for convalescents.

When he was fed at all he got pumpkin soup. Two bowls a day.

One week they had given him cabbage soup. But that petty change had been enough to revive his morale. So it was pumpkin soup or nothing.

The remnants of his most recent meal splashed the floor. Bile befilthed his mouth. He spat.

"Day will come," he promised in a whisper. "Is in balance of eternity, on great mandala. Reverse of fortunes will come."

His torturers spun him. Around and around and around, till he was drunk with dizziness and pain. Then they hoisted him to the ceiling, brought him down in a series of jerks. He heaved again, but there was nothing left in his stomach.

One of them washed his mouth.

This time was different, he realized. Radically different. This was new.

He paid attention.

The Man in the Mask moved.

He peered into Mocker's eyes, pulling each lid back as would a physician. Mocker saw eyes as dark as his own behind slits from which the jewels had been removed. No. Wait. This mask wasn't the one he usually saw. Instead of traceries of black on gold, this bore traceries of gold on black. A different man? He didn't think so. The feeling was the same.

There was no emotion, no mercy in those eyes. They were the eyes of a technician, the bored eyes of a peasant halfway through a day's hoeing midway through planting season.

That mask, though.... The changes were slight, yet, somehow, the alienness was gone. He began searching the burning attic of his mind.

The mask, the black robes, and the hands forever encased in the most finely wrought gauntlets he had ever seen, those were things he knew....

Tervola. Shinsan. He remembered them so well he was sure this wasn't a genuine Tervola.

Trickery was the way *he* would have programmed this had their roles been reversed.

That mask.... He remembered it now. He had seen it at Baxendala. It had lain abandoned on the battlefield after O Shing had begun his retreat. Gold lines on black, ruby fangs, the cat-gargoyle. That one, Mist had said, belonged to a man called Chin, one of the chieftains of the Tervola.

They had assumed, then, that Chin had perished.

Maybe he hadn't, though the eye-crystals had been removed from the mask. . . .

"Chin. Old friend to rescue," Mocker gasped, straining for a sarcastic smile.

The man's only response was a slight hesitation before he said, "There will be more pain, fat one. Forever, if need be. I can wait. Or you can listen. And learn."

"Self, am all ears. Head to toe, two big ears."

"Yes. You will be. The time of crudeness has ended. Now you begin listening and answering." He straightened, faced the door.

Two men pushed a wheeled cart through. Mocker ground his teeth though he didn't understand what he saw on the cart.

The Man in the Mask made him understand those sorcerer's tools.

The pain was worse than any he had known before. This agony was scientifically applied, to one purpose. To drive him mad.

Mocker never had been very stable. It took just two days to crack him completely.

They let him rave in darkness for a week.

Something happened then. More pain. Smoke smells, of flesh burning. Screams that weren't his own. Men struggling. A scream that was his own when he hit the floor of the cell. . . . Darkness. Peaceful, restful darkness.

The night whispers returned. They changed, becoming gentle, delicate whispers, happy, cheerful whispers, like those of a nymph beneath a waterfall. They calmed him. They shaped him.

Then there were gentle, feminine hands, and the distant murmur of grave-voiced men. But for a long time he was bound, his eyes blindfolded. His memories remained vague, confused. A man in a mask. El Murid's men . . . he thought. And Mercenary officers.

They kept him drugged and he knew that, but occasionally he came round long enough to catch snatches of conversation.

Once, evidently, a new nurse: "Oh, dear! What happened?" Horror filled her voice.

"He was tortured," a man replied. "Burned. I don't entirely understand it. From what he says, he was set up by men he

thought were his friends. Nobody knows why yet. Lord Chin
rescued him."

What? Mocker thought. His brains must be scrambled.
Wasn't Chin the torturer?

"It was a complicated plot. One of his friends apparently
tipped El Murid's agents, who kidnapped him. Then he sent
mercenaries who staged a rescue—then turned him over to this
Haroun, who wore the mask the Lord lost when the Dragon
tried invading the west."

"You said...."

"There's a link between man and mask. The Lord lost his, but
he still knows everything that happens if someone wears
it.... Hold it. I think he's coming around. Better give him
another sniff. He needs a lot more healing before we let him
wake up."

It may have been a day or week later. It was another man and
another woman. This time the man seemed to be the newcomer.

"...says Lord Chin transferred right into the dungeon. For
some reason bin Yousif wore the captured mask that day instead
of the one he'd had made to look like it. Lord Chin knew the
minute he put it on. He'd broken the eye crystals, apparently
thinking that was enough to end the connection."

"Bet the Lord caused an uproar."

The woman laughed musically. "They're still petrified,
thinking Shinsan's coming again. They're chasing their tails.
They don't know there's a new order here, that Ehelebe has
come."

"What happened?"

"The one called Haroun got away. Lord Chin punished the
others."

"Bin Yousif would. He's slippery."

"He can't run forever. Ehelebe has come. None shall escape
the justice of the Pracchia."

Even in his dazed state Mocker thought that a little preachy.
Perhaps the woman was a fanatic or recent convert.

"What were they trying to do?"

"Lord Chin thinks they were preparing him as a weapon
against Shinsan. The man called Ragnarson is paranoid about
it.... Get that cotton and the bottle. He's waking up."

People stirred. Mocker smelled something sweet.

"How much longer?"

"A month, maybe. The Lord...."

There were more, shorter episodes, quickly ended by sharp-eyed physicians and nurses.

Then came the day when they didn't put him back under.

"Can you hear me?"

"Yes," he whispered. His throat was dry and raw, as if his screams had never stopped.

"Keep your eyes closed. We're going to remove the bandages. Ming, get the curtain. He hasn't used his eyes for months."

Hands ran over his face. The cold back edge of a scalpel dented his cheek. "Don't move. I have to cut this."

The cloth slipped away. "Now. Open your eyes slowly."

For a while he saw nothing but bright and dim. Then shapes formed and, finally, vaguely discernible faces developed. Three men and five women surrounded him. They seemed anxious. One man's mouth became a hole. Mocker heard, "Can you see anything?"

"Yes."

A hand appeared. "How many fingers?"

"Three."

The women tittered.

"Good. Inform Lord Chin. We've succeeded."

They ran more simple tests, and freed him from the restraints. The speaker told him, "You've been laid up a long time. Don't try getting up without help. We'll start exercising you later."

The group fell silent when the Tervola entered. A man in black, wearing a mask. Black on gold, rubies, the cat-gargoyle.

Mocker shrank away.

A soft laugh escaped the mask. The Tervola sat on his bed, folding the sheet back. "Good. The burns healed perfectly. There won't be much scarring."

Mocker stared at the mask. This one had jewels where the other had been open.

"How...?"

"My fault. I apologize. I miscalculated. Your enemy controlled more power than I expected. He proved difficult. You were burned in the process. For that I offer my deepest apologies. You had suffered enough. A year of torture. Amazing. You're a strong man. Few of my colleagues could have endured."

"Self, being short of memories of interval incarcelated, am wondering, question being, where is same? Self."

"Ehelebe." The man examined Mocker's eyes. Mocker noted that he used his left hand. The Man in the Mask had been right-handed. Haroun was right-handed.

"Same being? Have never heard of same. Is where?"

"Ehelebe isn't a 'where'. It's a state of mind. I'm not being intentionally obscure. It's a nation without a homeland, its citizens scattered everywhere. We call ourselves The Hidden Kingdom. Wherever there are enough of us, we maintain a secret place to gather, to take refuge, to be at peace. This's such a place."

"Being same system known for cult of Methregul."

Methregul was a demon-god of the jungle kingdom of Gundgatchcatil. He had a small, secret, vicious following. The cult was outlawed throughout the western kingdoms. Its bloody altars were well-hidden. Today it was a dying creed. It had been more widespread in Mocker's youth.

"The structures are similar. But the ends are as different as day and night. Our goal is to expunge such darknesses from the world."

Mocker was regaining his wits quickly. "Self, self says to self, what is? Tervola saying same has mission to combat evil?" He laughed. "High madness."

"Perhaps. But who better to alter the direction of Shinsan? You'd be surprised who some of us are. I often am myself, when my work brings me into contact with brothers previously unknown to me."

Mocker wanted to ask why he had never heard of the organization. Old habit stifled the question. He would wait and watch. He needed data, and data not volunteered, on which to base conclusions.

"You've recovered remarkably. With a little wizardry and a lot of care from these good people." He indicated those watching. "You'll see when you get to the mirror. They repaired most of the damage. The bones and the flesh are fine now. You'll have a few scars, but they'll be hidden by your clothing. The only worry left is how you are up here." He tapped Mocker's head.

"Why?"

"Excuse me?"

"Have been told self was saved from wickedry. Am not ungrateful. But many persons labor many hours to repair ravishes—ravages?—of mad cruelty of captor who never says why self was imprisoned. Am wondering."

"Ah. Yes. *My* motives. No, they aren't entirely altruistic. I hope I can convince you to commit your talents to our cause."

Mocker sniffed. "Talent? Self? Lurker in dusty streets unable to support wife and child? Or morals only wafer thickness better than Tervola class? Of gambler habit capable of possessing self to point of self-destruction?"

"Exactly. You're a man. Men are weak. Ehelebe takes our weaknesses and makes them strengths serving Mankind."

Mocker wished he could see the man's face. His voice and apparent honesty were too disarming. He began reviewing everything that had happened from the moment he had received Bragi's invitation to the Victory Day celebration.

His mind froze on Nepanthe. What was she doing? Had she given up on him? What would become of her if Bragi and Haroun really were in cahoots against him?

"No. Self, have had gutsful of politics in time past. Year in dungeon with torturer for lover is final convincer."

"Sleep on it. We'll start your therapy when you wake up." Chin led everyone out.

Mocker tried to sleep, and did doze off and on. A few hours later, a slight sound brought him to the alert.

He cracked one eyelid.

His visitor was a bent old man.

Is old meddler himself, Mocker thought. Is infamous Star Rider.

The Star Rider's legends were as old as the world, older, even, than those of The Old Man of the Mountain, whom Mocker suspected was but the Star Rider's cat's-paw. Nobody seemed to know who this man was, or what motivated him. He moved in his own ways, keeping his own counsel. He was more powerful than the masters of Shinsan, or Varthlokkur. Bragi claimed he had made it impossible for sorcery to influence the course of battle at Baxendala. He meddled in human affairs, from behind the scenes, for no discernible reason. He was the subject of an entire speculative library at Hellin Daimiel's great Rebsamen university. He had become a mystery second only to the mystery of life itself.

So what the hell was he doing here?

Once is accident, twice coincidence. Three times means something is going on. This was Mocker's third encounter with the man.

He continued pretending sleep.

The bent old man stayed only seconds, considering him, then departed.

Was the Star Rider a sneak visitor? Or was he involved in this Ehelebe business? In times past, insofar as Mocker knew, the man had always meddled on behalf of the people Mocker considered the "good guys...."

Twice before the Star Rider had entered his life. Twice he had benefited. It was an argument favoring Lord Chin—assuming the old man wasn't here screwing up the clockwork.

A few weeks later, once he was able to get around and do some spying, Mocker overheard someone informing Chin that Bragi had just dumped Nepanthe and Ethrian into the old dungeons beneath Castle Krief.

He returned to his quarters and thought. The Star Rider had saved his life years ago. Varthlokkur had told him the man wouldn't have bothered if he hadn't had use for him in some later scheme. Was this the payoff?

Of one thing there was no doubt. Bragi and Haroun weren't going to get away with a thing.

NINE: A Short Journey

"Damned saddles get hard," Oryon grumbled. He, Bragi, Ragnar, and the wizard had just ridden up to the Bell and Bow Inn.

"Change of horses," Ragnarson told the innkeeper. "On the Crown Post." He showed an authority he had written himself. "We're over halfway there, Colonel. Twenty more miles. We won't make it till after dark, though. . . . In time?" he asked Varthlokkur.

"You ready to tell me what this's about?" Oryon demanded. Ragnarson had told him nothing.

"Trust me, Colonel."

Oryon was a short, wide bull of a man Bragi had first met during the El Murid Wars. He hadn't liked the man then, and felt no better disposed toward him now. But Oryon was a stubborn, competent soldier, known for his brutal directness in combat. He led his troops from the front, straight ahead, and had never been known to back down without orders. He made a wicked enemy.

Oryon neither looked it, nor acted it, but he wasn't unsubtle. Dullards didn't become Guild Colonels. He realized that a crisis was afoot, that Ragnarson felt compelled to separate him from his command.

Why?

"Something to eat, landlord. No. No ale. Not with my kidneys. Still got to make Baxendala tonight."

"Papa, do we have to?" Ragnar asked. "I'm dead."

"You'll get a lot tireder, Ragnar."

"Uhn," Varthlokkur grunted. "You know how long it's been since I've ridden?"

The innkeeper mumbled, "Five minutes, sirs."

Only Oryon seated himself immediately. Despite his complaint, he was more accustomed to saddles than the others. Oryon was, as he liked to remind Ragnarson, a field soldier.

Varthlokkur took up a tiny salt cellar. "A trusting man, our host." Salt was precious in eastern Kavelin.

Varthlokkur twitched his fingers. The cellar disappeared.

It was a trick of the sort Mocker might have used. Pure prestidigitation. But even the High Sorcery was half lie.

Ragnarson suspected the wizard was making a point. He missed it himself. And Ragnar merely remarked, "Hey, that was neat, Mr. Eldred. Would you teach me?"

Varthlokkur smiled thinly. "All right, Red." His fingers danced in false signs. He said a few false words. The salt reappeared. "It's not as simple as it looks." The salt disappeared. "You need supple fingers."

"He doesn't have the patience," Bragi remarked. "Unless he can learn it in one lesson. I gave him a magic kit before."

"I'll do it slowly once, Red. Watch closely." He did it. "All right, what did I do? Where is it?"

Ragnar made a face, scratched his forehead. "I still missed it."

"In your other hand," Oryon grumbled.

"Oh?" Varthlokkur opened the hand. "But there's nothing here either—except an old gold piece. Now where did that come from?"

Oryon stared at the likeness on that coin, then met Varthlokkur's eye. He had grown very pale.

"Actually, if you'll check behind the boy's ear, and dig through the dirt...." He reached. "What? That's not it." He dropped an agate onto the table. Then a length of string, a rusty horseshoe nail, several copper coins, and, finally, the salt. "What a mess. Don't you ever wash there?"

Ragnar frantically checked the purse he wore on his belt. "How'd you do that?"

"Conjuring. It's all conjuring. Ah, our host is prompt. Sir, I'll recommend you to my friends."

"And thank you, sir. We try to please."

Ragnarson guffawed. Somber Oryon smiled.

"Sirs?" asked the innkeeper.

"You don't know his friends," Oryon replied. Bragi read concern, even dread, in the taut lines the Colonel strove to banish from his face.

The innkeeper set out a good meal. It was their first since leaving Vorgreberg.

"Colonel," Ragnarson said, after the edge was off his hunger and he was down to stoking the fires against the future, "Any chance we can speak honestly? I'd like to open up if you will too."

"I don't understand, Marshall."

"Neither do I. That's why I'm asking."

"What's this about, then? Why'd you drag me out here? To Baxendala? To see the Queen?"

"I brought you because I want you away from your command if she dies while I'm there. I don't know what you'd do if it happened and you heard before I could get back to Vorgreberg. The Guild hasn't given me much cause to trust it lately."

"You think I'd stage a coup?"

"Maybe. There's got to be a reason why High Crag keeps pressuring me to keep your regiment. They know we can't afford it. So maybe the old boys in the Citadel want a gang on hand next time the Crown goes up for grabs. I know you have your standing orders. And I'll bet they cover what to do if the Queen dies."

"That's true." Oryon gave nothing away there. It took no genius to reason it out.

"You going to tell me what they are?"

"No. You know better. You're a Guildsman. Or were."

"Once. I'm Marshall of Kavelin now. A contract. I respect mine. The Guild generally honors its. That's why I wonder. . . . One word. Wasn't going to tell you for a while. But this is a good enough time. Your contract won't be renewed. You'll have to evacuate after Victory Day."

"This'll cause trouble with High Crag. They feel they have an investment."

"It'll bring them into the open, then. Every King and Prince in the west will jump on them, too. High Crag has stepped on a lot of toes lately."

"Why would they? The legalities are clear. Failure to fulfill a contract."

"How so?"

"Kavelin owes High Crag almost fifteen thousand nobles. The Citadel doesn't forgive debts."

"So you've said during our negotiations. They want payment

now? They'll have it." He laughed a bellybreaker of a laugh. "About four years ago Prataxis started applying a little creative bookkeeping at Inland Revenue, and some more in Breidenbach, at the Mint. We've been squirreling away the nobles, and now we'll pay you off. Every damned farthing you've imagined up." His smile suddenly disappeared. "You're going to take your money, sign for it, and get the hell out of my country. The day after Victory Day."

"Marshall. . . . Marshall, I think you're overreacting." Oryon's wide, heavy mouth tightened into a little knot. "We shouldn't be at cross-purposes. Kavelin needs my men."

"Maybe. Especially now. But we can't afford you, and we can't trust you."

"You keep harping on that. What do you want me to admit?"

"The truth."

"You were a Guild Colonel. How much did they tell you?"

"Nothing."

"And you think I'm told more? Once in a while I get a letter. Usually directions for the negotiations. Sometimes maybe a question about what's happening. Marshall, I'm just a soldier. I just do what I'm told."

"Well, I'm telling you. To march. Kavelin's in for rough times. The signs are there. And I don't need to be watching you and everybody else too."

"You're wrong. But I understand."

Varthlokkur continued demonstrating his trick to Ragnar while they argued. The wizard occasionally glanced at Oryon. The soldier shivered each time he did.

"You may not need a regiment after all," Oryon muttered at one point, nodding toward Varthlokkur.

"Him? I don't trust him either. We're just on the same road right now. Innkeeper. What's the tally here?"

"For you, Marshall? It's our pleasure."

"Found me out, eh?"

"I marched with you, sir. In the war. All the way from Lake Berberich to the last battle. I was in the front line at Baxendala, I was. Look." He bared his chest. "One of them black devils done that, sir. But I'm alive and he's roasting in Hell. And that's the way it should be."

"Indeed." Ragnarson didn't remember the man. But a lot of Wesson peasants had joined his marching columns back then.

They had been stout fighters, though unskilled. "And now you prosper. I'm pleased whenever I see my old mates doing well."

He often found himself in this situation. He had never learned to be comfortable with it.

"The whole country, sir. Ten years of peace. Ten years of free trade. Ten years of the Nordmen minding their own business, not whooping round the country tearing up crops and property with their feuds. Marshall, there's them here that would make you King."

"Sir! For whom did we fight?"

"Oh, aye. That was no sedition, sir. The only complaint could be raised 'gainst Her Highness is she's never wed and give us an heir. And now these strange comings and goings of a night, and rumors.... It worries a man, Marshall, not knowing."

"Excuse me," Ragnarson told his table mates. "Sir, I've just had a thought. Something in the kitchen...." He placed his arm round the innkeeper's shoulders and guided him thither.

"You whip up something. A dessert treat. Meanwhile, tell me what you don't know. Tell me the rumors. And about these comings and goings."

"Them others?"

"Not to be trusted. The boy's all right, though. My son. Too bull-headed and big-mouthed, maybe. Gets it from his grandfather. But go on. Rumors."

"'Tain't nothing you can rightly finger, see? Not even really a rumor. Just the feeling going round that there's something wrong. I thought you might ease my mind. Or say what it is so's I got the chance to be ready."

"Makes two of us. I don't know either. And I can't nail anything down any better than you. Comings and goings. What have you got there?"

"'Tain't much, really. They don't stop in here."

"Who doesn't?"

"The men what travels by night. That's what I calls them. From over the Gap. Or going over. Not many, now. One, two groups a month. As many coming as going, two, three men each."

"You seen them in the daytime?"

"No. But I never thought they was up to no good. Not when they skulks around in the night and skips the only good inn ten miles either way."

"Do they come by on the same nights every month?" Ragnarson's brain was a-hum. Thinking he might be on the enemy's track raised his spirits immensely.

"No. Just when they gets the feeling, seems like."

"How long has it been going on?"

"Good two years. And that's all I can tell you, excepting that some went past this morning. After the sun was up, too, come to think. Riding like Hell itself was after them. "Less they steals horses up the line, they's going to be walking by now."

"You said...."

"I never seen them by light? Yes, and it's so. These ones just showed me their backsides going away. Three of them, they was, and I knew it was the same kind 'cause of the way they just went on by."

"What's that got to do with it?"

"Everybody stops here, Marshall. I picked this spot the day we dragged ourselves back through here after we chased that O Shing halfway to them heathen lands in the east. It's right in the middle of everywhere. Gots water and good hayfields.... Well, never mind the what do you call it? Economics? People just stops. It's a place to take a break. You stopped yourself, and it's plain you're in as big a hurry as them fellows this morning. Even people what has no business stopping do. Soldiers. A platoon going up to Maisak? They stops, and you don't hear the sergeants saying nay. Just everybody stops. Except them as rides by night."

"Thanks. You've helped. I'll remember. You can do something else for me."

"Anything, Marshall. It was you made it possible for a man like me to have a place like this for himself...."

"All right. All right. You're embarrassing me. Actually, it's two things. We go back out, you put on a show of what a good choice of dessert I made."

"That's it?"

"No. It starts when we leave. You never saw us and you don't know who we were."

"True enough, excepting yourself, sir."

"Forget me too."

"Secret mission, eh?"

"Exactly."

"It's as good as forgotten now, sir. And the other thing?"

"Don't argue with me when I pay for my meal. Or I'll box your damned ears."

The innkeeper grinned. "You know, sir, you're a damned good man. A real man. Down here with the rest of us."

Ragnarson suffered a twinge of guilt-pain. What would the old veteran think if he found out about Elana and the Queen?

"That's why we followed you back then. Ain't why we joined, I grants you. Them reasons you can figure easy enough. Loot and a chance to break our tenantcy. But it's why we stuck. And there's plenty of us as remembers. The hill people too. Some of them comes in here of a time, and they says the same. You go up on the wall over there in Vorgreberg City sometime if'n you got trouble, and you stomp good and hard and you yell 'I needs good men' and you'll have ten thousand before the next sun shows."

He only wished it were true, dire as tomorrow smelled.

"You marks me, sir. There's men what never marched in the long march, and men what even missed Baxendala, but they'd come too. They maybe wouldn't have the sword you said they should have, because swords is dear, and everybody wanting one, and they wouldn't have no shields, except as some makes they own out of oak in the old way, or maybe green hide, and they wouldn't have no mail, but they'd come. They'd bring they rakes and hoes and butchering knives, they forge hammers and chopping axes...."

Ragnarson sniffed, brushed a tear. He was deeply moved. He didn't believe half of it, but just having one man show this much faith reached down to the heart of him.

"The hill people too, sir. 'Cause you done one thing in this here country, something not even the old Krief himself could do, and, bless him, we loved him. Something not even Eanred Tarlson could do, and him a Wesson himself and at the Krief's ear.

"Sir, you gave us our manhood. You gave us hope. You gave us a chance to *be* men, not just animals working the lands and mines and forges for drunken Nordmen. Maybe you didn't mean it that way. I don't know. We likes to think you did. You being down in Vorgreberg City, we judges only by what we seen in the long march. Coo-ee, we gave them Nordmen jolly whatfor, didn't we sir? Lieneke. I was right there on the hill, not fifty feet from you, sir."

"Enough. Enough."

"Sir? I've offended?"

"No. No." He turned away because the tears had betrayed him. "That's what I wanted. What Her Majesty wanted. What you say you've got. Down there in Vorgreberg, it's hard to see. Sometimes I forget that's only a little bit of Kavelin, even if it's the heart. Come on now. Let's go. And remember what I said."

"Right you are, sir. Don't know you from the man in the moon, and I'll gouge you for every penny."

"Good." Ragnarson put an arm around the man's shoulders again. "And keep your eyes open. There's trouble in those riders."

"An eye and an ear, sir. We've got our swords in this house, me and my sons. Over the door, just like it says in the law. We'll be listening, and you call."

"Damn!" Ragnarson muttered, fighting tears again.

"Sir?" But the Marshall had fled to the common room.

"What do you think?" Ragnarson asked, referring to the creamed fruit he had helped the innkeeper prepare. "Mixed. A trick my mother used to pull when I was a kid." And then, to Oryon, "Colonel, I don't think I'm as frightened of High Crag as I was."

"I don't understand."

"I thought of something when we were mixing the fruit. You know my old friend? Haroun?"

"Bin Yousif? Not personally."

"Five, six years ago he published a book through one of the colleges at Hellin Daimiel. You might read it sometime. Your answer is there."

"I've read it already. Called *On Irregular Warfare*, isn't it? Subtitled something like *The Use Of The Partisan In Achieving Strategic As Well As Tactical Objectives*. Excellent treatise. But his own performance discredits his thesis."

"Only assuming he *has* failed to do what he wants. We don't know that. Only Haroun knows what Haroun is doing. But that's not the answer. Now, innkeeper, the tally. We have to get going."

Somehow, now, the future looked a lot brighter.

TEN: Lord of Lords

"It's a whole new world, Tam," said Tran. The forester couldn't stifle his awe of Liaontung.

"What's that?" Tam asked their escort, an old centurion named Lo. Tam and Lang were as overwhelmed as Tran.

"Ting Yu. The Temple of the Brotherhood. It was there before Shinsan came."

Lo was their keeper and guide. Their month in his care hadn't been onerous. An intimate of Lord Wu and a senior noncom of the Seventeenth Legion, Lo had been a pleasant surprise. He was quite human when outside his armor.

"Where do you live, Lo?" Tam asked. "You said you had your own house that time we visited the barracks."

The boy's curiosity invariably amazed the centurion. He had never married, and had had no childhood himself. He knew only those children in legionary training. "It's not far, Lord." With a hint of embarrassment, "Would it please you to visit, Lord?" Behind his embarrassment lay a gentle, almost defiant pride.

Tran sipped tea and shook his head as Lo showed them his tiny garden.

"What's this one?" Lang asked, fingertip a whisker off the water.

Lo leaned over the pool. "Golden swallowtail." Sadly, "Not a prime specimen, though. See the black scales on this fin?"

"Oh!" Tam ejaculated as another goldfish, curious, drifted from beneath the lily pads. "Look at this one, Lang."

"That's the lord of the pool. That's Wu the Compassionate," Lo said proudly. "He *is* purebred. Here, Lord." He took crumbs from a small metal box, dribbled a few onto Tam's fingertips. "Put your fingers into the water—gently!"

Tam giggled as the goldfish sampled his fingerprints.

Tran studied the exotic plants surrounding the pool. There was a lot of love here, a lot of time and money. Yet Lo was a thirty-year veteran of the Seventeenth. Legionnaires quailed before him. But for an intense loyalty to Lord Wu, he could have become a centurion of the Imperial Standard Legion, Shinsan's elite, praetorian legion.

What was Lo doing breeding goldfish and gardening? Obviously, Shinsan's soldiers had facets outsiders seldom saw.

Tran wasn't happy. The revelation made it difficult to define his feelings. Soldiers shouldn't stop being sword-swinging automatons and start being human. . . .

Liaontung was a nest of paradoxes and contrasts. Once it had been the capital of a small kingdom. A century ago Lord Wu and the Seventeenth had come. Liaontung had become an outpost, a sentinel watching the edge of empire, its economy militarily dependent. Reduction in enemy activity had drawn colonists, then merchants. Yet the military presence persisted.

The Tervola, with their vastly extended lives, under the Princes, were patient conquerers. Take it a week or a century, they pursued operations till they won. They knew they would outlive their enemies. And no foe had their command of the Power.

Wu's latest foes, the Han Chin, were gone. The frontiers of his domains had drifted so far eastward that the Seventeenth soon would have to relocate. Liaontung would change, becoming less a border stronghold.

Lord Wu himself was an enigma. He could slaughter an entire race without reluctance or mercy, yet his subjects called him Wu the Compassionate.

Tran asked why.

"To tell the truth," Lo replied, "it's because he cares for them like a peasant cares for his oxen. And for the same reasons. Consider the peasant."

Now Tran grasped it. The poor man's ox was his most valued possession. It tilled his earth and bore his burdens.

"No," Lo said later, when Lang wandered too near a city gate. He gently guided them toward Liaontung's heart, Wu's citadel atop a sheer basaltic upthrust. It had been a monastery before Shinsan's advent.

Lo was the perfect jailor. He kept the cage invisible. Soon Tam had few opportunities to stray. Lord Wu directed him into intensive preparation for Tervola-hood and laying claim to the

Dragon Throne. Lo remained nearby, but seldom invoked his real authority.

Tam's principal tutors were Select Kwang and Candidate Chiang, Tervola Aspirants destined to join Shinsan's sorcerer-nobility. Both were older than Lo, and powerful wizards. Kwang had but a few years to wait to become full Tervola. His destiny was guaranteed. Chiang's future would remain nebulous till the Tervola granted him Select status.

His chances were excellent. Lord Wu was a powerful patron.

The Tervola of the eastern legions, including Wu, also contributed to Tam's education. He was the child of their secret ambitions.

Aspirants, usually the sons of Tervola, were selected for their raw grasp of the Power, and advanced by attaining ever more refined control.

Tam stunned his tutors.

He learned in weeks, intuitively, what most Aspirants needed years to comprehend.

His first few tricks, like conjuring balls of light, amazed Lang and Tran.

"His father is a Prince Thaumaturge," Lo observed, unimpressed.

Time marched. Tam's magicks ceased being games and tricks. And, despite the swiftness of his progress, his instructors grew impatient, as if racing some dread deadline.

"Of course they want to use you," Tran responded to an unexpectedly naive question. "They've never hidden that. Just don't let them make you a puppet."

"I can't stand up to them." Kwang and Chiang had shown him his limitations.

He could best neither, though his raw talent dwarfed theirs.

"True. And don't forget. Be subtle. Or suffer the fate they plan for your father."

Blood began to tell in a growing need to dominate.

"Lord Wu," Tam once protested, when the Tervola was his instructor, "can't I go out sometimes? I haven't left the citadel for months."

"Being O Shing is a lonely fate, Lord," Wu replied. He set his locust mask aside, took Tam's hands. "It's for your safety. You'd soon be dead if the agents of the Princes discovered you."

Nevertheless, Tam remained antsy.

The roots of his malaise lay in his treatment by minor

functionaries. They granted honors mockingly, treated him as O Shing only when Wu was present. Otherwise, they bullied him as if he were a street orphan. Till Tran cracked a few skulls. The persecutions, then, became more subtle.

When Tam was promoted to Candidate-nominee the bureaucrats tried separating him from his brother and Tran. He threw a fit, set his familiar on his chief tormentor, one Teng, and refused to study.

Wu finally intervened. He permitted Tam to retain his contacts and interviewed everyone who came in daily contact with Tam. Many left with grey faces. Then he summoned Tam.

"I won't interfere again," he said angrily. "You have to learn to deal with the Tengs. They're part of life. Remember: even the Princes Thaumaturge are inundated by Tengs. Only men of his choler, apparently, become civil servants."

There was something about Wu that Tam had, hitherto, seen in no one else. Maturity? Inner peace? Self-confidence? It was all that, and more. He awed Tam as did no other man.

The bitter years began when Tam was fourteen.

Treacheries took wing. Double and triple betrayals. A wizard named Varthlokkur destroyed Tam's father and uncle, Yo Hsi.

Lo brought the news. "Pack your things," he concluded.

"Why?" Lang demanded.

"The Demon Prince had a daughter. She's seized his Throne. It means civil war."

"I don't understand," said Tam, gathering his few belongings.

"You, you, get packing," Lo snapped at Lang and Tran. "The Throne, of all Shinsan, is up for grabs, Lord. Between yourself and Mist. And she's stronger than we are. The western Tervola support her." More softly, "I wouldn't give a glass diamond for our chances."

"She's that terrible?"

"No. She's that beautiful. I saw her once. Men would do anything for her. No woman like her has ever lived. But she's that terrible, too, if you look past her beauty. Lord Wu believes she conspired in the doom of the Princes."

"Why involve me?" Silly. This was the deadline Kwang and Chiang had been racing.

"You're Nu Li Hsi's son. Come on. Hurry. We have to hide you. She knows about you."

It was all too sudden and confusing. Willy-nilly, tossed by the whims of others, he fled a woman he didn't know.

O Shing was, Wu believed, the strongest Power channel ever born. But he hadn't the will to back it, nor the training to employ it. He had to be kept safe while he grew and learned.

"Oh, lord," Tam sighed. They were three miles from Liaontung. The band included Lo, Chiang, Kwang, and a Tervola named Ko Feng.

A black smoke tower had formed over Liaontung. Lightnings carved its heart. Here, there, hideous faces glared out.

"She's fast," Ko Feng snarled. "Come on! Move it!" He ran. The others kept up effortlessly. Being physically tireless was an axiom in Shinsan. But Tam....

"Damned cripple!" Feng muttered. He caught the boy's arm. Lo took the other.

The black tower howled.

"Lord Wu will show her something," Kwang prophesied.

"Maybe," Feng grumbled. "He was waiting."

Tam found most of the Tervola tolerable. He liked Lord Wu. But sour old Feng he loathed. Feng made no pretense of being servant or friend. He plainly meant to use Tam, and expected Tam to reciprocate. Feng called it an alliance without illusion.

Their flight took them to a monastery in the Shantung. Feng left to rejoin his legion. Elsewhere, the Demon Princess routed the Dragon Prince's adherents.

Her thoughts seldom strayed far from O Shing. She traced him within the month.

Tam sensed the threat first. Pressed, his feeling of the Power had developed swiftly.

"Tran, it's time to leave. I feel it. Tell Lo."

"Where to, Lord?" the centurion asked. He didn't question the decision. One of his darker looks silenced Select Kwang's protest. That made clear whom Wu had put in charge.

O Shing knew little about the nation being claimed in his name.

"Lo, you decide. But quickly. *She* is coming."

Kwang and Chiang wanted to contact Wu or Feng. "No contact," O Shing insisted. "Nothing thaumaturgic. It might help them locate us."

They didn't argue. Was Wu using this hejira to further his education?

Again they were just miles away when the blow fell. This time it was mundane, soldiers directed by a Tervola Chiang identified as Lord Chin, a westerner as mighty as Lord Wu.

"Tran," said Tam, as they watched the soldiers surround the monastery, "take charge. You're the woodsman. Get us out. Everyone, this man is to be obeyed without question."

There were complaints. Tran wasn't even a Citizen.... Lo's baleful eye silenced the protests.

Chin stalked them for six weeks. The party declined to six as the hunters caught a man here, a man there. Chiang went, victim of a brief, foredoomed exchange with Lord Chin. He didn't choose to go. Surprised, in despair, he fought the only way he knew.

His passing allowed the others to escape.

In the end there were Tam, Lang, Tran, Kwang, Lo, and another old veteran from the Seventeenth. They hid in caves in the Upper Mahai. Their stay lasted a year.

Men drifted to the Mahai, to O Shing. The first were regular soldiers from legions torn by the conflicting loyalties of their officers. Later, there were Citizens and peasants, fleeing homes and cities ruined by the Demon Princess's attacks.

Lord Wu, though far from Mist's match in the Power, won a reputation as a devil. Her chief Tervola, Chin, could defeat but never destroy him.

O Shing gave the recruits to Tran to command.

Tran played guerrilla games with them. His tactics were unorthodox and effective. Much enemy blood stained the rocky Mahai.

Tam learned to keep moving, to be where his foes least expected him. He learned to command. He learned to stand by his own judgment and will. He learned to trust his intuitions, Tran's military judgments, and Lang's assessments of character.

In the crucible of that nightstalk he learned to control and wield his awesome grasp of the Power.

He learned to survive in an inimical world.

He *became* O Shing.

Mist's attempts to hunt him down became half-hearted, though. Overconfident of her grip on Shinsan, sure time would bring the collapse of the eastern faction, she and her Tervola became embroiled in foreign adventures. Greedily, her Tervola devoured small states all round Shinsan's borders.

It was a different Shinsan without the balance and guidance

of the Princes Thaumaturge. Everything speeded up. Patience and perseverance gave way to haste and greed. Old ways of doing, thinking, believing, collapsed.

In one year six men became thirty thousand. More than the barren Mahai could support. Peasants and Citizens received war-training in their Prince's struggle to stay alive.

"It's time to move," Tam told his staff one morning. He seemed almost comical, commanding captains ages older than he. "We'll go to the forest of Mienming. It's more suited to Tran's war style."

Lord Chin was adapting. He was using a semisentient bat to locate and track Tran's raiders. Food could be stolen but concealment could not.

The old sorcerers returned to their commands and prepared for the thousand-mile march. No one questioned O Shing's wisdom.

Mist's troops met them at the edge of the Mahai. Skirmishing continued throughout the long march. A third of O Shing's army perished forcing a crossing of the Taofu at Yaan Chi, in the Tsuyung Hills. For three days the battle raged. Sorceries murdered the hills, and it seemed, toward the end, that O Shing would become one with the past, that his gamble had failed.

Tam redoubled his stakes, raising hell creatures few Tervola dared summon.

Mist's army collapsed.

Eyebrows rose behind a hundred hideous masks as the news spread. Chin defeated? By a child and a woodsman untrained in the arts of war? Six legions overwhelmed by half-trained peasants scantily backboned by the leavings of shattered legions?

The Tervola weren't bemused by Yo Hsi's daughter. They didn't enjoy being ruled by a woman. Quiet little missions penetrated the Mienming. This Tervola or that offered to slip the moorings of a hasty alliance if O Shing dealt her another outstanding defeat.

Seizing power wasn't the lodestone of Tam's life. Survival was the stake he had on the table. Chin was a tireless hunter.

O Shing was still in hunted-beast mind-set when Wu reentered his life.

Mist's Tervola had coaxed her into invading Escalon. Escalon was no impotent buffer state. The neutralist Tervola, constituting most of their class, joined the venture. Expansion was ancient national policy.

They weren't pleased with the war's conduct. Escalon was strong and stubborn. Mist had no feel for imaginative strategy. Her angry hammer blows consumed legions.

In Shinsan soldiers weren't, as elsewhere, considered fodder for the Reaper. Tervola loved spending men like a miser loved squandering his fortune. Two decades went into preparing a soldier. Quality replacements couldn't be conjured from beyond the barrier of time.

Divining future trouble, they had begun training enlarged drafts years ago, but those wouldn't be ready for a decade.

Their wealth and strength were being squandered.

They simmered with rebellious potential.

Wu and Feng wanted to take advantage.

"No!" Tam protested. "I'm not ready."

"*We* aren't ready," Tran growled. "You'll waste what little we've husbanded."

"It's now or never," Feng snarled.

Lord Wu tried persuasion. And O Shing acquiesced, overawed by Wu's age and ancient wisdom.

Tran got to choose the time.

Most of Escalon and a tenth of Shinsan lay under the shadow, terror, and destruction of Mist's assault on the Monitor and Tatarian, Escalon's capital. Lo led Tran's best fighters through the transfer....

O Shing followed minutes later. Mist had fled. Want it or not, he had inherited a war. The legions were in disarray. Tervola were demanding orders. He had no time to think. With Tran's help he battled the Monitor to a draw.

Afterward, Tran muttered, "We haven't gained anything. We're on the bull's-eye now, Tam." He indicated Wu and Feng, who were celebrating with small cups of Escalonian wine.

"Drink," Feng urged, offering Tam a cup. The professional grouch was radiant. "They say it's the world's finest wine."

"Sorry," Tam mumbled. This was the first time he had seen Feng without his mask. He was as ugly in fact as spirit. At one time fire had ravaged half his face. He hadn't fixed it. Tam feared that said something about the man within.

"Celebration's premature," Tran grumbled. "Somebody better stay sober."

O Shing's reign lasted a month.

Mist did as she had been done. Her shock troops transferred through during the height of a battle.

In the Mienming, Tam sat in the mud craddling Lo's head. The centurion was almost gone.

"This is the price of our lives," Tam hissed. Wu, maskless, moist of eye, knelt beside the man who, possibly, had been his one true friend. "Was a month worth it?"

Wu just held Lo's hand.

The centurion had fought like a trapped tiger. His ferocity had allowed O Shing, Wu, Feng, and the others to escape.

"No more, Wu," said Tam. He spoke in a tone suited to his title. "I've seen children more responsible. Amongst the forest people you despise." He indicated Tran, sitting alone, head between his knees. He and Lo had grown close.

"What'll satisify you? All our deaths? This time Lo and Kwang. Next time? Tran? My brother? If you persist, I promise I'll be the last. After you, My Lord."

Wu met his gaze, recoiled.

Neither he nor Chin seemed able to learn. They bushwhacked one another repeatedly. Chin finally got the upper hand.

O Shing remained in Mienming nursing his grudge against Tervola.

Mist completed her Escalonian adventure. Success stabilized her position, though not solidly. Her sex, the casualties, and her failure to capture the Tear of Mimizan remained liabilities.

O Shing first heard of the Tear from Wu. Wu wasn't sure what it was, just that it was important. It was the talisman which had made possible the Monitor's prolonged defense of Tatarian.

"It's one of the Poles of Power," Feng opined.

"Bah!" Wu replied. "Monitor's propaganda. There's no proof."

The Poles were legendary amongst the thaumaturgic congnoscenti. One, supposedly, was possessed by the Star Rider. The second had been missing for ages. Even the highest wizards had nearly forgotten it. During the recent conflict the Monitor had hinted that the Tear was the lost Pole.

Every sorcerer living would have bartered his soul to possess a Pole. The man who mastered one could rule the world.

In time, sensing the restlessness of the Tervola, Mist looked for another foe to divert them. She took up a program inherited from her father, which she had quietly nurtured since her ascension.

O Shing spent ever more time alone, or with Tran and Lang. Only those two still treated him as Tam. Only they considered him as more than a means to an end.

Lo's death cost Wu O Shing's love and respect.

Wu was changing. No one called him "the Compassionate" now. A poisonous greed, a demanding haste, had crept into his soul.

And O Shing was changing too, becoming cynical and disenchanted.

The man in the cat-gargoyle mask made his first presentation to the Pracchia. Nervously, he said, "Mist plans to invade the west now. She's suborned the Captal of Savernake. Maisak, the fortress controlling the Savernake Gap, will be Shinsan's. Ehelebe-in-Shinsan can assume control of the invasion whenever the Pracchia directs. We have moved with care, into leading positions in both political factions. I have become Mist's chief Tervola. Members of my Nine are close to the Dragon Prince. We still recommend that nominal rule be invested in the latter. He remains the more manageable personality." He detailed plans for eliminating Mist and making O Shing the Pracchia's puppet.

"Absolutely perfect," said he who was first in the Pracchia. "By all means encourage Mist's plans. She'll take care of herself for us."

O Shing, Lang, and Tran watched the commandos disappear. O Shing still shivered with the strain of a recently completed sorcery. Mist and the Captal certainly would be diverted.

"Why're we here, Tran?" he whispered.

"Destiny, Tam. There's no escape. We must be what we must be. How many of us like it? Even forest hunters ask the same question."

O Shing met Wu's eye. Lord Wu was in disguise. He wore no mask. His expression was taut, pallid, frightened.

Lang whispered, "Friend Wu is spooked." Lang took tremendous pleasure in seeing the mighty discomfited, perhaps because it brought them nearer his own insignificance. "That thing you called up.... He wasn't looking for that."

"The Gosik of Aubuchon? I was just showing off."

"You scared the skirts off him," Tran said. "He's having second thoughts about us."

Wu was frightened. Not even the Princes Thaumaturge, at the height of their Power, had dared call that devil from its hell. And, though O Shing hadn't gone quite that far himself, he *had* opened a portal through which the monster could cast a shadow of itself, a doorway through which it might burst if O Shing's Power weren't sufficient to confine it.

Wu wasn't certain whether O Shing had overestimated himself or was genuinely able to control the devil. Either way, he had trouble. If the Gosik broke loose, the world would become its plaything. If O Shing truly commanded it, the Dragon Prince was more powerful than anyone had suspected, and had trained himself quietly and well. Those who intended using him might find the tables turning.

Worse, the youth was winning allegiances outside the Tervola. He was popular with the Aspirants. This sudden Power might tempt him to replace Tervola with Aspirants he trusted.

But it was too late to change plans. Rectifications had to wait till Mist had been destroyed.

Wu felt like a man who bent to catch a king snake and discovered that he had hold of a cobra.

News filtered back. Mist had been completely surprised. Only a handful of supporters, all westerners, were with her. Tran's commandos were occupying Maisak. The woman would be theirs soon.

The same promises were still coming through two days later. The lives of Tervola had been lost, and the survivors kept saying, "Soon".

"This'll never end," Tam told Lang while awaiting their turn to transfer. "She'll get away. Just like we always did. There must be a reason."

Tran had been sitting silently, lost in thought. "May I hazard a guess?"

"Go ahead."

"I think there're other plots afoot. One catches things here and there if one listens."

"They'd *let* her get away?"

"Maybe. I'm not sure. She's smart and strong. Whatever, there's something happening. We'd best guard our backs."

O Shing would remember that later, when Wu brought Lord Chin to swear fealty.

Tam remembered escaping Mist's hunter almost miraculously. He graciously accepted Chin's oath, then became thoughtful. Tran was right.

He told Tran and Lang to be observant. No conspiracy could operate without leaving *some* tracks.

The battle at Baxendala upset everyone.

The preliminaries proceeded favorably enough. Chin assumed tactical command, quickly drove the westerners into their defense works. Then he had no choice but frontal attack. Nobody worried. The westerners were a mixed lot, from a half-dozen states, politically enmired, commanded by a man with little large-scale experience, and already had shown poorly against the legions. They would punch through.

The battle, as Shinsan's did, opened with a wizards' skirmish. O Shing, emboldened by Wu's reaction earlier, conjured the Gosik himself. . . .

A bent old man, high above the battlefield, became enraged. This wasn't in his plan. He took steps, knowing the result might delay his ends.

But O Shing was becoming dangerous. He was outside the control of Ehelebe-in-Shinsan. . . .

He ended the efficacy of the Power, using his Pole of Power, which had the form of a gold medallion.

The cessation of the Power rattled O Shing. His Tervola were dismayed. Never had they known the Power to fail.

"We retain our advantages," Chin argued. "They're still weak and disunited. We'll slaughter them." His confidence was absolute.

Chin's prediction seemed valid initially. The westerners were stubborn, but no match for the legions. Their lines crumbled. . . .

Yet Tam couldn't shake a premonition of disaster.

Tran felt it too. And acted. He ordered O Shing's bodyguard to be ready.

Then it happened. Western knights exploded from a flank long thought secured by local allies. They hit the reserve legion before anyone realized they weren't friendly.

The soldiers of Shinsan had never encountered knights. They stood and fought, and died, as they had been taught—to little real purpose.

Chin panicked. It communicated itself to O Shing.

"Stand fast!" Tran begged. "It'll cost, but we'll hold. They won't break."

Nobody listened. Not even the youth who had vowed to respect Tran's advice above all others'.

The horsemen turned on the legions clearing Ragnarson's defense works. Chin and Wu cried disaster.

Tran cajoled and bullied enough to prevent a rout.

That night O Shing ordered a withdrawal.

"What?" Tran demanded. "Where to?"

"Maisak. We'll retain control of the pass, transfer more men through, resume the offensive." He parroted Chin. "The Imperial Standard will reman here." His lips were taut. He hated that sacrifice. The legion would be lost if reinforcements didn't arrive in time.

"Stand here,".Tran urged again.

"We're beaten."

Tran gave up. When O Shing's ear went deaf there was no point in talking on.

Maisak greeted them with arrows instead of paeans for its overlord.

The King Without a Throne had gotten there first.

Chin blew. up. Never had soldiers of Shinsan been so humiliated.

"Attack!" he shrieked. "Kill them all!"

O Shing ignored Tran again.

The assault cost so many lives, uselessly, that Chin's standing with the Tervola plummeted. They wouldn't listen to him for years.

Tervola also questioned O Shing's acceding to Chin's folly when the barbarian, Tran, had foreseen the outcome....

After that secondary defeat O Shing put his trust in Tran again. The hunter guided the survivors across the wilderness, through terrible hardships. Two thousand men reached Shinsan. Of twenty-five thousand.

The western adventure, so optimistically begun, traumatized O Shing. The bitter trek across the steppes renewed his acquaintance with fear. Three times he had endured the fleeing terror: with the Han Chin, ducking Mist, and now escaping the west.

He wanted no more of it.

The terrors would shape all his policies as master of Shinsan.

That much he had gained. Mist had been beaten. She resided with the enemy now, lending her knowledge to theirs.

He became a dedicated isolationist. Unfortunately, the Tervola didn't see it his way.

ELEVEN: Marshall and Queen

Ragnarson's party reached Karak Strabger at midnight. Bragi grumbled about the castle's disrepair. It hadn't seen maintenance since the civil war. Something needed doing. Baxendala was crucial to Kavelin's defense.

Fortifications were like women past thirty. They required constant attention or quickly fell apart.

He gave his mount to one of the tiny garrison, glanced at Varthlokkur.

"Not time yet. She's resting. We have a day."

"I'll go see her. For a minute. Ragnar, stay with Mr. Eldred. The duty corporal will find you someplace to sleep."

"I need it," Ragnar replied. A shadow crossed his brow.

"I'll be down in a minute." He hugged his son. They had lost a lot, and had had too much time to remember while riding.

Ragnarson wasn't a demonstrative man. His hug startled Ragnar, but clearly pleased him. "Go on. And behave. Everybody in the army has permission to wax your ass if you act up."

It was a long climb. Gjerdrum and Dr. Wachtel had wanted Fiana inacessible.

She was alone except for a maid asleep in a chair. Only a candle beside her bed illuminated the room.

He stood over Fiana awhile, staring at beauty wasted by pain. She slept peacefully now, though. He wouldn't disturb her after what Varthlokkur suggested she had been through.

Gone was the elfin quality that had stunned him when first they met. But she had been barely twenty then, and tormented only by the cares of office.

The maid wakened. "Oh. Sir!"

"Shh!"

She joined him.

"How is she?"

"Better tonight. Last night.... We thought.... It's good you're here. It'll help. That you couldn't be..... That made it hard. Can you stay?"

"Yes. There's no reason not to anymore."

The maid's blue eyes widened.

"Do I sound bitter?" His attention returned to the pain lines on Fiana's face. "Poor thing."

"Wake her. I'll go."

"I shouldn't. She needs the rest."

"She needs you more. Goodnight, sir."

He settled on the edge of the bed, stared, thought. A good man, that innkeeper had said. And he had brought Fiana to this.

He liked to believe he was one of the good guys. Wanted—even needed—to think so. By the standards of his age, he was. So why was it that every woman who entered his life got nothing but pain for her trouble? How happy had he made Fiana? Or Elana? He never should have married. Pleasure he should have taken in chance encounters and houses of joy. Elana would have been better off with Preshka. The Iwa Skolovdan would have done right by her....

He was holding Fiana's hand. Too tightly. Her eyelids fluttered. He stared into pale blue eyes pleasantly surprised.

"You came," she murmured.

He thought of Elana. A tear escaped.

"What's wrong?"

"Nothing. Nothing to worry your pretty head about. Go back to sleep."

"What? Why? Oh! You look terrible."

"I didn't clean up."

"I don't care. You're here."

He smoothed her hair on her cerulean pillow. The blue framed her blondness prettily. The maid had taken good care of her hair. Good girl. She knew how to buoy sinking spirits.

"You're exhausted. What've you been doing?"

"Not much. Haven't slept for a couple days."

"Trouble? Is that why you came?"

"No. Don't worry about it. Come on. Go back to sleep. We'll talk in the morning."

She eased over. The mound of her belly was incredibly huge. Elana had never been that big. "Here. Lay down with me."

"I can't."

"Please? You've never stayed with me all night. Do it now."

"I brought my son. I told him I'd be back down."

"Please?"

He bit his lip.

"It might be the last time we can." Fear crossed her face. "I'm scared. I won't live through it. It's so bad...."

"Now wait a minute. There's nothing to worry about. You'll be all right. Funny. Women always get so scared. They go through it all the time. Elana..."

She wasn't offended. "It's not like before. It hurt last time, but only when the baby came." Her eyes moistened. Her daughter, a precocious, delightful blonde elf, had died mysteriously soon after the civil war. That had been one of Fiana's great sorrows. Another had been the passing of her husband, the old King, an event which had precipitated the civil war.

"Come on. Stay."

He couldn't refuse her. The look in her eyes....

"Now," she said after he slipped in beside her, "tell me what happened."

"Nothing. Don't worry."

She was persistent. And he didn't need much encouragement. He had to loose the grief sometime.

She cried with him. Then they slept.

And no one disturbed them. Her people were discreet.

It was afternoon when Ragnarson wakened. Fiana immediately asked, "You think it's Shinsan again?"

"Who else? Wish I had a way to hit back. If it weren't for you, and Kavelin, I'd head east right now, and not stop till I had my sword through O Shing's heart." Someday, he thought. Maybe with Varthlokkur's help. The wizard had his own grudge against Shinsan.

He hadn't mentioned Varthlokkur. What he had revealed had troubled Fiana enough. And had done her good. Worrying about Kavelin distracted her. Knowing her condition had drawn Varthlokkur from his eyrie might crack what control she retained.

"Darling, I've got to go downstairs. Ragnar will think I abandoned him. And Wachtel is probably dancing in the hall, trying to decide if he should stick his nose in."

"I know. Come back. Please? As soon as you can?"

"I will."

And he did, with Varthlokkur and Wachtel. Varthlokkur had conjured sorcerer's devices from Fangdred—and had frightened half the Queen's staff out of Karak Strabger.

What wild rumors were afoot in Baxendala?

Ragnarson kept his promise, but Fiana never knew. Her siege of agony had resumed. She screamed and screamed while Bragi and the doctor held her so she wouldn't hurt herself.

"It's worse this time," said Wachtel. He was a kindly old gentleman who winced with every contraction. He had been Royal Physician for longer than Fiana had been alive, was one of those rare Kaveliners of whom Ragnarson had heard no evil at all. Like Michael Trebilcock, he was unacquainted with fear. Varthlokkur didn't impress him except as a respectable physician.

Wachtel knew the wizard's history. Varthlokkur had learned life-magicks from the Old Man of the Mountain, who was believed to be the master of the field.

"Hold her!" Varthlokkur snapped. "I've got to touch her. . . ."

Bragi pressed down on her shoulders. She tried to bite. Wachtel struggled with her ankles. The wizard laid hands on her belly. "Never seen a woman this pregnant. You're sure it's only eight months?"

"That's what disturbs me," Wachtel said, nodding. His face was taut, tired. "You'd think she was delivering a colt."

"It's overdue. You're positive . . .? Oh!" He touched hastily, his face smeared with sudden incredulity. "Wachtel. You have anything to quiet her?"

"I didn't want to give her something and be sorry later."

"Give it to her. She'll need it. We'll have to cut. No woman could dilate enough to deliver this."

Wachtel eyed him—then released Fiana's ankles. The wizard assumed his place.

"Over twenty pounds," Varthlokkur murmured.

"Impossible!"

"You know it. I do. But that thing in her womb. . . . Tell it, Doctor. Marshall?"

"Uhm?"

"I don't know how to tell you. . . . I'm not sure *I* understand. This isn't your child."

A sneak attack with a club couldn't have stunned Ragnarson more. "But. . . . That's impossible. She. . . ."

"Wait! This's the part that's hard to explain."

"Go. I need something."

"Remember the plot hatched by Yo Hsi and the Captal of Savernake? As the Captal confessed it before you executed him?"

The Captal had been a rebel captain during the civil war. The Demon Prince had been his sponsor. Shinsan, to aid him, had put in the legions Ragnarson had defeated here at Baxendala. The plot had opened with the artificial insemination of Fiana, in her sleep, to create a royal heir controllable from Shinsan. To complicate their duplicity, the plotters had substituted another child for the newborn, ensuring a disputed succession.

Yo Hsi had made one grave error. Fiana's child had been a girl.

That had complicated matters for everyone.

Then Yo Hsi and Nu Li Hsi had been destroyed in Castle Fangdred. The plot lay fallow till Yo Hsi's daughter, Mist, resurrected it.

The ultimate failure of the rebel cause had brought the girl home to her mother. Then, during the winter, she had died of a spider bite.

"All right. Get to the point."

"This is the child meant to be born then."

"What? Bullshit. I ain't no doctor. I ain't no wizard. But I know for goddamned sure it don't take no fifteen years...."

"I confess to complete mystification myself. If this's Yo Hsi's get, then, necessarily, Carolan was your daughter."

Fiana's struggles lessened as Wachtel's drug took effect.

"Wizard, I can believe almost anything," Ragnarson said. "But there ain't no way I'll believe a woman could have my baby five years before I met her."

"Doesn't matter what you believe. You'll see when we deliver. Doctor. You agree we'll have to cut?"

"Yes. I've feared it all month. But I put off the decision, just hoping.... It should've been aborted."

"When?"

"I'll have your help?"

"If I can convince the Marshall...."

"Of what?"

"That this isn't your get. And that you should let me have it."

Ragnarson's eyes narrowed suspiciously.

"I know what you're thinking. You don't trust me. I don't

know why. But try this. We'll deliver the child. If you want to acknowledge it then, that's your choice. If you don't, I get it. Fair enough?"

Why would Varthlokkur lie? he wondered. The man was wiser then he.... "Do it, damnit. Get it over with."

"We'll need some...."

"I've been at birthings before. Nine." Elana had had three children who had died soon after birth. "Wachtel, have what's-her-name get it. Then explain why it's not ready already."

"It is ready. Sir." Wachtel was angry. No one questioned his competence or dedication.

"Good. Get at it." Ragnarson settled on a chest of drawers. "The man will be here watching." He rested his sword across his lap. "He won't be happy if anything goes wrong."

"Lord, I can't promise anything. You know that. The mothers seldom survive the operation...."

"Doctor, I trust *you*. You do the cutting."

"I plan to. The man's knowledge I respect. I don't know his hand."

Wachtel began. And, despite the drugs, Fiana screamed. They bound her to the bed, and brought soldiers to help hold her, but she thrashed and screamed....

Wachtel and Varthlokkur did everything possible. Ragnarson could never deny that.

Nothing helped.

Ragnarson held her hand, and wept.

Tears didn't change anything either.

Nor did the most potent of Varthlokkur's life-magicks. "You can't beat the Fates."

"Fates? Damn the Fates! Keep her alive!" Ragnarson seized his sword.

"Sir, you may be Marshall," Wachtel shouted. "You may have the power to slay me. But, by damned, this's my field. Sit down, shut up, and stay the hell out of the way. We're doing everything we can. It's too late for her. We're trying to save the baby."

There was a limit to what Wachtel would tolerate, and the soldiers saw it his way.

Ragnarson's aide, Gjerdrum, and two men got between Ragnarson and the doctor.

While Wachtel operated Varthlokkur began a series of quiet little magicks. He and the doctor finished together. The child, brought forth from a dead woman, floated above the bed in a sphere the wizard had created.

Its eyes were open. It looked back at them with a cruel, knowing expression. Yet it looked like a huge baby.

"That's no son of mine," Ragnarson growled sickly.

"I told you that," Varthlokkur snapped.

"Kill it!"

"No. You said...."

Gjerdrum looked from man to man. Wachtel confirmed Varthlokkur's claim.

"Child of evil," Ragnarson said. "Murderer.... I'll murder you...." He raised his sword.

The thing in the bubble stared back fearlessly.

Varthlokkur rounded the bed. "Friend, believe me. Let it be. This child of Shinsan.... It doesn't know what it is. Those who created it don't know it exists. Give it to me. It'll become our tool. This's my competence. Attend yours. Kavelin no longer has a Queen."

Kavelin. Kavelin. Kavelin. A quarter of his life he had given to the country, and it not the land of his birth. Kavelin. The land of.... What? The women who had loved him? But Elana had been Itaskian. Fiana had come from Octylya, a child bride for an old king desperately trying to spare his homeland the ravages of a succession struggle. Kavelin. What was this little backwater state to him? A land of sorrow. A land that devoured all that he loved. A land that had claimed his time and soul for so long that he had lost the love of the woman who had made up half his soul. What did he have to sacrifice to this land to satisfy it? Was it some hungry beast that ravened everything lovely, everything dear?

He raised his sword, that his father had given him when he and Haaken were but beardless boys. The sword he had borne twenty-five years, through adventures grim, services honorable and otherwise, and days when he had been no better than the men who had murdered his children. That sword was an extension of his soul, half of the man called Bragi Ragnarson.

He took it up, and whirled it above his head the way his father, Mad Ragnar, had done. Everyone backed away. He attacked the bed in which his Queen had died, in which he had lain with her, comforting her, her last night on earth. He hacked posts and sides and hangings like an insane thing, and no one tried to stop him.

"Kavelin!" he thundered. "You pimple on the ass of the world! What the hell do you want from me?"

Into his mind came a face. A simple man, an innkeeper, once had soldiered with a stranger from the north, whom he believed had come to set him free. Behind him were the faces of a hundred such men, a thousand, ten thousand, who had stood with him at Baxendala, unflinching. Peasant lads and hillmen, their hands virgin to the sword a year before, they had faced the fury of Shinsan and had refused to show their backs. Not many had been as lucky as that innkeeper. Most lay beneath the ground below the hill on which Karak Strabger stood. Thousands. Dead. Laid down because they had believed in him, because he and this woman who lay here growing cold had given them a hope for a new tomorrow.

What had Kavelin demanded of them?

"Oh, Gods!" he swore, and smashed that faithful blade against stone till it flew into a hundred shards. "Gods!" He buried his face in his hands, raked his beard with his fingers. "What do I have to do? Why must I endure this? Free me. Slay me. Keep the blades from going astray."

Wachtel, Varthlokkur, and Gjerdrum tried to restrain him.

He surged like a bear throwing off hounds, hurling them against the walls. Then he sat beside the torn body of his Queen, and again took her hand. And for a moment he thought he saw a tiny smile flicker through the agony frozen upon her dead face. He thought he heard a whisper, "Darling, go on. Finish what we started."

He threw himself onto her still form and wept. "Fiana. Please," he whispered. "Don't leave me alone."

Elana was gone. Fiana was gone. What did he have left?

Just one thing, a tiny mind-voice insisted. The bitch-goddess, the changeable child-vixen which he had come to love more than any woman.

Kavelin.

Kavelin. Kavelin. Kavelin. Damnable Kavelin.

His tears flowed.

Kavelin.

Henceforth there would be no other woman before her....

He lay there with his head on Fiana's breast till long after sundown. And when he rose, finally, with night in his eyes and tears dried, he was alone except for Gjerdrum and Ragnar.

They came to him, and held him, understanding.

Gjerdrum had loved his Queen more than life itself, though not with the love of a man for a woman. His was the love of a knight of the old romances for his sovereign, for his infallible Crown.

And Ragnar brought him the love of a forgiving son.

"Give me strength," said Ragnarson. "Help me. They've taken everything from me. Everything but you. And hatred. Stand with me, Ragnar. Don't let hate eat me. Don't let me destroy me."

He had to live, to be strong. Kavelin depended on him. Kavelin. Damnable Kavelin.

"I will, Father. I will."

TWELVE: The Stranger in Hammerfest

Hammerfest was a storybook town in a storybook land cozy with storybook people. Plump blonde girls with ribboned braids, rosy cheeks, and ready smiles tripped up and down the snowy streets. Tall young men hurried from one picturesque shop to another in pursuit of the business of their apprentice-ships, yet were never so hurried that they hadn't time to welcome a stranger. Laughing children sped down the main street on sleds with barrel staves for runners. Their dogs yapped and floundered after them.

The thin man in the dark cloak stood taking it in for a time. He ignored the nibbling of a wind far colder than any of his homeland. It was warmer than those he had endured the past few months.

Tall, steep-roofed houses crowded and hung over the rising, twisting street, yet he didn't feel as confined as he had in towns less densely built. There was a warm friendliness to Hammerfest, a family feeling, as though the houses were cuddling from love, not necessity.

His gaze lingered on the smoke rising from a tall stone chimney topped by a rack where storks nested in summer. He watched the vapors rise till they passed between himself and a small, crumbling fortress atop the hill the town climbed. Peace had reigned here for a generation. The brutal vicissitudes of Trolledyngjan politics had passed Hammerfest by.

A sled whipped past, carrying a brace of screaming youngsters. The dark man leapt an instant before it could hit him, slipped, fell. The snow's cold kiss burned his cheek.

"They don't realize, so I'll apologize for them."

A pair of shaggy boots entered his vision, attached to pillars of legs. A huge, grizzled man offered a hand. He accepted.

"Thank you. No harm done." He spoke the language well. "Children will be children. Let them enjoy while they can."

"Ah, indeed. Too soon we grow old, eh? Yet, isn't it true that all of us will be what we will be?"

The man in the dark clothing looked at him oddly.

"I mean, we must be what our age, sex, station, and acquaintances demand."

"Maybe...." A beer hall philosopher? Here? "What're you driving at?" He shivered in a gust.

"Nothing. Don't mind me. Everybody says I think too much, and say it. For a constable. You should get heavier clothing. Ander Sigurdson could outfit you. That all you wore coming north?"

The stranger nodded. This was a real fountain of questions. Nor was he as full of good-to-see-you as the others.

"Let's get you up to the alehouse, then. You're cold. You'll want something warming. A bite, too, by the look of you." He danced lightly as a sled whipped past.

The stranger noted his deftness. This would be a dangerous man. He was strong and quick.

"Name's Bors Olagson. Constable hereabouts. Boring job, what with nothing ever happening."

"I took you for a smith." The stranger refused the bait.

"Really? Only hammer I ever swung was a war hammer, back in my younger days. Reeved out of Tonderhofn a few summers, back when. That's why they picked me for this job. But it's just a hobby, really. Don't even pay. My true profession is innkeeper. I own the alehouse. Bought with my share of the plunder."

They passed several houses and shops before he probed again. "And who would you be?"

"Rasher. Elfis Rasher. Factor for Darnalin, of the Bedelian League. Our syndics are considering increasing profits by bypassing the Iwa Skolovdans in the fur trade. I've begun to doubt our chances. I didn't prepare well. As you noticed by my outfit."

"And you came alone? Without so much as a pack?"

"No. I survived. The Kratchnodians and rest of Trolledyngja aren't as friendly as Hammerfest."

"Indeed. Though it was worse before the Old House was restored. Here we are." He shoved a tall, heavy door. "Guro. A big stein for a new guest. The kids just knocked him into a snowbank." He grinned. "Yeah. Those were my brats."

The stranger surveyed the tavern. It was all warm browns, as homey and friendly within as the Hammerfesters were outside. He sidled to the fire.

Bors brought steins. "Well, Rasher, I admire you. I do. You're one of the survivors. Weren't always a merchant, were you?"

The questions were becoming irksome. "My home is Hellin Daimiel. I saw the El Murid wars. And I'm no countinghouse clerk. I'm a caravaneer."

"Thought so. Man of action. I miss it sometimes, till I remember drifting in a rammed dragonship with my guts hanging out on the oar bench...."

The stranger tried shifting the subject. "I was told Hammerfest was a critical fur town. That I might find men here who would be interested in making a better deal than the Iwa Skolovdans offer."

"Possibly. Those people are a gang of misers. I don't like it when they stay here. They fill the rooms and don't spend a groschen."

"When do they arrive?"

"You're ahead, if that's your idea. They're too soft to try the passes before summer. They'll be a month or two yet. But, you see, they'll bring trade goods. You've apparently lost yours."

"No real problem. A fast rider could correct that—if I find somebody interested. I'm the only foreigner in town now, then?"

The man's eyes narrowed. His mouth tightened. He wasn't much for hiding his thoughts. "Yes."

The stranger wondered why he lied. Was his man here? The trick would be to find him without bringing the town down on his head.

The best course would be to pursue his cover implacably, ignoring his urgency.

It had waited a year. It could wait a day or two more.

"Who should I see? If I can arrange something, I could get the goods through ahead of the Iwa Skolovdans. We've headquartered our operation at our warehouses in Itaskia...."

"You should get the frost out of your fingers first."

"I suppose. But I've lost my men and my goods. I have to recoup fast. The old boys who stay at home to tote up the profits and losses take the losses out of my pocket and put the profits in theirs."

"Oho! This's a speculative venture, then."

The stranger nodded, a quiet little smile crossing his lips.

"Gentlemen adventurers, perhaps? With the Bedelian League providing office space and letters of introduction, and you putting up the money and men?"

"Half right. I'm a League man. Sent to lead. I was supposed to get a percentage. Still can. If I find the right people, and make it back to Itaskia."

"You southerners. Hurry, hurry."

The stranger drew a coin from inside his cloak, then returned it. He searched by touch, found one which told no tales. It was an Itaskian half-crown, support for his story. "I don't know how long I'll stay. This should keep me a week."

"Six pence Itaskian, per day."

"What? Thief...."

The stranger smiled to himself. He had the better of the man for the moment.

Bors' wife brought ale and roast pork as they agreed on four pence daily. Pork! It was a difficult moment. But the stranger was accustomed to alien ways. He stifled his reaction.

"While you're making your rounds, could you ask that Ander to stop over?"

"His shop is just up the street."

"I'm not going out till I have to. I've had a couple months of snow and wind."

"It's a warm spring day."

"Well, all right then. But warm is a matter of opinion."

"I'll walk you up after you're settled."

"I'll need some other things, too. I'll be a boon to Hammerfest's economy."

"Uhm." The thought had occurred to Bors, apparently.

In the tailor's shop the stranger asked a few cautious questions. He had guessed right. No one would tell him a thing. This would take cunning.

Returning to the inn, alone because Bors was making his rounds, he had another sled encounter. He didn't see this one.

Its rider was a boy of six, scared silly that he had hurt the stranger. The dark man calmed him just enough to suit his purpose.

Then he asked, "Where is the other stranger? The one who stayed the winter."

"The man with black eyes? The man who can't talk?" The

Trolledyngjan idiom meant a man who couldn't speak the language. "In the tower." He pointed.

The dark man stared uphill. The castle was primitive. It had a low curtain wall and what looked like a shell keep piled on granite bedrock. One step better than the moat and bailey. "Thank you, son."

"You won't tell?"

"I won't if you won't."

He continued staring uphill. A man who walked like Bors was coming down. He smiled his little smile.

He was in the common room, drinking hot wine, when the constable returned. "All peaceful?" he asked.

"Nothing changes," Bors replied. "Last trouble we had was two years ago. Itaskian got into it with a fellow from Dvar. Over a girl. Settled it before it came to blows."

"Good. Good. I'll feel safe in my bed, then."

"Peace is what we sell here, sir. Don't you know? Every man in Hammerfest is pledged to die fighting if trouble comes from outside. We need peace. Where else, in this land, can you find shops like ours? The outback people won't even plant crops, let alone work with their hands. Except to make trinkets they bury with their dead, to placate the Old Gods. Silly. If the New Gods can't get a man's shade safely to the heroes' hall, then they can't be much."

"I don't know much about religion."

"Most folks here don't. They give to the priests mainly so they'll stay away. By the way. I talked to a couple fur-dealers. They're interested. In talking. They'll be round tomorrow."

The stranger moved to the fire. "Good. Then I shouldn't have to stay long."

"Oh, I think your stay will be short. They're eager, I'd say." There was something in his tone....

The stranger turned.

His cloak was back. Bors hadn't seen him open it. But he saw the worn, plain black sword hilt and the cold dark eyes and cruel nose. That wicked little smile played across the man's lips. "Thank you. You're most kind, going out of your way. I'll retire now. My first chance at a warm bed for weeks."

"I understand. I understand."

As the stranger climbed the stairs he caught the flicker of uncertainty crossing the big man's face.

He arranged a spell for his door, then went to bed.

They came earlier than he expected, though he hadn't been sure they would come at all. The ward spell warned him. He rose sinuously, hefted his weapon, concealed himself.

There were three of them. He recognized Bors' hulking shape immediately. One of the others was shorter and thinner than the man he sought.

He took Bors with a vicious throat swing, then gutted the short man, shoving a rag into his mouth before he could scream.

The third man didn't react in time to do anything. A sword tip rested at his adam's apple the instant it took the stranger to decide he wasn't the man. Then he died.

The stranger shrugged. He would have to visit the castle after all.

But first he lighted his lamp and studied the dead men.

He found nothing unusual.

Why would they commit murder for no more excuse than he had given?

He dressed in his new winter boots and coat, donned his greatcloak, sheathed his freshly cleaned sword.

Bors' wife waited in the common room.

The stranger's dark eyes met hers. There was no pity in his. "I'll be leaving early. I have a refund coming."

Terror restructured her face. She counted coins with fingers too shaky to keep hold.

The stranger pushed back two. "Too much." His voice was without emotion. But he couldn't resist a dramatic touch. He fished a coin from his purse. "To cover the costs of damage done," he said with a hint of sarcasm.

The woman stared at the coin as he slipped out the door. On one side a crown had been struck. On the reverse there were words in writing she didn't recognize.

Once the door slammed she flew upstairs, tears streaming.

They had been laid out neatly, side by side. On each forehead, still smoking, was a tiny crown-brand.

She didn't know what it meant, but there were others in Hammerfest who had paid attention to news from the south. She would learn soon enough.

She and Bors had entertained a royal guest.

THIRTEEN: Regency

Colonel Oryon had no idea what had happened at Karak Strabger. He did know he rode with a man possessed. His hard-faced, grim companion, closed of mouth, perpetually angry, wasn't the Ragnarson he had accompanied eastward. This Ragnarson was an avenger, a death-Messiah. There was the feel of doom, of destiny, about him.

Oryon watched him punish his mount, and was afraid.

If this man didn't mellow he could set a continent aflame.

He knew no pain, needed no comforts, wanted no rest. He plunged on till Oryon, who prided himself on his toughness, could no longer stand the pace. And still he rode, leaving his companions at an inn ten miles from Vorgreberg.

"Derel!" he roared through the Palace, as he stalked toward his office. "Prataxis! You south coast faggot! Where the hell are you? Get your useless ass up here on the double."

Prataxis materialized, partially dressed. "Sir?"

"The Thing. I want it assembled. Now."

"Sir? It's the middle of the night."

"I don't give a damn! Get those sons of bitches down there in two hours. Or they'll find out what it was like in the old days. We never threw out the hardware from the dungeons. And if you don't get it done yesterday, you'll be first in line."

"What's happened, sir?"

Ragnarson mellowed a little. "Yes, something happened. And I've got to do something about it before the whole damned house of cards falls in on us. Go on. Go, go, go." He waved a hand like a baker sending his boy into the streets, all rage gone. "I'll explain later."

He had arrived ahead of the news. And would stay ahead unless Oryon learned something, or Ragnar shot his mouth off. Ragnar had promised to say nothing, even to the ghost of his

115

mother. Gjerdrum and Wachtel would keep everyone else locked up in Karak Strabger.

"Before I leave," Prataxis said, "there's a woman in town looking for you. She showed up the day after you left."

"A woman? Who?"

"She wouldn't say. She gave the impression she was *very* friendly with bin Yousif."

"Haroun? About time we heard from that.... No. I won't say that. I think I understand him now. Go on. I'll see her after I talk to the Thing. How many of those bastards are in town, anyway?"

"Most of them. It's getting close to Victory Day and time to debate the Guild appropriations. They don't want to miss that."

"That won't be a problem anymore. I told Oryon to pack his bags. We'll pay them off. Thanks to you, Derel. You'll be rewarded."

"Service is my reward, Marshall."

"Bullshit. About two hundred Rebsamen dons fawning at your feet after you publish your thesis is what you're thinking about. You get the look a thief does when he sees loose gold whenever you talk about it."

"As you say, Lord."

"Get out of here. Wait! Before you go, send for Ahring, Blackfang, and Valther."

"The Queen, sir. She ... ?"

"Derel, don't even think about her. If they ask, say I need a vote of confidence on my army alert."

Blackfang and Valther arrived together.

"How're the kids, Haaken?" Bragi asked.

"Upset. You should see them."

"As soon as I can. Valther, you get anything yet?"

"Not a whisper. But there's a woman here...."

"Derel told me. Who is she?"

"Won't say. It looks like she wants us to think she's bin Yousif's wife."

"Wife? Haroun doesn't have.... Well, he never admitted it. But Mocker thought he might. That'd be his style. They keep their women locked up in Hammad al Nakir. And he wouldn't want El Murid to know. Not after killing his son, crippling his wife, and masterminding the kidnapping of his daughter. Yeah. He might have a wife. But I don't think she'd turn up here."

"I'm watching her," Valther told him. "And I'm backtracking her. I put a girl into her hostel. She's just waiting for you."

"Good. Haaken, send messengers to Kildragon and Altenkirk. I want their shock battalions moved here."

"Fiana . . . ?"

"Yes. Derel's getting the Thing together. I want to invoke martial law as soon as we're in session. Keep the Guild troops confined to barracks. Got that, Jarl?" he asked Ahring, who had just arrived.

"Uhm. Case Wolfhound?" Wolfhound was a contingency plan drawn up years ago, at Fiana's direction.

"Yes. Oh. Valther. Another problem for you. I met an innkeeper in Forbeck who said there's been men like our assassins going back and forth through the Gap. A gang went east right ahead of me. Catch a couple."

"And Maisak?"

"Better put somebody in."

The Savernake Gap, only good pass to the east for hundreds of miles north or south, controlled all commerce between east and west. Because Kavelin controlled the Gap, the kingdom and Gap-defending Fortress Maisak were constantly the focus of intrigue. Shinsan's plot to seize the Gap had been the root cause of Kavelin's civil war.

"You're spreading me awful thin," Valther complained.

"I'll try not to dump anything else on you. Wish Mocker was here. This's his kind of job. . . . Anything on that yet?"

"I came up with a Marena Dimura who saw him with three men in Ulhmansiek."

"Ah?"

"But the men are dead."

"What?"

"My man asked the Marena Dimura to describe them. Instead, he showed my man their graves. Two of them, and that of a man who wasn't with them originally. He's a good man, that Tendrik. Dug them up."

"And?"

"He identified one as Sir Keren of Sincic, a Nordmen knight who disappeared at the right time, and another as Bela Jokai, the battalion commander who vanished with Balfour. Judging from the size of the third body, and from the list of friends of Sir Keren who're missing, the other one was probably Trenice Lazen. He was Keren's esquire, but had connections with the underworld. He and Keren ran a little swords-for-hire business. They were riding with that one-eyed Rico creature who sometimes worked for El Murid's people."

"Any sign of him? Or Mocker? Or Balfour?"

"No. The Marena Dimura down there aren't very friendly. Tendrik thinks it went something like this: Keren, Lazen, and Rico were taking Mocker to Al Rhemish. Jokai and Balfour waylaid them. They fought. Rico turned out to be Balfour's man. They killed Keren and Lazen, and lost Jokai, then made off with Mocker."

"End of story?"

"Apparently. Not a trace after that. I've got the word out on what's left of the merchant network, but that hasn't turned up anything. And the Guild still wants to know what happened, so they aren't having any luck either."

"Unless they're smoke-screening."

"They're not that subtle. They're like your mean money-lender who comes round demanding the deed to the old homestead."

"We'll see. I told Oryon we're paying him off."

"We've got the money?"

"Thanks to Prataxis. Jarl, watch the Treasury. Haaken, the same at the Mint. In case somebody tries something."

"You're getting paranoid."

"Because people are out to get me. You were at the house that night."

"All right. All right."

"Jarl, I want to see Oryon when he gets back. I'll tell him about Jokai. See how he reacts. Now, it's time I wandered over to the Thing."

The Thing met in a converted warehouse. Its members kept whining for a parliament building, but Fiana had resisted the outlay. Kavelin remained too heavily indebted from the civil war.

Ragnarson waited in the office of the publican consul. One of the Vorgreberger Guards stood outside. Another remained on the floor. He would inform Ahring when the majority of the members had arrived.

Case Wolfhound included sequestering the Thing. Several delegates, especially Nordmen, were suspect in their loyalty. They would happily precipitate another civil scrimmage.

The Nordmen had been stripped of feudal privilege for rebelling, then offered amnesty. They had accepted only because the alternatives were death or exile.

No one had believed they would keep their parole, though Ragnarson and Fiana had hoped for an extended reign during which recidivists would pass away and be replaced by youngsters familiar with the new order.

The soldier knocked. "Most of them are here, sir. And Colonel Ahring's ready."

"Very good. Have you seen Mr. Prataxis?"

"He's coming now, sir."

Prataxis entered.

"How'd it go, Derel? What feeling did you get?"

"Well enough. All but three of them were in town. And they suspect something. No one refused to come."

"You look them over downstairs?"

"They're nervous. Grouping by parties."

"Good. Now, I need you to take a message to Ahring. I'll tell you what happened later."

Prataxis wasn't pleased. This would be one of the critical points in Kavelin's history.

"Here. A pass so you can get back in."

"All right. Stall. I'll run."

Ragnarson chuckled. "I'd like to see that." Prataxis, though neither handicapped nor overweight, was the least athletic person Ragnarson knew.

Bragi went downstairs slowly. Ahring would need time. His bodyguard accompanied him. The man was jumpy. A lot of hard men would glare at them from the floor, and debate there sometimes involved the crash of swords.

Pandemonium. At least seventy of the eighty-one members, in clusters, were arguing, speculating, gesturing. Ragnarson didn't ask for silence.

Word of his arrival gradually spread. The delegates slowly assumed their seats. By then Ahring's troops had begun to fill the shadows along the walls.

"Gentlemen," Ragnarson said, "I've asked you here to decide the fate of the State. It *will* be a fateful decision. You'll make it before you leave this hall. Gentlemen, the Queen is dead."

The uproar could have been that of the world's record tavern brawl. Fights broke out. But legislative sessions were always tempestuous. The delegates hadn't yet learned to do things in a polite, parliamentary manner.

The uproar crested again when the members became aware that the army had sealed them in. Ragnarson waited them out.

"When you're ready to stop fooling around, let's talk." They resumed their seats. "Gentlemen, Her Majesty passed on about forty hours ago. I was there. Doctor Wachtel attended her, but couldn't save her." His emotion made itself felt. No one would accuse him of not feeling the loss. "Every attempt was made to prevent it. We even brought in a wizard, an expert in the life-magicks. He said she's been doomed since the birth of her daughter. The breath of Shinsan touched her then. The poison caught up."

His listeners began murmuring.

"Wait! I want to talk about this woman. Some of you did everything you could to make her life miserable, to make her task impossible. She forgave you every time. And gave her life, in the end, to make Kavelin a fit place to live. She's dead now. And the rest of us have come to the crossroads. If you think this's a chance to start something, I'm telling you now. I won't forgive. I am the army. I serve the Crown. I defend the Crown. Till someone wears it, I'll punish rebellion mercilessly. If I have to, I'll make Kavelin's trees bend with a stinking harvest.

"Now, the business at hand."

Prataxis hustled his way in burdened with writing materials. He *had* run. Good. Ahring and Blackfang would be sealing the city perimeter against unauthorized departures.

"My secretary will record all votes. He'll publish them when we make the public announcement."

He grinned. That would give him an extra ten votes from fence-sitters. He should be able to aim a majority any direction.

"Our options are limited. There's no heir. The scholars of Hellin Daimiel have suggested we dispense with the monarchy entirely, fashioning a republic like some towns in the Bedelian League. Personally, I don't relish risking the national welfare on a social experiment.

"We could imitate other League towns and elect a Tyrant for a limited term. That would make transition smooth and swift, but the disadvantages are obvious.

"Third, we could maintain the monarchy by finding a King among the ruling Houses of other states. It's the course I prefer. But it'll take a while.

"Whichever, we need a Regent till a new head of state takes power.

"All right. The session is open for arguments from the floor. Mind your manners. You'll all get a say. Mr. Prataxis, handle the Chair."

Someone shouted, "You forgot a possibility. We could elect one of our own people King."

"Hear hear," the Nordmen minority chanted.

"Silence!" Prataxis bellowed. Ragnarson was startled by his volume.

"Let me speak to that, Derel."

"The Marshall has the floor."

"'Hear hear' you shout, you Nordmen. But you can't all be King. Look around. You see anybody you want telling you what to do?"

The point told. Each had, probably, considered himself the logical candidate. Kavelin's nobles were never short on self-appreciation.

"Okay. Derel?"

"The commons delegate from Delhagen."

"Sirs, I think the Barons missed the point of the suggestion. I meant the Marshall."

That precipitated another barroom round. Ragnarson himself denied any interest. His denial was honest. He knew what trying to break this rebellious bronc of a kingdom had done to Fiana.

He understood the delegate's motives. There was a special relationship between between himself and Delhagen and Sedlmayr, the city there. They operated almost as an autonomous republic federated with Kavelin, under a special charter he had urged on Fiana. In return the commons there had remained steadfastly Royalist during the civil war. Sedlmayr, with the similarly chartered "Sieges" of Breidenbach and Fahrig, were nicknamed "The Marshall's Lap Dogs."

Ragnarson smiled gently. The man had made the suggestion so he could gradually back down. Relieved, some opponent would propose the Marshall as Regent instead.

And that task he would accept. He had, in reality, been Regent since Fiana's seclusion. He could handle it. And a Regent could always get out.

Once, years ago, Haroun had tried to tempt him with a kingship. The notion had been more attractive then. But he had seen only the comforts visible from the remote perspective.

The moment gone, he fell asleep in his chair. It would be a long session. Nothing important would get said for hours.

Kaveliners were a stubborn lot. The arguing lasted four days. Weariness and hunger finally forced a compromise. The Thing named Ragnarson Regent by a fat majority—after every alternate avenue had been pursued to a dead end.

Ragnarson left the hall physically better than when he had entered. He had made a vacation of it, getting involved only when delegates threatened to brawl.

Vorgreberg anxiously awaited the session's end, sure the news would be bad.

When it came out Kildragon and Altenkirk were on hand. Vorgreberg was secure. Loyal troops were poised at the kingdom's heart, ready to smash rebellion anywhere.

FOURTEEN: Lady of Mystery

"Show him in," Ragnarson told Prataxis. He rose, extended his hand. "Colonel. Sorry I took so long with the Thing."

"I understand," Oryon replied. "Congratulations."

"Save it for a year. Probably be sorry I took the job. I wanted to talk about Balfour. My people came up with something."

"Oh?"

Ragnarson hoped Oryon's response would betray something about Guild thinking. He related the tale Valther had told. "Will you want Captain Jokai's body?"

"I'd have to ask High Crag. What the hell was Balfour doing in Uhlmansiek? His log says he was taking the week to go hunting around Lake Berberich. Something's going on here. And I don't like it."

"I've been saying that for a long time. Any idea why he'd kidnap my friend?"

"No. This Rico creature.... The whole thing baffles me. I'll ask High Crag, of course."

"I still won't renew the commission."

Oryon's thick lips stretched in a grin. "I noticed the guards at the Treasury."

"I get some strange ideas sometimes."

Oryon shook his head. "Wish I could understand why you're scared of us. Maybe I could change your mind."

"Wish *I* understood it. Just an intuition, I guess. Victory Day is coming up, by the way."

"My staff is planning the evacuation. We'll move out come sunrise Victory Day. We expect to be out of Kavelin within five days. Because of the confinement to barracks, I haven't informed High Crag or made transit arrangements. I doubt there'll be any problems."

"Good enough. We'll put on a going-away party for your boys."

"Can't bitch about that."

"Don't want any hard feelings."

"Keep me posted about Balfour. Or our agent after I leave."

"Will do. Thanks for coming." He followed Oryon to the door. "Derel, want to find that woman for me? The one who wants to see me?"

"All right."

Ragnarson selected one of the mountain of requests that already had appeared on his desk. Everything held in abeyance during the Queen's indisposition was breaking loose. Every special interest was trying to get his attention first. "Hey, Derel. Get me a big box."

"Sir?"

"So I can file the stuff I want to 'put aside for further consideration.' Like this one. Guy wants me to come to the opening of his alehouse."

"Sir? If I might? Act on ones like that if you have time. Chuck the ones where some Nordmen insists on his right to collect ford tolls. Giving breaks to important people and cronies is a deathtrap. It's Wessons like that soldier-turned-innkeeper who are your power base. Keep them on your side. I'll get that woman. Half an hour?"

He took ten minutes. The word had reached her. He encountered her downstairs.

"Marshall? The lady."

"Thank you, Derel." He rose, considered her. She wore traditional desert costume. Dark almond eyes peered over her veil. There were crow's feet at their corners, though cunningly hidden. She was older than she liked.

"Madam. Please be seated. Kaf? I'm sure Derel could scare some up."

"No. Nothing is necessary." She spoke a heavily accented Itaskian of the Lower Silverbind.

"What can I do for you? My secretary says you hinted it has to do with Haroun bin Yousif."

A sad little laugh stirred her veil. "Excuse me for staring. It has been so long. . . . Yes. Haroun. He is my husband."

Ragnarson settled into his chair. "I never heard of any wife."

"It is one of the unhappy secrets of our lives. But it is true. Twenty-three years. . . . It seems an eternity. Most of that I was wife in name only. I did not see him for years at a time."

Ragnarson's skepticism was obvious. She responded by dropping her veil. It was an act which, in her culture, was considered incredibly daring. Women of Hammad al Nakir, once married, would rather have paraded nude than reveal their naked faces.

Ragnarson was impressed. He didn't have Derel throw her out.

"You do not recognize me still?"

"Should I? I never met a woman with a claim on Haroun."

"Time changes us. I forget that I'm no longer the child you met. She was fourteen. Life has not been easy. Always his men run—when they do not ride the desert to murder my father's men."

Ragnarson still didn't understand.

"But you *must* remember! The day the fat man brought me to your camp in Altea? When I was so much trouble you pulled up my skirts and paddled me in front of your men? And then Haroun came. He scared me so much I never said another word."

Why couldn't women just say things straight out? He tried to remember Mocker dragging a tart into some wartime camp....

"Gods! You're Yasmid? El Murid's daughter? Married to Haroun?" He strangled a laugh. "You think I'll swallow that?"

"So! You call me a liar? You had my skirts up. You saw." She bent and raised her skirts.

Ragnarson remembered the winestain birthmark shaped like a six-fingered baby hand.

"And this!" Angrily, she bared small, weary breasts. Over her heart lay the Harish tattoo worn by El Murid's chosen.

"All right. You're Yasmid."

Incredible. The daughter of El Murid, missing twenty years, appearing here. As Haroun's wife.

The marriage was the sort of thing Haroun would do to drive little knives into his enemy's heart. Why hadn't he ballyhooed it over half the continent?

"I did not expect you to be easily convinced. I made that my first task. I brought these." She showed him jewelry only Haroun could have given her and letters he couldn't read because they were in the script of Hammad al Nakir, but which bore Haroun's King Without a Throne seal.

"I believe you. So why're you here?" He decided to check with

Valther. Men of the desert didn't let their women roam free. Not
without an uproar.

"My husband has disappeared "

"I know. I've been trying to get in touch."

That startled her. "He has sworn to kill my father."

"Not exactly the news of the century."

"No. Listen. Please. After he came back, after the war in your
country, after he started to attack my father, but turned north
against your enemies instead. . . ."

"That hurt him. He had it in his hands. Al Rhemish. But he
let love for friends sway him. He surrendered his dream to help
you."

Haroun had come out of nowhere with thousands of
horsemen to harry O Shing through the Savernake Gap and into
the plains east of the Mountains of M'Hand. Bragi hadn't
understood Haroun then, nor did he now. For friendship?
Haroun would murder his mother for political expedience.

"So?"

"When he came home, a year later, he was so tired and
old. . . . He didn't care. I made him promise he wouldn't hurt my
father if my father didn't harm him."

"Ah! That's why he's been laying low. Been a long time since
he's done anything. Just skirmishing to keep his people
interested."

"Yes. That's my fault."

"He's changed his mind?"

"Yes. He told Beloul and Rahman to prepare the final
offensive. He sent El Senoussi and El Mehduari to collect the
wealth and fighters of the refugees in the coastal states. He
ordered the deaths of my father's agents wherever they are
found. It will be bloody."

"It's been that for years. It'll go on till Haroun or your father
dies."

"Or longer. We have a son. Megelin. The boy is filled with
hatred."

"I don't see what you're after. Or why Haroun made this
about-face. He keeps his word."

"He thinks my father broke the armistice. My father's men
here, Habibullah and Achmed, kidnapped your fat friend."

"Mocker. What's become of him? I sent him to see Haroun a
year ago. He disappeared." He wouldn't say more till he heard
her version.

"I'm not sure. Maybe Haroun is. The Marena Dimura told him what happened.

"Habibullah was one of my guards when Mocker kidnapped me. What they called kidnap. I wasn't very smart then. And he could talk, that fat man. I came willingly. I thought I could make peace. Anyway, your friend almost killed Habibullah that night. I suppose he's wanted revenge ever since."

"Derel," Ragnarson called. To Yasmid, "Could you face Habibullah now?"

"But why? Won't that make trouble? They have all forgotten me now. If they knew.... It would just make trouble."

"Sir?" Prataxis asked.

"See if Habibullah what's-it can come over."

"Now?"

"As soon as possible."

"I don't think...." But Prataxis went.

"I'm running that man half to death," Bragi muttered. "Wish Gjerdrum would get back." Prataxis was supposed to be arranging appointments for ambassadors and factors for the caravan companies.

"Pardon me," Ragnarson said. "You needn't reveal yourself. You think Habibullah had Mocker kidnapped because Mocker embarrassed your father? Because of it Haroun plans to start fighting again?"

"One operation. One planned for years. All or nothing. He thinks the tribes will rise to support him."

"Yes. So. But El Murid doesn't have Mocker. And Haroun knows it. The Marena Dimura down there are his spies."

"I'll tell you what I know. Some men killed Habibullah's men. They handed the fat man over to a man in black. Haroun believed the killers went into the north to hide."

"Wait. The man in black. Tell me about him."

"The Marena Dimura say he was tall and thin. He wore a mask."

"Mask?"

"A metal mask. Maybe gold. With jewels. Like those creatures on the walls of the temples in the jungle cities. The killers were afraid of him."

Ragnarson buried his face in his hands.

"Haroun has vanished. I fear he will try to murder my father so there'll be confusion when he invades Hammad al Nakir. I came here because I hoped you could do something."

"What?"

"Stop him."

"I don't understand."

"I love my father. He was a good father. He's a good man. He means no evil. . . ."

"Nearly a million people died during the wars."

"My father didn't do that. He didn't want it. That was the fault of men like Nassef. His generals were brigands."

Ragnarson didn't contradict her. She was partly right. But her father had given the order to convert the west, and to slay anyone who didn't accept his faith.

"What could I do? I don't know where Haroun is. I've only seen him once in the last ten years."

She wept. "The Fates are cruel. Why do the men I love spend their lives trying to kill each other?

"I shouldn't have come. I should have known it was useless. All that planning, that trouble getting away, hiding from Haroun's men. . . . . All for nothing."

"Maybe not. There's a possibility. . . . . The old story of the enemy of my enemy."

"Excuse me?"

"There's a greater enemy. One your husband and your father could agree to be more dangerous than one another."

"You're being mysterious."

"I hate naming the name. I've seen the men in black before. I've fought them. They call themselves Tervola."

The color left Yasmid's face. "Shinsan! No."

"Who would impersonate a Tervola?" But then, why would Shinsan grab Mocker? What was the connection between Balfour and Shinsan? Did that permeate the Guild? And this Willis Northen, who used a Marena Dimura name, was a Kaveliner Wesson. . . . . Had Shinsan penetrated Kavelin?

"Derel!"

But Prataxis was gone. Ragnarson wrote names. Oryon. Valther. Mist. Trebilcock. It was time he found out if Michael had learned anything.

"Does anybody know where Haroun went?"

"No. He just disappeared. He didn't even tell Beloul or Rahman. He does that. Everybody complains. He promises, but keeps doing it. I think he will try to get my father."

"If I could contact him, this war might be averted. Your father. Would he listen to you?"

"Yes."

How confident she was after all these years. "He's changed. He's a fat old man now. They say he's crazy."

"I know. People come from the desert to Haroun. They all say that. They say he's betraying the ideals he seized the Peacock Throne for.... Men like Nassef changed him."

"Nassef died a long time ago. I killed him."

"A bandit named Nassef is dead. But there are more Nassefs. They have walled my father off and taken control."

"He still has his voice. The Faithful would support him if he spoke publicly. Disharhûn is coming, isn't it?"

Disharhûn was the week of High Holy Days celebrated in Hammad al Nakir. Pilgrims went to Al Rhemish to hear El Murid speak.

Ragnarson was thinking only of Kavelin. If Haroun launched an incursion from Kavelin and Tamerice, and failed, El Murid would have a legitimate case for counteraction. It might initiate a new round of wars.

"Don't I have trouble enough?" he muttered. "Haroun, Haroun, maybe I should've cut your throat years ago."

He still considered Haroun a friend. But he had never really *liked* the man much. A paradox.

Haroun had always been too self-involved.

"Marshall?"

"Derel? Just a minute." To Yasmid, "Will you reveal yourself?"

She replaced her veil. "I'll decide after I see him."

Bragi went to the door. "Ah. Ambassador. Glad you could come."

"I need to speak with you, too, Marshall. Our intelligence...."

"Excuse me. Derel, send for Valther, his wife, and Colonel Oryon."

"He just...."

"I know. Something came up. On Balfour. I need to see him again. And see if anybody knows where Trebilcock is."

"On my way." Prataxis wasn't pleased. His own work suffered more and more while he handled tasks Gjerdrum should have done.

"Thank you, Ambassador. Come in."

Habibullah cast a suspicious glance at the woman.

"Yes. That bandit bin Yousif...."

"I know. And you know why, too, don't you?"

"What?"

"There's an interesting story going around. About a man who paid to have a friend of mine kidnapped. Who also happens to be a friend of the bandit you mentioned."

Habibullah refused to react.

"You've probably heard the story yourself. Especially the part about the kidnappers failing to deliver their goods." He retold Yasmid's tale.

"Where did you hear this fairy tale?"

"Several sources. Today, from this lady."

Habibullah eyed her again. "Why would Shinsan kidnap a fat fakir?"

"Good question. I've even wondered why El Murid's agents would try it."

Habibullah started to make excuses.

"Yes, I know. But these days we're pretending to have forgiven and forgotten. Doesn't El Murid say that to forgive is divine?"

"What the fat man did was a crime against God Himself. . . ."

"No, Habibullah."

The ambassador turned.

Yasmid said, "You hate him because he made a fool of you." To Ragnarson, "The men of my people can forgive a wound, an insult, a murder. Habibullah has. But he can't forget the pain of being made a fool before his friends in the Invincibles. No. Habibullah, admit it. He told you those stories and showed you those tricks, and you believed he was your friend. You spoke for him to me. And he tricked you. That's why you risked another war to get him."

"Who are you? Marshall?"

Ragnarson smiled, licked his lips. "Mr. Habibullah, I think you suspect already."

Yasmid dropped her veil.

Habibullah stared. And it wasn't her boldness that astonished him. "No. This's some trick, Marshall. Have you leagued with the minions of Hell? You call up the dead to mock me?"

"I think Habibullah was in love with me. I didn't realize it then. I think a lot of them were."

"My Lady."

Ragnarson gaped as Habibullah knelt, head bowed, and extended his arms, wrists crossed. It was an ultimate gesture, the surrender to slavery.

Ragnarson could no longer doubt her genuineness.

"Rise, Habibullah." She replaced her veil.

"What would My Lady have of me?"

"Speak honestly with the Marshall."

"I've gotten what I needed. Except this: Can you escort the lady to her father? More successfully than you did my friend?"

Habibullah became El Murid's ambassador once more. "Why?"

"I've got no use for your boss. I wouldn't shed a tear if somebody stuck a knife in his gizzard. The world would be better off. That's why I don't bother bin Yousif any more than I have to to keep the peace with Hammad al Nakir.

"But that peace is critical to me now, with Shinsan sticking its nose into Kavelin. I'm grasping at straws. I need my flanks free. Yasmid implies that she'll be the go-between in arranging a truce between her father and her husband."

"Her husband?"

"Bin Yousif. You didn't know?" Got him now, Ragnarson thought.

"It's true," Yasmid said. "And it was my choice, Habibullah." She explained how she had engineered the recent peace.

"Unlike the Marshall, I'm not concerned with Shinsan. But I'll play his game to keep my men from murdering each other."

"Are there children?" Habibullah asked. "He mourns the fact that he has no grandchildren. The wars cost him that hope."

"A son. Megelin Micah bin Haroun."

"That would please him." El Murid's name had been Micah al Rhami before the Lord had called him.

"It would make more sense to send your son," Ragnarson observed. "That way each principal holds the other's child hostage."

"No. Megelin would murder his grandfather."

"The risks should be equalized."

"I've decided, Marshall. I'll take the risks."

"Ambassador?"

"Yes?"

"Will you escort her? Or are you committed to this war you've made almost inevitable?"

"I haven't kissed the Harish dagger. I didn't realize the results would be so grave. One fat man. A nothing, from the slums. Who'd notice? Who'd care? I still don't understand."

"And I don't understand why you want him after so long."

"I'll do it. For the Lady Yasmid."

"Good. Let me know how it goes. Oh. A favor. Whenever you get another wild hair, get approval from Al Rhemish."

Habibullah smiled thinly. "My Lady?" He offered a hand. "Is there anything else?"

"No." She rose.

"Then we'll go to the embassy. We'll leave as soon as guards can be assembled."

Ragnarson saw them past the door of Derel's office. Already they were playing remember when.

He settled in to wait for Oryon, Valther, and Mist. He should get at that paperwork.... Instead, he closed his eyes.

It was strange, the twists fate could take. So Haroun had a wife. Amazing.

FIFTEEN: The Stranger's Appointment

They jumped him when he left the inn. There were three of them again, and this time he wasn't ready. But they weren't professionals.

He was.

The plain-hilted sword made a soft *schwang* sound as it cleared his scabbard.

One of them knicked his arm, but that was it. They weren't very good. Peace had reigned for a long time in Hammerfest. He cut them up and laid them down in twenty seconds, before they could scream for help.

Then he stepped inside. "Guro."

He spoke softly, but his voice brought the woman rushing downstairs. She looked at him, and her face became a study in horror.

He tossed a coin. "Three more. In the street."

"You. . . . You. . . ."

"I didn't draw the first blade, Guro. I came to see a man. I'll see him. Why did they die? Must I slay every man in Hammerfest? I will. Tell them. I'm leaving now. I hope I won't have to pay for any more funerals."

He stepped over the neatly ranked bodies. Each bore a small crown-shaped brand on its forehead.

He strode uphill, his blade sheathed once more. He doubted that anyone would be bold enough to attack him now. He had already killed the best men in town.

When he passed the last building he looked back. Storybook town, storybook houses, filled with storybook people—till the sun went down.

Hammerfest would lose its fairy tale luster as the news spread.

Hell had visited this night.

He lifted his gaze to the crumbling little castle.

His man was there.

Was he awake? Waiting?

Certainly. *He* would be, in the man's position. Waiting for word of success—or of failure. Or for the intended victim to come asking questions.

A thin, cruel little smile crossed his lips.

It was a cold, chill walk. Each time he glanced back more windows showed light. Guro was busy.

Would they have the nerve to come after him? To save a man who had sent six of them to their deaths?

He came within bowshot of the curtain wall. His guerrilla's sensitivities probed for another ambush. Senses beyond the human also reached out. He detected nothing outside the keep. Inside, there were three life-sparks.

Just three? Even a tumbledown, cruddy little shed of a castle rated a bigger garrison. Especially when one of the sparks was female.

He paused, thought. There seemed to be a numerological relationship.... Three assassins in his room. Three outside the inn. Three here.

Woman or not, she was part of it.

How? Women seldom bore swords in Trolledyngja.

A witch. That had to be the answer.

Then they knew he was coming.

Though he knew where they waited, he poked around like a man carefully searching. They knew a hunter was coming, but not who.

He used the time to prepare himself for the witch.

He readied his most powerful, most reliable spells. Though these Trolledyngjan wild women had little reputation, he hadn't survived thirty years under the sword without being cautious.

He probed. Still all in one room. And nothing sorcerous waiting anywhere else.

Whatever, it would happen there.

Again, they couldn't know who he was, only that he had come from the south. They would want to know who and why before they killed him.

They were going to be surprised.

He approached their room with right hand on sword hilt and left protruding from his greatcloak. He had the position of the woman fixed clearly in mind.

Now!

His left forefinger felt as though he had jabbed it into fire.

The woman screamed.

He stepped inside. The thin, cruel smile was on his lips. He tipped back his hood.

The woman kept screaming. She was strong. She had survived.

The others stared. The fat one with the mane gone silver had to be the Thane of Hammerfest.

"Bin Yousif!" the other gasped.

"Colonel Balfour. You seem surprised." He threw back his cloak. "He was my friend."

Balfour didn't reply.

"He has other friends," said Haroun. "I'm just the first to arrive." His left forefinger jabbed again. The woman stopped screaming. Another cruel smile. "You. Do you want to see the sun rise?"

The heavy man nodded. He was too frightened, too shocked, to speak.

"Then get up—carefully—and go down to Bors' inn. They need someone to tell them what to do. And don't look back."

The man went out like a whipped dog.

"He'll find his courage," Balfour predicted.

"Possibly. Having a mob behind you helps. Now. We talk."

"You talk."

"You have one chance to get out of this alive, Balfour. It's remote. It requires the leopard to change its spots. It requires you to tell me the truth despite your training. You want to be stubborn, you won't live out the night. And I'll get what I want anyway."

"You'll starve up here before you can break me."

"Perhaps. If I restrict myself to the physical." Haroun shifted to the tongue of ancient Ilkazar, now used only liturgically in Hammad al Nakir and by western sorcerers. He made a lifting gesture with his left hand.

The dead woman stood.

Haroun's fingers danced.

The witch took a clumsy step.

"You see? I master the Power now. The King of Hammad al Nakir is also his people's chief shaghûn."

The shaghûn belonged to a quasi-religious sorcerer's brotherhood. He served with military units, aided priests, advised leaders. He seldom was powerful.

Haroun had been born a fourth son. Distant not only from the Peacock Throne but from his father's Wahligate, he had started training to become chief shaghûn of his father's province.

Time and the efficiency of El Murid's assassins had made him chief claimant to the Peacock Throne. He had been smart enough, quick enough, murderous enough, to stay alive and maintain his pretense to the crown. After a two-decade interruption he had resumed his studies, and now he bent the Power to pursuit of his usurped Throne.

Balfour didn't respond.

"You see?" Haroun said again.

Balfour remained firm.

Haroun again spoke the tongue of emperors.

A dark umbra formed round the witch's head. She spoke.

She hadn't much to tell. This was a minor Nine, its only noteworthy member the man who had come north to hide.

Haroun squeezed his fingers into a fist. The woman dropped, tightened into a fetal ball.

"Colonel? Must I?"

Despite the draft in that old stone pile, Balfour was wet with sweat. But he was a hard man himself. Suddenly, he sprang.

Haroun expected it.

Below, villagers filled Hammerfest's streets, their torches painting the storybook houses with terrible, crawling shadows. They watched the castle, and shuddered each time it reverberated to one of those horrible cries.

They were being torn from a throat which couldn't respond to the will trying to control it.

Balfour was stubborn. He withstood Haroun's worst for hours. But Haroun's torments weren't physical, which a stubborn man could school himself to ignore. These were torments of the mind, of the soul. Witch-man Haroun bin Yousif conjured demons he sent into the soldier. They clawed through mind and soul and took control of his mouth, babbling both truth and lies. Haroun repeated his questions again and again. In the end he thought he had gotten everything to be had. He thought there were no more secrets....

He finally used his sword.

Then he slept, with corpses to frighten off evil dreams.

Haroun bin Yousif had lived this way for so long that it hardly disturbed him.

He wakened shortly before nightfall, finished what needed finishing, went down the hill.

The Hammerfesters remained in the streets, frightened. The fat man stood before them, shaking.

Haroun drew back his cloak. "You may return to your castle, Thane. I have no need of it now. Wait." He tossed a coin. "Bury them."

That cruel smile crossed his lips.

Nearly twenty men faced him, but eased out of his path. His unrelieved arrogance assured them that they had no choice. This dread man would pay for their funerals too if they argued.

"Thane."

"Yes?"

"Forget your game of Nines. It brings on the dire evils."

"I will, sir."

"I believe you will." Smiling, Haroun went to Bors' inn, took a room. He paid his due, as ever he did—be it in silver or evil.

He fell asleep thinking this Nine had been a puerile little conspiracy, fit for nothing but hiding men who had grown too hot elsewhere. But there were other Nines that might shake the roots of mountains.

Next morning he purchased a horse and rode southward. Traveling alone.

He knew no other way. Even in crowds this dread, deadly man traveled alone.

SIXTEEN: Deaths and Disappearances

Ragnarson woke with a start. "Eh?"

"Colonel Oryon, Marshall."

"Thank you, Derel."

His dream had been grim. He had been trapped at the heart of a whirling mandala with good and evil chasing one another around him, the champions of one as vicious as those of the other. The struggle had consumed everything he loved.

Fiana. Elana. Two children. Mocker. Already gone. Who would be next?

Rolf? What had become of Rolf, anyway? Bragi hadn't seen him since returning from Karak Strabger. Commanding the Palace Guard wasn't much, but it was a job, with its duties.

Would it be Haaken? Or Reskird, a friend of two decades? Haroun?

The Haroun he knew and loved was an idealization of the Haroun with whom he had adventured. He didn't know the Haroun of today. Today's Haroun was a different man.

Who else? His children. Especially Ragnar, in whom he saw his immortality. Ahring. Altenkirk. Gjerdrum. . . . They were friends, but they hadn't gotten the grip on his soul the others had, perhaps because he had met them later, after the world had hardened him. Likewise Valther and Mist. Nepanthe, though. . . . He had a soft spot for Nepanthe and Ethrian, his godson.

And for Kavelin. Kavelin had its claws in him. And he couldn't comprehend it.

"Marshall? You wanted to see me?"

"Oh, I'm sorry." Ragnarson's hair had grown shaggy through inattention. He brushed it from his eyes. "Grab a chair. Derel, bring something to sip."

"Your secretary says you've got something new on Balfour."

"Yes. But hang on a minute. There's a couple people I want to sit in."

Valther and Mist were a long time arriving. More than an hour later than he expected. He tried to make small talk, reminiscing about the El Murid wars, the civil war, basic training at High Crag, whatever he and the Colonel had in common. Oryon waited it out. But he got antsy. He had his evacuation to prepare.

"Derel, what's taking them so long?"

"I don't know, sir. I was told they'd be here as soon as possible."

"Must be a family crisis," Ragnarson told Oryon. "Pretty sickly, their kids. Derel, have you seen Captain Preshka?"

"No sir. I've been meaning to mention it. He hasn't turned in his pay sheets. He's gone to pieces the last week."

"I'll talk to him."

"Here's Valther now, sir."

Valther and Mist filed in, Valther slump-shouldered, pale.

"What happened? You look like death warmed over."

"Trouble. Nepanthe and Ethrian are gone."

"What? How?"

"I don't know. Gundar was the only one who saw what happened. He doesn't make much sense. Says a man came. Nepanthe went away with him. She packed for herself and Ethrian, and went. Gundar thinks the man said he was supposed to take her to Mocker, who's hiding because you and Haroun want to kill him."

"I'll talk to him later. There's got to be more. Derel. Put out the word. How long have they been gone?"

Valther shrugged. "Since this morning. They've got at least four hours' start."

"Another move against us?"

"Probably. This's starting to look big, isn't it?"

"Yeah. I found a new angle, too. That's why I wanted you.

"I had a visitor. Right after you left, Colonel. Bin Yousif's wife."

Bragi let them settle down before adding, "She's also El Murid's daughter. That's not as important as what she told me. About why Haroun has been so peaceful. And about Mocker and Balfour."

He told the story. It elicited a covey of questions.

"Look, I don't have any answers. Valther, fit the pieces into your puzzle. Mist. The man in black. Tervola?"

"He must be. But the mask isn't familiar. It sounds like Chin's, but the black and gold are wrong.... We could check. Didn't you capture Chin's mask at Baxendala?"

"There was a mask. I don't know whose."

"Chin. I remember. Get it for me. I'll tell you if it was Chin."

"Derel. See if you can dig the thing up. It's in the Treasury vault. We were going to display it when the army got rich enough to afford its own museum."

Prataxis bowed and departed. His writing materials he left lying in a sarcastic scatter.

"I'm getting that man's goat," Bragi observed. "If Gjerdrum don't get back pretty soon, he'll quit on me. I don't think I can manage without him. Colonel. You haven't said anything."

"I don't know. I don't like it. Our people conspiring with Shinsan? If that came out it could destroy the Guild's credibility."

"Yet you don't dismiss the possibility. How come?"

Three pairs of eyes fixed on Oryon.

"Because of something my adjutant told me. We talked a long time, after this morning."

"Ah?"

"He didn't know what it was about, but he once found a message to Balfour, from High Crag, partially destroyed in the Colonel's fireplace. The little he made out violated standing orders. The message was signed 'The Nine.' I'd heard rumors before that Balfour might be one of the Nine."

"What's that? I've never heard of it."

"Not many people have, even inside High Crag. It's a story that's been going around for several years. It says there's a cabal of senior officers trying to grab control. Whenever one of the old boys dies, you hear somebody say the Nine murdered him.

"The rumors started maybe three years ago. Jan Praeder claimed he had been invited to join the plot. To replace a member who had died. He said he looked into it, didn't like what he saw, and refused. He didn't say much, though, before he was posted to Simballawein, to replace Colonel Therodoxos, supposedly the member who had died. There was no mystery about Therodoxos's passing. He was killed when he interrupted a gang rape. Killed most of them before they finished him. But there were a lot of questions when Praeder died. He was supposedly poisoned by a jealous husband two weeks after arriving."

"Strong circumstantial evidence," said Ragnarson.

"Yes. Circumstance two: there have been eleven deaths in the Citadel since Praeder went down. That's a lot even for old men. Those guys are tough old geezers. Hawkwind is up in his eighties now. Lauder is right behind him. And they're as mean as ever. They go on like they're immortal. The others usually do too.

"The name, the Nine, I guess, comes from the fact that that would make a majority in Council. To grab control you'd have to have nine conspirators at Councilor level. Balfour was a prime suspect because he was close, despite his youth, and because he was so damned impatient with the traditional mysteries."

"That I can understand," Ragnarson observed. "That was always hokey to me. But I only made the Third Circle. Maybe there's more to it later. I'm supposed to be a general now. Maybe I could go find out."

"You'd start where you left off. You don't short-cut the Seven Steps. Your Guild rank wouldn't mean much inside the Order."

"Why not? Why would they promote me, then?"

"The same reason you don't turn them down. It makes people think you've got the Guild behind you. They want your success to reflect on High Crag.

"I'll never get into the Citadel myself. I can't master the Mysteries of the Sixth Circle. Oh, well. The organizational table is top-heavy anyway."

"Valther? Mist? What do you think?"

Valther shrugged.

His wife replied, "Colonel Oryon sounds honest. He may even sympathize a little. He has stretched his conscience today." She flashed a smile that could melt hearts of bronze. Oryon responded.

She was, simply, inarguably, the most beautiful woman in the world. Before her fall from power in Shinsan she had spent ages engineering her perfection.

"What action will you take, Colonel?" Ragnarson asked.

"I don't know. If I inform High Crag, I'll either start worse rumors or warn the conspiracy—depending on who gets my letter. I'll have to investigate myself, when I get back."

"Well, I've done what I could. Wish we could lay hands on Balfour. Valther. I've given you a whole list of things. Got anything yet?"

"No. I sent a couple men to that inn just before we came over. Told them to grab the next bunch of riders."

"Mist. We need your help. First, locate Nepanthe. Then see if you can call in Visigodred and Zindahjira, and get Varthlokkur cracking."

For an instant the woman's cold beauty gave way to pique. "You can't trust a woman? You don't think I can handle...."

"No. Because you don't want to be involved in this sort of thing anymore. And because I don't think one wizard will be enough. Not when we're toe to toe with Shinsan.... Ah. Derel. Well?"

"It's not there."

"It's got to be."

"You find it then. I took the place apart."

"Hey, cool off. I believe you. Mist?"

"Someone took it."

Ragnarson snorted. He needed an expert to tell him that? "Another job for you, Valther."

"I know. Find out who. When am I going to get some sleep?"

"Any time I'm in bed, you steal all you want. I won't be there to raise hell. Mist can help you. Can't you? At least to find out where the mask is now?"

"Yes."

"All right. Derel, I've got two more jobs for you, then I'll leave you alone. One I think you'll like. First, scare up Haaken. Have him meet me at the cemetery. It's time I saw what he did for Elana." He spoke with a throat suddenly tight. "Then write Gjerdrum. Tell him to quit farting around and get his ass back here." He signed a blank piece of paper. "That do you?"

Prataxis's smile was wicked. "Perfect, sir. Absolutely perfect. Oh. I couldn't find Trebilcock."

"Probably whoring around. He runs with a strange crowd. He'll turn up." But Ragnarson was worried. Too many people were out of sight. Michael might have found something and been silenced.

"I'll look for him too," Mist offered.

"You want to find me someone, find Haroun. Valther, you be home later?"

"I imagine."

"Okay. I'll be out to see how the house is coming. And to talk to Gundar."

"What?"

"I told you to take the house apart to find this Tear of Mimizan, didn't I?"

"Yes."

"Well?"

"Haven't made any headway. My people are all in the field."

"Uhm." Valther was going to have to show more initiative. "Borrow them from Ahring. Or Haaken."

"All right. All right."

"You needn't destroy the house," said Mist. "I'll find it if it's there. I know it well. . . ." Her eyes clouded as she remembered a cruel past, when she had been mistress in Shinsan and warring with the Monitor of Escalon.

She must be getting restless, Ragnarson thought. Being a housewife isn't what she thought. She might need watching too.

This was getting touchy. The people he *knew* he could trust were being stripped away. Those who, potentially, could help most he didn't dare trust. Wizards. Witches. Mercenaries. People whose prime loyalties were to themselves.

And somebody wanted him dead. He didn't doubt for an instant that the false Harish Cultists' primary mission had been to murder him.

"Enough. There're a thousand things we can discuss. But not now. I'm going to the cemetery. Derel?"

"I'll have a horse readied."

"Someday you'll be rewarded."

"Thank you, sir."

To the others, "Sorry I ran you all over. I'm getting desperate, trying to make sense out of things. I feel like a fly in a spider web, and can't make out the spider."

He strapped on his new sword, donned a heavy coat. The nights were still chilly. He left ahead of his guests.

The cemetery lay on a hill north of Vorgreberg, beginning about a mile beyond the city gates. It was large, having served the city since its founding. All Vorgreberg's dead were buried there. Rich or poor, honored or despised, they lay in the same ground. There were divisions, family areas, parts set off for different religions, ethnic groups, and paupers put down at city expense, but all bodies ended up there somewhere. There were graves in the tens of thousands, mostly marked by simple

wooden wands, but some in vast and ornate mausoleums like
that of the family Krief, Kavelin's Kings. It was there that,
before long, Fiana would be laid to rest.

The sun was on the horizon. A chill wind had come up.
Ragnarson entered the open gate. Time and weather seemed
appropriate.

"Bigger than I remembered." He had forgotten to ask where
Elana lay. He spied gravediggers working in the paupers'
section, asked them.

It was near the top of the hill. Haaken had gone all out.

The three new graves were easily spotted. There were no
markers yet. Ragnarson decided to keep them simple.
Ornateness didn't suit Elana.

He didn't see the leg till he tripped. He felt around.

He had found his missing Commander of the Palace Guard.

Preshka had been dead for hours. At least since morning.
Ragnarson rose. His anger was indescribable.

There were flowers under Rolf, wild flowers, the kind Elana
had loved. It must have taken him hours to gather them. The
season was early.... Someone had cut him down on his way to
respect the dead.

Ragnarson tripped again.

He found another corpse.

This one he didn't recognize.

He scrambled around in the gloaming, searching amongst
the headstones and decorative bushes.

"What're you doing?" Haaken asked.

Ragnarson jumped. He hadn't heard his brother come up.
"Counting bodies."

"Eh?"

"Somebody jumped Rolf here, last night or this morning. He
did a job on them before they finished him. I found three
already."

Haaken searched too. "That's all you'll find," he said a
minute later.

"Why?"

"He was crawling toward her grave when he died. If there'd
been any of them left, they wouldn't have let him."

"I wonder."

"What?"

"If they'll run out of assassins before we run out of us." He
paused. "Let him lie where he fell."

Haaken understood. "It'll cause talk."

"I don't care. And I won't be buried beside her. I'll die on a battlefield. She always knew that. She should have someone.... And he was more true than I."

"He was a tough buzzard," said Haaken. "Lived ten years longer than he had any right. And crippled he takes three of them with him."

"They'd sing him into the sagas at home. I'll miss him."

"You don't seem very upset."

"I halfway expected it. He was looking for it. Anyway, there's been too much. They got Nepanthe and Ethrian this morning."

"What?"

"Somebody talked her into going off with them. Gundar saw them. I'm going over there from here. Why don't you come too? We've got things to talk about."

"Okay."

"Wait down the hill a minute, then."

Haaken moved off a short distance.

Ragnarson wept then. For his wife and children, and for Rolf. Rolf had been both a true friend and a loyal follower. No one could have asked more of the man than he had given voluntarily. Again Ragnarson affirmed his determination to avenge the dead.

Then he joined Haaken.

"The first thing I need," he said, "is a plan for partial mobilization. I want to start after Oryon crosses into Altea and there's nobody left to argue with me."

Haaken commanded the Vorgreberger Guards, a heavy infantry regiment begat by the force Ragnarson had commanded during the civil war. He was also Bragi's chief of staff.

Jarl Ahring commanded the Queen's Own Horse Guards, consisting of one "battle" of heavy cavalry and two of light. The army Ragnarson was building included another five regular regiments, each numbering six hundred to seven hundred and fifty men organized in three battles. Each regiment regularly drilled twice its number of volunteers, who could be integrated in case of mobilization. The volunteers, in turn, were responsible for training their neighbors. Counting Nordmen and retainers, Marena Dimura scouts and mountain troops, and regular garrisons and border guards, Kavelin could muster a field army of twelve thousand five hundred overnight, and be assured of a steady supply of partially trained replacements.

"How broad a mobilization?" Haaken asked.

"Just alert the ready people at first. But don't bring them in.
Let them finish planting. Step up the training."

"You'll scare hell out of our neighbors."

"If they've got guilty consciences.... No. The enemy is
Shinsan. Let that leak when you issue the orders. No more
leaves. Training in full swing from now on. And reinforce
Maisak and Karak Strabger. We've got to hold the Gap. I'll do
what I can diplomatically. We'll have a first class plenipoten-
tiary."

"Who?"

"Varthlokkur. If they don't listen to him, they won't listen."

"You won't get much backing. I mean, I can take your word
that Shinsan is moving again. But you'll have to produce hard
evidence to convince other folks."

"I'll work on it. And about two thousand other things. You
know, Haroun wanted me to take over as King here. The bastard
is crazy. And look what *he* wants to be king of. Hammad al
Nakir is a hundred times bigger than Kavelin."

"Hammad al Nakir runs itself. It's got a whole different
tradition."

"Could be."

They reached Valther's home. "Any news?" Bragi asked.

"Not much. Nepanthe, Ethrian, Haroun, Rolf.... She
couldn't find a trace. They're either shielded, or...."

"Or?"

"Dead."

"Rolf's dead. Definitely. We found him in the cemetery. He
took three of them with him."

"Three of who?"

"Ones like we had at my house."

"Harish?"

"No pretense this time. But they were the same breed. What
about the jewel?"

"It's not there."

"Where'd it go?"

"She doesn't know."

"It keeps piling up, and that's the best we can come up with?
Nobody knows anything for sure? But I do. I'll get them if they
don't get me first."

"That goes without saying," Haaken remarked sarcastically.

"Eh?"

"They knew that before they started. That's why they tried to kill you first."

"Oh. Where's Gundar? Let's see what he's got to say."

Gundar didn't tell them anything new. His description of Nepanthe's visitor fit the six dead assassins.

"Guess we can kiss her off," Haaken whispered.

"Quiet!" Bragi muttered. "This'll give Valther a bigger stake. Maybe get some action out of him." He felt that Valther was dragging his heels. Why? His brother-in-law kidnapped, his brother murdered.... That should have been motivation enough. If Nepanthe didn't move him, Ragnarson reflected, he would have to find a new chief spy.

His paranoia had reached the point where he suspected everyone. Anyone he didn't see working as hard as he— irregardless of how hard they hit it when out of his sight—was somehow betraying him.

That, too, may have been part of the enemy plan. A cunning adversary operated on many levels.

SEVENTEEN: Michael's Adventure

Michael Trebilcock lay as still and patient as a cat. His gaze never left the house across Lieneke Lane.

He had stumbled onto the foreigners while visiting his friend Aral, whose father had known his own in their younger days. Aral's father was a caravan outfitter fallen on hard times. He survived on military supply contracts given because the family had remained loyal during the rebellion.

The three had left an inn down the block, looking so much like the men Michael had seen at Ragnarson's that he had felt compelled to follow them.

His investigation had been luckless till then. Even with Aral's help he hadn't discovered anything of interest.

Everybody in Vorgreberg believed something was afoot. But anyone who *knew* anything was keeping quiet. There was an undercurrent of fear. Knives had flashed by moonlight; bodies had turned up in rain-damp morning gutters. Few people were interested in risking a premature visit from the Dark Lady.

"Aral!" he had yelled, and they had followed the three here. One was inside. The others were out of sight, hiding.

Aral Dantice was a short, wide, tough little thug, tempered in the streets during his father's hardship. He didn't look bright. Scars complimented his aura of thuggishness. His problem, his weakness, was a lack of patience. He wouldn't have taken half his scars if he had had enough self-control.

"Let's grab them," Dantice whispered. "If they're the same gang...."

"Easy. Let's find out what they're up to first."

"What they're up to is no good. Let's just cut them up."

"Suppose they're all right? You want to hang?"

Aral was straightforward, Trebilcock thought. You always knew where he stood.

148

Michael didn't understand their friendship. They had little in common but curiosity and itchy feet, and the past friendship of their fathers. They were opposites in virtually everything.

But Trebilcock didn't understand himself. He was a man without direction. He didn't know why he had come to Kavelin. Friendship for Gjerdrum? Plain wanderlust? Or just his intense need for an excuse not to take over his father's business? He had turned that over to the family accountants to manage and followed Gjerdrum to this incredibly complex little kingdom, never knowing what he was seeking.

There had been few of the adventures he had anticipated. Life had been pretty dull. But now.... It had begun to move. His blood, finally, was stirring.

Aral started to rise.

Trebilcock pulled him down. "Hey! Come on!"

"One of them just left."

Michael peered at the house. The man who had gone inside was on the porch, watching the lane. One of his henchmen was running toward town.

"Okay. Follow him. But don't bother him. Let him do whatever he wants. I'll stick to this one."

"Where should we meet?"

"They'll get together again. When they do, so will we. If they don't, I guess we'll meet at your place."

"Right." Dantice scampered along the backside of the hedge where they had hidden. He was built so low that keeping down wasn't difficult.

A woman and boy joined the man on the porch.

The fat man's wife, Michael thought. The boy must be his son.

The woman said something. She seemed nervous. The man nodded. She ducked inside, returned with a bundle. All three hastened along the lane.

Trebilcock crept along behind the hedge, waiting for the third man to act. Nepanthe seemed extremely upset, though she was accompanying the man by choice. She was sneaking away, and was afraid someone would notice.

"That dark guy must've done some fancy talking," Trebilcock muttered.

The third man then followed Nepanthe and her escort once they rounded a bend. When he had made the same turn, Michael went back to the road. He kept his head down. He was passing the Marshall's home. A half-dozen soldiers were there, and might. . . .

"Hey! Michael!"

"Damnit!" It was one of the Horse Guards he bummed with. For once in his life he wished he didn't have so many friends. "'Lo, Tie. How goes it?"

"Fine. Except I think they're getting carried away trying to find things for us to do. Squaring away the Marshall's house, you know what I mean? He's got a wife, he's got a maid and butler and all. Don't seem right. . . ."

So. The word wasn't out. "That's a shame. But you could be out riding around the Gudbrandsdal in the rain."

"You got it. I don't complain to the sergeant. He'd come up with something like that."

"I'd like to hang around and see what's happening, Tie, but I've got a job."

"You?"

"Sure. Not much. Running messages for the Marshall's secretary. But he expects me to get them moved."

"Yeah. All right. Catch you later. Why don't you plop in at the Kit 'N Kettle tonight? Got some girls from Arsen Street coming down. . . . But don't bring that chunky guy. What's his name? Dantice. He busted the place up last time."

"Okay. I'll see. If Prataxis don't keep me running."

"What's with that guy anyway, Mike?"

Trebilcock glanced up the lane. How far ahead were they? "Aral? Don't mind him, Tie. He isn't so bad when you get to know him. Hey. I've got to go."

"Sure. See you later."

Trebilcock walked briskly till his soldier-friend could no longer see him. Then he jogged, glancing down the cross lanes to make sure they hadn't turned aside.

He hoped they were headed back to their inn. In Aral's part of town they would be easier to trail.

Luck was with him. That was their destination, and he picked up the rear guard in West Market Street, which was packed with shoppers.

He found Dantice lounging around outside his father's place. That, for Aral, was a near career. "What happened?"

"Not a damned thing. The guy came back to the inn. The others just showed up."

"What're they up to?"

"Mike, I don't know. You're the one playing spy. Ho! Hang on. Here's the first one again."

A dusky man had come to the inn door leading a half-dozen horses.

"Oh-oh," Trebilcock muttered. "What do we do now?"

"How should I know? You're the brains."

"Aral, they're leaving town. I never thought of that. I just thought.... Never mind. Here." He slapped a gold piece into Dantice's hand. "Get us a couple horses. Some food and stuff. I'm going to talk to your father."

"Are you crazy?"

"Come on. Why not?"

"You're nuts. All right. You straighten it with the old man."

"Right. Yes. Come on. Hurry. We'll lose them."

"I'm going."

Trebilcock slammed through the door of the Dantice establishment, knocking the bell off its mounting. "Mr. Dantice! Mr. Dantice!"

The older Dantice came from the little office where he kept his accounts. "Hello, Michael. How are you?"

"Mr. Dantice, I need some money. All the money you can give me. Here." He seized pen and paper. "I'll write you a letter of credit. You can take it to Pleskau Brothers. They handle my finances in Vorgreberg."

"Michael, boy, calm down. What's this all about?"

"Mr. Dantice! Hurry!" Trebilcock raced to the door, peeped out. Nepanthe, Ethrian, and the dark men were mounting up. "There's no time. They're leaving. I'm doing a job for the Marshall. I've got to have money. I'm going out of town."

"But...."

"Isn't my credit good?"

"The best." The old man scratched the back of his head. "I just don't understand...."

"I'll explain when we get back. Just give me what you can." He wrote hastily, leaving a blank for the amount.

Puzzled, but wanting to help his son's friend—whom he thought a bit strange, but felt to be a good influence—Dantice retrieved his cash box from hiding.

"Michael, I don't have much here today. 'Bout fifteen nobles, and change."

"That's good. Whatever. We'll only be gone a couple days. It's just so we can eat on the way." He flung himself to the door again. "Hurry. They're almost gone. Come on, Aral. Where are you?"

"Twelve and seven. That's all I can spare, Michael. I have to keep some just in case...."

"Fine. Fine. Ten is plenty, really. If I can't get by....." He signed the credit for ten nobles, scooped coins as fast as the older man could count them out. "Thanks, Mr. Dantice. You're a gem." He kissed the old man.

"Michael!"

"Hey, we'll see you in a few days."

He whipped out the door. Aral was just coming with the horses. "They're all Trego had left."

"We'll switch later. You see where they headed?"

"Up the street. If they leave town, they'll have to use a gate. Different than the west one, right? From here that means the east or south."

"But which? Never mind. Let's see if we can catch up."

They made no friends that day, pushing through the streets the way they did, as if they were the Nordmen of old. They caught Nepanthe's party as it turned into the Palace Road, which ran straight to the east gate.

"Got them now," Trebilcock enthused. "We can swing around and get ahead."

"Why not just pass them?"

"The woman knows me."

"Whatever. You're the boss. What'd the old man say when you told him?"

"What?"

"That I'm going off with you. He's still trying to dump those account books on me."

"Oh, hell. I clean forgot, Aral."

"You didn't tell him?"

"I was too busy trying to get some money."

"Well, he'll live. He's used to me taking off for a couple days whenever I find me a new slut."

But this adventure would last longer than either expected.

Their path wound eastward, through Forbeck and Savernake provinces, often by circuitous routes. The group they tracked avoided all human contact. The two expended a lot of ingenuity maintaining contact while escaping notice.

"They're sure in a hurry," Aral grumped the third morning.

He hadn't complained yet, but his behind was killing him. He wasn't accustomed to long days in the saddle.

"Don't worry. They'll slow down. You'll outlast the woman and boy."

Michael picked the right note. There was no way Aral Dantice was going to be outdone by a kid and a broad in her forties.

Michael finally realized they were getting in deep after they passed Baxendala at night and were approaching Maisak, the last stronghold of Kavelin, high in the Savernake Gap.

There, between Maisak and Baxendala, stood several memorials of the civil war. It was said that broken swords and bones could still be found all through the area.

Two weeks after sneaking past Maisak, Michael and Aral reached a point from which they could see the eastern plains.

"My God! Look, Mike. There's nothing out there. Just grass."

Trebilcock grew nervous. How did people keep from getting lost out there? It was a green grass ocean. Yet the caravans came and went. . . .

They met caravans every day. Traders were racing to get through with early loads, to obtain the best prices. Sometimes the two overhauled an eastbound train and encountered someone they knew. Thus they kept track of their quarry. Later, when they reached the ruins of Gog-Ahlan, they would have to close up. The other party might strike out toward Necremnos, or Throyes, or any of the cities tributary to them. And who knew where they would go from there?

They traded for better horses, foodstuffs, equipment, and weapons along the way, and always got a poor deal. Trebilcock had no mercantile sense whatsoever. He finally surrendered the quartermaster chores to Aral, who was more intimidating in his dickering.

It was in potentially violent confrontations that Michael Trebilcock was intimidating. Men tended to back down when they saw his eyes.

Michael didn't understand, but used it. He felt it was his best weapon. He had trained in arms, as had everyone at the Rebsamen, but didn't consider himself much good. He didn't consider himself good at anything unless he was the best around.

They reached Gog-Ahlan. Aral found a man who was a

friend of his father. With Michael's help he wrote the elder
Dantice, and wrote a credit on House Dantice, which Michael
promised to repay. And they learned that Nepanthe's party was
bound for Throyes.

There was no holding Aral to an unswerving purpose that
night. Old Gog-Ahlan lay in ruins, a victim of the might of
Ilkazar four centuries earlier. On the outskirts, though, a trading
city had grown up. Vices were readily available. Aral had
energies to dissipate.

It took him two nights. Bowing to the inevitable, Michael
tried to keep up. Then, heads spinning, they rode on.

Their quarry moved more leisurely now, safely beyond the
reach of Kavelin's Marshall.

The two overhauled them within the week, a hundred miles
from Throyes. "Now we go ahead," Michael said. "We'll swing
around, too far away to be recognized." That was what two
riders overtaking a larger party would do anyway. Out on those
wild plains no one trusted anyone else.

Throyes was a sprawl of a city that made Vorgreberg look
like a farming village. Most of it wasn't walled, and no one cared
who came or went.

Here, for the first time in their lives, they felt like foreigners.
They were surrounded by people who were different, who owed
them no sympathy. Aral behaved himself.

Four days passed. Their quarry didn't show. Dantice began
fretting.

Michael had begun to consider hitting their back trail when
Aral said, "Here they come. Finally."

Only one man remained. He was wounded. The woman and
boy, though, were hale if still a little frightened.

"Bandits," Trebilcock guessed. "Let's stay behind after this.
In case we need to rescue the lady."

"Hey, Mike, I'm ready. Let's do it. My old man must be out
of his head by now. You know how long we've been gone?"

"I know. And I think we should stay gone until we find out
what's happening."

"We won't get a better chance. That guy's bad hurt."

"No. Let's see where he goes."

The wounded man went to a house in the wealthiest part of
town. There he turned the woman and boy over. The man who
received them wasn't happy. Neither eavesdropper understood
the language, but his tone was clear, if not his reasons.

"What now?" Aral asked.

"We see what happens."

They watched. Aral daringly climbed the garden wall and listened at windows. But he heard nothing of importance.

Two days later the woman and boy returned to the road with a new escort.

"Oh, no," Aral groaned. "Here we go again. We going to follow them to the edge of the world?"

"If we have to."

"Hey, Mike, I didn't sign on for that. A couple days, you said."

"I'm not dragging you. You can go back. Just give me half the money."

"What? You'd be in debtor's prison by tomorrow night. And I ain't riding around out here without nobody to talk to."

"Then you'd better stick with me."

"They can't go far anyway. Argon is the end of the road."

"How do you know?"

"They're heading for the Argon Gate. If they were headed east, they'd go to Necremnos. So they'd head for the Necremnos Gate."

"How do you know where they're heading?"

"You know my old man."

"So?"

"His stories?"

"Oh. Yeah."

Dantice's father bragged endlessly about his youthful adventures, before the El Murid Wars, when he had made a fortune in the eastern trade. Aral, having heard the tales all his life, had a fair notion of where they were.

They reached Argon two weeks later.

Argon, in summer, was an outpost of Hell. The city lay in the delta of the River Roë. That vast river ran in scores of channels there, through hundreds of square miles of marshland.

The city itself, twice the size of Throyes, had been built on delta islands. Each was connected by pontoon bridges to others, and some had canals instead of streets.

The youths' quest took them to the main island, a large, triangular thing with its apex pointing upriver. It was surrounded by walls rising from the river itself.

"Lord, what a fortress," Trebilcock muttered.

Aral was even more impressed. "I thought Dad was a liar.

That wall must be a hundred feet high." He pointed toward the northern end of the island, where the walls were the tallest. "How did Ilkazar conquer it?"

"Sorcery," Michael replied. "And there weren't any walls then. They thought the river was enough."

Aral looked back. "Rice paddies. Everywhere."

"They export it to Matayanga mostly. We studied it at school, in Economics. They have a fleet to haul it down the coast."

"Better close it up. We might lose them in the crowd."

The pontoon was crowded. They couldn't find anyone who spoke their language, so couldn't ask why.

The trail led to a huge fortress within the fortress-island.

"The Fadem," Aral guessed. The Fadem was the seat of government for the Argonese imperium, and was occupied by a nameless Queen usually called the Fadema or Matriarch. Argon had been ruled by women for four generations, since Fadema Tenaya had slain the sorcerer-tryant Aron Lockwurm and had seized his crown.

The men escorting Nepanthe were expected.

"Don't think we'd better try following," Michael said. Nobody had challenged them yet. The streets were full of foreigners, but none were entering the inner fortress.

Trebilcock led the way round the Fadem once. He could study only three walls. The fourth was part of the island wall and dropped into the river. "We've got to get in there," he said.

"You're crazy."

"You keep saying that. And you keep tagging along."

"So I'm crazy too. How do you figure to do it?"

"It's almost dark. We'll go down there on the south end where the wall is low and climb in."

"Now I know you're crazy."

"They won't expect us. I'll bet nobody ever tried it."

He was right. The Argonese were too much in dread of those who dwelt within the Fadem. They would have labeled the plan a good one for getting dead quick. Suicides traditionally jumped from the high point of the triangular outer wall, where the memorial to the victory over Lockwurm stood.

Trebilcock and Dantice chose the Fadem, though. About midnight, without light, during a driving rain.

"No guards that I can see," Michael murmured as he helped Aral to the battlements.

"Must be the weather."

It had been raining since nightfall. They would learn that, in Argon, it rained every night during summer. And that by day the humidity was brutal.

It took them two hours of grossly incautious flitting from one glassless window to another, attending only those with lights behind their shutters, to find the right room.

"It's her," Aral whispered to Michael, who had to remain behind him on a narrow ledge. They had clawed eighty feet up the outside of a tower to reach that window. "I'll go in and...."

"No! She'd turn us in. Remember, she came because she wanted to. Let's just find out what's up."

Nothing happened for a long time. After resting, Michael slipped a few feet back down and worked his way across beneath the window so he could reach the ledge at the window's far side.

Three hours dragged through the stuttering mills of time. Neither man had ever been more miserable. The rain beat at them. Hard stone below dared them to fall asleep. There was no room to move, to stretch....

Someone entered the room.

Trebilcock came alert when he heard a woman say, "Good evening, Madame," in heavily accented Wesson. "I'm sorry you had to wait so long."

Trebilcock and Dantice peeked through the slats of the shutters. Why the hell don't they put glass in these things? Michael wondered. But Castle Krief, too, had unglazed windows, and weather in Kavelin was more extreme.

Glass was a luxury even kings seldom wasted on windows.

Nepanthe rose from a bed. Ethrian lay sleeping on a couch. "Where is he? When can I see him?"

"Who?"

"My husband."

"I don't understand."

"The men who brought me to Throyes.... They said they were taking me to my husband. He sent for me. They had a letter."

"They lied." The woman smiled mockingly. "Permit me. I am Fadema. The Queen of Argon."

No "Pleased to meet you" from Nepanthe. She went to the point. "Why am I here?"

"We had to remove you from Vorgreberg. You might have embarrassed us there."

"Who is us?"

"Madame." Another visitor entered.

"Oh!"

Trebilcock, too, gasped.

He had never seen a Tervola, but he recognized the dress and mask. His heart redoubled its hammering. The man would discover them with his witchery....

"Shinsan!" Nepanthe gasped. "Again."

The Tervola bowed slightly. "We come again, Madame."

"Where's my husband?"

"He's well."

Nepanthe blustered, "You'd better send me home. You lied to me.... I have Varthlokkur's protection, you know."

"Indeed I do. I know exactly what you mean to him. It's the main reason we brought you here."

Nepanthe sputtered, fussed, threatened. Her visitors ignored her.

"Madame," said the Tervola, "I suggest you make the best of your stay. Don't make it difficult."

"What's happened to my husband? They told me they were taking me to him."

"I haven't the faintest idea," the Fadema replied.

Nepanthe produced a dagger, hurled herself at the Tervola.

He disarmed her easily. "Fadema, move the boy elsewhere. To keep her civil. We'll speak to you later, Madame."

Nepanthe screamed and kicked and bit, threatened and pleaded. The Tervola held her while the Fadema dragged Ethrian away.

Michael Trebilcock suffered several chivalrous impulses. He didn't fear the Tervola. But he did have a little common sense. It saved his life.

After the Fadema left, the Tervola said, "Your honor and your son are our hostages. Understand?"

"I understand. Varthlokkur and my husband...."

"Will do nothing. That's why you're my captive."

In that he was mistaken. Varthlokkur ignored extortion, and Mocker just became more troublesome. It was in the blood.

"*Your* captive? Isn't this *her* city?"

"She seems to think so. Amusing, isn't it?" His tone grew harsh. "One year. Behave and you'll be free. Otherwise.... You know our reputation. Our language has no word for mercy." He departed.

Michael waited five minutes, then crept forward to whisper to Aral. . . . And found Dantice dead asleep.

The idiot had slept through almost the whole thing.

"Ssst!"

Nepanthe responded to his third hiss by approaching the window fearfully.

"What? Who are you? I. . . . I know you."

"From Vorgreberg. My name is Michael Trebilcock. My friend and I followed you here."

"Why?"

"To find out what you were up to. Those men were the same sort who killed the Marshall's wife. And your brother."

She became angry anew. He had a hard time calming her.

"Look, you're in no real danger while they think they can use you to blackmail the wizard and your husband."

"What're you going to do?"

"I thought about bringing you out the window. But they've got your son. You probably wouldn't go. . . ."

"You're right."

"There's nothing I can do for you, then. I can only go home and explain what happened. Maybe the Marshall can do something."

Nepanthe leaned out the window. "The rain's stopped. It's getting light."

Trebilcock groaned.

He and Aral would have to spend the day on that ledge.

Then the Fadema returned. But she stayed only long enough to taunt Nepanthe.

Michael thought he would die before daylight failed. That ledge was murderous. The sun was deadly. . . . Damnable Arnal simply crowded the wall and snored.

Trebilcock waited till the rain cleared the streets, then wakened Aral. He spoke with Nepanthe briefly before departing, trying to buoy her hopes.

"We'll ride straight through," he promised. "It won't take long."

Aral groaned.

"Wait," she said. "Before you leave. I want to give you something."

Her captors hadn't bothered searching her effects even after the dagger episode. That arrogant confidence led to a crucial oversight.

She gave Michael a small ebony casket. "Give this to Varthlokkur. Or my brother if you can't find the wizard."

"What is it?"

"Never mind. Just believe that it's important. No matter what, don't let Shinsan get their hands on it. Turran called it the last hope of the west. Someone gave it to me to take care of because she was thinking about. . . . Never mind. Get it to Varthlokkur or my brother. Make sure it don't fall while you're going down." She checked his shirt to see if it was safely tucked in. "Oh, was I stupid! If he'd just stay home like normal people. . . . Those men knew just what to say to me. I'm lucky I've got friends to look out for me."

She gave each man a little kiss. "Good luck. And remember about the casket. It's easy to forget."

"We will," Trebilcock told her. "And we'll be back. That's a promise."

"You're bold." She smiled. "Remember, I'm a married lady. Good-bye." She left the window. There was a bounce to her step that would puzzle her jailors for months.

Michael and Aral returned home. And the worst of their journey was getting down that eighty feet of tower.

Exhausted, they reached Vorgreberg during the first week of August. They had been gone nearly three months.

EIGHTEEN: The Unborn

For a week no one dared enter the chamber where Fiana lay, where her child-of-evil was being nurtured by one of the older wickednesses of the world. Even Gjerdrum lacked the courage to intrude. He carried meals to the door, knocked, retreated.

Varthlokkur was indulging in those black arts which had made him so infamous. By week's end he had terrorized both Karak Strabger and Baxendala.

During the day the castle was obscured by a whirling, twisting darkness which throbbed like a heart beating. Its boundaries were sharply defined. The townspeople called it a hole through the walls of Hell. Some claimed to see the denizens of an Outer Domain peering out at the world with unholy hunger.

That was imagination. But the darkness was real, and by night it masked the stars over Karak Strabger. Eldritch lights from within sometimes cast red shadows on the mountains surrounding castle and town. And always there were the sounds, the wicked noises, like the roar of devil hordes praising some mighty demon-lord....

On the floor of the little chamber the sorcerer had laid out a pentagram which formed one face of an amazing construct. Eight feet above the floor floated another pentagram, traced in lines of fire. Rising like the petals of a flower, from the luminescent design on the floor, were five more pentagrams, sharing sides with five pentagrams depending from the design above. The whole formed a twelve-faced gem. Every apex was occupied by a silvery cabalistic symbol which burned cold and bright. Additional symbols writhed on the surfaces of the planes.

The dead Queen lay on a table at the construct's heart. Upon

her breast lay the monster she had died to bring into the world.
Outside, the wizard worked on.

He called his creation the Winterstorm, though it had
nothing to do with weather or season, but, rather, a dead
magician's mathematical way of looking at sorcery. It was a gate
to powers undreamt even in Shinsan. It had enabled the
destruction of the Princes Thaumaturge in times of yore.

Like so many evils, it was terribly beautiful.

For a week Varthlokkur had labored, taking no rest, and
little food. Now his hands trembled. His courage wavered. His
sense of morality recoiled. The thing he was trying to create
would be more evil than he. Darker, possibly, than the
incalculable evils of Shinsan. What it did to the world would be
determined by his ability to control it—especially in the critical
moments approaching. If he failed, he would be just the first to
die a grisly death. If he succeeded only partially, it would be but
a matter of time till he lost control.

Success had to be complete and absolute. And he was so
tired, so hungry, so weak....

But he had no choice. He couldn't stop now. Nor could he
turn back. He was committed.

On the edges of his consciousness, out where his heightened
senses met the Beyond, he heard the Lords of Chaos chuckling,
whispering amongst themselves, casting lots for him.... He
wasn't that kind of wizard. He refused to make deals. He
increased the might of the Winterstorm and *compelled* them to
respond to his will. He ordered, and they performed.

They hated him for it. And forever they would wait,
tirelessly, patiently, for his fatal slip.

His fiery wand touched several floating symbols. Those
beings on the edges of his senses screamed. Agonized, they
awaited his commands.

The symbols blazed brighter. Colored shadows frothed over
the barren walls. The dark cloud shuddered and swirled round
the stronghold. The people of Baxendala locked their shutters
and doors. The handful of castle servants huddled downstairs.
They would have fled if Gjerdrum had let them.

The Marshall had told him not to let anyone leave till he
heard otherwise. The news was to be stifled till Ragnarson had
stabilized the political response.

Gjerdrum was devoted to his Queen and Marshall. Though
wanting nothing more than to flee himself, he kept his flock

inside. Now, with the howl above redoubling, he again prepared to block a rush toward freedom.

Varthlokkur raised his arms and spoke softly to the denizens of the netherworlds. He used the tongue of his childhood.

Those things would respond to any language. But the old tongue, shaped by the wizards of ancient Ilkazar, was precise. It didn't permit ambiguities demons could exploit.

He commanded.

The things on the Other Side cringed, whined—and obeyed.

The Queen's corpse surged violently. The terrible infant, englobed in a transparent membrane, still in a fetal curl, levitated. Its head turned. Its eyes opened. It glared at Varthlokkur.

"You see me," the wizard said. "I see you. I command you. You are my servant henceforth." For seven days he had been shaping its hideous mind, teaching it, building on the knowledge of evil stamped on the thing's genes. "Henceforth you shall be known as Radeachar, the Unborn."

The name, Radeachar, meant only "The One Who Serves," without intimations of actual servitude. It had overtones of destruction, of sorcery held ready as a swordsman holds a ready blade. In olden times those sorcerers who had marched with Ilkazar's armies had been entitled Radeachar. The nearest modern equivalent was the shaghûn of Hammad al Nakir.

It fought him. The things he compelled to aid him battled back. He pitted his will and power against the Unborn....

He had to win beyond any shadow of compromise.

It lasted thirteen hours.

Then he collapsed.

But not before Radeachar had become his lifelong slave, virtually an extension of his own personality.

He slept, unmoving, on the cool stone floor for two days. And, though the blackness had freed the castle, and spring silence reigned, no one dared waken him.

The distraction of Varthlokkur's undertaking allowed Nepanthe, and those who followed her, to slip through the Gap during the time the wizard slept.

Varthlokkur never sensed the nearness of the woman who meant more to him than life itself.

She was married to his son now, but he and she had an agreement. When Mocker died—unless Varthlokkur himself were responsible—she would become his wife. The bargain, woven on the looms of Fate, had made it possible to destroy Nu Li Hsi and Yo Hsi.

He awakened almost too weak to move. From amongst his paraphernalia he secured a small bottle, drank it dry. A warm, temporary strength flooded him. He lay down again, let it work. A half hour later he went downstairs.

"You can turn them loose now," he told Gjerdrum. "What needed doing is done. And Ragnarson has finished in Vorgreberg."

"I haven't had word from him yet."

"You will."

Gjerdrum considered. Varthlokkur was probably right. "Okay. I won't tell them they can leave. But if they get away while my back is turned, that's all right."

"They won't go far. They won't be welcome in Baxendala. They'll stay around till you're ready to leave for Vorgreberg."

Varthlokkur insisted on showing Gjerdrum his masterwork.

Eanredson took one look and retched.

Varthlokkur was hurt. "I'm sorry." He had been proud, forgetting that it took a peculiar breed to appreciate his artistry.

"Come, then," he said. "We'll be needed in Vorgreberg."

"You're going to take that.... That.... With us?"

Puzzled, Varthlokkur nodded.

"Better do it on the quiet. The very damned quiet, else you'll start a revolution. The black arts aren't popular with the man in the street."

Varthlokkur's feelings were bruised again. His greatest work had to remain hidden? "All right. I'll leave it here."

"Good." Gjerdrum glanced at the Unborn. This time he forced his gorge down.

"You'll get used to it."

"I don't want to. It should've been killed when Wachtel saw what it was."

"You're being very narrow...."

Gjerdrum refused to argue. "If we're going, let's go. I've been away too long. That foreigner, Prataxis, has probably screwed everything up."

They left that afternoon. Gjerdrum kept going through the night. They reached Vorgreberg the next evening, exhausted. Gjerdrum had to invoke the wizard's reputation to keep the servants from scattering with their horror stories.

Gjerdrum and Varthlokkur got no rest. Prataxis dragged them to the Marshall's office immediately.

"About time," Ragnarson said. "You got Derel's letter?"

"No," Gjerdrum replied.

"Must've crossed paths. Just a note telling you to get your butt home."

"I was waiting on him."

"Everything taken care of?"

"I still have to make the servants forget," the wizard replied.

"Won't be necessary. The news is out. The Thing elected me Regent. They're already forming a committee to consider royal candidates."

"There're some things he *should* make them forget," Gjerdrum growled.

Ragnarson glanced at Varthlokkur.

"I performed a few sorceries. They upset him. Before we left, I performed a divination. Very unclear, but two names came through. Badalamen. The Spear of Odessa Khomer."

"Meaning what?"

"I don't know. Badalamen may be a person. The Spear sounds like a mystical weapon. It isn't one I've heard of. And that's unusual. Those things are pretty well known."

"Neither means anything to me," Ragnarson said. He related recent events in Vorgreberg, concluding, "I've prepared for mobilization."

"Before the mercenaries leave?" Gjerdrum asked. "They'll come at you twice as hard...."

"No problem. Oryon wants to go. To poke around High Crag for the connection with Shinsan. Meanwhile, we're going to turn Kavelin upside down. These assassinations and kidnappings have got to stop."

Varthlokkur glowed. "I have the perfect device. The perfect servant, the perfect hunter...."

"Gjerdrum? What's the matter?"

"I saw his perfect hunter."

Ragnarson looked from one to the other.

"The baby," Gjerdrum said. "The demon thing. He kept it alive."

Ragnarson leaned back, closed his eyes, said nothing for a long time. Then, softly, suppressing his revulsion, "Tell me about it."

"I merely salvaged it," the wizard replied. "I did what was necessary so it survived, bound it to me, taught it. It's not as bad as your friend thinks."

"It's horrible. You should have killed it."

"I go with Gjerdrum emotionally. How can it help?"

"It can find the men you want found. And kill them, or bring them to you."

"How'll it tell enemies from friends? When can you begin?"

"I could call it right now. It detects enemies by reading their minds."

The hairs on Bragi's neck bristled. Read minds? In all likelihood it would read everyone, friend or foe. "Let me think about it. Gjerdrum. You brought Fiana?"

Eanredson nodded.

"Good. Set up the funeral. Big as a coronation. With open house here. The works. Vorgreberg is restless. It's time we distracted it some. I've got a feeling there won't be time for fun much longer." He turned to Varthlokkur. "Can we possibly hit Shinsan first?"

"A spoiler? No. They're moving. The old destiny call is echoing from border to border. They've recovered from the war with Escalon and the feud between O Shing and Mist. They're ready. They're short just one element. An enemy. The Tervola want us."

"How do you know?"

"It's no secret. Baxendala shattered the myth of their invincibility. They want to regain that. You just said a Tervola was seen in the Kapenrungs. They're doing the obvious. Softening up. Eliminating men who would resist. Trying for a sure thing. I suggest we loose Radeachar now—before they reach anyone else who shapes the power. Did you find the Tear?"

"Gjerdrum, would you step outside please?" Once Eanredson left, "It hasn't turned up. Mist can't find a trace. She and Valther can't find our enemies, either. They're either well shielded or gone."

"Why did you ask the boy to go?"

"They got Nepanthe."

The sorcerer rose slowly, face darkening.

"Wait! She's not dead. They kidnapped her. So to speak. My son Gundar heard a man tell her he could take her to Mocker.

She and Ethrian went with him. Mist couldn't locate her, though."

"Excuse me. I've got work to do. I'll summon Radeachar. He'll begin bringing your enemies in soon. Then I'll gather the Brotherhood. And see if anyone will loan troops for another Baxendala. This time, I think, we'd better keep after O Shing till he's done for."

He dropped back into the chair. "I'm tired. Weary unto death. This constant struggle with Shinsan has got to end. Us or them, for all time."

Ragnarson countered, "Would that settle anything? Permanently? Aren't there always more evils? If we destroy Shinsan, won't something else arise? Somebody once said that evil is eternal, good fleeting."

"Eternal? I don't know. It's relative. In the eye of the beholder. The Tervola don't think they're evil. They feel we're wicked for resisting destiny. Either way, though, I want rid of Shinsan. A force of equal magnitude isn't likely to rise in my lifetime."

"Wizard, I'm tired too. And emotionally exhausted. I have trouble caring anymore. I've lost so much that I'm numb. Only Kavelin is left. Till we find a new king. . . . Well, I'll keep plugging."

The wizard smiled. "I believe you've found a home, Marshall."

"What? Oh. Yes. I guess. Yes. I still care about Kavelin. But I don't know what to do."

"Trust me. Not forever, but for now. Our interests are congruent. I want peace. I want to escape the machinations of this pestilence in Shinsan. I want Nepanthe. . . ."

"Did *you* grab Mocker?"

"No. I promised Nepanthe. My promises are good. And he's my son. . . ." There was no resentment in his response.

"What?"

"It's true. It's a long story, that doesn't matter now. But he is."

"Uhm. That explains why he isn't afraid of you. . . . Does he know the other thing?"

"No. And he'd better never find out. But back to our congruency of interest. You have my pledge to remain a steadfast ally till Shinsan falls. Or destroys us."

"All right. Destruction seems most likely."

"Maybe. They have the advantages. Unity. Power. A huge army. . . . Why dwell on it? The die is cast. The doom is upon us. The Fates speed us from their bows. I'll go now. You may not see me for a while."

This was the point, according to Prataxis, when the First Great Eastern War began. He selected it primarily because histories need milestones. First causes could be traced back, and back, and back. And heavy, massed combat didn't occur till the Second Great Eastern War. Some authorities argued that Baxendala should be called the First Great Eastern War, and seen separately from Kavelin's civil war. Though the rebels accepted aid from Shinsan, Shinsan's objective in intervening was eventual mastery.

Whatever, this was the moment when, irrevocably, Ragnarson and Varthlokkur committed themselves to destruction of the Dread Empire.

NINETEEN: Funerals and Assassins

Haaken rode at his brother's side. Gjerdrum and Derel trailed them. It was the morning after the day following Eanredson's return. He had arranged the funeral quickly, for Victory Day, for whatever symbolic value that might have.

Behind them, Dr. Wachtel rode in a small carriage. He was too fragile for a horse. He would be an important speaker. His honesty was beyond question. His testimony would dispel rumors surrounding the Queen's passing—though he wouldn't tell the whole truth.

The word had spread quickly. The streets were human rivers flowing northward.

Ragnarson told Haaken, "Keep a sharp watch. This mess is perfect for an assassination."

"I'm watching." He glanced around. "Something we should talk about. Ragnar."

"Oh?"

"He's bound for trouble. And he won't listen."

"What is it?"

"A girl."

"That all? Well. The little devil. Ain't fifteen yet.... You remember Inger, Hjarlma's daughter, back home? I was about his age when...."

"If you won't take it serious either...."

"Wait. Wait. I do. These southerners worry about that crap. Never understood why. She somebody's daughter?"

"No. Her father's one of Ahring's sergeants. It wouldn't be a political thing. I'm just thinking we've got trouble enough already."

"Okay. I'll talk to him. Where is he, anyway?"

"With Valther and his bunch."

"Maybe I'll keep him closer."

"You keep saying that."

"I get distracted. Damn, I miss Elana." He sagged in his saddle, momentarily overwhelmed by past emotions.

They encountered Valther on the road. Ragnarson asked, "You found anything, Valther?"

"No. Except that there were three men involved in Nepanthe's disappearance. I found their hostelry. The landlord thought they were guards off a caravan from Throyes."

"Ah. And Throyens look pretty much like desert people."

"Same stock. But they wouldn't have told the truth, would they?"

"Why not? Still, even if they were, they were just hired blades. Anything else? Mist?"

"I can't find much. No Nepanthe. No Haroun. No Mocker. Nothing here in Kavelin. . . ."

"Trebilcock," Valther said.

"I'm getting to it."

"What about him?"

"I located him. He and a man named Dantice are in the Savernake Gap. Apparently following Nepanthe."

"What the hell? I told him to keep his ears open, not to. . . . Following? You sure?"

"No."

"I hope so. This could be a real break."

"You want I should send a squadron after them?" Haaken asked. "In case they need help?"

"Let them run free. Trebilcock don't attract much attention. They might lead him to the guy running the assassins. But I'm not doing this right. Valther. She's your sister. What do you think? Should we risk it?"

The spymaster pondered, looked to his wife for support, thought some more. "She seems safe, doesn't she? If they meant her harm, they'd have done it already. . . . I don't know. Using your own sister. . . ."

"You've done it before. For smaller stakes."

"All right. Let it ride. We have Turran to avenge. And my other brothers. Brock. Luxos. Ridyeh. Okay. But I hope this Trebilock is competent."

"I think so. There's a man under that weird facade."

"I'm trusting you. Now, what about Oryon? He going peacefully?"

"Yes. He's in a hurry to find out what's up at High Crag. I don't like him, but he's okay. He believes in the Guild. Which's a plus now. If someone in the Citadel is conspiring with Shinsan he'll root them out. He'll leave at sunrise. Which reminds me. Gjerdrum. What's planned for tonight?"

There was little festivity this Victory Day, despite Ragnarson's proclamation asking Vorgreberg to give the Guildsmen a good send-off.

"Won't be much," Gjerdrum replied. "Nobody's interested. This." He indicated cemetery and mob. "And politics."

Ragnarson had been elected Regent but his position wasn't unshakeable. The Nordmen already were accusing him of dictatorial excess. And he *had* been high-handed occasionally, especially in preparing for mobilization. He had explained to a handful of supporters in the Thing, but hadn't yet taken his case to the opposition.

He would have to make time. The sympathy generated by his announcement of Elana's murder wouldn't last.

They went up to the Royal Mausoleum. "Everybody in town must be here," Haaken observed. Crowds packed the hillside.

Trumpets sounded in the distance.

"Jarl's coming," Gjerdrum said.

The procession could be seen clearly from the hilltop. The Queen's Own Horse Guards, in full dress, rode ahead of the hearse, behind the heavy battle of Haaken's Vorgrebergers. Immediately behind the hearse were scores of knights in gleaming armor, many of them carefully chosen Nordmen barons. Behind them, afoot, came the leaders of the other ethnic groups, including chieftains of the Marena Dimura. Bringing up the rear was another battle of light horse. So that the glory of the knights wouldn't be eclipsed, no regular heavy cavalry had been included.

This wasn't just a send-off for a monarch, it was a major political event, with shows of unity and fence-mending. Key men had to be honored. Selected loyalists from each ethnic group would deliver eulogies. Members of the diplomatic community would contribute remarks—and watch closely for weaknesses.

Ragnarson's heart throbbed with the measured beat of Vorgreberger drums. "Derel, Gjerdrum, I appreciate this. What would I do without you?"

"You'd make do," Prataxis replied. "You got along without me before I came." Yet he was pleased. His employer tended to take for granted the competence of his associates.

It was a beautiful morning. The sky was intensely blue. A few stately cumulus towers glided sedately eastward. A gentle, chilly breeze teased through the graveyard, but the morning promised a comfortable afternoon. It was that sort of spring day which made it hard to believe there were shadows in the earth. It was a day for lying back in the green, courting cloud castles, thinking how perfect life was. It was a day for dreaming impossible dreams, like the brotherhood of man, world peace, and freedom from hunger.

Even a funeral that was a national enterprise couldn't blunt spirits sharpened by the weather.

The blunting came later, with the endless speeches already wearing the edge off.

Ragnarson had made his speech earlier. Like every speaker before and since, he had been windier than necessary. He had discarded the unification theme prepared by Derel, speaking instead of Fiana and her dreams, then of the threat Kavelin faced. He revealed almost everything, which unsettled his associates.

"Just trying to warn them," he told Valther. "And let them know it's not hopeless."

Secrecy was a fetish with Valther. He didn't tell anybody anything the person didn't absolutely have to know.

The crisis came during acting ambassador Achmed's strained praise of Fiana.

Three men plunged from the crowd, short swords in hand. One went for Valther, one for Mist, the third for Ragnarson. Bragi, arguing with Valther, didn't see them.

Haaken threw himself in front of his brother. He took a stroke along his ribs while dragging Bragi's assailant down. He also tripped the man going for Valther.

Gjerdrum and Derel tried to intercept the third assassin. Both failed.

Mist's eyes widened. Surprise, fear, horror plundered her beauty. The sword bit deeply....

Something like a shouted song parted her lips.

Thunder rolled across the blue sky.

Haaken, two assassins, Gjerdrum, and Prataxis stopped rolling across the hillside. Ragnarson gave up trying to smash heads. Valther stumbled, flung headlong from the impetus of his charge toward his wife. The crowd stopped yelling.

For an instant Mist was enveloped by fire. Then the fire stepped away, leaving behind a feminine silhouette in thick fog. The fire wore Mist's shape.

The assassin screamed and screamed, thrashing like a broken-backed cat. The fire-thing was merciless. It grew brighter and brighter as its victim became a wrinkled, sunburned husk sprinkled with oozing sores.

Finally, it left him.

And turned to the man who had tried for Valther.

The crowd began withdrawing, threatening panic.

"Wait!" Ragnarson bellowed. "It's the enemy of our enemies. It won't harm anybody else."

Nobody believed him. Common folk didn't trust anything about sorcerers and sorcery.

The man who had attacked Haaken ran for it. He and his comrades had been pledged to die, but not like this.

The fire-thing caught him.

"You all right?" Bragi asked Haaken.

"In a minute. He kneed me."

Bragi examined the sword cut. Haaken would need new clothes, and his hauberk the attention of an armorer, but his only injury would be a bruise.

Mist's fire avatar finished the third assassin, floated up thirty feet, hovered. Ragnarson again tried to calm the crowd. A few braver souls listened. The panic began dying.

The fire avatar drifted, hunting enemies.

"Mist," Ragnarson growled, "stop it. You might nail somebody we don't want to lose."

The fire thing seemed interested in the Nordmen knights. With Nordmen, sedition was a way of thought.

It drifted to the shadow-Mist. They coalesced.

Ragnarson ordered the ceremonies resumed, joined Valther.

Mist was badly wounded, but didn't seem concerned. "I'll heal myself," she gasped. "Won't be a scar." She touched Valther's cheek. "Thank you for trying," she told Gjerdrum.

Then Ragnarson noticed Prataxis. He rushed to the man. What would he do without Derel's steady hand directing the everyday work of his offices?

But Prataxis wasn't dead. He had the same problem as Haaken.

Those who spoke after Achmed gave short speeches. Crowd noise settled to a buzz.

Then the Unborn made its public debut.

It followed the road from Vorgreberg, floating twenty feet high. Beneath, three men marched with jerky steps, frequently stumbling.

The people didn't like what they saw.

Neither did Ragnarson.

The thing in the milky globe was a malformed fetus thrice normal birth-size, and it radiated something that drove people from its path. Its captives, strutting like the living dead, wore faces ripped by silent screams.

Straight to Ragnarson they came. Haaken's Guards interposed themselves. They had seen the Gosik of Aubuchon at Baxendala, had seen fell sorceries, but they were frightened. Yet they stood, as they had stood at Baxendala, while facing the terrible might of the Dread Empire.

"Easy," Ragnarson said. "It's on our side."

Unhappy faces turned his way. Men muttered. It wasn't right to form alliances like this.

The automaton-men halted five paces away. Ragnarson saw no life in their eyes.

One's mouth moved. A sepulchral voice said, "These are your enemies. Ask. They will answer."

Ragnarson shuddered. This *thing* of Varthlokkur's.... Powerful. And terrifying.

The crowd began evaporating. Fiana had been popular, especially with the majority Wessons, but folks weren't going to bury her if it meant suffering a constant barrage of unpleasant surprises. All they wanted was to run their homes and shops and pretend, to hide from tomorrow.

"What's your name?" Ragnarson demanded.

"Ain Hamaki."

"Why are you here?"

"To slay our enemies."

"Who sent you?"

No response. Ragnarson glanced at the Unborn.

Another captive replied, "He doesn't know. None do. Their leader brought them from Throyes."

"Find the leader."

"He lies behind you."

Ragnarson glanced at the withered bodies.

One husk twitched. Its limbs moved randomly. Slowly, grotesquely, it rose.

The more bold and curious of the crowd, who had waited to see what would happen also left for town. Even a few soldiers decided they had seen enough.

"Ask," said the dead man.

Ragnarson repeated his questions. He received similar answers. This one had had orders. He had tried to carry them out.

He collapsed into the pile.

Another spoke. He was a leader of Nine. He believed there were eight more Nines preparing Kavelin.

"Preparing Kavelin for what?"

"What is to come."

"Shinsan?"

The Unborn replied, "Perhaps. He didn't know."

"Uhm. Scour the kingdom for the rest of these.... Whatever they are."

The three collapsed.

The Unborn whipped away so rapidly the air shrieked.

"Grab them," Ragnarson ordered. "Throw them in the dungeons."

He worried. Their organization had the earmarks of a cult like the Harish, or Merthrgul, being used politically. He didn't recognize it, though he had traveled the east in his youth.

"Derel. Gjerdrum. You're educated. That tell you anything?"

Both shook their heads.

"We keep getting information, but we're not learning anything. Nothing fits together."

"If that thing really is going to help," Valther said, "I'd say we've taken the initiative. It should free us of assassins."

Ragnarson smiled thinly. "And save you some work, eh?"

"That too. It dredges up all those people, I'll have time to concentrate on my real job. Keeping tabs on home-grown troublemakers."

"How's Mist?"

"Be like new in a week." Softly, "I'd hoped she wouldn't get involved. Guess our enemies don't see it my way."

"O Shing owes her."

"I know. Nobody ever believes a wizard has retired. We'd better be careful," he added. "When they realize they're doomed, they might try to do as much damage as they can."

He was right. Before week's end Ragnarson had lost Thom Altenkirk, who commanded the Royal Damhorsters, the regiment garrisoning Kavelin's six westernmost provinces, plus three of his strongest supporters in the Thing, his Minister of Finance, the Chairman of Council in Sdelmayr, and a dozen lesser officials and officers who would be missed. There were unsuccessful attacks on most of his major followers. His friend Kildragon, who commanded the Midlands Light in the military zone immediately behind Altenkirk's, established a record by surviving four attacks. The bright side was that the enemy wasn't overly selective. They went for Ragnarson's opponents too. For anyone important.

Many of the assassins taken were native Kaveliner hirelings. Terrorism declined as the Unborn marched foreigner after foreigner into imprisonment. He captured sixty-three. A handful escaped to neighboring states. Radeachar followed. When its actions couldn't be traced, it amused itself by tormenting them as a cat might.

Kavelin soon became more peaceful than at any time in living memory. When Radeachar patrolled the nights, even the most blackhearted men behaved. A half dozen swift bringings-to-justice of notorious criminals convinced their lesser brethren that retribution was absolute, inevitable, and final.

It was a peaceful time, a quiet time, but not satisfying. Beneath the surface lay the knowledge that it was just a respite. Ragnarson strove valiantly to order his shaken hierarchy and prepare for the next round. He trained troops relentlessly, ordered the state for war, yet pressed the people to extend themselves in the pursuits of peacetime, trying by sheer will to make Kavelin strong militarily and economically.

Then Michael Trebilcock came home.

TWENTY: The Dragon Emperor

Shinsan had no recognized capital. Hadn't had since the murder of Tuan Hoa. The Princes Thaumaturge had refused to rest their heads on the same pillows twice. Life itself had depended on baffling the brother's assassins and night-sendings.

The mind of Shinsan's empire rested wherever the imperial banner flew.

Venerable Huang Tain constituted its intellectual center. The primary temples and universities clustered there.

Chin favored Huang Tain. "There's plenty of space," he argued. "Half the temples are abandoned."

They had been in the city a month, recuperating from the flight homeward. "I'm not comfortable here," O Shing replied. "I grew up on the border." He couldn't define it precisely. Too refined and domesticated? Close. He was a barbarian prince amongst natty, slick priests and professors. And Huang Tain was much too far west....

Lang, Wu, Tran, Feng, and others shared his discomfort. These westerners weren't their kind of people.

While touring Tuan Hoa's palace and gardens—now a museum and park—O Shing paused near one of the numerous orators orbiting the goldfish ponds.

"Chin, I can't follow the dialect. Did he call the Tervola 'bastard offspring of a mating of the dark side of humanity and Truth perverted'?"

"Yes, Lord."

"But...."

"He's harmless." Chin whispered to a city official accompanying them. "Let him rave, Lord. We control the Power."

"They dare not challenge that," said Feng. A sardonic laugh haunted his mask momentarily.

"They call themselves slaves—and enjoy more freedom than scholars anywhere else," Chin observed. "Even in Hellin Daimiel thinkers are more restrained."

"Complete freedom," said Wu. "Except to change anything."

Both O Shing and Chin wondered at his tone.

The official whispered to Chin, who then announced, "This's Kin Kuo-Lin. A history teacher."

The historian raved on, opposing the wind, drawing on his expertise to abominate the Tervola and prove them fore-doomed. His mad eyes met O Shing's. He found sympathy there.

I'm incomplete, O Shing thought. As lame in soul as in body. And I'll never heal. Like my leg, it's immutable. But none of us are whole, nor ever will be. Chin. Wu. Feng. They've rejected their chance for wholeness to pursue obsessions. Tran, Lang, and I spent too much time staying alive. Our perspectives are inalterably narrowed to the survival-reactive. In this land, in these alum-flavored times, nobody will have the chance to grow, to find completeness.

Some lives have to be lived in small cages. Tam was sure the walls of his weren't all of others' making.

He chose to show the imperial banner at Liaontung. He was comfortable with that old sentinel of the east. And Liaontung was a long, long way from the focus of the Tervola's west-glaring obsession.

"I swear. Wu rubbed his hands in glee when Tran told him." Lang giggled. "Chin like to had a stroke. Feng sided with Wu. Watch Wu, Tam. I don't think he's your friend anymore."

"Never was," Tran growled. He still resented Tam's having trusted Tervola expertise before his own.

"That's not fair, Tran. Wu is a paradox. Several men. One *is* my friend. But he isn't in control. Like me, Wu was cut from the wrong bolt. He's damned by his ancestry too. He has the Power. He yields to it. But he'd rather be Wu the Compassionate."

Tran eyed him uncertainly. The changed, more philosophi-cal, more empathetic Tam, tempered in the crucible of the flight from Baxendala, baffled him. Tran's image of himself as a man of action, immune to serious thought, became a separating gulf in these moments.

To defend his self-image Tran invariably introduced military business.

"The spring classes will graduate twenty thousand," he said, offering a thick report. He still hadn't learned to read well, but had recruited a trustworthy scribe. "Those are Feng's assignment recommendations. Weighted toward the eastern legions, but I can't find real fault. I'd say initial it."

No one could fault O Shing and his Tervola for reinforcing the most reliable legions first.

"Boring," Tam declared five pages in. "These reports can be handled at subordinate levels, Tran. Sometimes I think I'm being swamped just to distract me."

"You want to rule these wolves, you'd better know everything about them," Lang remarked.

"I know. Still, there's got to be a way to get time for things I *want* to do. Tran. Extract me a list of Tervola and Aspirants linked with legions being shorted. And one of Candidates I don't know personally. Lang, arrange for them to visit Liaontung. Maybe I can pick the men who get promoted."

"I like that," said Tran. "We can move the Chins out."

About Chin Tran had developed an obsession. He *knew* their former hunter remained a secret foe. He went to absurd lengths to make his case. Yet he could prove nothing.

O Shing already pursued a policy of favoritism in promotions. He was popular with the Aspirants. He became more so when he pushed the policy harder. The machinery of army and empire drifted to his control. His hidden enemies recognized the shift, could do little to halt it.

One thing Tam couldn't accomplish. He couldn't convince one Tervola to repudiate the need to avenge Baxendala.

It was a matter of the honor and reputation of an army unaccustomed to defeat.

Feng, in a rare, expansive mood, explained, "The legions had never been defeated. Invincibility was their most potent weapon. It won a hundred bloodless victories.

"They weren't defeated at Baxendala, either. We were. Their commanders. To our everlasting shame. Your Tran understood better than we did, not having had the shock of losing the Power to impair his reason. Our confusion, our panic, our irrational response—hell, our cowardice—killed thousands and stigmatized the survivors."

A moment of raw emotion burned through when Feng declared, "We sacrificed the Imperial Standard, Lord!"

"While Baxendala remains unredeemed, while this Ragnarson creature constitutes living proof that the tide of destiny can be stemmed, our enemies will resist when, otherwise, they'd yield. We're paying in blood.

"Lord, the legions are the bones of Shinsan. If we allow even one to be broken, we subject the remainder, and the flesh itself, to a magnified hazard. In the long run, we risk less by pursuing revenge."

"I follow you," O Shing replied. Feng spoke for Feng, privately, but his was the opinion of his class. "In fact, I can't refute you."

Tran, who disagreed with the Tervola by reflex, supported them in this. Every Tervola who managed an audience had a scheme for requiting Baxendala. Stemming the tide devoured Tam's time, making his days processions of boring sameness only infrequently relieved by change or intrigue.

Yet he built.

Five years and six days after the ignominy of Baxendala, Select Fu Piao-Chuong knelt and swore fealty to O Shing. Not to Shinsan, the Throne, or Council, but to an individual. His emperor assigned him an obscure post with a western legion. He bore, under seal, orders to other Aspirants in posts equally obscure.

The night-terrorist *Hounds of Shadow* struck within the week.

After a second week, Lord Wu, maskless, agitated, appealed, "Lord, what's happening?" He seemed baffled and hurt. "Great men are dying. Commanders of legions have been murdered. Manors and properties have been destroyed. Priests and civil servants have been beaten or killed. Our old followers from the days of hiding are inciting rebellion around the Mienming and Mahai. When we question a captured terrorist he invariably names an Aspirant as his commander. The Aspirant cites you as his authority."

"I'm not surprised."

"Lord! Why have you done this? It's suicide."

"I doubt it."

"Lord! You've truly attacked your Tervola?"

Lang and Tran were surprised too. They weren't privy to all of O Shing's secrets either. He was developing the byzantine thought-set an emperor of Shinsan needed to survive.

"I deny attacking *my* Tervola, Lord Wu. You'll find no loyal names among those of the dead. The evidence against each was overwhelming. It's been accumulating for years. Years, Lord Wu. And I reserved judgment on a lot of names. I indicted no one because he had been an enemy in the past. Lord Chin lives. His sins are forgiven. The Hounds will pull down only those who stand against me now."

"Yes, Lord." Wu had grown pale.

"It'll continue, Lord Wu. Until it's finished. Those who remain faithful have nothing to fear.

"My days of patience, of gentleness, of caution, have ended. I *will* be emperor. Unquestioned, unchallenged, unbeholden, the way my grandfather was. If the Council objects, let it prove one dead man wasn't my enemy. Till then the baying of the Hounds of Shadow will keep winding on the back trails of treachery. Let those with cause fear the sound of swift hooves."

Wu carefully bowed himself out.

"There goes a frightened man," Tran remarked. His smile was malicious.

"He has cause," Lang observed. "He's afraid his name will come up."

"It won't," said Tam. "If he's dirty, he's hidden it perfectly."

"Chin's your ringleader," Tran declared.

"Prove it."

"He's right," Lang agreed.

"Is he? Can I face the Council with that? Bring me evidence, Tran. Prove it's not just bitterness talking. Wait! Hear me out. I agree with you. I'm not asleep. But he *looks* as clean as Wu. He doesn't leave tracks. Intuition isn't proof."

Tran bowed slightly, angrily. "Then I'll get proof." He stalked out.

Tam *did* agree. Chin was a viper. But he was the second most powerful man in Shinsan, and logical successor to the empire. His purge would have to be sustained by iron-bound evidence presented at a perfectly timed moment.

Chin would resist. Potential allies had to be politically disarmed beforehand.

The Council, increasingly impatient with O Shing's delay in moving west, were growing cool. Some members would support any move to topple him.

It was a changed Shinsan. A polarized, politicized Shinsan. Even Wu admitted his suspicion that the empire had been better off under the Dual Principate. It had, at least, been stable, if static.

While Tran obsessively rooted for evidence damning Chin, Tam healed old wounds and opened new ones. He studied, and quietly aimed his Hounds at their midnight targets. And futilely persisted in trying to draw the venom of the Tervola's western obsession.

Then, without Tran there to advise them otherwise, he and

Lang began riding with the Hounds.

Select Hsien Luen-Chuoung was a Wu favorite, a Commander-of-a-Thousand in the Seventeenth. Such a post usually rated a full Tervola. The evidence was irrefutable. O Shing had, for the sake of peace with Wu, avoided acting earlier.

The unsigned, intercepted note sealed Chuoung's doom.

"Go ahead. Deliver it," Tam told a post rider who was one of his agents. "We'll see who his accomplices are. Lang, start tracing it back." The note had come to his man from another post rider, who in turn had received it at a way station in the west.

The message? "Prepare Nine for Dragon Kill."

O Shing was The Dragon. It was his symbol, inherited from his father. The sign in the message was his, not the common glyph for dragon, nor even the thaumaturgic symbol.

So, Tam thought. Tran was right, after all, in mistrusting learning. His advice about suborning the post riders had paid off.

"Lang, I want to go on this one myself. Let me know when the wolves are in the trap."

Chuoung, unsuspicious, gathered his co-conspirators immediately.

"It looks bad for Lord Wu," Lang averred as he helped Tam with his armor. The conspirators were all officers of the Seventeenth or important civilians from Wu's staff.

"Maybe. But nobody contacted him. He hasn't shown a sign of moving. And the message came from the west. I think somebody subverted his legion."

"Chin somebody?"

"Maybe. Remembering their confrontations back when, he might want Wu more vulnerable if there were a next time. Come. They'll be waiting."

Twelve Hounds loafed in the forest near the postern. Tam examined them unhappily. These scruffy ruffians were the near-Tervola he had recruited? He had insisted on having the best for this mission. These looked like they were the bandits the Council accused them of being.

Chuoung occupied a manor house a few miles southwest of Liaontung. As Commander-of-a-Thousand he rated a body-guard of ten. And there would be sorcery. Most of Chuoung's traitor-coven were trained in the Power.

O Shing sent a black sleeping-fog to those guards in barracks.

Thus, six would never know what had happened. To distract the conspirators themselves he raised a foul-tempered arch-salamander....

They were guilty. He listened at a window long enough to be sure before he attacked.

Pure, raging hatred hit him then. Nine men squawked in surprise and fear when he lunged into the room, his bad foot nearly betraying him.

Their wardspells had been neutralized unnoticed by a greater Power.

The salamander blasted through the door.

They weren't prepared. The thing raged, fired the very stone in its fury. Screams ripped through melting Tervola-imitative masks. Scorched flesh odors conquered the night. O Shing retched.

Chuoung tried to strike back.

Lang, from over Tam's shoulder, drove a javelin through a jeweled eye-slit.

"Keep some alive," O Shing gulped as the Hounds swept in.

Too late. The surprise had been too complete, the attack too efficient. In seconds all nine were beyond answering any questions ever. The salamander didn't even leave shades which could be recalled.

O Shing banished the monster before it could completely destroy the room, then searched Chuoung's effects.

He found nothing.

He interrupted his digging an hour later, suddenly realizing that the screaming hadn't stopped. Why not? The conspirators were dead.

He went looking for his Hounds.

They were behaving like western barbarians, murdering, raping, plundering. And Lang was in the thick of it.

Tam spat, disgusted, and limped back to Liaontung alone.

Lang became addicted. He was a born vandal. He began riding every raid, ranging ever farther from Liaontung, using his fraternal ties to acquire ever greater command of the Hounds.

O Shing didn't pay any heed. He was happy to have Lang out of his way.

Lang did love it, making the Hounds his career....

The men attacked didn't accept their fates passively. O Shing lost followers. Yet every raid encouraged recruiting.

A plague swept Shinsan. Rejection of the established order

became endemic. And O Shing didn't see the peril, that rebels are always against, never for, and rebellion becomes an end in itself, a serpent devouring its own tail.

It got out of hand. His tool, his weapon, began cutting at its own discretion.

Lords Chin and Wu came to O Shing. Backing them were Ko Feng, Teng, Ho Lin and several other high lords of the Council of Tervola. They were angry, and didn't bother hiding it.

Their appearance was message enough, though Wu insisted on articulating their grievance.

"Last night men wearing the Hound Badge invaded Lord Chin's domains. You challenged the Council to prove you in error. Today the Council insists that you produce proof of Lord Chin's perfidy."

O Shing didn't respond till he had obtained absolute control of his emotions. He had authorized no action against Chin.

He didn't dare be intimidated. "Those were no men of mine. Were they once, I repudiate them now. I said before, I bear Lord Chin no malice. Till he gives me cause otherwise, his enemies will be mine. I'll find these bandits and punish them." He doubted that that would mollify the Council, though.

"They have been punished, Lord," Chin replied. "They're dead. All but one." He gestured.

Soldiers dragged a chained Lang into the presence. The bravado of the night rider had fled him. He was scared sick, and more terrified of Tam than of his captors.

O Shing stared, tormented. "I'll issue orders. Henceforth any who raid, anywhere, any time, will be outlawed. They'll be my enemies as well as the enemies of my enemies." Tran misbehaving he would have believed more readily than Lang. "The Terror ends. Henceforth, the Hounds will course outlaws only. Lord Chin, restitution will be made."

"And this one?"

"His actions convict him. I gave my word. The Hounds would strike only where the proof was *absolute*." He didn't flinch from the Tervola's gaze. He wanted Chin to *know* he dared make no mistake.

Lang, Chin, and Wu all seemed astonished because he didn't ask for the gift of a life.

It hurt, but he meant it. To bend these people to his will he was going to have to stop being indecisive and vacillatory. The future demanded a demonstration. Lang had convicted himself.

Tam could ache with temptation, but O Shing dared reveal no weakness. The vulture wings of chaos shadowed his empire. He had to take control.

"Lang. Do you have something to say?"

His brother shook his head.

Tam was glad Tran was absent. The hunter's accusatory stare might have withered his resolve. He needed time to develop the habits of autocracy. "Your judgment, Lord Chin. You're the injured party."

Ruby eye-crystals tracked brother and brother. Then one gloved hand removed the cat-gargoyle mask. "It ends here, my Lord. I yield him to you. There's been enough unhappiness between us."

"A good thought, Lord Chin." You guileful snake. "Thank you. Is there anything else?"

"When do we avenge the Imperial Standard?" Feng snarled.

Wu took Feng's elbow. Chin said, "Nothing, Lord. Good day."

The door closed behind Chin. Lang whined, "Were you really going to . . .?"

"Yes." Tam limped to his communications devices. "I won't tolerate disobedience from anyone. Not even you. I didn't ask to be emperor. I didn't want to be. But here I am. And emperor I'll be. Despite all of you. Understand?"

The following week he ordered the deaths of seventy Hounds. His revolution had to end.

This was the inevitable blood purge of the professional rebels, men for whom the raiding, the fighting, was cause enough. Now the insurrectionists had to give way to the administrators. All Shinsan, he vowed, would become as steady and responsive as it had been during Tuan Hoa's reign. If he could just remain decisive. . . .

Lang's indiscretion precipitated the Change, the Day, the Final, Absolute Decision.

Henceforth Tam would *be* O Shing. Completely, in the manner pioneered by Shinsan's founding tyrant. He would yield, minimally, only to absolute political necessity.

Shinsan's First Nine met in extraordinary session. Every member made sure he could attend. The Nines themselves were imperiled.

The last was still in the doorway when the cat-gargoyle said,

"O Shing suspects. His Hounds weren't indulging in random violence. There was a pattern. He was trying to get a fix on who we are and what we're doing. He's suddenly a liability instead of an asset. Tally against him, too, his unremitting resistance to western operations. And his popular support. Question: Has he outlived his usefulness?"

The man in a fanged turtle mask (Lord Wu's current Nine disguise) countered, "I disagree. He's young. Still malleable. He's been subjected to too much pressure in too little time. Remember, he's risen to emperor from slavery in a few short years, without benefit of Tervola time-perspective. We're being too hasty. Ease the pressure. He'll mellow. Don't discard this tool before it's finish-forged. We're close to him. Eliminate his companions so he becomes dependent on our guidance."

Wu argued from the heart, from the identical weak streak that had earned him the sobriquet "The Compassionate." He felt more for O Shing than the youth had ever suspected.

Wu had no sons of his own.

He also argued from ignorance. He didn't know that Lord Chin had to conform to the timetable of a higher Nine.

Chin knew Wu's blind spots.

"I shouldn't have to admonish our brother about security discipline. Yet what he says deserves consideration. I propose a week's recess for reflection before we redefine our policies and goals. Remain available. In the name of the Nine."

One by one they departed, till only Chin and a companion remained. "Do we need another promotion?" the companion asked.

"Not this time, Feng. He spoke from his heart, but he won't desert the Nine. I know him that well."

Chin couldn't say that Wu, probably, couldn't be killed anyway. Mist had failed. And Chin himself, fearing future confrontations, had made several more serious attempts, in Mist's behalf, than his Ehelebe role had demanded. Wu could be slippery, and a terrible, determined enemy.

"As you will."

The bent man appeared after Feng left. "Delay action," he ordered. "But lay the groundwork. O Shing will have to go sometime. He'll resist when the Pracchia's hour arises."

Chin nodded. He needed no orders to do what he planned anyway. Hadn't he sniffed the breeze with Select Chuoung already? The cretin had muffed everything.... "And his replacement? He has no heir, and the Pracchia dares not operate openly."

"Shall we say someone with direct responsibility to the Pracchia? Someone seated with the High Nine?"

Chin bowed. He hoped he put enough subservience into what, really, was a restrained gesture of victory. Soon, Shinsan. Later, perhaps, Ehelebe.

"Step up your western operations. The hour of Ehelebe approaches."

This time Chin bowed with more feeling. He enjoyed the intrigues he was running out there. They presented real challenges, and provided genuine results. "I'm handling it personally. It proceeds with absolute precision."

The bent man smiled thinly. "Take care, Lord Chin. You're the Pracchia's most valuable member."

The man in the cat-gargoyle didn't respond. But his mind darted, examining possibilities, rolling the old man's words around to see how much meaning dared be attached. They were playing a subtle, perilous game.

The armies had begun gathering. The storm was about to break upon an unsuspecting west. O Shing had exhausted the tactics of delay. His excuses had perished like roses in the implacable advance of a tornado. The legions had healed. Shinsan was at peace with itself. The Tervola were strong and numerous.

Liaontung bulged with Tervola and their staffs. O Shing had chosen Lord Wu to command the expedition. Wu was putting it together quickly and skillfully, abetted by hungry, eager, cooperative Tervola. Their obsession was about to be fulfilled.

O Shing could no longer back down.

Sometimes he wondered about the consequences of another Baxendala. More often, he worried about those of victory. For a decade, anticipation of this war had colored the Tervolas' every action and thought. It had become part of them. After the west collapsed, what? Would Shinsan turn upon itself, east against west, in a grander, more terrible version of the drama briefly envisioned in the struggle with Mist?

And sometimes he wondered about that eldritch lady. She had given up too easily. For the well-being of Shinsan? Or because she wanted him to play out some brief, violent destiny of his own before renewing her claims?

Neither Tran nor Lang had unearthed any nostalgic sentiment surrounding Mist, but in this land, with its secrecies, sorceries, and conspiracies, anything was possible.

She would have to be eliminated. Merely by living she posed a threat.

Tran returned from the Roë basin, where he had been watching the progress of a curious war. He brought some unusual news.

"It's taken me years," he enthused, bursting into Tam's apartment still filthy from the road. "But I've got Chin. Not enough to prove him your enemy, but enough to nail him for insubordination. Acting without orders. Making policy without consulting the Throne."

Lang arrived. "Calm down. Start from the top. I want to hear this." He gave Tam a wicked look.

O Shing nodded.

"The war in the Roë basin. Chin is orchestrating it. He's been busy the past couple years. Look. Here. He's been skipping all over the west. Chaos followed him like a loyal old hound dog." He offered several pages of hastily scribbled report.

"Lang? Read it. Tran, watch the door. Chin's out of town, but he and Wu are getting like that." He crossed his fingers.

Lang droned through Tran's outline of an odd itinerary. There were numerous gaps, when Chin's whereabouts simply hadn't been determinable, but, equally, enough non-gaps to damn the Tervola for violating his emperor's explicit orders.

They fell to arguing whether action should wait till after the western campaign. O Shing felt Chin would be valuable in that.

Tam dogged the relationship between Wu and Chin, wondering if, for so slight a cause, Lord Wu ought to be put to the question. . . .

They forgot the door.

Lang's eyes suddenly bulged.

O Shing looked up. The moment at the Hag's hut flashed through his mind.

"Wu!" they gasped.

TWENTY-ONE: The King Is Dead.

Long Live the King

The lean, dark man came like a whirlwind from the north. Horses died beneath him. Men died if they tried to slow him. He was more merciless with himself than with anyone else. He was half dead when he reached his headquarters in the Kapenrungs.

Beloul let him sleep twelve hours before telling him about his wife.

He hardly seemed to think before replying, "Bring Megelin."

The boy was his father reflected in a mirror that took away decades. At nineteen he already had a reputation as a hard and brilliant warrior.

"Leave us, Beloul," Haroun said.

Father and son faced one another, the son waiting for the father to speak.

"I have made a long journey," Haroun said. His voice was surprisingly soft. "I couldn't find him."

"Balfour?"

"Him I found. He told me what he knew."

Which wasn't strictly true. Balfour had answered only the questions asked, and even in his agony had shaded his answers. The Colonel had been a strong man.

All during his ride Haroun had pondered what he had learned. And he had planned.

"I didn't find my friend."

"There is this that I cannot understand about you, my father. These two men. Mocker and Ragnarson. You let them shape your life. With victory at your fingertips you abandoned everything to aid Ragnarson in his war with Shinsan."

"There is this that you have to learn, my son. Into each life come people who become more important than any crown. Believe it. Look for it. And accept it. It cannot be explained."

They stared at one another till Haroun continued, "More-over, they have aided me more than I them, often when it flew in the face of their own interest. For this I owe them. Question. Have you ever heard Beloul—or any of my captains— complain?"

"No."

"Why? I'll tell you why. Because there would be no Peacock Throne for anyone, even El Murid—may the jackals gnaw his bones—if Shinsan occupied the west."

"This I understand. But I also understand that that was not your motive for turning north when you were upon the dogs at Al Rhemish."

"One day you will understand. I hope. Tell me about your mother." Pain marred his words. His long love with the daughter of his enemy made a tempestuous epic. Her defection seemed anticlimactic.

"That, too, I try to understand. It is difficult, my father. But I begin to see. Our people bring scraps of news. They draw outlines for a portrait."

Eyes downcast, Megelin continued, "Were she not my mother, I would not have had the patience to await the information."

"Tell me."

"She means to forge an armistice with the Beast. She went to your friend, Ragnarson. He sent her."

"Ah. She knows my anger. My other friend vanished. She knew I would swoop on the carrion at Al Rhemish. She knew I would destroy them. They have no strength now. They are old men with water for bones. I can sweep them away like the wind sweeps the dust from the Sahel."

"That too."

"She is his daughter."

"The head understands, my father. The heart protests."

"Listen to your head, then, and do not hate her. I say again, she is his daughter. Think of your father when you think to judge her."

"So my head tells me."

Haroun nodded. "You are wise for your years. It is good. Summon Beloul."

When the general returned, Haroun announced, "I am leaving my work to my son. Two duties war for me. I pass to him the one that may be passed. The one that came upon me in Al

Rhemish, so long ago, when Nassef and the Invincibles slew all others who had claim to the Peacock Throne."

"Lord!" Beloul cried. "Do I hear you right? Are you saying you abdicate?"

"You hear me, Beloul."

"But why, Lord? A generation, more, have we fought.... We have it in our grasp at last. They are waiting for us, shaking in their boots. They weep in the arms of their women, wondering when we will come. Ten thousand tribesmen have buried swords beneath their tents. They await our coming to dig them up and strike. Ten thousand wait in the camps, eager, knowing the tree of years is to bear fruit at last. Twenty thousand more stir restlessly in the heathen cities, awaiting your summons. Home! A home many have never seen, Lord!"

"Beseech me not, Beloul. Speak to your King. It is in his hands. I have chosen another destiny."

"Should you not consult with the others? Rahman? El Senoussi? Hanasi?..."

"Will they oppose me? Will they stop me?"

"Not if it is your will."

"Have I not said so? I am compelled in another direction. I must discharge old debts."

"Whither, my father? Why?"

"The Dread Empire. O Shing has my friend."

"Lord!" Beloul protested. "Sheer suicide."

"Perhaps. That is why I pass my crown before I go." He knelt before a low table. His hands went to his temples. Immense strain clouded his face. His neck bulged.

Beloul and Megelin thought it a stroke.

Haroun's hands rose suddenly. Something hit the table with a thud.

Lo! A crown materialized.

"The crown of the Golmune Emperors of Ilkazar," Haroun said. "The Crown of Empire. And of what survives. Our Desert of Death. It is incalculably heavy, my son. It possesses you. It drives you. You do things you would loath in any other man. It's the bloodiest crown ever wrought. It's a greater burden than prize. If you take it up your life will never be your own—till you find the strength to renounce it."

Megelin and Beloul stared. The crown seemed simple, almost fragile, yet it had scored the table.

"Take it up, my son. Become King."

Slowly, Megelin knelt.

"This is best for Hammad al Nakir," Haroun told Beloul. "It will ease the consciences of men of principle. He is not just my son, he is the grandson of the Disciple. Yasmid's story should be well-known by now."

"It is," Beloul admitted. The return of El Murid's daughter was the wonder of the desert.

Megelin strained harder than had Haroun. "My father, I cannot lift it."

"You can, have you but the will. I couldn't lift it my first try either."

His thoughts drifted to that faraway morning when he had crowned himself King Without a Throne.

He, at fifteen, with the man for whom Megelin had been named, and a handful of survivors, had been fleeing El Murid's attack on Al Rhemish.

His father and brothers were dead. Nassef, El Murid's diabolical general, called Scourge of God so terrible was he, was close behind. Haroun was the last pretender to the Peacock Throne.

Ahead, in the desert, the ruin of an Imperial watchtower appeared. Something drew him. Within he found a small, bent old man who claimed to be a survivor of the destruction of Ilkazar, who claimed to have been charged with protecting the symbols of Imperial power till a proper candidate arose among the descendants of the Emperors. He begged Haroun to free him from his centuries-long charge.

Haroun finally took the crown—after having as much difficulty as would Megelin later.

Though he was to encroach upon Haroun's life many times, bin Yousif never again encountered that old man. Even now he had no idea whom he had met then, and who had defined his destiny.

Nor did he suspect that the tamperer was the same "angel" who had found a twelve-year-old desert wanderer, sole survivor of a bandit raid on a caravan, had named him El Murid and had given him his mission.

That old man meddled everywhere, more often than anyone suspected. He often added a twist on the spur of the moment. He remembered, kept his plot-lines straight, and got found out only in retrospects of a century or more.

Things didn't always go his way, though, because he worked with a cast of millions. The imponderables and unpredictables were always at work.

Haroun wouldn't give up his crown just to rescue a friend. Would he?

Beloul's feeling exactly. He became quite difficult while Megelin wrestled the crown.

"Enough!" Haroun declared. "If you won't accept it, and follow Megelin with the faith you've shown me, I'll find an officer who will." Haroun wasn't accustomed to having a decision debated.

"I'm just concerned for the movement...."

"Megelin will lead. He is my son. Megelin. If you feel the need, go to my friend in Vorgreberg. Explain. But tell no one else. Westerners have tongues like the tails of whipped dogs. They wag all the time, whether there is need or not."

With that a barrier broke. Though Megelin's strain remained herculean, he raised the crown, stood, hoisted it overhead, crowned himself.

He staggered, recovered. In a minute he seemed the Megelin of old. The Crown was no longer visible.

"The weight vanishes, my father."

"It's only a seeming, my son. You will feel it again when the crown demands some action the man loathes. Enough now. This is no longer my tent. I must rest. Tomorrow I travel."

"You cannot penetrate Shinsan," Beloul protested. "They will destroy you ere you depart the Pillars of Ivory."

"I will pass the mountains." When Haroun said it it sounded like accomplished fact. "I will find the man. I have mastered the Power."

He had indeed. He was the strongest adept his people had produced in generations. Yet that had little real meaning. The practice of magic, except in the wastes of Jebal al Alf Dhulquarneni, had been abandoned by the children of Hammad al Nakir. He had become the best for lack of competition.

Varthlokkur, O Shing, Chin, Visigodred, Zindahjira, Mist—they could have withered him at a glance. Excepting O Shing, they were ancient in their witchcraft. He would need a century to overtake the least and laziest.

Haroun still suffered from his ride, yet when he chose a place to rest, he sat and sharpened his sword instead of sleeping again.

Sometimes he considered Mocker, and sometimes wandered among his memories. Mostly, he longed for his wife. The peaceful years hadn't been bad.

He hadn't been much of a husband. If he came through this maybe he could make it up to her.

He left before next dawn, slipping away so quietly that only one sentry noticed. The man bid him a quiet farewell. There were tears in both their eyes.

That was why he had chosen to depart stealthily. Some of his men had been fighting for twenty years. He didn't want to feel their grief, to see the accusation in their eyes.

He knew he was betraying them. Most were here for him. They were his weapons. And he was yielding them to an unfamiliar hand....

He wept, this dark, grim man. The years had not dessicated that faculty.

He rode toward the rising sun, and, he believed, out of the pages of history, a free man at last, and less happy than ever.

There were times, too, when he would visit Turran's grave. his face clouded. Once they had been enemies, and had become allies. He had considered the man almost a brother.

Yet strange things happen.

He felt no resentment, except against himself.

The days passed into we...

time on his...

Protect...
common folk a...

At the Palace they s...
the tempest, yet couldn't keep ...
possessive.

Even problems like Altea's refusal to permit ...
didn't alter the atmosphere of well-being. Ragnarson q... y
arranged transit through Anstokin and Ruderin, and asked
caravaneers headed west to follow Oryon. Altea's mercantile
houses depended on the eastern trade as much as Kavelin's. The
new Altean leadership quickly became less obdurate.

The swift-flying rumor that Haroun had abandoned his
armies to his son disturbed no one either. Ragnarson didn't
believe it. He felt it a ploy to lull Al Rhemish.

The Thing did little to find a new King. Their one candidate,
Fiana's baby brother, fourteen-year-old Lian Melicar Sardygo,
didn't want the job. He and his father were downright rude in
their refusal of the committee's invitation to visit Kavelin. They
said they would come only to visit Fiana's tomb.

Ragnarson, often with Ragnar and Gundar, made a daily
pilgrimage to the cemetery. He had the boys pick wild flowers
along the lane. Then, till after dark, he would sit by Elana's
grave. Too often, he counted headstones. Elana. Inger. Soren.
Rolf. And two earlier children who had died soon after birth,
before they could be named. He had had them moved here.

Sometimes he took a few flowers to the Royal Mausoleum,
to Fiana's plain, glass-topped casket. Varthlokkur's artifices
had restored her beauty. She looked as though she might
waken.... The old, secret smile lay on her lips. She looked
peaceful and happy.

...himself.

...ks and months. He spent ever more ...morbid jaunts. Prataxis, Gjerdrum, Haaken, Ahring assumed more of his duties. Ragnar began to worry. He had idolized his mother, and, though a little frightened by him, loved his father. He knew it was unhealthy to spend so much time mourning.

He went to Haaken. But Haaken had no suggestions. Blackfang remained steadfast in his belief that the family should return to Trolledyngja. The political compulsion for exile no longer obtained. The Pretender had abdicated—by virtue of a dagger between his ribs. The Old House had been restored. Heroes of the resistance were collecting rewards. Lands were being returned.

Bragi never considered returning, neither when the news first came down, nor now.

Someday he would go. He had family obligations there. But not now. There were greater obligations here.

Except that he was getting nothing accomplished.

Then Michael Trebilcock returned.

Trebilcock finally sought Haaken at the War Office. He had waited hours with Prataxis, and Ragnarson hadn't shown.

Haaken listened. An evil, angry smile invaded his face. It exposed the discolored teeth that had given him his name.

"Boy, this's what we've been waiting for." He strapped on his sword. "Dahl!" he called to his adjutant.

"Sir?"

"It's war. Spread the word. But quietly. You understand? It'll be a call-up."

"Sir? Who?"

"You wouldn't believe me if I told you. Get on it. Come on, man," he told Trebilcock. "We'll find him."

Dantice had remained to one side all afternoon. Now he said, "Mike, I'd better see my father."

"Suit yourself. He could wait another day, couldn't he? If you want to see the Marshall...."

"Marshall, smarshall. What's he to me? My Dad's probably half-crazy worrying."

"Okay."

After they parted with Aral, Haaken observed, "I like that boy. He's got perspective." He didn't elaborate, nor did he speak again till they reached the cemetery. Blackfang was no conversationalist.

Trebilcock replied, "The trip changed him."

They found Bragi, Ragnar, and Gundar at Elana's grave, with the usual flowers and tears. Haaken approached quietly, but the boys heard him. Ragnar met his gaze and shrugged.

Haaken sat beside his foster brother. He said nothing till Bragi noticed him.

"What's up, Haaken?" Ragnarson tossed a pebble at an old Obelisk. "More bureaucratic pettifoggery?"

"No. It's important this time."

"They've got it made, you know."

"Huh? Who?"

"These people. Nothing but peace under the ground."

"I wonder."

"Do you? Damnit, when I say. . . ."

"Father!"

"What's your problem, boy?"

"You're acting like an ass." He wouldn't have dared had Haaken not been there. Haaken always took his part. He thought.

Ragnarson started to rise. Haaken seized his arm, pulled him back.

Bragi was big. Six-five, and two hundred twenty-five pounds of muscle. His years at the Palace hadn't devoured his vitality.

Haaken was bigger. And stronger. And more stubborn. "The boy's right. Sit down and listen."

Trebilcock seated himself facing them. He wrinkled his nose. He was fastidious. He picked dirt and grass, real and imagined, off his breeches the whole time he told his tale.

Ragnarson wasn't interested, despite Michael's rending the veils of mysteries that had plagued him for months.

"Why didn't you bring them out?" Haaken asked. Michael hadn't told it all earlier.

"They separated her from Ethrian. She wanted to stay. And they had a man there, who wore black, and a golden mask. . . . He would've found us in minutes if he'd known we were there. Probably before we could get out of town."

Ragnarson looked thoughtful when Michael mentioned the

man in the mask, then lapsed into indifference again.

"I never saw a city that big. . . . It made Hellin Daimiel look like a farm town. Oh. I almost forgot. She said to bring you this. Well, Varthlokkur, but he isn't around. It might not wait till he finds me." He handed Ragnarson an ebony casket.

Bragi accepted with a slight frown. "Elana's thing." He turned it over and over before trying to open it.

The lid popped up. . . .

The ruby within was alive, was afire. It painted their faces in devil shades.

"Please close it."

They jumped. Swords whined out. They looked upward.

"Close it!"

Ragnarson kicked the lid shut.

Varthlokkur descended from the sky, his vast cloak flapping about him. Above him floated the Unborn.

Trebilcock, Ragnarson thought, at least had the decency to be surprised. Hopefully, someday, he would be afraid too.

"Where the hell did you come from?" Haaken demanded.

"Afar. Radeachar came for me when he saw the pale man and his companion coming through the Gap. You were hard to locate. What're you doing here?"

Haaken made a gesture which included Ragnarson, Elana's grave, and the Royal Mausoleum.

Meantime, Bragi lost interest again. He sat down, reopened the casket.

"Damnit, I said close it!" Varthlokkur growled.

Ragnarson quietly drew his sword.

High, high above, a tiny rider on a winged steed spied another red flash. He circled lower, passing over unseen because he was invisible from below. He recognized three of the men. "Damn!" he spat. He soared, and raced northward. He didn't notice the great bird which circled higher still.

Varthlokkur shuddered and glanced around, feeling something. But there was nothing to see.

The Unborn darted this way and that. It had felt the presence too. After a moment it settled into position above Varthlokkur's head.

The others felt it too. Bragi lowered his blade, looked around, realized what he was doing. Attacking Varthlokkur? With simple steel?

It was getting dark. Ragnar lighted the torches he always

brought because his father so often dallied till after nightfall.

The flames repulsed the encroachment of night....

Something shifted, made a small mewling sound beyond the light.

Weapons appeared again. A soft, hissing voice said, "Enough. I come in friendship."

Ragnarson shuddered. He knew that voice. "Zindahjira."

That sorcerer's life-path had crossed his before. The first time had been once too often. Zindahjira wasn't even human—or so Bragi suspected. When this wizard went abroad by daylight, he wrapped himself in a blackness which reversed the function of a torch.

Varthlokkur was the more powerful, the more dread magician, but, at least, came in human form.

Must be what we sensed, Ragnarson thought.

Something else moved at the edge of the firelight. Bragi had the satisfaction of seeing Michael Trebilcock startled.

Two more *things* appeared. One went by the name The Thing With Many Eyes, the other, Gromacki, The Egg Of God. Each was as inhuman as Zindahjira, though not of his species.

They were sorcerers of renown and had gathered from the far reaches of the west. With them were a half-dozen men in varied costume. Not a one spoke. Each seated himself on the graveyard grass.

"This's the right place," Haaken muttered.

"Who are they?" Ragnar asked, terrified. Gundar, luckily, had fallen asleep during Michael's story.

Trebilcock kept his sword ready. He was wondering too.

"The Prime Circle. The chief sorcerers of the west," Haaken whispered.

Cold steel fingers stroked Ragnarson's spine. Fear stalked his nerves. It was a dark day when this group covened, putting their vicious grievances in abeyance. "One's missing," he observed.

When last they had gathered it had been for Baxendala, to greet the eastern sorcery with their own.

An implacable enmity for the Tervola was the one thing they had in common.

"He comes," said the mummylike being called Kierle the Ancient. His words hung on the air like smoke on a still, muggy morning.

An inhuman scream clawed the underbelly of the night. Torchlight momentarily illuminated the undersides of vast wings. A rush of air almost extinguished Ragnar's brands. Anxiously, he lighted more.

The flying colossus hit ground thunderously. "Goddamned clumsy, worthless, boneheaded.... Sorry, boss."

A middle-aged dwarf soon strutted into the light. "What the hell is this? Some kind of wake? Any of you bozos got something to drink?"

"Marco," said a gentle voice.

The dwarf shut up and sat. Ragnarson rose, extended a hand. The newcomer was an old friend, Visigodred, Count Mendalayas, from northern Itaskia. Their lives had crossed frequently, and they almost trusted one another.

"We're all here," Varthlokkur observed. "Marshall...."

"Who was that on the winged horse?" Visigodred asked.

Everyone looked puzzled. Including Varthlokkur, who should have understood.

Ragnarson caught it, though. He remembered seeing a winged horse over Baxendala missed by everyone but himself. He remembered thinking the rider was a mystery which needed solving.... But by someone else. Even this convocation couldn't excite him for long.

Varthlokkur went on. "Marshall, I tracked bin Yousif into Trolledyngja, where he had overtaken Colonel Balfour. He's back in the south somewhere now."

Since Bragi didn't ask, Haaken did. "What happened?"

"I don't know. Bin Yousif was thorough. He didn't even leave a shade I could call up. But he got something, fast as he rode south."

"Michael," said Haaken, "tell the wizards your story."

Varthlokkur was in a state before Trebilcock finished. "Shinsan, Shinsan," he muttered. "Always Shinsan. They've done this to force me to obey. How is it that they always cloud my mind? Must be something they did while I studied there.... Was she well? Was she safe? Why Argon? Why not Shinsan? Marshall, what'd you do with the jewel? That we must unravel if we're to repulse O Shing again. It won't be just four legions this time."

His words gushed. The man in the golden mask—he must be one of O Shing's craftiest Tervola—had conjured one hell of a dilemna for Varthlokkur.

Dull-eyed, staring at Elana's grave, Ragnarson handed him

the casket. Varthlokkur frowned, not understanding Bragi's lassitude.

Haaken touched his cloak diffidently. He beckoned Visigodred, led both a short distance away, explained Bragi's problem.

Behind them, having grown bored, Zindahjira created balls of blue fire, juggled them amongst his several hands. He threw them into the air. They coalesced into a whirling sphere which threw off visible words like sparks flying from a grindstone.

He was a show-off. A loudmouth and a braggart. For some quirky reason, he liked being called Zindahjira the Silent.

The blue words were in many languages, but when they queued up in sentences they invariably proclaimed some libel on Visigodred's character.

Their feud was so old it was antique. What irritated Zindahjira most was that Visigodred wouldn't fight back. He simply neutralized every attack and otherwise ignored the troglodytic wizard.

Visigodred ignored him now, though his assistant, the dwarf, made a few remarks too softly to reach his master's ears. Zindahjira became furious. . . .

This sort of thing had driven Ragnarson to distraction in the past. It symbolized the weakness of the west. The wolves of doom could be snuffling at the windows and doors and everyone would remain immersed in their own petty bickerings. Right now Kiste and Vorhangs were threatening war. The northern provinces of Volstokin were trying to secede to form an independent kingdom, Nonverid. The influence of Itaskia was the only stabilizing force in the patchwork of little states making up the remainder of the west.

It was hard to care about people who didn't care about themselves.

Visigodred and Varthlokkur came to an agreement. The former returned with Haaken. The other went to the Mausoleum of the Kings.

The Prime Circle watched in silence.

The necromancy didn't take long. Neither woman had been dead long.

Even now, with ghosts walking, Michael Trebilcock showed no fear. But Ragnar whimpered.

That alerted Bragi. He drew his sword. What devilment...?

He recognized the wraiths, saw the sadness in their faces,

their awareness of one another. "Have you no decency?" he thundered, whirling his blade.

Invisible hands seized him. His weapon slipped from numbed fingers, falling so that it stuck in the soft graveyard earth. The hands compelled him to face the ghosts.

A voice said, "Settle it. Finish it. Make your peace. Slay your grief. A kingdom can't await one man's self-pity." It was no voice he knew. Perhaps it was no voice at all, but the focused thought of that dread circle.

Both women reached out to him. Hurt crossed their faces when they couldn't touch him.

He was compelled to look at them.

There was no hatred, no accusation in his Queen. She didn't blame him for her death. And in Elana there was no damnation for his having failed her, in life or in death. She had known about Fiana. She had forgiven long before her death. In each there was a stubborn insistence that he was doing himself no good with his morbid brooding. He had children to raise and a kingdom to defend. All Elana asked was that he try to understand and forgive her, as she had done for him.

He had forgiven her already. Understanding was more difficult. First he had to understand himself.

He believed he had always done poorly by women. They always paid cruel prices for having been his lovers....

He tried to tell Elana why he had buried Rolf Preshka near her....

She began fading back into her new realm. As did Fiana. He shouted after one, then the other, calling them back. Fiana left him with the thought that the future lay not in a graveyard. He had maneuvered himself into a Regency. Now he must handle it.

Kavelin. Kavelin. Kavelin. Always she thought of Kavelin first.

Well, almost. She had allowed Kavelin to come second occasionally, and had paid a price, her belly ripped by the exit of a thing conceived in the heart of darkness. That darkness was responsible for Elana, too. And two dozen others. His friend Mocker....

Something could be done.

Tendrils of the anger, the outrage, the hatred which had driven him during his ride from Karak Strabger insinuated themselves through his depression. He glanced round, for the first time fully grasped the significance of this gathering.

Kavelin's peace was a false peace behind which darkness marshaled. This mob would not be here were the confrontations not to begin soon.

Nepanthe. Argon. It was all he had to work on. He would pick it up from there....

"Michael. Walk with me. Tell me about Argon." He recovered his sword and strode from the circle, eyes downcast but mind functioning once more.

Early next morning, as the sun broke over the Kapenrungs, he figuratively and literally followed an innkeeper's advice. He went onto the ramparts of Castle Krief and stomped and yelled. This was no quiet alert to the army and reserves, this was a bloody call to a crusade, an emotional appeal calculated to stir a hunger for war.

That innkeeper had been right about the mood of the country folk, the Wesson peasants and Marena Dimura forest-runners.

TWENTY-THREE: The Hidden Kingdom

The winged horse settled gently into the courtyard of Castle Fangdred. The fortress was even more desolate and drear now that Varthlokkur had departed. The small, bent man stalked its cold, dusty halls. When he came to them, he had no trouble passing the spells that had kept Varthlokkur from the chamber atop the Wind Tower.

He paused but a moment there, apparently doing nothing but thinking. Then he nodded and went away.

The winged horse flew eastward, to the land men named Mother of Evil when they didn't call it Dread Empire. From there he flew on to a land so far east that even the Tervola remained ignorant of its existence. The bent man believed it time to employ tools named Badalamen and Magden Norath.

It was morning, but light scarcely penetrated the overcast. Great shoals of cloud beat against the escarpments, piled up, and were driven upward by the Dragon's Teeth. From their dark underbellies they shed heavy, wet snow.

The air stirred in the chamber atop the Wind Tower. Dust moved as if disturbed by elfin footfalls.

A single muscle twitched in the cheek of the old man on the stone throne. Varthlokkur had said his former friend neither lived nor was dead. He was waiting. And his next passage through the world would be his last. He had been burned out in a life extended beyond that of any other living creature (excepting the Star Rider), and by the things he had had to do.

He had even died once and, a little late, been resurrected.

It remained to be seen how much the Dark Lady had claimed of him.

204

An eyelid, a finger, a calf muscle, twitched. His naked flesh became covered with goose bumps.

His chest heaved. Air rushed in, wheezed out. Dust flew. Minutes passed. The old man drew another breath.

One eye opened, roved the room.

Now a hand moved, creeping like an arthritic spider. It tumbled a glass vial from the throne's arm. The tinkle of breakage was a crash in a chamber that had known silence for years.

Ruby clouds billowed, obscuring half the room. The old man breathed deeply. Life coursed through his immobile limbs. It was a more powerful draft than ever he had wakened to before, but never before had he been so near death.

He heaved himself upright, tottered to a cabinet where his witch tools were stored. He seized a container, drained it of a bitter liquid.

He operated almost by instinct. No real thoughts roiled his ancient mind. Perhaps none ever would. Lady Death had held him close.

The liquid refreshed him. In minutes he had almost normal strength.

He abandoned the room, descended a spiral stair to the castle proper. There he drew waiting, ready food from a spell-sealed oven and ate ravenously. He then carried a platter up to the tower chamber.

Still no real thoughts disturbed his mind.

He went to a wall mirror. With sepulchral words and mystic gestures he brought it to life.

A picture formed. It showed falling snow. He placed a chair and small table before it. He sat, nibbled from his tray, and watched. Occasionally, he mumbled. The eye of the mirror roamed the world. He saw some things here, some there. Like a navigator taking starshots he eventually got enough references to fix his position in time. Bewilderment creased his brow. It had been a short sleep. Little more than a decade. What had happened to necessitate his return?

Thoughts were forming now, though most were vagaries, trains of reasoning never completed. The Dark Lady had indeed held him too tightly.

Much of what he had lost could be called will and volition. Knowledge and habit remained. He would be a useful tool in skilled hands.

The hours ground away. He began uncovering events of interest. Something mysterious was happening at the headquarters of the Mercenaries' Guild, where soldiers ran hither and yon, parodying an overturned anthill. Smoke billowed and drifted out to sea. Curious debates were underway at the Royal Palace in Itaskia, and in the Lesser Kingdoms princes were gathering troops. The tiny state called Kavelin was a-hum.

Something was afoot.

A footfall startled him. He turned. A tall, massive man in heavy armor, in his middle twenties apparently, dark of hair and eye, met his gaze. "I am Badalamen. You are to come with me."

The absolute confidence of the man was such that the old man—his only name, that he could remember, was The Old Man of the Mountain—rose. He took three steps before balking. Then, slowly, he turned to his sorcery cabinet.

The warrior looked puzzled, as if no human had ever failed to respond to his commands.

He had been born to command, bred to command, trained from birth to command. His creator-father, Magden Norath, Master of the Laboratories of Ehelebe and second in the Pracchia, had designed him to be unresistible when he issued orders.

His amazement lasted but a moment. He revealed the token Norath had given him. "I speak for he who gave me this."

That medallion changed the Old Man. Radically. He became docile, obedient, began packing an old canvas bag.

There was an island in the east. It was a half-mile long and two hundred yards at its widest, and lay a mile off the easternmost coast. It was rugged and barren. An ancient fortress, erected in stages over centuries, rambled down its stegosaurian spine. The coast to the west was lifeless.

It had been built during the Nawami Crusades, which had broken upon these shores before Shinsan had been a dream.

This land and its ancient wars were unknown in the west. Even the people of the so-called far east were ignorant of its existence. A band of lifeless desert a hundred miles wide scarred that whole coast.

No one remembered. There were few written histories. But the Crusades had been bitter, enduring wars.

The great ones always were. The man who orchestrated them made certain. . . .

The born soldier led the Old Man from the transfer portal to

a room where a man in a grey smock leaned over a vast drawing
table, sketching by candlelight. Badalamen departed. The man
on the stool faced the Old Man.

This was the widest man he had ever seen. And tall. His head
was bald, but he had long mustachios and a pointed chin beard.
His facial hair and eyes were dark. There was a hint of the
oriental to his features, yet his skin was so colorless veins showed
through. Dark lines lurked at the corners of his eyes and mouth,
and lay across his forehead like a corduroy road. His head was
blockish. He was a gorilla of a man. He could intimidate anyone
by sheer bulk.

The Old Man wasn't dismayed. He had seen many men,
including some who had exuded more *presence* than this one.

"Hello." Any other visitor might have snickered. The man's
high, squeaky voice was too at odds with his physique.

There was a scar across his throat from an attempt on his life.

"I'm Magden Norath." He flashed the medallion Badalamen
had shown before. "Come." He led the Old Man to the
battlements.

The Old Man began remembering. The near past was gone,
but, like a senile woman reliving her childhood, he had no
trouble recalling remote details. He had been a player in the
drama of the Crusades.

"It's changed," he said. "It's *old*."

Norath was startled. "You've been here before?"

"With Nahamen the Odite. The High Priestess of Reth."

Norath was puzzled. He had been led to believe that no one
knew who had built the fortress.

He knew nothing about it himself, nor did he care. He saw it
only as a refuge where he could continue the researches that had
caused him to be driven from his homeland, Escalon, a decade
before it fell to Shinsan.

"There is no need, then, to explain where we are."

"K'Mar Khevi-tan. It means 'The Stronghold on Khevi
Island.'"

Norath eyed him speculatively. "Yes. So. It's that for the
Pracchia." A smile bruised his lips. "If Ehelebe has a homeland,
this is it. Come. The others have arrived by now."

"Others?"

"The Pracchia. The High Nine."

Enfeebled though his mind was, the Old Man didn't like what
he saw.

They had gathered, sure enough, and most wore disguises. Even the bent man, whom he recognized instantly.

Only Badalamen and Norath didn't hide. They had no need.

Norath was the creative genius of the society. Beside Badalamen, he had filled the fortress with the products of other experiments. Most had to be caged.

There was a Tervola in a golden mask. A woman of middle-eastern origins. A masked man clothed as a don of the Rebsamen. A masked general from High Crag. Two more, whose origins the Old Man couldn't place. And one empty seat.

"Our brother couldn't join us," said the small man. "He couldn't leave his bed. It behooves us to consider replacements. He has cancer of the blood. No one survives that—though he whom I have summoned, had he his whole mind, might have arrested it. Sit, my friend."

The Old Man took the empty chair.

The Tervola spoke. "Question. How do we deal with this monster created by Varthlokkur? It betrays our agents everywhere."

Others agreed. The Mercenary added, "It's demoralized th working Nines. We're on the run. Our people are cowering in the Hidden Places to escape the Unborn. In Kavelin it merely collected them. Now that it haunts the entire west, it's killing. Cruelly. It's kept us from moving for weeks. I've lost touch with what's going on in Kavelin. Maybe our brother from Shinsan, with his sight, has seen."

Golden Mask shook his head. "Not only the Unborn is there. Varthlokkur is. Mist is. They've veiled the country. Only the living eye itself can see there."

And a certain mirror, but the Old Man volunteered nothing.

He who was first said, "I was there last night. In the evening. I was bound toward High Crag when I noticed a red light. Descending, I saw Varthlokkur, the Regent, and three more men gathered over the Tear of Mimizan...."

A susurrus ran through the room. Norath growled, "I thought it had disappeared."

"It reappeared. In a cemetery, with five men. And, about to join them, every wizard of consequence in those parts."

The susurrus ran round again.

"They're forewarned. And forearmed. We'll have to move fast," said the general.

"That will require the strength of Shinsan. And Shinsan is not yet ours," said Golden Mask. "O Shing remains reluctant."

"Then we have to buy time."

"Or convince O Shing."

"I can't overcome the Unborn," said Golden Mask. "We can't buy time without that."

"We could," said the bent man. "Unless O Shing moves, they have the edge—while their sorcery holds. But they're not united. My Lady," he said to one woman, "prepare your army. General, move your Guild forces east. Find a provocation. Secure that pass and hold it till O Shing arrives. Itaskia won't interfere. El Murid's no threat either. He's fat and weak. We may use him to add to the confusion."

"And their wizards?" Golden Mask asked.

"They'll be neutralized."

The Tervola peered intently. "And ourselves? Will we be deprived too?"

"There are cycles of Power. We're entering an epoch of irregularity. My contribution is the ability to predict the shifts. Unfortunately, the effect isn't localized. But we can take advantage. It becomes a plain military matter, then, for the general and Badalamen. Why worry so?"

"Because things are happening that surpass my understanding. I feel forces working and can't control them. There're too many unpredictables."

"That gives it spice, my friend. Spice. There's no pleasure in the sure thing."

The man in the mask said no more. But spice didn't interest him.

"Enough," said the other. "Return home, to your assignments. We'll meet monthly after this. Quickly, now. The Power will wane soon."

When the last had departed, the bent man shed his disguise, approached the Old Man. "Well, old friend, here we are again. Am I too secretive? Would they tear me apart if they knew? You say nothing. No. I suppose not. You're not the man you were. I'm sorry. But there's too much to keep up with. It seems the scope of things, to be successful, has to be bigger each time. And the bigger, the harder to control. And these days there's ever less time to plan, to prepare. Now I have to keep several currents running, have to anticipate next stages before present ones are finalized. The Shinsan era is still a-building toward climax, and already I have to input Ehelebe. Time was, we had centuries. We had almost four between the Ilkazar and El Murid epics. The birth epic of Shinsan lasted two generations. The Nawami crusades spanned five hundred years. Remember Torginol and The Palace of Love? A masterwork, that was.... Old friend, I'm tired. Old and tired. Burned out. The sentence, surely, must be near its end. Surely *They* must free me if there's nothing left when this's done."

He whispered in the Old Man's ear. "This time it's the holocaust. There are no more ideas. No more epics to play out on this tortured stage.

"Old friend, I want to go home."

The Old Man sat like a statue. A handful of memories had been cast into the turgid pool of his mind. He struggled to catch them.

He had lost a lot. Even his name and origins.

The bent man took his hand. "Be with me for a time. Help me not to be alone."

Loneliness was a curse that had been set upon him ages past.

Once, in some dim, unremembered yesterday, he had sinned. His punishment was countless corporeal centuries, alone, directing diversions which would please *Them*, and possibly move *Them* to forgive....

He had said it himself. Things had become too complex to control.

The Guild general stepped from the portal into his apartment—and the cauldron of an unbelievable battle. He had no opportunity to learn what had happened. Two elderly, iron-hearted gentlemen, to whom the Guild meant more than life itself, awaited him.

"Hawkwind! Lauder! What...?"

They said nothing. Sentence had been passed.

They were old, but they could still swing swords.

TWENTY-FOUR: Kavelin A-March

The volunteers poured in. Campfires dotted every patch of unused land.

"They must be coming out of the ground," Ragnarson observed.

Haaken stood beside him on the wall. "It is hard to believe. So many. Who's doing the work?"

"Yeah. Some will have to go home. You sorted out the ones we want?" Haaken, Reskird, and his other staffers had found trebled work dumped upon them. Kavelin, preparing for war, could no longer proceed on inertia.

Ragnarson had to devote his entire energy to being Regent. He had to browbeat the Thing into accepting this venture, and to prepare a caretaker regime for his absence. Gjerdrum had gotten that job, primarily because his father, Eanred Tarlson, had been a national hero trusted by every class.

Gjerdrum thought being left behind worse than being accused of treason.

Haaken, Reskird, and the other zone commandants had selected six thousand men for Ragnarson's expeditionary force. On a backbone of regulars they had fleshed a corpus of the best reserves and most promising volunteers. A force of equal strength would be left with Gjerdrum.

It would be essentially an infantry force. The venture had raised little enthusiasm among the Nordmen, whence the trained knights came. Ragnarson would take a mere two hundred fifty heavy cavalry, counting those of the Queen's Own. Fleshed out, Ahring would field a thousand men, only half of whom were real horse soldiers. Most were light horse, skirmishers, messengers, and the like.

The infantry would be the Vorgrebergers, the Midlands

Light, the South Bows, a battle each from the Damhorsters, Breidenbachers, and Sedlmayr Light, plus a hodgepodge of engineers, select skilled bowmen, and Marena Dimura auxiliaries.

Ragnarson was an inveterate tinkerer. He would have fiddled till he had his force balanced to the last billet. Only Haaken's nagging got him moving.

Ragnarson understood what few of his contemporaries did. That training and discipline were the critical factors in winning battles. That was why little armies whipped big ones. Why Shinsan was so dreaded a foe. Her army was the most disciplined ever formed.

Ragnarson's plan depended on trickery and surprise, and his cabal of wizards.

"I'm nervous," he told his brother. "We're not ready for this."

"We'll never be ready," Haaken countered.

"I know. I know. And it pains me. All right. Get them moving. I'm going back to the Palace."

He soon joined Gjerdrum in the empty War Room. Every available map of the east was posted there. Scribes directed by Prataxis had made copies for field use. His intended route was sketched in red on a master.

He kept worrying. Could he make it without being detected? Could he feed his men on the wild eastern plains?

What about water? Could he trust the maps to show genuine creeks and water holes?

I've got to stop this, he thought. What will be will be.

There was no turning back. If nothing else, even failure would startle Shinsan. His spunk might make O Shing back off awhile, giving the west time to respond to Varthlokkur's warnings.

This was the second time Kavelin had had to be the bulwark. It wasn't fair.

Varthlokkur arrived. He was a pale imitation of the wizard of a week earlier.

"It's still dead?" Bragi asked.

"Absolutely. Even the Unborn is weakened."

For no reason the wizards could determine, the Power had ceased to function six days past. Only the Unborn retained any vitality, and that because it drew on the Winterstorm, partially tapping different sources of energy.

The weakened Radeachar was busy. A spate of enemies had

pelted against Kavelin's borders after the Power's failure. Visigodred's assistant, flying the huge roc, was as pressed, scouting beyond the borders.

Radeachar would stay with Gjerdrum. His presence would keep the Nordmen in line.

"Marshall," Prataxis called from the door, "you have a minute? There's a man here you should see."

"Sure. Come on in."

Derel's man wore a Guild uniform. Ragnarson frowned, but let him have his say.

"Colonel Liakopulos, General. Aide to Sir Tury."

Ragnarson shook his hand. "Hawkwind, eh?" He was impressed. Hawkwind was the most famous of High Crag's old men, and justifiably so. He had performed military miracles.

"Colonel Oryon asked me to come. The General approved."

"Yes?"

"Oryon was my friend."

"Was?"

"He died last week."

"Sorry to hear it. What happened?"

"Trouble at High Crag. Oryon was in the thick of it. You know how he was."

"Yes. I know." The main message wouldn't register. Guildsman fighting Guildsman. It couldn't happen. "What?... Explain."

"He threw some wild charges around after he got back. Not at all in character. He always kept his mouth shut before. So people listened. And started digging. I believe he mentioned rumors of a junta trying to take over?"

"He did."

"There was one. We cleaned it out. The leader, General Dainiel, had disappeared from his apartment just before Oryon's return. Hawkwind and Lauder moved in. Six days ago Dainiel reappeared out of thin air. A transfer. It had that Shinsan smell. They cut him down. None of his intimates knew for sure, but thought he'd been to Shinsan to meet with other cabal heads. Dainiel had hinted that they were ready to grab control of the west."

Ragnarson looked for someone to tell "I told you so." Derel was the only one handy. Telling him wouldn't give any satisfaction.

"Thank you for your courtesies. Thank the General. I feel

better about the Guild now. Oryon probably mentioned my suspicions."

"He did. The General apologizes for the pressures. The Citadel never planned to force its protection on anyone. That's Dainiel's doing. He wanted a strong force kept near the Savernake Gap.

"We can't offer much restitution right now. It's not much, but Hawkwind offers *my* talents."

Ragnarson raised an eyebrow. "How?"

"Training soldiers is my forte, Marshall. You appear to be mounting an expedition. Yet your men aren't ready. It'll take imaginative leadership to teach on the march."

"It's my biggest headache."

"I can handle it."

There was no arrogance in his manner.

"All right." Ragnarson made the snap decision based on Hawkwind's reputation. "Derel, take Colonel Liakopulos to Blackfang. Tell Haaken to put him in charge of training, and don't bother him."

He remembered the name Liakopulos now. The Colonel had a reputation equal to his self-confidence.

"Thank you, Marshall."

"Uhm." He returned to his maps.

Too late to turn back. Advance parties were already in the Gap. A force had occupied Karak Strabger, to stop eastbound traffic at Baxendala so word wouldn't cross the mountains. Maisak backed the play. No one not authorized by the Marshall traveled east of that stronghold.

The cessation of eastbound trade would itself be a warning that something was happening in Kavelin. Bragi had sent loyal mercantile factors through to hint that another civil war was brewing. The trade community expected something savage to follow Fiana's death.

He had run himself and everyone else ragged. What more could he do?

Go, of course. And hope.

He went.

A post rider overtook him slightly east of Maisak. He brought news from Valther.

"Haaken, listen to this. That kid of Haroun's has invaded Hammad al Nakir." He hadn't anticipated that. "Twenty-five thousand men, Valther says, in six columns. Headed for Al Rhemish."

And Ragnarson had expected Haroun's movement to collapse without him.

This Megelin bore watching.

"What about it?" Haaken asked.

"Will it affect us?"

"How? Unless people think we closed the Gap to cover his rear."

"Possible." His friendship for bin Yousif was well known.

"I hope Megelin makes it. This'll give El Murid an excuse for war."

"Should I turn back?"

"Go on," Varthlokkur advised. "Megelin will hurt him even if he loses. El Murid won't be able to do anything. Cooler heads will prevail before he recovers."

"The numbers worry me," Ragnarson told Haaken. "I didn't realize Haroun could scare up that many men." He turned to Visigodred. "Could Marco fly down there occasionally? To keep track?"

"Too damned much trouble," Marco protested. "Got me hopping like the one-legged whore the day the fleet came in now. What do you think I am? I need to sleep too. You guys think because I'm half size I can do twice the work?"

"Marco," said Visigodred.

The dwarf shut up.

"Skip some of your visits to your girlfriends."

"Boss! What'll they do? They can't manage."

Haaken rolled his eyes. Bragi whispered, "He's for real. I've seen him in action.

"So," he said aloud, "we continue. Ragnar, let's catch Jarl."

Ahring commanded the vanguard, a day ahead. He filtered westbound caravans through, then kept anyone from turning back.

The entire Gap was confusion. This was the height of the caravan season. In places several were crowded up nose to tail, their masters muttering obscenities about being shoved around. Ragnarson saw more than one wound. Jarl had had trouble here and there.

He asked questions. Kaveliners returning home answered.

His advent in the east remained unanticipated.

After riding with Ahring a day he took Derel, Ragnar, Trebilcock, and Dantice and forged ahead, to overtake the scouts. In time he passed them, too.

He knew the risk was wild, yet his spirits soared. He was in the field again. Political woes lay a hundred miles behind. He let his beard go feral. Boldly, he took his friends to Gog-Ahlan. He and Ragnar spent a day prowling the ruins and ramshackle taverns and whorehouses.

Rumors of unrest in Kavelin were thick. Less daring traders were staying put till they knew what was happening.

Kavelin's army turned north twenty miles short of the town, following a side valley. It debouched on the plains away from routes frequented by caravans. A screening force broke contact and began herding cognizant caravaneers westward.

Ragnarson tightened his formation. He allowed his light horse troops to roam only a few miles. Marco would watch the plains nomads. Bragi increased the pace, and turned away whenever Marco reported riders approaching.

Marco also patrolled their back trail, to frighten off any nomads threatening to discover it.

A hundred miles east of the ruins of Shemerkhan, following marches of forty miles per day, the Power reasserted itself. The wizards scrambled to take advantage, but it faded before they could get organized.

The Power quickened again next afternoon, and again it faded rapidly.

The sorcerers debated its meaning for hours.

Ragnarson suspected that little man on the winged horse. In the lonely, quiet hours of riding he tried to think of ways to capture the man, to find out who he was and what he was up to. If legends were to be believed, that would be impossible. It had been tried a thousand times. Anyone who attempted it came to grief.

Nearing lands tributary to Necremnos, the army turned south. Bragi took Varthlokkur, Prataxis, Trebilcock, Dantice, and Ragnar into the city. He left Haaken with orders to move to the Roë halfway between Necremnos and Argon, in the narrow zone beholden to neither city.

People lived there. He counted on Marco and the horsemen to cut their communication with Argon.

He didn't plan on staying long. Just while he visited an

acquaintance, a Necremnen wizard named Aristithorn.

He wasn't sure the man still lived. His own wizards had heard no reports of Aristithorn's death, though the man had seemed on his last legs back when Bragi had helped him make Itaskia's King Norton honor a debt.

Necremnos hadn't changed in twenty-some years. Varthlokkur said it hadn't since his own last visit, centuries earlier. Old buildings came down and new ones arose, but the stubborn Necremnens refused to borrow from foreigners. New buildings were indistinguishable from those demolished.

Aristithorn maintained a small estate outside the city proper. A miniature castle graced its heart. Continuous moans and wails echoed from within.

"He's very dramatic," Bragi told Varthlokkur. The wizard didn't know Aristithorn.

Aristithorn's door was tall and massive. Upon it hung a knocker of gargantuan proportions. It struck with a deep-voiced boom. That was followed by a sound like the groan of a giant in torment.

"Is this the man who married that princess?" Ragnar asked. "The one that you. . . ."

"Tch-tch," Bragi said. "You forget I told you that story. He's old and retired, but he's still a wizard. And a cranky one."

The massive door swung inward. A voice which could have been that of the tormented giant boomed, "Enter!"

"He's changed the place some," Ragnarson observed.

They stood in a long, pillared chamber done in marbles. The only furnishings were several dozen suits of armor. Even whispers echoed there, playing around the chuckling of a fountain at the center of the hall.

Varthlokkur stood at Ragnarson's left. Trebilcock and Dantice remained a step behind, to either flank, facing the walls, their hands on their weapons. Prataxis and Ragnar tucked themselves into the pocket thus formed. The place was intimidating.

"Cut the clowning and get your ass out here," Bragi yelled. "That'll get him in here," he whispered. "He's got this this about scaring people. Bet you he runs a bluff about turning us into frogs."

He was right, though newts were the creatures mentioned. Decades had passed, but Aristithorn hadn't changed. He had become more of what he had always been. Older, meaner, crankier. He didn't recognize Ragnarson till the third time Bragi interrupted to explain who he was.

And then Aristithorn wasn't pleased. "Back to haunt me, eh? Ye young ingrate. Thought ye got away with it, didn't ye? I tell ye, I knew it all along. . . ." He was speaking of a woman. One of his wives.

Ragnarson had had even less sense about women when he was twenty.

"Let me introduce my companions. Michael Trebilcock. Aral Dantice. Soldiers of fortune. Derel Prataxis, a don of the Rebsamen. Ragnar, my son. And a colleague, Varthlokkur."

". . . saw ye two and yere wickedness. . . . Eh?"

"Varthlokkur. Also called The Silent One Who Walks With Grief and Empire Destroyer."

Varthlokkur met Aristithorn's gaze. He smiled a smile like the one worn by the mongoose before kissing a cobra.

"Eh? Oh, my. Oh. Oh my god. Pthothor preserve us. Now we know. The visitation of Hell. I recant. I plead. Give me back my soul. I should have known when the Power failed me. . . ."

"Was he always like this?" Trebilcock asked. "How'd he stand up to that King Norton?"

"Don't pay any mind. It's all act. Come on, you old fraud. We're not here to hurt you. We want your help. And we'll pay." To the others, "He's got a lot of pull here. I don't know why. Guess they haven't figured out he's ninety percent fake."

"Fake? You. . . . You. . . . Young man, I'll show you who's fake. Don't come croaking in my pond when you're a frog."

"You admitted the Power deserted you."

"Ha! Don't you believe it!"

Varthlokkur interrupted. "Marshall, can we get to the point? Seconds could be critical now. You! Be silent!"

Aristithorn's lips kept moving but no sound came forth. He was doing as directed while indulging an old vice. He had to talk, but didn't have to say anything.

"Old friend," said Ragnarson, "I've risen in the world since our adventure. I'm Marshall and Regent of Kavelin in the Lesser Kingdoms now. I'm marching to war. My army lies just beyond Necremnen territory. No. No worry. Necremnos isn't my target. I'm going to Argon. Yes. I know. Argon hasn't been invaded since Ilkazar managed it. But nobody has gone about it seriously. . . . Why? Because they attacked me. On orders from

Shinsan. They murdered my wife, two of my kids, some of my friends. And they kidnapped a friend of mine's wife and son. And maybe the friend, too. They're locked up in Argon's Royal Palace. I'm going to punish Argon."

Aristithorn's gaze flitted to Varthlokkur whenever the urge to verbalize became strong. Varthlokkur merely stared.

Aristithorn seemed a mouse, but that was pure show. He was a mortal danger to his enemies.

"What I want is boats. All the boats I can lay hands on. And don't forget, we'll be in your debt. Varthlokkur's ability to meet his obligations has never been questioned."

Ragnarson smiled to himself, pleased with his double entendre. A threat and a promise in one simple declarative sentence—which meant little. Varthlokkur was accepting no obligations himself. This wriggling in the worm pile of politics was making a politician of him too.

Aristithorn changed. He sloughed the pretense, stood tall and arrogant. "You say Shinsan has its hooks in the Fadem? That would explain some strange things."

"Fadem?" Bragi asked.

"What they call their Royal Palace in Argon," Trebilcock reminded.

"Yes," Aristithorn continued, "Argon has behaved oddly the past few years. And I've heard that a man resembling a Tervola visits there frequently, and came here once. Pthothor gave him short shrift, the story goes. This's bad—if it's true. This's a sad enough earth without Shinsan creeping into its palaces like some night cancer. Yes. This explains things that puzzle the wise. Particularly about the Fadema."

"Queen of Argon," said Trebilcock.

"Boats? Did I hear right?"

"Boats, yes. As many as possible. Big, little, whatever can be had. But quickly. So I can arrive before they know I'm coming, before the Power returns and they can see me with their inner eyes."

"Ye might work it. Argon's defenses be meant to stop land-bound armies."

"Told you he was sharp. Figured it without me telling him a thing."

"Yes, this must be stopped. And Pthothor, with his fear of things Shinsan, and his lust to be remembered as a conqueror.... He may join ye."

The old coast reever in Ragnarson became wary instantly. Somebody was hinting about divvying the plunder. Before the booty was gained. "That might be useful," he said, trying to sound noncommittal. "As later support. But the enemy has agents everywhere. We dare not risk ourselves by including anyone in our plan just now. In a week...?"

"My sense of rectitude compels me to assist ye. But there must be balance."

"Derel. The man's ready to dicker. Don't give him the Royal silverware."

Prataxis was a master. With Varthlokkur to handle the intimidation he soon got Aristithorn to agree to what Ragnarson considered bargain terms. A modest amount of cash. A few items believed to be in possession of the Fadema. Kavelin to sponsor his children's educations at the Rebsamen. The university's fame had spread far and wide, and a man from these parts who could honestly claim to have been educated there was guaranteed a high, happy life.

What Ragnarson didn't realize was that Aristithorn had children in droves. His wives were always pregnant, and often bore twins.

Later, as they strolled to the waterfront with the babbling wizard, they were spotted by a chunky brown man who scrambled into shadows and watched them pass. His face contorted into a mixture of surprise and bewilderment. Only Aral Dantice noticed him. He had no idea who the man was. Just another curious easterner....

TWENTY-FIVE: The Assault on Argon

Aristithorn did better than Ragnarson expected. His reputation locally was as nasty as Varthlokkur's worldwide. Boat owners, merchant captains, no one refused him more than once. No one quibbled over the vow of silence he extracted. Boats and ships departed, fully crewed, without question of payment being raised, though Ragnarson promised owners and crews a portion of the loot of Argon.

Aristithorn claimed that didn't matter. This was war. If Ragnarson failed, Pthothor would take over. There were old grievances between Necremnos and Argon. The cities were overdue for one of their periodic scrimmages.

So Ragnarson led an armada down the Roë and met Haaken. Three thousand men boarded the vessels, more than he had hoped. His spirits rose. If he remained unnoticed he had a chance.

Aristithorn virtually guaranteed that the Necremnen army would be right behind him. Ragnarson soon hoped so. Argon was huge. A million people lived in its immediate environs. Six thousand men could disappear quickly if the populace fought back.

As Argon drew closer, Bragi found ever more reasons for forgetting the whole thing. But he went on. Worrying was his nature. Haaken had chided him for it since childhood. Sometimes you had to ignore potential difficulties and forge ahead. Otherwise nothing got done.

The first wave consisted of the smallest boats, carrying Marena Dimura mountaineers, attacking at two points. One group drifted down to where the walls of the Fadem rose from the river. The other remained at the apex of the island.

The Marena Dimura scaled the rough walls and established bridgeheads. Their boats returned upriver to Haaken, whose

men, weary from slogging through marshes and swimming delta
channels, awaited their turns to ride. One battle of the Queen's
Own had taken the horses and train back into the plains, to erect
a fortified camp a few miles above the Argon-Throyes road.

Ragnarson traveled aboard a galley which served Necrem-
nos's trade in the Sea of Kotsüm. He had filled a dozen such with
Haaken's Vorgrebergers, Reskird's Damhorsters, and bowmen.
The assault captains were ex-mercenaries who had come to
Kavelin with him years ago. They were the shock troops who
would expand the bridgeheads.

It went so smoothly he suspected he had a friendly god
perched on his shoulder. The Argonese were expecting nothing.
As always, when the evening rains came, the wall sentries had
scurried for cover. Argon lay as defenseless as a virgin thrown by
her protectors to barbarian raiders. Two thousand men were
over the walls before they attracted any attention.

The fighting broke out, as Ragnarson had hoped, at the apex
of the island. Kildragon, in charge there, immediately began
raising the biggest fuss possible.

Ragnarson took his party into the second bridgehead.

There the troops were lying low. The Fadema maintained a
personal guard of a thousand, and had regular army units
quartered in the Fadem too. Ragnarson wanted to be as strong
as possible before the Argonese counterattacked.

He cleared the top of the wall, scuttled out of the way,
gasped, "Didn't think I'd make it. Getting old for this. Jarl?
How's it going? You spreading out yet?"

Here the Marena Dimura were doing what they did best,
skulking, stabbing in the dark, occupying strongpoints by
stealth.

"We've taken everything you can see from here. This's the
sloppiest defense I ever saw. We haven't found anybody awake
yet. It's too bad Reskird's raising hell up there. We might've
grabbed the whole damned place before anybody knew we were
here."

"Uhm. Keep moving. Grab what you can while you can.
Gods, it's big."

The Fadem alone seemed as big as Vorgreberg. Trebilcock
said it had thirty thousand permanent residents.

"Michael. Aral," Bragi whispered. "Where's this tower?"

"The squarish one yonder, with the spire sticking up from the
corner," Dantice replied.

"Let's see if she's still there."

They descended to street level and slipped through narrow passages between buildings, making of a two-hundred-yard crow flight a quarter mile walk. They won the distinction of being first to face wakened opponents.

It was over before Ragnarson realized what had happened. The parties stumbled into one another at a sharp turn. Trebilcock disposed of the Argonese in an eye's blink.

Ragnarson's eyebrows rose. Michael could handle a blade damned well.

"It's sixty feet to the first ledge," Trebilcock whispered. "And twenty more to the one by her window. I'll drop a line from the first one...."

"Kid, if you and Aral can make it, so can I." Bragi sheathed his sword, felt for hand and toeholds.

He quickly regretted his bravado.

Trebilcock and Dantice went up like rock apes. Ragnarson had thirty feet to go when they reached the first ledge. His muscles threatened cramps. His fingers were raw when he heaved himself onto the ledge. Looking down, he muttered, "Bragi, you're a fool. You've got men who get paid to do this."

A clash of arms sounded here and there. The defenders still weren't reacting except locally.

Reskird had a good fight going. The uproar reached the Fadem, and the bellies of the rain clouds glowed with firelight.

The last twenty feet were worse. Now he was conscious of how far he could fall. And of his age. And his sword kept beating the backs of his legs.

"We're going down by the stair," he muttered when he rolled onto the upper ledge.

Trebilcock smiled, a thin, humorless thing in the reflected firelight. "Would've been easier if we'd gotten here before the rain."

Ragnarson's stomach flip-flopped as he realized how easily he could have slipped.

Dantice crept back from the window. "Can't tell if there's anybody inside."

A head popped out. Bragi recognized Nepanthe. She didn't see them. "Inside," he growled. "Quick."

Dantice went. They heard his sword clear its scabbard. Trebilcock and Ragnarson plunged after him.

Sounds of struggle, of steel against stone. Dantice cursed. "She bit me!"

"Nepanthe!" Bragi snapped. "Settle down!"

"She started to yell," Dantice said.

"Michael, find a lamp." Ragnarson moved the other way. "Damn!" He bruised his shin on something low.

Someone crashed to the floor. Metal skittered across stone. "Marshall, I'm going to clout her!"

"Easy, son. Nepanthe! It's me. Bragi. Behave yourself."

Cang-chang. Sparks flew. A weak light grew, illuminating Trebilcock's face. As the flame rose, it revealed Nepanthe and Dantice on the floor. Aral had one hand on her mouth, his legs scissored around her. He was fending a dagger with his free hand. Bragi kicked the weapon away.

He grabbed handfuls of Nepanthe's hair and forced her to look at him. "Nepanthe. It's me."

Her eyes widened. Her fear subsided. She relaxed.

"Can you keep quiet now?"

She nodded. He grinned as Dantice's hand bobbed with the motion. "Let her go, Aral. Michael, look at his hand."

Dantice winced when he put weight on that hand while rising. Ragnarson helped Nepanthe up.

"Take a minute," he said as she started babbling. "Get yourself together."

After she calmed down, she explained how the stranger had come to Valther's house and convinced her that Mocker had gone into hiding because Haroun had tried to murder him. He feared Bragi was in on it. The messenger had brought Mocker's dagger as a token. And she had always suspected Haroun of the worst.

"He could do it if he thought he needed to," Bragi observed. "But how would Mocker have been a threat to him?"

"I never thought about it. Not till I found out they tricked me." She started crying. "Look what I got you into. What're you doing here, anyway? Who's watching things at home? I heard about Fiana. They tell me all the bad news."

"I'm here because you are. Because Argon seems to be behind all our trouble."

"No. It's Shinsan. Bragi, there's a Tervola. . . . He controls the Fadema. . . . I think. Maybe they're partners."

"I mean to find out."

"But. . . . You're only one man. Three men." To Michael she said, "Thank you. Did you get the casket to Varthlokkur? And you. I'm sorry. I was scared."

Dantice smiled. "No matter, ma'am." He sucked his injured hand.

"He brought the Tear back, yes. Tell me about the Tervola. Does he wear a golden mask?"

"Yes. How'd...?"

"He keeps turning up. Must be O Shing's special bully boy. And I didn't come by myself. That's our army kicking ass out there."

"But.... *Argon*? They took me out once. I think the Fadema wanted to show me what a hick I was. Bragi, you can't get in a war with Argon. Not over me...."

"Too late to back off. The boys are probably too loaded with loot to run." He chuckled. "I don't want to take the city. Just the Fadem. Just to spoil whatever they're up to. I'm no conquerer."

"Bragi, you're making a mistake...."

"Somebody coming," Trebilcock said. He had one ear against the door. "Sounds like a mob."

"Get out of sight. Aral! Your sword."

Dantice scampered back for the weapon.

"Nepanthe, pretend we're not here. They must be coming for you. They'll want their prize counter safe. Get by the window. Make them come to you. Michael, Aral, we'll hit them from behind."

Dantice was a street fighter. He understood. But Michael protested.

"We're here to win, Michael, not get killed honorably."

Ragnarson concealed himself just in time. The door creaked inward. Six soldiers entered, followed by the Fadema.

"Well, Madam," said the woman, "your friends are more perceptive and less cautious than we anticipated. They're here."

"Who?" Nepanthe asked, cowering against the window frame.

"That bloody troublesome Marshall. He's attacked Argon. What gall!" She laughed. It was forced.

Things must be going good, Bragi thought.

"You stay away," Nepanthe told the soldiers. "I'll jump."

"Don't be a fool!" the Fadema snapped. "Come. We have to move you. The tower is threatened."

"I *will* jump."

"Grab her."

Four soldiers advanced.

"Now," Ragnarson said. Leaping, he took out a man who had remained with the Fadema.

Dantice went for the man on her far side instead of the four. Trebilcock got another, but quickly found himself in trouble.

Ragnarson smacked the Queen to shut her up, turned to help Michael.

Somebody hit him from behind.

He turned as he fell, looked up into a golden mask.

The Tervola had hit him with a wooden statuary stand. "Finish them!" he ordered. "This's the man we want. The Marshall himself."

Trebilcock was fencing a man who was good. Dantice rolled across the floor with one of the others. The third soldier pranced around looking for a chance to strike a telling blow.

Ragnarson kicked the Tervola's legs from beneath him, dragged him nearer. The stand rolled away.

The Tervola had the combat training of every soldier of Shinsan. And he had staying power, though Ragnarson was stronger. They rolled and kicked and gouged, and Bragi bit. He kept trying to yank the man's mask off so he could go for his eyes.

That usually put a superior opponent on the defensive. And this Tervola was a better fighter than he.

The extra soldier almost got Dantice. But Nepanthe stabbed him from behind, turned on Aral's antagonist, stabbed him too. Aral muttered, "We're even, lady," recovered his sword, took a wild chop at the head of Michael's opponent.

Meanwhile, the Fadema recovered and fled.

Ragnarson got a thumb under the golden mask. By then he was sure he was dead. The Tervola had a hold of his neck and he was losing consciousness.

Dantice and Trebilcock closed in. The Tervola saw them. The Power was dead. There was nothing he could do. He threw himself after the Fadema. His mask remained in Bragi's hand.

Dantice helped Ragnarson up. "That was close. Mike, better make sure of those guys."

"But...."

"Never mind. I'll do it." While Nepanthe and Trebilcock supported Ragnarson, he cut throats. "I don't understand you, Mike. It ain't beer and skittles. It ain't no chess game. You want to come out alive, you got to be meaner than the other guy. And you don't leave him alive behind you."

Ragnarson groaned. Nepanthe massaged his neck. "See if any of our people are outside. We'll have half an army on us in a minute."

Dantice leaned out the window. "Nope. They're all down the street."

"You and Michael pile stuff in front of the door. No. Let me go! I'm okay. I'll make something to lower Nepanthe down."

"Wait!" she protested. "What about Ethrian?"

Bragi hurt. It made him cranky. "What do you want me to do? We've got to get out of here first. Then we'll worry about Ethrian."

She kept arguing. He ignored her. There was a racket in the hall already.

A party of Marena Dimura came up the street as he dropped his rope of torn blankets. "You men. Hold up. It's me. The Marshall. Aral, hand me that lamp." He illuminated his face. "Hang onto the end of that down there, and stand by."

Several Wesson bowmen joined the Marena Dimura. They stood around watching.

"Nepanthe, come here."

Still complaining, she obeyed. He turned his back. "Put your arms around my neck and hang on."

"You'd better let me do that," Dantice offered.

"I can handle it. I'm not all the way over the hill." He did leave his sword belt, though, remembering what a hazard it had been coming up.

Going down was a pain too. He hadn't made it halfway before he wished his pride had let him yield to Dantice.

"Hurry up," said Trebilcock. "The door's giving."

Dantice started down the instant Bragi's feet hit pavement. He came like a monkey.

"Boy, you'd make a good burglar."

"I am a good burglar." They watched Trebilcock lever himself over the window sill.

Someone yelled inside. Michael stared, then threw himself aside, barely managing to cling to the ledge.

Men appeared in the window.

"Bowmen," said Ragnarson. "Cover him."

Arrows streaked through the window. The Argonese withdrew, cursing. Ragnarson asked the Marena Dimura captain, "Where's Colonel Ahring?"

The man shrugged. "Around."

"Yeah. Michael, hurry up." Trebilcock had reached the lower ledge. Someone upstairs was throwing things out the window. A vase smashed at Bragi's feet.

Trebilcock kicked away from the wall and dropped the last fifteen feet, grunting as he hit cobblestones. "Damn. I twisted my ankle."

"Teach you to show off," Aral growled.

"Come on," said Ragnarson. "Back to the wall. You men. Go on wherever you were going."

Ahring had left. His men had penetrated the Fadem deeply in several directions. Runners said some defenders were fleeing the fortress for the city.

Haaken had arrived. He was directing operations now.

"What's happening?" Ragnarson asked.

"They're running. All our people are in now. But we've got a problem. Most of those Necremnens are heading out. We'll be in big trouble if we don't win this."

"Michael, where's the nearest causeway?"

Trebilcock leaned over the battlements. "Upriver a quarter-mile."

"Haaken, scare up some men and grab it. Michael. Is there a causeway Reskird could use?"

"Inside his area. Shouldn't be any problem."

Ragnarson stared northward. The entire apex of the island seemed to be burning. The rain had let up. Nothing held the flames in check.

"Getting bad up there," he observed. "Could be as rough for Reskird as the Argonese."

"Bragi." Haaken had unrolled a crude map atop a merlon. He shaded an area with charcoal. "This's what we've taken. Half." Dark salients stuck out like greedy fingers. There were white islands throughout the area already captured.

"How're they fighting?"

"Us or them?"

"Both."

"Our guys are having fun. Theirs.... Depends on the unit. The officers, I guess. Some are tromping each other trying to get away. Some won't budge. I'd say our chances of carrying it are better than even. But then we'll have to hold off counterattacks while we mop up."

"Keep after them. Any Necremnens have balls enough to stick?" He leaned over the wall. A dozen smaller boats rocked against the base of the wall.

"Why?"

"I want to go get Reskird. Watch Nepanthe. And keep an eye out for Ethrian. They've got him here somewhere."

TWENTY-SIX: Battle for the Fadem

Reskird had an overachievement problem. "Bragi, I've got them whipped. I could clean up on them. Only I can't get to them. Damned fire...."

A curtain of flame thwarted Kildragon's advance. It spanned the base of an acute isosceles triangle. Whole blocks were infernos, drawing a strong breeze. Neither side could get close enough to combat the blaze.

"I can't leave you here while it burns itself out. Might be days."

The devastation was stunning. Even during the El Murid Wars Ragnarson had seen nothing to equal it. "Jarl and Haaken need help."

"Those damned Necremnens took off like rabbits afraid of a fox."

"You taken that causeway there yet?"

"The gatehouse guards won't give up. But we'll get it. It's all we've got to work on anymore."

"Michael. Does it hook up to the same island as the one by the Fadem?"

"I think so."

"You see?" Bragi asked Kildragon.

Reskird's sandy hair flew as he nodded.

Bragi laughed.

"What?"

"Look at us. Me, you, Haaken. We've gotten civilized. We never cut our hair short before we came to Kavelin. And we didn't shave, except you."

"It's a strange country. I'd better go get things moving before it's light enough for them to see what we're up to."

They didn't join Haaken before dawn. The causeways didn't

229

connect to the same island. They had to cross three. There were
skirmishes. And then the right causeway turned out to still be in
Argonese hands.

Haaken hadn't had a chance to grab it. The garrison had
counterattacked.

Bragi's old veterans carried the bridge in a short, brisk battle,
only to find Argonese troops forming up beyond. The melee
lasted several hours. Haaken's bowmen, when they could,
plinked from the Fadem. Ragnarson advanced till he screened
the Fadem's main gate, which remained in enemy hands.

"Who's got who trapped?" he wondered aloud. "How long
before the whole city turns on us?"

Tactically, it was going magnificently. Yet the strategic
situation looked worse and worse.

Kildragon considered the houses and shops facing the
fortress-palace. "A lot of wood in those places. Maybe another
fire. . . ."

"Go to it."

Kildragon's fire masked their flank. Bragi had men climb the
wall where Blackfang and Ahring were already established.
They took the main gate from behind.

Weary, he joined Haaken at another merlon. The map now
showed only a few white islands.

"The gate completes the circuit," said Blackfang. "The whole
wall is ours."

"Think that's smart?" Ragnarson asked. "They'll fight harder
if they can't get away."

"If they could, the Fadema might get out. Shouldn't we get a
hold of her?"

"She'd be a good bargaining counter if things got hairy. You
found Ethrian yet?"

"No. Else I'd say let's get out now."

"Another reason to get our hands on the lady. They'll chase
us all the way home if we don't."

"Those wizards want to see you."

"They come up with something?"

"I don't know. They've been everywhere, getting in the way."

"How are the men? Any problems?"

"Not yet. Still think they can lick the world as long as you're
in charge. But it's daytime now. They've seen how big the place
is. I'm scared they'll start thinking about it."

The western soldier was flighty, and totally unpredictable. One day he might, if inspired, stand against impossible odds and fight to the death. Another day some trivial occurrence might spook an entire army.

"Keep them too busy to think. These pockets. What are they?"

"Citadels within the citadel. They've locked themselves in. Don't look like it'll be easy digging them out."

"Where's the Queen? Keep the others from sallying. Go after her. On the cheap."

"Been doing that. Lying about Pthothor's intentions. Got more prisoners than I can handle. Reskird showed up just in time. We'll need men on the wall."

"Keep the fires going. What about casualties?"

"Not bad. Mostly new men, the way you'd expect. Enough to be a problem if we have to fight our way out."

"Where're those wizards?"

Haaken was skirting the question of leaving the wounded. Ragnarson didn't want to think about it, let alone verbalize it. It always gnawed at his guts, but sometimes it had to be done.

"Wherever you find them. Just prowl around till one bites your ankle."

He did. Trebilcock and Dantice followed, playing their bodyguard role to the hilt.

Ragnarson found a courtyard where a thousand prisoners sat in tight ranks on the cobblestones, heads bowed, thoroughly whipped. In a second courtyard he found his dead and wounded, in neat rows on mattresses looted from a barracks room. The dead and mortally wounded were pleasingly few.

On one mattress lay the innkeeper met during the ride to Baxendala.

"Hey, old man, what're *you* doing here? You should be home minding the tavern."

"Old? I'm younger than ye are, sir."

"My job. I get paid for being here."

"My job, too, sir. It's my country, ye see. My sons, Robbie and Tal, have ye seen them, sir? Are they all right, do you think?"

"Of course. And heroes, too. Be taking home a double share of loot." He hadn't the faintest idea where they were. But the innkeeper hadn't many hours left. "When it lets up a little, I'll send them down."

"Good, sir. Thank ye, sir."

"Get better, innkeeper. We'll need you again before this's done."

"Be up and around in a day or two, sir. These Argonese can't cut ye bad when they're showing their backs."

Ragnarson moved on before his tears broke loose. Again and again he saw familiar faces, men who had followed him so long they were almost family. The same men were always at the forefront, always where the killing was worst.

He couldn't help himself. More than once he shed a tear for an old comrade.

Three wizards handled the doctoring. The Thing With Many Eyes, strange though he appeared, was a sympathetic, empathetic soul. He hated watching pain. He, Kierle the Ancient, and Stojan Dusan, were performing surgery on an assembly line. With the Power they would have defeated Death and pain more often.

"Michael, our species is a paradox," Ragnarson observed as they departed. "All sentience is paradoxical."

"Sir?" The hospital court hadn't fazed Trebilcock. Dantice, though, had grown pale.

"Those wizards. They get mad, they can rip up a city, wipe out twenty thousand people, and never bat an eye. But look at them now. They're killing themselves for men they don't even know."

"That's part of being human. We're all that way, a little. I saw you weep in there. Yet you'd destroy Shinsan to the last babe in arms. Or reduce Argon to ashes."

"Yes. Is a conundrum, as my fat brown friend would say. What's the difference between the innkeeper and the man I killed last night? Each did his duty.... No. Enough. Let's find Varthlokkur."

The downhill side of, and aftermath of, battles always pushed him into these moods. If he didn't catch himself, didn't become otherwise preoccupied, he would plunge into a nihilism from which he wouldn't recover for days.

Night threatened before they tracked Varthlokkur down. He and Visigodred were in a library, searching old books. Zindahjira was there too, though Ragnarson never saw him. From back in the stacks he fussed and cursed and tried to get Visigodred's goat.

"What's that all about?" Trebilcock asked.

"I don't know," Ragnarson replied. "It's been going on as long as I've known them."

Ragnar materialized from the stacks. "Dad!"

After hugging him, Bragi held him at arms' length. The boy was festooned with loot. "Somebody been breaking plunder discipline?"

"Aw, Dad, I just picked up a couple things for Gundar and the kids."

"What if everybody did that? Who'd do the fighting?"

Ragnar posed cockily. "Varthlokkur's still alive."

To keep him out of trouble Ragnarson had convinced him the wizard needed a bodyguard. An amusing notion. Varthlokkur, Visigodred, and Zindahjira all were damned formidable even without the Power.

"He's been invaluable," said Varthlokkur. "How goes the fighting?"

"So-so. We're on top. But we've got to lay hands on the Fadema. Haaken said you wanted to talk to me. Problems?"

"Not sure," Visigodred said. "I heard from Marco this morning. He visited Hammad al Nakir."

"So?"

"El Murid hasn't collapsed. For a while Haroun's boy won everywhere but at Al Rhemish. He had help from the tribes. After that last surge of the Power, though, things turned around."

"How?"

"Rumor says El Murid appealed to the angels. Because he claims a direct commission from heaven, I guess. The angels apparently responded. They sent him a general. The Royalist offensive bogged down."

"Only a matter of time before weight of numbers tells."

Varthlokkur took it up. "Megelin learned from the best. But he's losing. Three battles last week, all to inferior forces. This angelic general is superhuman."

"And?"

"Two points. What happens if Megelin loses? Another round of El Murid wars? The man is old and fat and crazier than ever. He'll want to get even with everybody who helped Haroun. Second point. The general calls himself Badalamen."

"Badalamen? Never heard of him."

"You have. In a divination, remember? So cloudy, but the name came through as dangerous. . . ."

"Yeah. Now I remember."

"We've reasoned thus: Badalamen was furnished by O Shing, to reverse El Murid's fortunes because Shinsan isn't ready to move. This business with Argon was probably geared to an attack next summer. But we've wrecked that.

"Oh. I heard about your fight with the Tervola. He's still here. With the Fadema. Haaken gave me the mask. I didn't recognize it. It does look a lot like Chin's. He might have changed it after Baxendala. If it is Chin, he's as dangerous as Tervola come. We'd save a lot of grief by killing him. But to the matter in Hammad al Nakir.

"It's my guess that your reaction has been more effective than O Shing expected. And there's Radeachar. So he's put this Badalamen in to threaten your flank."

"He another Tervola?"

"No. Marco says he's pretty ordinary. You've seen the eastern martial arts artists? The way they use an opponent's strengths against him? That's the way Badalamen operates.

"I don't think he's human at all. Nu Li Hsi and Yo Hsi both tried to breed superhuman soldiers. O Shing was the result of one experiment. I'd guess Radeachar is another. I doubt the work stopped with the passing of the Princes Thaumaturge."

Ragnarson pursed his lips, sucked air across his teeth. "There's not a lot we can do about it, is there?"

"No. I just wanted you to know. I'd say it makes it imperative that we kill the Tervola here. He's bound to be one of O Shing's top men."

"And the Fadema," Ragnarson added. "Whoever takes over might think twice about being Shinsan's stalking horse."

"Marco went to Necremnos, too," Visigodred said. "Pthothor has gathered an army. But he's in no hurry to get here. Waiting to hear how we did. Doesn't want to throw live men after dead."

"Can't blame him. Well, I'd better tell Haaken we've got to get that tower."

Having admonished Ragnar again, Bragi departed. Zindahjira resumed fulminating in the stacks. Bragi chuckled. Someday he'd have to find out what had started that.

The Fadema stubbornly refused to surrender. Days passed. The impasse persisted. Ragnarson worried.

The city garrisons recovered. Troops from out of town

reinforced them. Ragnarson had to lock his force into the Fadem. His men stayed busy defending its walls. He expected a major assault.

There could be no escape, now, without victory. And that appeared to be slipping away—unless Necremnos came.

The first week ended. Except for the Queen's stronghold, the Fadem was his. Outside, the Argonese seemed content to wait, to starve him out. Their probes he beat back with heavy losses. Necremnos was moving, but slowly, willing to let Kavelin do the heavy dying.

The stalemate persisted, though Ragnarson didn't sit still. His engineers worked round the clock to tunnel into the Queen's tower. He battered its walls with captured engines. He tried sending Marena Dimura up its wall by night.

The sappers completed the tunnels the last day of the second week.

Ragnarson chose his assault teams carefully. Haaken and Reskird each led one, and he took the third. Ahring mounted a vicious diversion outside.

The bailey was a cylindrical tower with thick walls and little room inside. The easiest entry, once the single door had been sealed, was over the top—almost a hundred feet above the encircling street.

Unless one penetrated its basements. An obvious and antici-pated tactic. The defenders would be waiting. It would be rough.

Bragi didn't doubt the outcome. His concern was keeping costs down.

His engineers tested to see if the basements had been flooded. They hadn't. Some other greeting waited.

Bragi expected fire.

It didn't materialize. Again, Argon's initial lack of readiness told.

It was a savage melee, fought through dim passages and narrow doors, Ragnarson's men advancing by sheer mass. The defenders remained stubborn despite the hopelessness of their situation.

It went floor by floor, hour by hour.

"Why the hell don't she give up?" Bragi asked Kildragon. "She's just wasting lives."

"Some people keep hoping."

"Marshall! We're at the top."

"Okay! Reskird, Haaken, this's it. Send for Varthlokkur."

The wizard appeared immediately. Ragnarson and his friends forced themselves into the Fadema's last redoubt.

She had but two soldiers left. Both were wounded, but remained feisty.

And the Tervola was there. Ethrian, bound and gagged, stood behind him.

"My Lord Chin," said Varthlokkur. "It's been a while."

Chin bowed slightly. "Welcome to Argon, old pupil. You learned well. Someday you'll have to teach me the secret of the Unborn."

"I have no taste for teaching. Is there anything you'd care to tell us, My Lord? So we can avoid the rough parts?"

"No. I think not." Chin glanced at an hourglass. He didn't seem worried.

Ragnarson grew wary. These people always had something up their sleeves. . . .

He collected a fallen javelin, pretended to examine it. "Something's going to happen," he whispered to Reskird. "Start moving the men out."

Chin responded to the withdrawal with the slightest of frowns and a touch of nervousness.

"My Lord," said Ragnarson. "Could you tell me why you killed my people? My wife never did anything to you." Iron and pain tinged his voice.

Chin glanced at the hourglass, brought his sword to guard. "Nothing personal. You're in the way. But we'll correct that soon enough. The hour has come."

For an instant Ragnarson thought that the Tervola meant it was his moment to die. Then, when Varthlokkur gasped and staggered, he realized Chin had been warning his companions.

The Power had come alive. A portal had opened behind Chin and the Fadema.

The Tervola attacked. Haaken and Michael met him, prevented his blade from reaching the Marshall. The Fadema came at Bragi with a dagger identical to that he had taken off the leader of the assassins who had killed Elana. A trooper savaged her knife hand with a wild swing, kicking the dagger toward his commander. He tried to follow up. Bragi grabbed his arm, yanked him away from Chin's blade.

"Thanks." He slapped the dagger into the soldier's hand. It was rich booty, a spell-blade worth a fortune.

Chin hurled the two Argonese soldiers, the Fadema, and Ethrian into the portal's black maw, chanting a hasty spell. Varthlokkur responded with a warding spell.

Chin jumped for the portal. His magick roared through the chamber.

Bragi hurled the javelin, then dropped to the floor, rubbed his eyes. He couldn't see. His skin felt toasted.

He moaned.

"Easy," said Varthlokkur. "You'll be all right. I blocked most of it."

Ragnarson didn't believe him. "Did I get him?" he demanded. "Did I get him?" Chin's life almost seemed worth his eyes.

"I don't know. I'm sorry. I don't."

TWENTY-SEVEN: Mocker Returns

The brown man watched from the shadows. He shivered, sure Varthlokkur would notice him. But only one man glanced his way, a squat, hard looker he didn't recognize. The youth didn't react to his stare.

His breath hissed away. Relieved, he waited till they rounded a corner, then followed.

What were they up to? Bragi and Varthlokkur had no business being in Necremnos. And who was the Necremnen? Everyone seemed to know and fear him.

The brown man interrupted a street cleaner.

"Self, beg thousands pardon, sir. Am foolish foreigner, being ignorant of all things Necremnen. Am bestruckt by puzzlement. Am seeing man pass, moment gone, ordinary, with foreign companions, and people hide eyes from same. Am wondering who is same?"

"Huh?"

Necremnen was one of the languages of Mocker's childhood. He could reduce any tongue to unintelligibility.

He tried again.

"Him? That's the high and mighty Aristithorn, that is. Him what makes himself out to be a little toy god, out in his little toy castle.... Here now. Where're you going already?"

Mocker had heard enough. He had never met Aristithorn, but he knew the name. Bragi had mentioned it often enough.

So the big bastard was recruiting old accomplices into his schemes, eh?

He slid hurriedly through the crowds. But he had wasted too much time with the street cleaner. He had lost them.

He traced them to the waterfront. Again he was too late. He

238

did learn that they had visited shipping firms and the master of the fishers' guild.

Boats. A lot of them. That had to be it.

Why would Bragi be in Necremnos trying to build a navy? It didn't make sense—unless he was on some adventure with Kavelin's army.

It seemed possible, with Argon a probable target, but reason failed him at that point. He could conceive of no cause for Kavelin to attack Argon. Nor could he figure how Bragi hoped to get away with it. Bragi had pulled off military miracles before, but this was unrealistic.

Mocker knew Argon. Ragnarson didn't. The brown man knew that the city boasted a population greater than that of Kavelin. The biggest force Kavelin could muster would simply vanish into the crowds....

But Bragi had Varthlokkur with him. That could make all the difference. It had for Ilkazar.

He might be guessing wrong. Bragi might need boats to ferry across the Roë.

He kept on the trail. This needed investigation.

It was time he started moving. He had been here for a month and a half accomplishing nothing. He had gambled away almost the entire fortune Lord Chin had provided him before transferring him here. He knew what he was supposed to do, but old habits, old thought patterns, died hard.

Chin would throw a fit next time they met. He should have been in Kavelin by now.

Hunger taunted him. He touched his purse. Empty again. It was a long walk to his room, where his final emergency reserve lay hidden. He considered stealing, didn't try. He wasn't as quick as he used to be. Age was creeping up. Soon he'd be able to commit robbery only by the blade. He hadn't lost his skill with a sword.

Cursing all the way, he trudged across town, retrieved his poke, bought a meal twice too big, downed it to the last drop of gravy. Overindulgence was his weakness, be it in food, gambling, or drink.

He finally overtook Aristithorn three days later. Bragi and Varthlokkur were long gone. Their visit had caused little public comment.

But something was happening.

The half-ruined stone pile palace of Necremnos's King had

come alive. The captains of Necremnos's corrupt, incompetent army swarmed there, coming and going with ashen faces. They were hobby soldiers, allergic to the serious practice of their craft. They hadn't signed on to die for their country, only to bleed its treasury. In the taverns soldiers patronized, there was both grumbling and anticipation.

Mocker was there, listening.

The subject was war with Argon. No one seemed to care why. Pessimists argued that penetrating Argon's defenses was impossible. Optimists verbally spent the booty they would bring home.

Regiments mustered at the Martial Fields south of the city, slothfully, in the tradition of all Necremnen state activity.

Mocker was there, too. He wasted no time insinuating himself into the camp following. He recruited a half-dozen young, enthusiastic, attractive girls capable of drawing the big-spending officers. He put them to work. And listened.

He quickly determined that the high command was stalling. The generals would never admit it, but they knew they were incompetent. They knew they couldn't manage forces like these against Argon. That city's army was poorly trained and equipped, and its officers as corrupt as they, but it did take war seriously.

Finally, sluggishly, like a bewildered amoeba, the Necremnen host stumbled southward, following the east bank of the Roë. A hundred thousand regulars, levies, allies, and plunder-hungry auxiliaries had responded to the raising of Pthothor's war baton. The movement went forward in dust and confusion. Despite Aristithorn and the King, the mass never did quite sort itself out.

Its first skirmish nearly resulted in disaster, though the enemy numbered no more than ten thousand. The regulars and levies almost panicked. But hard-riding auxiliaries from the plains tribes finally harried the Argonese border force into retreating, then swept ahead, burning and pillaging.

After the near-disaster the army began suffering seizures of near-competence. Pthothor hanged fifty officers, dismissed a hundred more, and demoted scores. When someone grumbled about losing traditional prerogatives, Pthothor referred him to Aristithorn.

No one challenged the cranky old wizard.

The army eventually blundered into the Valley of the Tombs,

where countless generations of Argonese nobility lay with their death-treasures. The Argonese came out to forestall looting and vandalism.

An unimaginative battle raged among the tombs and obelisks from dawn till dusk. Thousands perished. The thing came to no conclusion till the steppe riders broke free, circled the valley, and began plundering Argon's suburbs. They captured the pontoons to a dozen outlying islands. During the night the Argonese command brought up thousands of hastily mobilized citizens, and might have turned the tide had the news not come that the Queen's bastion had fallen.

Mocker whooped when he heard that Bragi's banners flew everywhere over the Fadem.

The Necremnens took courage. The Argonese began melting away, running to salvage what they could from their homes.

Pthothor pushed on, occupying islands which had failed to destroy their pontoons and bridges.

Mocker couldn't believe the confusion on both sides. This had to be why Bragi believed he could best Argon. Kavelin's troops were superb compared to these, and the quality of their leaders was incomparable.

Haaken and Reskird would be here, he knew, with the Vorgreberger Guards and the Midlands Light. Ahring and Altenkirk, too, probably with the Queen's Own and the Damhorsters. And, knowing Bragi's fondness for archers, TennHorst and the King's Memory Bows.... Maybe even the Breidenbachers and the Sedlmayr Light, and who knew what from the Guild....

The more Mocker thought, the bigger the army he conjured from imagination, till he pictured the Fadem crawling with the entire adult male population of Kavelin....

His depression began receding. He showed flashes of the Mocker of old, amazing his girls with his lighthearted nonsense. For a time he forgot the pressure....

The officers he entertained knew little about Bragi. Aristithorn and Pthothor were tight-lipped, trusting none of their staff. Mocker wished he could get the wizard into his tent.

His girls went along most of the time, but that they wouldn't tolerate. Aristithorn had a reputation. He took home girls who caught his fancy. They were never seen again.

So Mocker just tagged along, the officer's best friend, and awaited the opportune event.

His moment came soon after The Valley of the Tombs.

A Necremnen barge came meandering up a delta channel. Aboard were Bragi, his son, Varthlokkur, Haaken, Reskird, Trebilcock and his squat friend, and—Nepanthe!

They were hunting Aristithorn and Pthothor, allegedly to arrange coordinated action against Argon, most of which remained unconquered.

Mocker spotted Nepanthe long before she saw him. And couldn't believe what he saw. She was laughing with Haaken and Reskird about the clown army of their allies. The immaculate, perfectly disciplined troopers of the Queen's Own made the ragtag Necremnen loafers at Pthothor's headquarters look pathetic. Like poorly organized bandits.

Mocker eased as close as he could without revealing himself.

Nepanthe was supposed to be in the dungeons of Castle Krief.

He didn't see Ethrian, and that disturbed him more than his wife's presence. The boy seldom strayed from his mother's side. She wouldn't let him.

She was going to make Ethrian a mama's boy in spite of himself.

He was so intrigued by his wife's presence, and by trying to eavesdrop, that he ignored everything else—especially the others in Bragi's party.

Beyond being able to get into trouble anywhere, Aral Dantice had one noteworthy talent. He remembered. Now he remembered a dark face seen only momentarily in Necremnos when he noticed the same face peeping from an ornamental hedge. He whispered to Trebilcock.

It didn't occur to them that they shouldn't nab suspects on Necremnos's turf. They decided, they split, they drifted round till they could take the watcher from behind.

Mocker's first warning was a grip of iron closing on his shoulder.

He squealed, "Hai!" and jumped, kicked, sent Dantice sprawling—and found himself staring into the cold, emotionless eyes of Michael Trebilcock, along the blade of a saber.

He whipped out his own blade, began fencing. In silence, which was one of the most un-Mocker-like things he had ever done.

The clash of steel drew a crowd.

He had meant it to be a quick passage at arms, perhaps wounding the boy as he whipped by and fled across the yards and hedges. . . .

But Trebilcock wouldn't let him.

Mocker's eyes steadily widened. Trebilcock met his every stroke and countered, often coming within a whisker of cutting him. Nor did the younger man give him any respite in which to calculate, or regain his wind.

Trebilcock was *good.*

Mocker's skill with a blade was legend among his acquaintances. Seldom had he met a man he couldn't best in minutes.

This time he had met one he might not best at all. He managed to touch Trebilcock once in ten minutes, with a trick never seen on courtly fields of honor. But Trebilcock wasn't daunted, nor did he allow the trick a second chance.

Trebilcock couldn't be intimidated. Mocker couldn't perturb him. And that scared Mocker. . . .

"Enough!" Ragnarson shouted. "Michael, back off."

Trebilcock stepped back, lowered his guard. Perforce, Mocker did likewise.

He was caught.

Wham!

Nepanthe hit him at a dead run. "Darling. What're you doing? Where've you been?" And so on and so on. He couldn't get in a word.

"Come on," said Ragnarson. "Back to the barge. It's time we moved out. Nepanthe, keep a hold of him."

Mocker looked everywhere but at Bragi. He could feel Bragi searching his face.

He considered pretending amnesia, rejected it. He had given himself away by responding to Nepanthe. Some fast thinking was in order.

As he clambered aboard the barge, Ragnarson said, "Michael, you handle a blade damned good."

"Sir?"

"I've never seen anybody go to draw with Mocker."

"Wasn't a draw. He was tiring."

"That's why I stopped you. Where'd you learn?"

"My father's fencing master. But I'm not that good, really. At the Rebsamen. . . ."

"You impressed me. You men. Get this sonofabitch cast off. We've got to disappear before they find out I told them a pack of lies."

Nepanthe slackened her fussing. Mocker took the opportunity to look around.

He didn't like what he saw.

Haaken leaned against the deckhouse, a piece of grass between his dark teeth, staring. Varthlokkur stared from the bows. Reskird, directing the bargemaster, stared. They didn't have friendly eyes.

The safest course would be to tell ninety percent of the truth.

He was confused. Nepanthe was babbling all the news since his capture. It piled up dizzyingly. She and Ethrian had been kidnapped by agents of Shinsan? Possibly by Chin, his supposed rescuer. Though he tried, he couldn't make the evidence of his own kidnapping indict Chin. If the Tervola had stacked it against Haroun, he had stacked it perfectly. The accusation against Bragi could be due to misinformation....

When it came to question time he told the exact truth. All he held back was his feeling that it hadn't ended, that he still had to make up his mind which way to jump.

For the moment he leaned toward his old companions, despite bin Yousif's apparent perfidy. He could be on Bragi's side without being on Haroun's.

"Get those lazy bastards rowing," Bragi yelled at Reskird. "Damn." He slapped at a mosquito. It was everybody's hobby. "Let's get some miles behind us before those clowns change their minds."

Mocker frowned puzzledly.

"Stealing a march, old buddy. One from Haroun's book. Kind of hate doing it to Aristithorn. He's not a bad guy. The others.... They deserve whatever they get."

"Self, am wondering what old friend blathers about. Is getting more governmentalized all time, till cannot speak with meaning."

"I made a deal with the junta that took over when we got rid of the Fadema. We finished what we came for. We got Nepanthe. Only reason we've been hanging around is we couldn't get out. So I told them, let us go home, we'll leave without bothering you anymore. If they didn't, I'd whip on them from behind the whole time they were trying to handle Necremnos. Argon's in a bad way. They'd didn't have much

choice. My boys have been turning them every way but loose.
They didn't have any stomach left for storming the Fadem,
against my bows, with the Necremnens behind them. So they
agreed. Ahring and TennHorst are moving out already.

"Of course, if they saw a chance to plunder us back, they'd
jump on it. So hurry, damnit, Reskird."

"What about Necremnens?" Mocker asked.

Ragnarson grinned. "Their bad luck. They didn't show up
because we needed help. They came to plunder. And they'd jump
us too, if they thought they could get away with it. Old Pthothor
hedged every time I tried to pin him down about designating
plunder areas."

"Old friend is right. Trick is worthy of Haroun."

"Think they'll report to Pthothor?" Haaken asked after they
debarked and joined the escort Ahring had left for them. The
Necremnen rivermen were wasting no time heading upstream.

"Not unless he heads them off," Bragi replied. "Those boys
are scared. They're homeward bound."

Later, as they hurried along a road raised above rice paddies,
Visigodred's roc made a clumsy landing a few hundred yards
ahead. Marco tumbled off, landed with a hearty splash and
heartier cursing. He came boiling up the embankment, blood in
his eye. He fell back. Sputtering, he tried again.

"Goddamned overgrown buzzard, you did that on purpose.
We're gonna bring this pimple to a head. You're lower than
snake puke, you know that, you big-ass vulture?"

He slipped again. Splash!

"Throw him a rope," Ragnarson suggested.

The bird quietly preened, ignoring everyone.

"I'm gonna carve out your gizzard and make me giblet stew,"
Marco promised. Soldiers helped him dry off. He bowed
mockingly toward Ragnarson.

"Got a word for you, chief," he said. "And that's get your butt
home. That creep Badalamen is kicking ass all over Hammad al
Nakir. And El Murid told him to wale on Kavelin next." He
snatched a lance from a trooper, rushed the bird, whacked it
between the eyes. "Listen, bird, if I wasn't allergic to
walking...."

Ragnarson waved his companions past and hurried onward.
Marco was still cursing when they passed out of earshot.

The army gulped huge distances daily. Ragnarson walked
himself, to demonstrate that anyone could manage. The column

became strung out. Plains riders came for a look, but withdrew
when they saw the Thing and the Egg prowling the column's
flanks.

Ragnarson halted near Throyes, sent a party to the city for
supplies, and to inform the Throyens of Varthlokkur's presence.
The Throyens might have been tempted otherwise. The loot of
the Fadem was considerable.

Mocker went along.

He had been given plunder money and he knew Throyes of
old. He knew its gaming houses well.

It was in one of those that the Throyen Nine contacted him.

The emissary was fatter than he. Sweat rolled off him in
rivers, and he smelled. Flies loved him. Yet men made way for
him when he approached the table where Mocker, having an
apparent run of luck, was amazing the house with his bets.

The man watched during three passes of the dice. Then he
whispered, "I would speak with you, fat man."

"Hai! Is case of kettles calling pot black. Begone, ponderous
interrupter of. . . ."

"You want these people to check your dice?"

Mocker rattled the bones slowly, wondering if he could
resubstitute without the fat man noticing.

"Come. We have to talk."

Mocker collected his winnings, apologized to the onlookers.
The house didn't object, which was surprising. He was into it
deep.

He did manage to switch dice before departing.

He followed the fat man outside and into an alley. . . .

He grabbed the fatter man, laid a dagger across his throat.
"Self, being old skulker of alleys, take steps first, before trap
springs," he murmured. "Speak. Or second, redder mouth opens
under first."

The bigger man didn't seem perturbed. "I speak for the
Hidden Kingdom."

Mocker had wondered if the contact would ever come. He
hadn't done much to please Lord Chin.

"Speak." He didn't relax.

"The message comes from the Pracchia. A directive. Dispose
of the man named Ragnarson."

"And in case of possibility former adherent, self, has changed
mind?"

"They have your son. You choose which dies."

"Pestilential pig!" He drew the blade across the fat man's throat.

But when he turned to flee he found someone blocking his path. The man threw dust into his face.

He collapsed.

Endlessly repetitive, droning voices told him what he had to do....

"Here he is," Haaken called. Several Kaveliners joined him in the alley. "The fat guy must be the one he left with. Poul, look out for the Watch. This other one looks like Mocker nailed him before he went down."

A soldier knelt beside Mocker. "He's alive, Colonel. Looks like he got knocked in the head."

"Check his purse."

"Empty."

"Funny. It's not like him to get caught this easy. Here. Blood. Looks like he hurt a couple more, but they got away." He stirred a third body with his foot. Mocker's sword still pierced its heart. "What the hell was he doing down an alley with somebody he didn't know? With that much money on him? And why the hell didn't they kill him?"

"Colonel...." Poul shouted too late.

The Watch identified the man with Mocker's blade in him as a notorious cutpurse. The fat man was an important magistrate. They took detailed depositions. Their mucking around enraged the managers of the gaming house. The police wanted to hold Mocker. Blackfang fumed and stormed and threatened to have Varthlokkur roast their tongues in their mouths. They finally released Mocker on condition that his deposition would be presented as soon as he recovered.

When Mocker came round he found Bragi, Varthlokkur, Nepanthe, and Haaken waiting over him.

"What happened?" Bragi demanded.

"Give him a chance," Nepanthe pleaded. "Can't you see...?"

"All right. Get some of that soup down him."

Mocker took a few spoonfuls, desultorily, while trying to remember. Voices. Telling him he had to.... To what? Kill. Kill these men. Especially Bragi. And Varthlokkur, if he could.

He felt for his missing dagger.

The compulsion to strike was almost too much for him.

Varthlokkur eyed him suspiciously. He had been doing so since the island encounter. This would take cunning. He had to get himself and Nepanthe out alive.

He had to do it. For Ethrian.

His friend of more than twenty years, and his father.... Already the necessities gnawed his vitals like dragon chicks eating their ways out.

Varthlokkur was the illegitimate son of the last King of Ilkazar. He had killed his father, indirectly. It was the curse of the Golmune line. The sons slew the fathers.... Mocker had slain Varthlokkur once already, long ago, over Nepanthe.... But that spooky little man with the winged horse had revived him.

Mocker told his lies, and his mind strayed to his own son. Ethrian. Would he, too, someday, be responsible for the death of his father?

TWENTY-EIGHT: A Friendly Assassin

Marco brought the news to Ragnarson at Gog-Ahlan. Megelin had retreated to the Kapenrungs. The blood of half his followers stained the desert sands.

El Murid had suffered as bitterly. Nevertheless, he had ordered Badalamen to lead the ragged, war-weary victors into Kavelin.

Ragnarson increased the pace again.

As the army entered the Savernake Gap, Varthlokkur told him, "We have a problem. Mocker. Something was done to him. He's lying...."

"He's acting strange, yeah. Wouldn't you if Shinsan had had a hold of you?"

"Shinsan has had a hold of me. That's why I'm suspicious. Something happened in Throyes that he's not admitting."

"Maybe."

"I know what you're thinking. The spook-pusher is getting antsy about moving in on Nepanthe. Keep an eye on him anyway."

Later, after the army had passed Maisak and started eagerly downhill into its homeland, Varthlokkur returned. "Nepanthe is gone," he announced.

"What? Again?"

"Your fat friend did it this time."

"Take it from the beginning." Ragnarson sighed.

"He left her at Maisak."

"Why?"

"You tell me."

"I don't know."

"To remove her from risk?"

"Go away."

He didn't like it. Varthlokkur was right. Something had happened. Mocker had changed. The humor had gone out of him. He hadn't cracked a smile in weeks. And he avoided his friends as much as possible. He preferred remaining apart, brooding, walking with eyes downcast. He didn't eat much. He was a shadow of the man who had come to the Victory Day celebration.

Challenging him produced no answers. He simply denied, growing vehement when pressed. Haaken and Reskird no longer bothered.

Ragnarson watched constantly, hoping he could figure out how to help.

Kavelin greeted them as conquering heroes. The march lost impetus. Each morning's start had to be delayed till missing soldiers were retrieved from the girls of the countryside.

"I don't like it," said Haaken, the morning Bragi planned to reach Vorgreberg.

"What?" There had been no contact with Gjerdrum. Vorgreberg seemed unware of their approach.

"How many men have you seen?" Haaken's way was to let his listeners supply half the information he wanted to impart.

"I don't follow you."

"We've been back for three days. I haven't seen a man who wasn't too old to get around. When I ask, the people say they've gone west. So where are they? What happened to the garrison Gjerdrum was supposed to send to Karak Strabger?"

"You're right. Even the Nordmen are gone. Find Ragnar. And Trebilcock and Dantice. We'll ride ahead."

Varthlokkur joined them. They reached Vorgreberg in midafternoon. The city lay deserted. They found only a few poorly-armed old men guarding the gates. Squads of women drilled in the streets.

"What the hell?" Ragnarson exploded when first he encountered that phenomenon. "Come on." He spurred toward the girls.

Months in the field had done little to make him attractive. The girls scattered.

One recognized Ragnarson. "It's the Marshall!" She grabbed his stirrup. "Thank God, sir. Thank God you're back."

The others returned, swarmed round him, bawled shamelessly.

"What the hell's going on?" Ragnarson demanded. "You!" he jabbed a finger at the girl at his stirrup. "Tell me!" He seized her wrist. The others fled again, through quiet streets, calling, "The Marshall's back! We're saved."

"You don't know, sir?"

"No, damnit. And I never will unless somebody tells me. Where're the men? Why're you girls playing soldier?"

"They've all gone with Sir Gjerdrum. El Murid.... His army is in Orthwein and Uhlmansiek. They came through the mountains somehow. They might be in Moerschel by now."

"Oh." And Gjerdrum had little veteran manpower. "Haaken...."

"I'll go," Ragnar offered.

"Okay. Tell Reskird to pass the word to the men. One night is all we'll spend here. Nobody to wander. Go on now."

He watched his son, proud. Ragnar had become a man. He was nearly ready to fend for himself.

"Thank you, Miss. To the Palace. We'll fill in the gaps there. Varthlokkur, can you reach Radeachar?"

"No. I'll have to wait till he comes to me."

"Damn. Ought to take ages to cross those trails. How did they get through? Without Radeachar noticing?"

They hadn't. Badalamen had, simply, moved more swiftly than anyone had believed possible, and Gjerdrum, unsure if he were attacking Megelin or Kavelin, had waited too long to respond. Then, thoughtlessly, he had ordered his counterattacks piecemeal. Badalamen had cut him up. He had taken to Fabian tactics while gathering a larger force in hopes of blocking the roads to Vorgreberg.

Two days had passed since there had been any news from Gjerdrum. Rumor had a big battle shaping up. Gjerdrum had drawn every able-bodied man to Brede-on-Lynn in the toe of Moerschel, twenty-five miles south of the capital.

Ragnarson had passed through the area during the civil war. "Gjerdrum smartened up fast," he told Haaken. "That's the place to neutralize big attacking formations. It's all small farms, stone fences, little woods and wood lots, some bigger woods, lots of hills.... And a half-dozen castles within running distance. Lots of places to hide, to attack from if he loses, and no room for fancy cavalry maneuvers. Meaning, if that's the way this Badalamen wants to fight, he'll have to meet our knights head on."

Varthlokkur observed, "He'll refuse battle if the conditions are that unfavorable."

"He wants Vorgreberg. He'll have to fight somewhere. Us or Gjerdrum. The maps. They'll tell us." They moved to the War Room, set out maps of Moerschel and neighboring provinces. "Now," Ragnarson said, "try to think like Badalamen. You're here, over the Lynn in Orthwein. There's a big mob waiting at Brede. The ground is bad. What do you do to get to Vorgreberg?"

"I might split my strength," Trebilcock replied. "Hold Gjerdrum at Brede and circle another group around. If he has enough men. Gjerdrum couldn't turn even if he knew what was happening."

"Till we hear from the Unborn, or the dwarf, we're guessing. I'd bet he's outnumbered. Gjerdrum's probably mustered twenty, twenty-five thousand men. But Badalamen's soldiers are veterans."

Trebilcock fingered a map. "If he circles, he'll go east, up the Lynn." He traced the stream which formed the southern boundary of Moerschel. It ran toward Forbeck and the Gudbrandsdal Forest, approaching the Siege of Vorgreberg, emptying into the Spehe. As a river it wasn't much, yet it formed a barrier of sorts. An army crossing would be vulnerable.

Ragnarson joined Trebilcock. "Yeah. The hills and woods are rough in Trautwein. The roads would be easy to hold. But that don't mean he won't go that way. He's never been to Kavelin."

Haaken snorted. "You think Habibullah and Achmed were sleeping the last five years? He probably has maps better than ours."

"Yeah. Well. I agree with Michael. I'd come up the south bank of the Lynn too. So we'll get lost in the Gudbrandsdal. He should cross the Lynn at Norbury, where it runs into the Spehe. There're bridges both sides of town. We'll hit his flank while he's crowded up to cross. The woods aren't a hundred yards from the one bridge. They run right down to the banks of the Spehe."

The arguments continued. Ragnar returned, bringing Mocker.

"We're fussing too much," Bragi declared later that evening. "We can't plan to the last arrow. We shouldn't. We'd get too set on a plan. We'd try sticking to it no matter what. Sleep will do us more good. Mocker, the room you and Nepanthe used before should be empty. Make yourself to home."

Jarl Ahring arrived, drew Haaken aside. A moment later they approached Ragnarson. "Sir," said Ahring, his steely eyes evasive.

"Well?"

"A problem."

"What?"

"One of my sergeants wants to talk to you. A personal matter."

"Important enough that I should see him?"

"I think so," Haaken said.

"All right. Bring him up."

"I warned you," Haaken muttered as Ahring departed.

"Oh-oh. Ragnar and that girl. . . ."

"She's pregnant."

"Get Ragnar back here. He know?"

"Probably. I expect he made time to see her."

Sergeant Simenson was a tough buzzard Bragi wouldn't have wanted to face in a fracas. His scars showed he had been in the thick of it throughout his service, which had begun before Ragnarson's appearance in Kavelin. Nevertheless, he was as nervous as a child asked to explain a broken vase.

Haaken brought Ragnar. Ragnar nearly panicked when he saw Simenson.

Bragi growled, "Boy, you've been aping a man. Let's see if you can be one. You and the sergeant have some talking to do. Do it. I'll just listen—till somebody acts like an ass. Then I'll crack heads." Simenson he admonished, "It's too late to change anything. So confine yourselves to the future. Sergeant, did you talk to your daughter?"

Simenson nodded. He was angry, but was a good father, mainly worried about his daughter's welfare.

Ragnarson exited that confrontation admiring Ragnar. His son hadn't tried weaseling. He was truly enamored. He got down to cases and worked out a marriage agreement. Bragi couldn't have handled it as well himself. He hadn't with Fiana.

That was that. Except that the story leaked, and eventually won support for Ragnarson's Regency. Prataxis-generated tales showed Bragi as incorruptible. He wouldn't bend to benefit his own son.

It was late when he retired, a return to the field awaiting him beyond the dawn. He fell asleep hoping his men wouldn't waste themselves drinking and skirt-chasing, and knowing the hope vain.

Something wakened him. It wasn't a sound. The intruder moved with the stealth of a cat.

Dawn would soon break. The slightest of grey lights crept through the window.

He sensed rather than saw the blow, rolled away. The knife ripped through the bearskins and slashed his back, sliding over ribs and spine. He bellowed, pulled the covers with him to the floor.

The assassin pitched onto the bed.

Ragnarson staggered to his feet. Warm blood seeped down his back. He whirled the bearskins into the killer's face, wrapped him in his arms, bore him off the far side of the bed.

He was a short man, heavy, yet agile as a monkey. His knee found Bragi's groin as they hit the floor. Bragi grunted and clung, smashed the man's knife hand against the bed post. The blade skittered under a wardrobe.

The assassin kicked, gouged, bit. So did Ragnarson, and yelled when he could.

His antagonist was tough, skilled, and desperate. He began getting the best of it. Bragi grew faint. His wound was bleeding badly.

Where the hell were the guards. Where was Haaken?

He stopped blocking blows, concentrated on getting an unbreakable hold. He managed to get behind the assassin and slip an arm around the man's throat. He forced his hand up behind his own head. He arched his back and pulled with his head.

"Now I've got you," he growled.

It was a vicious hold. Applied suddenly, to an unsuspecting victim, it could break a man's neck.

The assassin kicked savagely, writhed like an eel out of water. He slapped and pounded with his free hand. Bragi held on. The assassin produced another dagger, scarred Ragnarson's side repeatedly.

Where the hell was Haaken? And Varthlokkur? Or anybody?

The murderer's struggles weakened.

That, Bragi suspected, was feigned.

Slowly he dragged the man upright....

The assassin exploded, confessing his fakery.

Enough, Bragi thought. He leaned forward till the man was nearly able to toss him, then snapped back with all the strength and leverage he could apply.

He felt the neck go through his forearm and cheek. He heard the crunch.

The door burst inward. Haaken, Varthlokkur, and several soldiers charged in. Torchlight flooded the room. Bragi let the would-be murderer slide to the floor.

"Oh, my gods, my gods." He dropped to his bed, wounds forgotten, tears welling.

"He's alive," said Varthlokkur, touching the pulse in Mocker's throat.

"Get Wachtel!" Bragi ordered.

Varthlokkur rose, shedding tears of his own. "Stretch out," he told Ragnarson. "Let me stop that bleeding. Come on! Move!"

Ragnarson moved. There was no resisting the wizard's anger.

"Why?" He groaned as Varthlokkur spread the cut across his back.

"This will lay you up for a while. Wachtel will use a mile of thread. Cut to the bone. Side, too."

"Why, damnit? He was my friend."

"Maybe because they have his son." The wizard's examination wasn't gentle. "I had a son once...."

"Damnit, man, don't open me up."

"... but I think he died in an alley in Throyes. The Curse of the Golmunes again. But for Ethrian he wouldn't be lying there now."

Wachtel bustled in. He checked Mocker's pulse, dug in his bag, produced a bottle, soaked a ball of wool, told Haaken, "Hold this under his nose." He turned to Bragi.

"Get hot water. Have to clean him before I sew." He poked and probed. "You'll be all right. A few stitches, a few weeks in bed. It'll be tender for a while, Marshall."

"What about Mocker?"

"Neck's broken. But he's still alive. Probably be better off dead."

"How come?"

"I can't help him. No one could. I could only keep him alive."

While Wachtel washed, stitched, and bandaged Bragi, Varthlokkur reexamined Mocker carefully. Finally, he ventured, "He won't recover. He'll stay a vegetable. And I don't think you'll keep him that healthy long. You'll have trouble feeding him without severing his spinal cord." His tone betrayed his anguish, his despair.

Wachtel also reexamined Mocker. He could neither add to nor dispute Varthlokkur's prognosis.

"He'd be better off if we finish him," the wizard said. His eyes were moist. His voice quavered.

Bragi, the doctor, and Haaken exchanged looks.

Ragnarson couldn't think straight. Crazy notions kept hurtling through his mind....

Mocker twitched. Weird noises gurgled from his throat. Wachtel soaked another ball of wool, knelt.

The others exchanged glances again.

"Damnit, I'll do it!" Haaken growled. There was no joy in him. He drew a dagger.

"No!" Varthlokkur snapped. His visage would have intimidated a basilisk.

"I'm the doctor," said Wachtel.

"No," the wizard repeated, more gently. "He's my son. Let it be on my head."

"No," Ragnarson countered. "You can't. Think about Nepanthe and Ethrian." He struggled up. "I'll do it. Let her hate me.... She's more likely to listen if it was me.... Doctor, do you have something gentle?"

"No," said Varthlokkur.

"It has to be done?" Bragi surveyed faces. Haaken shrugged. Wachtel agreed reluctantly. Varthlokkur nodded, shook his head, nodded, shrugged.

"You men," Ragnarson growled at the soldiers who had come with Haaken and the wizard. "If you value your lives, you'll never forget that he was dead when you got here. Understood?"

He knelt, grunting. The cuts were getting sensitive. "Doctor, give me something."

Wachtel reluctantly took another bottle from his bag. He continued digging.

"Hurry, man. I've got a battle to get to. And I'm about to lose my nerve."

"Battle? You're not going anywhere for a couple weeks." Wachtel produced tweezers. "Lay one crystal on his tongue. It'll take about two minutes."

"I'll be at the fight. If somebody has to carry me. I've got to hit back or go mad."

He fumbled the little blue crystal three times.

Ragnarson stared across the Spehe at Norbury. Tears still burned his cheeks. He had scourged himself by walking all the way. His wounds ached miserably.

Wachtel had warned him. He should have listened.

He glanced up. It might rain. He surveyed Norbury again. It was a ghost town. The inhabitants had fled.

He fretted, waiting for his scouting reports. The Marena Dimura were prowling the banks of the Lynn.

Again he considered the nearer bridge. It was a stout stone construction barely wide enough for an ox cart. A good bottleneck.

Behind him archers and infantry talked quietly. Haaken and Reskird roamed among them, keeping their voices down. Up the Spehe, Jarl and the Queen's Own waited to ford the river and hit the enemy's rear.

If he came.

Not today, Ragnarson thought as the sun settled into the hills of Moerschel. "Ragnar, tell the commanders to let the men pitch camp."

He was still standing there, ignoring his pain, when the moon rose, peeping through gaps in scurrying clouds. It was nearly full. Leaning on a spear, he looked like a weary old warrior guarding a forest path.

Trebilcock, Dantice, and Colonel Liakopulos joined him. No one said anything. This was no time to impose.

Mostly he relived his companionship with Mocker and Haroun. They, with the exception of Haaken and Reskird, had been his oldest friends. And the relationship with his fellow Trolledyngjans hadn't been the same. Haaken and Reskird were quieter souls, part-time companions always there when he called. There had been more life, more passion, and a lot less trust with the other two.

He reviewed old adventures, when they were young and couldn't believe they weren't immortal.

They had been happier then, he decided. Beholden to none, they had been free to go where and do what they pleased. Even Haroun had shown little interest in his role of exiled king.

"Somebody's coming," Trebilcock whispered.

A runner zipped across the gap between village and stream.
He splashed into the river.

"Get him, Michael."

Trebilcock returned with a Marena Dimura. "Colonel
Marisal, he comes, The Desert Rider, yes. Thousands. Many
thousands, quiet, pads on feets of his horses, yes."

"Michael, Aral, Colonel, pass the word. Kill the fires.
Everyone up to battle position. But quietly, damn it. Quietly."
Of the scout, "How far?"

"Three miles. Maybe two now. Slow. No scouts out to give
away."

"Uhm." Badalamen was cunning. He looked up. The gaps in
the clouds were larger. There would be light for the bowmen.

"Ragnar. Run and tell Jarl I want him to start moving right
away." Ahring's task would be difficult. His mounts wouldn't
like going into action at night.

The men had barely gotten into position. Shadows were
moving in the town. El Murid's horsemen came, leading their
mounts. Soon they were piling up at the bridge.

Ragnarson was impressed with Badalamen. His maneuver
seemed timed to reach Vorgreberg at sunrise.

A hundred men had crossed. Ragnarson guessed three times
that would have crossed upriver. Five hundred or so had piled
up on the south bank here.

"Now!"

Arrows hit the air with a sound like a thousand quail
flushing. Two thousand bowmen pulled to their cheeks and
released as fast as they could set nock to string.

The mob at the bridge boiled. Horses screamed. Men cursed,
moaned, cried questions. In moments half were down. Fifteen
seconds later the survivors scattered, trying to escape through
brethren still coming from the town.

"Haaken!" Bragi shouted. "Go!"

Blackfang's Vorgrebergers hit the chill Spehe. Miserably
soaked, they seized the far bank, formed up to prevent those
already over the bridge from returning. Once bowmen joined
them they forced it, compelling the horsemen to withdraw
upstream or swim back.

Badalamen reacted quickly.

Horsemen swept from the village in a suicidal, headlong
charge, startling the infantrymen screening Haaken's bridge-

head. Arrows flew on both sides. More horses went down by
stumbling than by enemy action.

Another force swept up the north bank of the Lynn, against
the Kaveliners there.

The south bank riders hit the thin lines protecting the Spehe
crossing, broke through. The arrows couldn't get them all.

The struggle became a melee. Ragnarson's troops, unaccustomed to reverses, wavered.

"Reskird!" Bragi called. "Don't send anyone else over.
Spread out. Cover them if they break." With Liakopulos,
Dantice, and Trebilcock helping, he scattered his forces along
the bank, made sure the archers kept plinking. Victory or defeat
depended on Ahring now.

Across the river Haaken Blackfang bawled like a wounded
bull, by sheer thunder and force of will kept the Vorgrebergers
steady. He seemed to be everywhere.

Something drifted down from the north. It glowed like a
small moon, had something vaguely human within it. . . .

The fighting sputtered. Both sides, awed, watched the
Unborn. Here, there, El Murid's captains silently toppled from
their saddles.

Haaken started bellowing again. He took the fight to the
enemy.

A huge man on a giant of a stallion cantered from the village.
In the moonlight and glow of the Unborn Ragnarson saw him
clearly. "Badalamen," he guessed. He was surprised. The man
didn't wear Tervola costume.

His appearance rallied his men. Ragnarson yelled at his
bowmen. Some complained they were short of arrows.

"It's in the balance," he told Trebilcock. "Tell Reskird to send
more men over."

Radeachar and Haaken cleared the west bank again. The
Midlanders didn't have to fight their way ashore.

"Wish I could get my hands on that bastard," Ragnarson said
of Badalamen. The reinforcements hadn't made much difference. Badalamen's men were, once more, confident of their
invincibility, of their god-given destiny.

For Radeachar had attacked the eldritch general with no
more effort than a bee stinging the flank of an elephant.
Badalamen had hardly noticed. His only response was to have
archers plink at the Unborn's protective sphere.

Soon, despite their numbers, the Kaveliners were again on the verge of breaking.

Then Ahring arrived.

Not at the point of greatest danger, but up the Lynn, at the other bridge.

He led with his heavy cavalry. His light came behind and on his flanks. The knights and sergeants in heavy plate were unstoppable. They shattered the enemy formation, leaving the survivors to the light horse, then came against Badalamen from behind. The news reached him scarcely a minute before the charge itself.

Here Ahring had more difficulty. He was outnumbered, faced an inspired leader, and had little room to gain momentum. Nevertheless, he threw the desert riders into confusion. Haaken and Reskird took immediate advantage.

Ahring and his captains drove for Badalamen himself, quickly surrounding the mysterious general and his boydguard.

Ragnarson laughed delightedly. His trap had closed. He had won. While his men slaughtered his enemies, he planned his march down the Lynn to relieve Gjerdrum.

In the end, though, it proved a costly victory. Though the last-gasp might of Hammad al Nakir perished, Bragi lost Jarl Ahring. Badalamen cut him down. The born general himself escaped, cutting his way through the Queen's Own as though they were children armed with sticks.

Radeachar was unable to track him.

His entire army he abandoned to the untender mercies of Kavelin's soldiers.

TWENTY-NINE: A Dark Stranger in the Kingdom of Dread

The dark man cursed constantly. The Lao-Pa Sing Pass, the Gateway to Shinsan, penetrating the double range of the Pillars of Heaven and the Pillars of Ivory, had no visible end. These mountains were as high and rugged as the Kratchnodians, and extended so much farther....

He was tired of being cold.

And damned worried. He had counted on using the Power to conceal himself in enemy territory. But there was no Power anymore. He had to slip around like a common thief.

His journey was taking longer than he had expected. The legions were active in the pass. He had to spend most of his time hiding.

When the Power had gone, he had learned, turmoil had broken loose in Shinsan, rocking the domains of several despotic Tervola. Peasants had rebelled. Shopkeepers and artisans had lynched mask-wearers. But the insurrections were localized and ineffectual. The Tervola owned swift and merciless legions. And, in most places, the ancient tyranny wasn't intolerable.

Haroun made use of the confusion.

He traveled east without dawdling, yet days became weeks, and weeks, months. He hadn't realized the vastness of Shinsan. He grew depressed when he reflected on the strength pent there, with its timeless tradition of manifest destiny. Nothing would stop these people if O Shing excited them, pointed them, unleashed them....

O Shing, it seemed, had hidden himself so far to the east that Haroun feared that he would reach the place where the sun rose first. Autumn became winter. Once more he trudged across snowy fields, his cloak pulled tight about him.

His horse had perished on the Sendelin Steppe. He hadn't replaced it. Stealing anything, he felt, would be tempting Fate too much.

He had entered Lao-Pa Sing thinking the journey would last a few hundred miles at most.

His thinking had been shaped by a life in the west, where many states were smaller than Kavelin. Shinsan, though, spanned not tens and hundreds, but thousands of miles. Through each he had to march unseen.

In time he reached Liaontung. There, based on the little he understood of Shinsan's primary dialect, he should find O Shing. And where he found O Shing he should find Mocker.

In happier circumstances he might have enjoyed his visit. Liaontung was a quaint old city, like none he had seen before. Its architecture was uniquely eastern Shinsan. Its society was less structured than at the heart of the empire. A legacy of border life? Or because Wu was less devoted to absolute rule than most Tervola? Haroun understood that Wu and O Shing were relatively popular.

O Shing's reputation didn't fit Haroun's preconceptions. The emperor and his intimates, Lang and Tran, seemed well-known and accessible. The commons could, without fear, argue grievances with them.

Yet O Shing was O Shing, demi-god master of the Dread Empire. He had been shaped by all who had gone before him. His role was subject to little personal interpretation. He had to pursue Shinsan's traditional destinies.

He was about to move. Liaontung crawled with Tervola and their staffs. Spring would see Shinsan's full might in motion for the first time since Mist had flung it at Escalon.

The holocaust was at hand. Only the direction of the blow remained in doubt.

O Shing favored Matayanga. Though he realized the west was weak, he resisted the arguments of the Tervola. Baxendala had made a deep impression.

Haroun hid in a wood near the city, pondering. Why did O Shing vacillate? Every day wasted strengthened his enemies.

He scouted Liaontung well before going in. Hunger finally moved him.

His eagerness for the kill had faded.

He hadn't heard one mention of Mocker yet.

He went in at night, using rope and grapnel to scale a wall

between patrols. Once in the streets he took it slow, hanging in shadows. Had it been possible, he would have traveled by the rooftops. But the buildings had steeply pitched tile roofs patched with snow and ice. Stalactites of ice hung from their ornate corners.

"Getting damned tired of being cold," he muttered.

The main streets remained busy despite the hour. Every structure of substance seemed to have its resident Tervola. Aides rushed hither and yon.

"It's this spring," he mumbled. "And Bragi won't be ready."

He stalked the citadel, thoughts circling his son and wife obsessively. His chances of seeing them again were plummeting with every step.

Yet if he failed tonight, they would be trapped in a world owned by O Shing.

It didn't occur to him that he *could* fail. Haroun bin Yousif never failed. Not at murder. He was too skilled, too practiced.

Faces paraded across his mind, of men he thought forgotten. Most had died by his hand. A few had perished at his direction. Beloul and El Senoussi had daggers as bloody as his own. The secret war with El Murid had been long and bloody. He wasn't proud of everything he had done. From the perspective of the doorstep of a greater foe the Disciple didn't look bad. Nor did his own motives make as much sense. From today the past twenty years looked more a process of habit than of belief.

What course had Megelin charted? Rumors said there was heavy fighting at home. But that news had come through the filter of a confused war between Argon and Necremnos which had engulfed the entire Roë basin, inundating dozens of lesser cities and principalities.

Argon, rumor said, had been about to collapse when a general named Badalamen had appeared and gradually brought the Necremnens to ruin.

Haroun wondered if O Shing might not be behind that war. It was convenient for Shinsan, and he had heard that a Tervola had been seen in Argon.

He could be sure of nothing. He couldn't handle the language well.

Liaontung's citadel stood atop a basaltic upthrust. It was a massive structure. Its thirty-foot walls were of whitewashed brick. Faded murals and strange symbols, in places, had been painted over the whitewash.

The whole thing, Haroun saw after climbing seventy feet of basalt, was roofed. From a distance he had thought that a trick of perspective.

"Damn!" How would he get in? The gate was impossible. The stair to it was clogged with traffic.

The wall couldn't be climbed. After a dozen failures with his grapnel he concluded that the rope trick was impossible too. He circled the base of the fortress. There was just the one entrance.

Cursing softly, he clung to shadow and listened to the sentries. He retreated only when certain he could pronounce the passwords properly.

It was try the main entrance or go home.

He waited in the darkness behind the mouth of a narrow street. In time a lone Tervola, his size, passed.

One brief, startled gasp fled the man as Haroun's knife drove home. Bin Yousif dragged him into the shadows, quickly appropriated his clothing and mask.

He paid no heed to the mask. He didn't know enough to distinguish Tervola by that means.

The mask resembled a locust.

In complete ignorance he had struck a blow more devastating than that he had come to deliver.

Haroun hadn't known that Wu existed. Nor would he have cared if he had. One Shinsaner was like another. He would shed no tears if every man, woman, and child of them fell beneath the knives of their enemies.

Haroun was a hard, cruel man. He wept for his enemies only after they were safely in the ground.

He mounted the steps certain something would go awry. He tried to mimic the Tervola's walk, his habit of moving his right hand like a restless cobra. He rehearsed that password continuously.

And was stunned when the sentries pressed their foreheads to the pavement, murmuring what sounded like incantations.

His fortune only made him more nervous. What should his response have been?

But he was inside. And everyone he encountered repeated the performance. He remained unresponsive. No one remarked on his behavior, odd or not.

"Must have killed somebody important," he mumbled. Good. Though it could have its disadvantages. Sooner or later someone would approach him with a petition, request for orders, or....

He ducked into an empty room when he spied another Tervola. He dared not try dealing with an equal.

His luck persisted. It was late. The crowds had declined dramatically.

He stumbled across his quarry by accident.

He had entered an area devoted to apartments. He encountered one with its door ajar and soft voices coming through....

A footfall warned him. He turned as a sentry entered the passage, armed with a crossbow. For a moment the soldier stared uncertainly.

Haroun realized he had made some mistake. The crossbow rose.

He snapped the throwing knife underhand. Its blade sank into the soldier's throat. The crossbow discharged. The bolt nipped Haroun's sleeve, clattered down the hallway.

"Damn!" He made sure of the man, appropriated his weapon, hurried back to the open door.

To him the action had seemed uproarious. But there was no excitement behind the door.

He peeped in. The speakers were out of sight. He slipped inside, peeped through a curtain. He didn't recognize the three men, nor could he follow a tenth of their argument. But he lingered in hopes he could learn the whereabouts of his target, or Mocker.

O Shing told Lang and Tran, "I'm convinced, Tran. There's too much smoke for there not to be fire. Chin's it. And Wu must be in it. You identify anyone else, Tran?"

"Feng and Kwan, Lord." He used the Lord of Lords title.

Haroun stepped in.

"Wu!" the three gasped.

Haroun was the perfect professional. His bolt slew Lang before his gasp ended. He finished Tran a second later, with the knife he had thrown before.

O Shing hobbled around a bed, pulled a cord.

Haroun cursed softly.

"You.... You're not Wu."

Haroun discarded the locust mask. The cruel little smile tugged his lips as he cranked the crossbow.

"You!" O Shing gasped. He remembered who had harried him through the Savernake Gap. "How did you...?"

"I am the Brother of Death," Haroun replied. "Her blind brother. Justice."

Running feet slapped stone floors.

Haroun fired. The bolt slammed into O Shing's heart.

The dark man drew his sword and smiled his smile. Now there might be time for Bragi and the west. He was sad, though, that he hadn't found Mocker. Where the hell *was* that little tub of lard?

He couldn't know that his bolt had removed the only obstacle to Pracchia control of Shinsan. His action would have an effect exactly opposite his intent.

He fought. And broke through, leaving a trail of dead men.

He stayed to find and free Mocker.

He remained at liberty long enough to bloody the halls of that fortress, to learn that Mocker wasn't there, and had never been. Long enough to convince his hunters that he was no man at all, but a blood-drinking devil.

THIRTY: The Other Side

The Old Man watched dreamily as the Star Rider reactivated the Power and opened a transfer stream.

A gang tumbled through immediately. A bewildered boy and a maskless Tervola followed. Curses pursued them. Then a javelin flickered through, smashed into the Tervola's skull.

The Old Man and Star Rider froze, stunned. Then, cursing, the bent man scuttled after the boy. Catching him, he demanded, "What happened?" Panic edged his voice.

Everything was going wrong. The leukemia victim had expired. The Mercenary's Guild had cleansed itself. There had been no time to replace Pracchia members. Now Chin, his most valuable tool, lay dead at his feet. "Help him!" he roared at the Old Man, before the Fadema could answer his question.

The Old Man knelt beside the Tervola. It was hopeless. The javelin had jellied Chin's brain.

"Ragnarson," the Fadema whined.

"What? What about him?"

"He crossed the steppes. He made an alliance with Necremnos. He came down the Roë and attacked from boats. He captured the Fadem. We barely held on till transfer time."

The others began arriving. They milled around, trying to comprehend the latest disaster.

"Move along! Move along!" the Star Rider shouted. "Get to the meeting room." Badalamen came through. He looked dashing dressed as a desert general.

"Who's this?" the bent man demanded, indicating the boy.

"The fat man's son. His wife got away."

"Take him to the meeting room." He kicked Chin's corpse. "Incompetent. Can't get anybody to do anything right. Argon was supposed to be ready for war." Pettily, viciously, he used the Power to murder the Fadema's soldiers.

He asked the Old Man, "How will I ever get out of here?" Then, "Drag the bodies to Norath's pets." He kicked Chin again.

While working, the Old Man slowly put together the thought that he had never seen his master behave this irrationally.

He wandered to the meeting room once he finished, arriving amidst a heated discussion.

The setbacks were gnawing at Pracchia morale. The stumbling block, the man responsible for the delays, was O Shing. He wouldn't move west. Nor would he be manipulated.

"Remove him," Badalamen suggested.

"It's not that simple," the Star Rider replied. "Yet it's necessary. He's proven impossible to nudge. If he weren't more powerful than Ehelebe-in-Shinsan.... Most of the Tervola support him. And we've lost our Nine-captain there. He died without naming a successor. Who were the members of his Nine? We must locate them, choose one to assume his Chair. Only then can we take steps against O Shing."

"By then he may have moved west voluntarily," Norath observed.

"Maybe," the bent man replied. "Maybe. Whereupon we aid him insofar as he forwards our mission. So. We must proceed slowly, carefully. At a time when that best serves our western opponents."

"What about Argon?" the Fadema demanded.

"What can we do? You admit the city is lost."

"Not the city. Only the Fadem. The people will rally against them."

"Maybe. Badalamen."

The born general said, "Megelin has been stopped. It was difficult and expensive. It will continue to be difficult and expensive if El Murid is to be maintained. The numbers and sentiment oppose him. But it can be done."

"The point was to weaken that flank of the west. That's been accomplished. Continued civil war will debilitate the only major western power besides Itaskia."

"There will be nothing left," Badalamen promised.

"Win with enough strength left to invade Kavelin," said the bent man. "Seize the Savernake Gap. Make of yourself an anvil against which we can smash Ragnarson when we come west."

After the meeting the Star Rider went into seclusion, trying to reason how his latest epic could be brought back under control. At last he mounted his winged steed and flew west, to examine Argon.

He drifted over the war zone and cursed. It was bad. Not only had Ragnarson done his spoiling, he had extricated himself cheaply. The Argonese were too busy with the Necremnens to pursue him.

He fluttered from city to city, hunting Chin's little fat man. He finally located the creature in company with Ragnarson. He raced to Throyes, gave instructions to order the fat man to eliminate Ragnarson before Kavelin's army returned home. When Badalamen finished Megelin he could move north against limited resistance....

Then he butterflied about the west, studying the readiness, the alertness, of numerous little kingdoms. Some, at least, were responding to Varthlokkur's warning.

He was pleased. Western politics were at work. Several incipient wars seemed likely to flare. Mobilizations were taking place along the boundaries of Hammad al Nakir too, in fear that El Murid might reassume his old conqueror's dream.

The raw materials for a holocaust were assembling.

He nudged a few places, then returned to his island in the east. He began hunting Chin's replacement.

Lord Wu was initiated into the Pracchia minutes before Badalamen announced his defeat in Kavelin. Wu showed no enthusiasm for his role. Badalamen blamed a lack of reliable intelligence. Both men, supported by Magden Norath, petitioned the return of the Power.

"What can I do about it?" the bent man demanded. "It comes and goes. I can only predict it.... Fadema. Are you ready to go home?"

"To a ruin? Why?"

"It's no ruin yet. Your people are still holding out. Necremnos's leaders are too busy one-uping each other to finish it. A rallying point, a leader, a little supernatural help, should turn it around. Badalamen. Go with the Fadema. Destroy Necremnos. They're too stubborn ever to be useful. Then head west. Seize the Savernake Gap. Throyes will help."

Badalamen nodded. He had this strength, from the viewpoint of the bent man: he didn't question. He carried out his orders.

He was, in all respects, the perfect soldier.

"What supernatural aid?" the Fadema demanded. "Without the Power...."

"Products of the Power, my lady. Norath. Your children of darkness. Your pets. Are they ready?"

"Of course. Haven't I said so for a year? But I have to go with them, to control them."

"Take a half-dozen, then." He buried his face in his hands momentarily. To the Old Man, who sat silently beside him, he muttered, "The fat man. He failed. Or refused. Throw the boy to Norath's children."

A pale vein of rebellion coursed through the Old Man as he rose.

The boy gulped, shivered in the Old Man's grip. He stared across the mile-wide strait. A long swim. With desert on the farther shore.

But it was a chance. Better than that offered by the *savan dalage*.

Shaking, he descended to the stony beach.

It was the turning of the year and, the bent man hoped, the shifting of luck to the Pracchia. Wu would have finalized plans for the removal of O Shing. Badalamen's report on the war with Necremnos would be favorable....

The Pracchia gathered.

Badalamen's report could have been no better. Norath and his creatures had turned it around. When Shinsan marched, the Roë basin would be tributary to the Hidden Kingdom. The holocaust had swept the flood plain and steppes. Argon was closing in on Necremnos.

But Lord Wu didn't show. The Pracchia waited and waited for Locust Mask to come mincing arrogantly into the room.

Later the bent man wearily mounted his winged steed. His flight was brief. It ended at Liaontung.

THIRTY-ONE: Baxendala Redux

"Man, I don't know," said Trebilcock. He surveyed Ragnarson's captains.

"What's that?" Kildragon asked. Reskird was still grey around the gills from wounds he had received at Norbury. His left arm hung in a sling. Badalamen had overcome a dozen champions in fighting free.

"Might as well wait for everybody. Save telling it twice." Trebilcóck approached Ragnarson.

"Where's your shadow, Michael?"

"At his father's. Learning bookkeeping."

"Last summer took the vinegar out of him, eh?"

"His father claims it gave him perspective. What I wanted to say.... I should tell everybody. Old friend of Aral's dad showed up while I was there. First man through the Savernake Gap this year."

"Oh? News?"

Ragnarson didn't ask if it was bad. There wasn't any other kind these days.

"Go ahead. Latecomers can hear it from somebody else." He pounded his table. "Michael has got some news."

Trebilcock faced the captains, stammered.

"I'll be damned," Bragi muttered. "Stage fright."

"I just talked to a man from Necremnos." Michael eyed his audience. Half he didn't know. Many were foreign military officers. Most of his acquaintances were recovering from wounds. Gjerdrum still couldn't walk without help. He'd had a savage campaign of his own.

"He says Argon is kicking Necremnos all over the Roë basin. The Fadema reappeared with a general named Badalamen and a wizard named Norath. Since then everything's gone her way."

A murmur answered him.

"Yes. The same Badalamen we whipped a couple months ago. But Norath, even without the Power, was the real difference." He glanced into the shadows where the Egg of God lurked. It seemed excited. Did it know Norath?

"Magden Norath?" Valther asked.

"Yes."

"I heard about him in Escalon. The Monitor exiled him for undertaking forbidden research. Everybody thought he was dead."

"He's running some nasty creatures ahead of the Argonese army," Trebilcock continued. "The worst is called a *savan dalage*."

"Means 'beasts of the night' in Escalonian," Valther interjected.

"They're supposedly invulnerable. They prowl at night, killing everything. Aristithorn has only found one way to control them. He lures one into a cave or tomb and buries it."

"I hope our friends from the Brotherhood can find a better solution," said Ragnarson. "I expect we'll get a look at them ourselves. Anything else, Michael?"

"Necremnos probably won't last through spring."

"Anything about our friend in the mask?"

"No. But the man said there's been a palace revolution in Shinsan. O Shing was killed. The Tervola are feuding."

"Varthlokkur. That good or bad?"

The wizard stepped up behind Ragnarson. "I don't know enough about what's happening to guess."

"Mist?"

The woman sat in an out-of-the-way seat. When she rose, the foreigners gawked. Few had encountered a beauty approaching hers.

"It's bad. They'd overthrow him only if he were too timid. The Tervola have grown anxious to grab Destiny. They're tired of waiting. As soon as they've decided who'll take over, they'll be here. The shame of Baxendala."

"Michael, bring this Necremnen to Varthlokkur. Varthlokkur, if you can get in touch with Visigodred, ask him to send Marco to see what's going on around Necremnos."

Visigodred had returned home after Badalamen's defeat in Moerschel. He was a genuine Itaskian count and couldn't abandon his feudal duties forever.

"I'll have Radeachar tell him." The wizard left with

Trebilcock. Varthlokkur was developing a liking for Michael simply because the man wasn't afraid of him.

Varthlokkur had lived for centuries in a world where mere mention of his name inspired terror. He was a lonely man, desperate for companionship.

Ragnarson peered after them, frowning. An hour earlier Varthlokkur had asked him to be best man at his wedding.

The pain hadn't yet eased. Thoughts of Mocker made him ache to the roots of his soul. And in the wounds his friend had inflicted.

Wachtel insisted he had healed perfectly, yet he often wakened in the night suffering such agony that he couldn't get back to sleep.

The temptation to drink, to turn to opiates, was maddening, yet he stubbornly endured the pain. Other voices whispered of his mission.

He turned to the Nordmen baron who was the Thing's observer here. "Baron Krilian, haven't you people found a candidate yet?"

Ragnarson hadn't visited the Thing since his eastern expedition. There hadn't been time. Derel Prataxis handled all his business with the parliament now.

"No, Regent. We've gotten refusals from everyone we've contacted. Quite offensive, some of them. I don't understand."

Ragnarson grinned. Men like Baron Krilian were why. "Anybody interested?"

"The Kings of Altea, Tamerice, Anstokin, and Volstokin have all hinted. Volstokin even tried to bribe old Waverly to push him in committee."

"Good to hear you and the old man agree on something." Waverly, a Sedlmayr Wesson, was the Regency's whip in the Thing.

"We're all Kaveliners, Marshall."

That truism had faltered during the civil war. Previously, the tradition had been to close ranks against outsiders. The Siluro minority had plotted with El Murid and Volstokin. The Nordmen had been in contact with Volstokin and Shinsan.

The Queen's side hadn't been above it either. Fiana had received aid from Haroun, Altea, Kendel, and Ruderin. Ragnarson himself had come south partly at the urging of the Itaskian War Ministry.

Itaskia wanted a strong, sympathetic government controlling

the Savernake Gap and lying on the flank of Hammad al Nakir. The then War Minister had been paranoid about El Murid.

Ragnarson turned to the agenda, finally got his neighbors to lend him token forces. As the group dispersed, he asked, "Derel, what'd we get?"

"Not much. Fifteen thousand between them." Prataxis leaned closer. "Liakopulos said the Guild will contribute. If you're interested. He says Hawkwind and Lauder are still angry about Dainiel and Balfour."

"I'll take whatever help I can get."

He didn't expect to best Shinsan this time. Not without a hell of a lot more help than he was getting.

That evening he visited his home in Lieneke Lane, where Ragnar and his new wife were staying with Gundar and Ragnarson's other children. The real ruler of the household was a dragoness named Gerda Haas, widow of a soldier who had followed him for decades, and mother of Haaken's aide. Bragi didn't visit his children much, though he loved them. The little ones exploded all over him, ignoring his guilt-presents to sit in his lap. Seeing them growing, seeing them become, like Ragnar, more than children, was too depressing. They stirred too many memories. Maybe once the pain of Elana's loss finally faded. . . .

Marco arrived two weeks later. He had overflown the middle east. He brought no good news.

Necremnos had fallen. The Roë basin was black with Shinsan's legions. Tervola had allied with Argon and Throyes. The Throyens were camped at Gog-Ahlan.

O Shing *was* dead. And, apparently, Chin as well. The latest master of the Dread Empire was a Ko Feng. Varthlokkur spoke no good of him. Mist called him a spider.

"How did they get out?" Bragi demanded. "Marco says the Lao-Pa Sing is still snowed in."

"Transfers," Varthlokkur replied. "The Power has been coming and going, oscillating wildly, for months. They must be sending people through with every oscillation. They seem random, but maybe Feng can predict them."

"They'll come early, then. Damn. We might not get the crops planted."

He planned to meet Shinsan as he had before, at the most defensible point in the Savernake Gap west of fortress Maisak. Baxendala.

Work there had been going forward all winter, when weather

permitted. Civilians had been removed to Vorgreberg. Karak Strabger was being strengthened. New fortifications were being erected. Earthen dams were being constructed to deepen the marshes and swamps which formed a barrier across part of the Gap. A major effort was being made to construct traps and small defensive works which would hold the enemy while bowmen showered them with arrows, and siege engines bombarded them from their flanks.

Farther east, at Maisak—unreachable now—the garrison were striving to make the Gap impassable there. The fortress had fallen but once in its history, to Haroun, who had grabbed it by surprise while it was virtually ungarrisoned.

Ragnarson didn't expect it to survive this time. He did hope it would hold a long time.

Every minute of delay would work to Kavelin's advantage. Every day gained meant a better chance for getting help.

Wishing and hoping. . . .

It wasn't the season of the west. Already Feng's Throyen allies were at the drudgery of opening the Gap road. They brought Feng to Maisak a week early.

Ragnarson stood in the parapet from which he had directed the first battle of Baxendala. His foster brother leaned on the battlements. General Liakopulos snored behind them. Varthlokkur paced, muttering. Below Karak Strabger soldiers worked on the defenses. Fifty thousand men, half Kaveliners. Five thousand Mercenaries, Hawkwind himself commanding. Nineteen thousand from Altea, Anstokin, Volstokin, and Tamerice, the second-line states. The remainder were Itaskian bowmen, a surprise loan. They would make themselves felt.

Wagons swarmed behind the ranked earthworks, palisades, traps, incomplete fortifications. Long trains labored up from the lowlands. Baxendala had been converted to a nest of warehouses.

Bragi meant to compel Feng to overcome an endless series of redoubts in close fighting, under a continuous arrowstorm. Attrition was his game.

Marco said there would be twenty-eight legions supported by a hundred thousand auxiliaries from Argon, Throyes, and the steppe tribes. Ragnarson couldn't hope to turn such a horde. He aimed only to cut them up so badly they would have bitter going after they broke through.

Bragi wasn't watching the work. He stared eastward, over the peaks, at a pale streamer of smoke.

It was a signal from Maisak. While it persisted the fortress held.

Ragnarson used mirror telegraphy and carrier pigeons too. Shinsan had learned. The Tervola brought dismantled siege engines. For a week they pounded Maisak. The Marena Dimura reported encounters with battered patrols which had forced the Maisak gauntlet. They finished those patrols.

Those little victories hardly mattered. The patrols were forerunner driblets of the deluge.

"Smoke's gone!" Liakopulos ejaculated.

The mirror telegraph went wild.

"Damn! Damn-damn-damn! So soon." Ragnarson turned his back, waited for the telegraphists to interpret.

It was a brief, unhappy message. *Maisak betrayed. TennHorst.*

The last pigeon bore a note almost as terse. *Enemy led over mountains into caverns. Last message. Good luck. Adam TennHorst.*

It spoke volumes. Treachery again. Radeachar hadn't rooted it all out.

"Varthlokkur, have Radeachar check everybody out again. A traitor in the right place here would be worth a legion to them."

The weather was no ally either. A warm front accelerated the snow melt. Bragi's patrols reported increasingly savage skirmishes.

Then Ko Feng attacked.

Two things were immediately apparent. Shinsan had indeed noted the lessons of the previous battle. And the Tervola hadn't understood them.

Cavalry had ruined O Shing. So cavalry came down the Gap, steppe riders who had come for the plunder of the west.

Ragnarson countered with knights. Though grossly outnumbered, they sent the nomads flying, amazed at the invincibility of western riders.

Three days later it was an infantry assault by the undisciplined hordes of Argon and Throyes. Again the knights carried the day. The slaughter was terrible. Hakes Blittschau, an Altean commanding Ragnarson's horse, finally broke off the pursuit in sheer exhaustion.

Feng tried again with every horseman he could muster. Then he used his auxiliary infantry again. Neither attack passed Blittschau. The troops in the redoubts grumbled that they would never see the enemy.

When knights fought men untrained and unequipped to meet them, casualty ratios favored the armored men ridiculously. In five actions Blittschau killed more than fifty thousand of the enemy.

Ravens darkened the skies over the Gap. When the wind blew from the east the stench was enough to gag a maggot. After each engagement the Ebeler ran red.

Blittschau lost fewer than a thousand men. Many of those would recover from their wounds. Armor and training made the difference.

"Feng must be crazy," Ragnarson mused. "Or wants to rid himself of his allies."

Liakopulos replied, "He's just stupid. He hasn't got one notion how to run an army."

"A Tervola?"

"Put it this way. He's not flexible. The pretty woman. Mist. Says they call him The Hammer. Just keeps pounding till something gives. If it doesn't, he gets a bigger hammer. He's been holding that back."

"I know." Twenty-eight legions. One hundred seventy thousand or more of the best soldiers in the world.

When Feng swung that hammer, things would break.

The legions came.

The drums began long before dawn, beating a cadence which shuddered the mountains, which throbbed like the heartbeat of the world.

The soldiers in the works knew. They would meet the real enemy now, dread fighters who had been defeated but once since the founding of the legions.

Ragnarson gave Blittschau every man and horse available.

The sun rose, and the sun set.

Hakes Blittschau returned to Karak Strabger shortly before midnight, on a stretcher. His condition reflected that of his command.

"Wouldn't believe it if I didn't see it," Blittschau croaked as Wachtel cleansed his wounds. "They wouldn't give an inch. Let us hit them, then went after the horses till they got us on the ground." He rolled his head in a negative. "We must've killed twenty. . . . No, thirty, maybe even forty thousand. They wouldn't budge."

"I know. You can't panic them. You have to panic the Tervola." Ragnarson was depressed. Feng had broken his most valuable weapon. Blittschau had salvaged but five hundred men.

The drums throbbed on. The hammer was about to fall again.

It struck at dawn, from one wall of the canyon to the other. Stubbornly, systematically, the soldiers in black neutralized the traps and redoubts, filled the trenches, demolished the barriers, breached the palisades and earthworks. They didn't finesse it. They simply kept attacking, kept killing.

Ragnarson's archers kept the skies dark. His swordsmen and spearmen fought till they were ready to drop. Feng allowed them respites only when he rotated fresh legions into the cauldron.

The sun dropped behind the Kapenrungs. Bragi sighed. Though the drums sobbed on, the fighting died. His captains began arriving with damage reports.

Tomorrow, he judged, would be the last day.

The archers had been the stopper. Corpses feathered with shafts littered the canyon floor. But the arrows were nearly gone. The easterners allowed no recovery of spent shafts.

Mist was optimistic, though. "Feng has gone his limit," she said. "He can't waste men like this. The Tervola won't tolerate it. Soldiers are priceless, unlike auxiliaries."

She was correct. The Tervola rebelled. But when they confronted Feng they found. . . .

He had yielded command to a maskless man named Badalamen. With Badalamen were two old-timers: a bent one in a towering rage, and another with dull eyes. And with them, the Escalonian sorcerer, Magden Norath.

The bent man was more angry with himself than with Feng. His tardiness had given Feng time to decimate Shinsan's matchless army.

Feng grudgingly yielded to the Pracchia. The transition was smooth. Most Tervola chosen to come west were pledged to the Hidden Kingdom.

At midnight the voice of the drums changed.

Ragnarson exploded from a restless sleep, rushed to his parapet. Shinsan was moving. No precautions could completely squelch the clatter.

Reports arrived. His staff, his wizards, his advisors crowded onto the parapet. No one could guess why, but Shinsan was abandoning positions they had spent all day taking. Sir Tury Hawkwind and Haaken attacked on their own initiative.

"Mist. Varthlokkur. Give me a hint," Ragnarson demanded.

"Feng's been replaced," Mist said.

"Yeah? Okay. But why back down?"

"Oh!" Varthlokkur said softly.

Mist sighed. "The Power...."

"Oh, Hell!"

It was returning. Ragnarson decided he was done for.

The Unborn streaked across the night. Beneath it dangled Visigodred. After delivering the shaken wizard, it communed with Varthlokkur. "Gather the Circle!" Varthlokkur thundered. "Now! Now! Hurry!"

The monster whipped away too swiftly for the eye to follow.

Visigodred said, "Something is coming down the Gap. Creatures this world has never before seen. The ones Marco said turned Argon's war around. We can't stop them."

"We will!" Varthlokkur snapped. "The Unborn will! We have to." He, Visigodred, and Mist staggered. "The Power!" they gasped.

"Clear the parapet," Varthlokkur groaned, handling it more easily than the others. "We need it."

Kierle the Ancient arrived, followed by the Thing and Stojan Dusan. Radeachar rocketed in with The Egg of God. Ragnarson hustled his people downstairs.

He didn't want to stay either. There was little he dreaded so much as a wizard's war. But his pride wouldn't let him turtle himself.

Screams erupted from the canyon.

"They're here. The *savan dalage*," said Visigodred. "Varthlokkur. Unleash the Unborn before they gut us." He threw his hands overhead, chanted. A light-spear stabbed from his cupped hands. He moved them as though he were directing a mirror telegrapher. The earth glowed where the light fell. "Too weak," he gasped.

Here, there, Ragnarson glimpsed the invaders. Some were tall, humanoid, fanged and clawed, like the trolls of Trolledyngian legends. Some were squat reptilian things that walked like men. Some slithered and crawled. Among them were a hundred or so tall men who bore ordinary weapons. They reminded him of Badalamen.

And there was something more. Something shapeless, something which avoided light like death itself.

Radeacher swooped and seized one, soared into the night. Ragnarson saw an ill-defined mass wriggling against the stars.

"*Savan dalage*," Visigodred repeated. "They can't be killed."

Radeachar departed at an incredible speed.

"He'll haul it so far away it'll take months to get back," Varthlokkur said.

"How many?" Ragnarson asked.

"Ten. Fifteen. Be quiet. It begins."

A golden glow began growing up the Gap.

All the Circle had arrived. They babbled softly, in their extremity even welcoming Mist to their all-male club. This was no time for masculine prerogatives. Their lives and souls were on the gaming table.

Radeachar reappeared, undertook another deportation.

Ragnarson briefly retreated to the floor below, where a half dozen messengers clamored for his attention.

His formations were shambled. His captains wanted orders. The troops were about to panic.

"Stand fast," he told them. "Just hang on. Our wizards are at work."

Back on the parapet he found the human sorcerers all imitating Visigodred, using light to herd the *savan dalage*.

The Egg, Thing, and Zindahjira concentrated on the remaining monsters.

"The men-things," Zindahjira boomed. "They're immune to the Power."

Ragnarson remembered Badalamen's indifference to Radeachar.

"They're human," he observed. "Sword and spear will stop them."

True. His men were doing so. But, like Badalamen, the creatures were incredible fighters, as far beyond the ordinary soldier of Shinsan as he was beyond most westerners.

"Arrows!" he thundered from the parapet. "Get the bowmen over there!" No one heard. He ducked downstairs to the messengers.

The struggle wore a new face when he returned. The Tervola had unleashed a sorcery of their own.

At first he believed it the monster O Shing had raised during

First Baxendala. The Gosik of Aubuchon. But this became a burning whirlwind with eyes.

Mist responded as she had then. A golden halo formed in the night. Within its confines an emerald sky appeared. From that a vast, hideous face leered. Talons gripped the insides of the circle.

The halo spun, descended. The ugly face opened a gross mouth, began biting.

The screams of the ensuing contest would haunt Bragi's dreams forever. Yet the struggle soon became a sideshow. Other Tervola-horrors rose. Ragnarson's sorcerers unleashed terrors in response.

Through it all the Unborn pursued its deportations in a workmanlike manner.

The whirlwind and halo rampaged up and down the Gap, destroying friend and foe. Once they crashed into Seidentop, the mountain opposite Karak Strabger. The face of the mountain slid into the canyon. In moments the defense suffered more than in all the previous fighting.

Shinsan tasted the bitterness of loss too. Stojan Dusan conjured a seven-headed demon bigger than a dozen elephants, with as many legs as a centipede. Each was a weapon.

"It's the battle for Tatarian all over again," someone murmured. Ragnarson turned. Valther had come up. He had served Escalon in its ill-fated war with Shinsan.

The mountains burned as forests died. Smoke made breathing difficult.

"Pull out while you can," Valther advised. "Use this to make your retreat."

"No."

"Dead men can't fight tomorrow. Every death is a brick in his house of victory." Valther stabbed a finger.

High above, barely discernible, a winged horse drifted on updrafts.

"That damned old man again," Bragi growled.

Visigodred's apprentice suddenly struck from even higher. The winged horse slipped aside at the last instant. Marco kept dropping till Bragi was sure he would smash into a flaming mountainside. But the roc whistled along Seidentop's slope, used its momentum to hurl itslef into the undraft over another fire.

Surprise gone, Marco tried maneuver. And proved he had

paid attention to his necromantic studies. His sorceries scarred the night air. The winged horse weaved and dodged and fought for altitude.

Ragnarson asked Valther, "Who's winning? The battle."

"Us. Mist and Varthlokkur make the difference. Watch them."

Oh? Then why the admonition to get out?

They were holding the Tervola at bay and still grabbing moments for other work. Varthlokkur developed the Winterstorm construct. Mist opened and guided another, smaller halo. It cruised over the defensive works, snatching the creatures of Magden Norath. It even gobbled one *savan dalage*. Just one.

"Must have a bad taste," Ragnarson muttered sardonically.

Radeachar returned from a trip east and was unable to find another unkillable. He joined the assault on the Tervola.

"We've got them now," Valther crowed, and again Bragi wondered at his earlier pessimism.

The Tervola went to the defensive. Above, Marco harried the winged horse from the sky.

But, as Valther had meant, that old man *always* had another bolt in his quiver.

Fires floated majestically in from the eastern night, from beyond the Kapenrungs, like dozens of ragged-edged little moons.

Mist spied them first. "Dragons!" she gasped.

"So many," Valther whispered. "Must be all that're left."

Most dragons had perished in the forgotten Nawami Crusades.

Straight for the castle they came. The glow of their eyes crossed the night like racing binary stars. One went for Marco. He ran like hell.

The Unborn took over for him.

The leaders of those winged horrors were old and cunning. *They* remembered the Crusades. They remembered what sorcery had done to them then, when they had served both causes, fighting one another more often than warlocks and men. They remembered how to destroy creatures like those atop the castle.

"Get out of here!" Valther shouted. "You can't handle this."

Bragi agreed. But he dallied, watching the saurians spiral in, watching Radeachar drive the winged horse to earth behind Shinsan's lines.

The Unborn turned on its dragon harrier.

The beast's head exploded. Its flaming corpse careened down the sky, crashed, thrashing, into a blazing pine grove. Flaming trunks flung about. A terrible stench filled the Gap.

Varthlokkur completed his Winterstorm construct as a dragon reached the tower.

Ragnarson dove downstairs, collecting bruises and a scorching as dragon's breath pursued him.

"Messengers, Valther," he gasped. "You were right. It's time to cut our losses."

Ragnarson's army, covered by the witch-war, withdrew in good order. By dawn its entirety had evacuated Baxendala. Shinsan had redeemed its earlier defeat.

The wizard's war ended at sunrise, in a draw. Kierle the Ancient, Stojan Dusan, and the Egg had perished. The others scarcely retained the strength to drag themselves away.

Radeachar had salvaged them by driving the dragons from the sky.

The Tervola were hurt too. Though they tried, they hadn't the strength or will to follow up.

The bent old man ordered Badalamen to catch Ragnarson, but Badalamen couldn't break Bragi's rear guard.

Ragnarson had bought time. Yet he had erred in not trying to hold.

As he debouched from the Gap he encountered eastbound allies from Hellin Daimiel, Libiannin, Dunno Scuttari, the Guild, and several of the Lesser Kingdoms. Auric Lauder commanded about thirty thousand men. Ragnarson borrowed Lauder's knights to screen his retreat.

He didn't try correcting himself. Baxendala was irrevocably lost. Shinsan still outnumbered him three to one, with better troops.

Lauder followed the example of previous allies and accepted Bragi as commander.

In thought, Ragnarson began laying the groundwork for the next phase, Fabian, accepting battle only in favorable circumstances, playing for time, trying to wear the enemy down.

THIRTY-TWO: Defeat. Defeat. Defeat.

Fahrig. Vorgreberg. Lake Turntine. Staake-Armstead, also called the Battles of the Fords. Trinity Hills, in Altea. The list of battles lost lengthened. Detached legions, supported by Magden Norath's night things, conquered Volstokin and Anstokin. Badalamen, by slim margins, kept overcoming the stubborn resistance of Ragnarson's growing army.

He reinforced his northern spearhead. It drove through Ruderin and curved southward into Korhana and Vorhangs. Haaken Blackfang, with a hasty melange of knights, mercenaries, and armed peasants, stopped the drive at Aucone. Ragnerson extricated himself from envelopment in Altea. Badalamen ran a spearhead south, through Tamerice, hoping eventually to meet the northern thrust at the River Scarlotti, behind Bragi.

Reskird Kildragon harried the Tamerice thrust but refused battle. Tamerice's army had been decimated in Kavelin.

Then Badalamen paused to reorganize and refit. He faced Ragnarson across a plain in Cardine just forty miles short of the sea and cutting the west in two.

In the Kapenrungs, Megelin bin Haroun chose to ignore the threat behind him. He launched another campaign against Al Rhemish and El Murid.

"Damn! Damn! Damn!" Ragnarson swore when the news arrived. "Don't he have a lick of sense?" He had counted on Megelin thinking like his father, had anticipated that the Royalists would conduct guerrilla war behind Badalamen's main force.

He sat before his tent with Liakopulos, Visigodred, his son, and officers from most of the nations which had sent troops.

This ragtag army was the biggest gathered since the El Murid Wars.

"I think we've done well," said Liakopulos. Hawkwind and Lauder nodded. "We've managed to keep from being destroyed by the best army in the world."

Lord Hartteoben, an Itaskian observer, agreed. "The persistence of your survival continues to amaze everyone."

"Uhm." Bragi surveyed his army.

It wasn't especially dangerous, despite its size. The demands of constant retreat hadn't given him time to organize and integrate. New contingents had to be thrown in immediately. Often his captains didn't speak the language of their neighbors in the line.

"Why shouldn't he?" Ragnar asked. "El Murid *is* Shinsan's client now." He stirred the fire with the tip of a crutch. He had been injured at Aucone. Haaken had sent him south to keep him from getting himself killed. He was too impetuous.

"Maybe. But I wish he'd helped us instead. Haroun would've seen that getting El Murid ain't worth a damn if the rest of the west goes."

At least the west now believed an eastern threat existed. But mobilizations hadn't helped yet. A battalion arrived now, a regiment then. Too little relative to the task.

The political question of who should be the supreme commander hadn't yet been posed. That the generals of major nations should be commanded by the Marshall of a country village-state like Kavelin seemed implausible to Ragnarson. He considered Hawkwind the best man. But his allies remained impressed with his ability to evade disaster.

Hawkwind didn't want the job anyway. He had had enough of command politics during the El Murid Wars.

"When'll we see help from Itaskia?" Bragi asked Visigodred. The wizard had been home several times and been able to produce just Lord Hartteoben and another thousand bowmen. Itaskia was husbanding her resources to fight on home ground.

Ragnarson had rebuilt his cavalry advantage. He pressed it mercilessly, compelling the legions to remain close and their allies to stay within the protective umbrella of Badalamen's genius.

Marco and Radeachar hunted and exterminated the creatures of Magden Norath—excepting the *savan dalage*, the disease without a cure. The Tervola transported them back almost as fast as Radeachar hauled them away. Varthlokkur and the Unborn tried burying them in caverns on islands in the ocean, but even there the Tervola found them.

Shinsan's sorcerers had to be exterminated before the *savan dalage* could be solved permanently.

The Tervola wouldn't permit that.

For the time being, then, there was a thaumaturgic impasse.

At least, Bragi thought, if defeated, he would fall to force of arms.

The nearest town was Dichiara. The battle took its name.

It was the nadir of Ragnarson's career.

Badalamen announced himself with drums. Always Shinsan marched to the voice of drums, grumbling directions to legion commanders.

Bragi had had two weeks to prepare, to plan. He was as ready as time permitted.

Varthlokkur, privately, told him, "Back off. The omens aren't right."

Ragnarson remained adamant. "This far and no farther. This's the best position for leagues around. We'll hurt him here."

His army held a rough hill facing a plain on which cavalry could maneuver easily. His bowmen could saturate climbing attackers who survived the horsemen. Once Badalamen came to grips and drove him back, as was inevitable, he would withdraw into woods on the west slope, where Shinsan's tight formations would become less effective. He would re-form beyond the trees.

Attrition. That remained the game. Quick victory was out of the question. He worked against the day the power of the north took arms. Till then he had to stay alive.

His espionage was poorer than he thought.

Badalamen started his first wave.

Bragi, as always, responded with knights. That had worked well in every confrontation. He saw no reason to change.

Badalamen counted on that.

The knights swept over the plain—and into destruction ere striking a blow. Badalamen had cut a trench across his front, by night, and had camouflaged it.

The legions hit the tangle before the riders could extricate themselves. Half the knighthood of the coastal states and the Lesser Kingdoms perished.

Badalamen circled the debacle, rolled toward the hills. Ragnarson began falling back.

"I warned you," Varthlokkur said.

"Warned me, my ass! You could've been specific. Damned wizard never says anything straight out. Come on, Klaust. Get those men moving." He studied a map. "Hope we can ferry the Scarlotti. Else we're trapped at Dunno Scuttari."

The sun hadn't been up an hour. Radeachar, till now occupied deporting *savan dalage*, brought his first scouting report.

The legions in Tamerice weren't. They were racing north, having begun at sunset, and now were just ten miles away. They might beat him to the far side of the woods.

The withdrawal became a rout. Bragi desperately tried to keep control, to blunt the legions from Tamerice. The Guildsmen and his Kaveliners responded, but hadn't enough strength.

Their effort prevented total disaster. Most of the army escaped. Half reached the Scarlotti, where Ragnarson regained control and ferried them over.

Thousands of escapees joined Kildragon, who fled toward Hellin Daimiel.

Legions pushed south as far as Ipopotam, leaving enclaves at Simballawein, Hellin Daimiel, Libiannin, and Dunno Scuttari. The garrisons hadn't the strength to sally. The Itaskian Navy ran supplies in, as it had done during the sieges of the El Murid Wars.

Badalamen brought reinforcements through the transfers. Valther identified elements of seven legions not seen at Baxendala.

Badalamen beefed up the force in Vorhangs while facing Ragnarson across the Scarlotti near Dunno Scuttari. Blackfang strove valiantly, but hadn't the resources for success. He lost a battle at Glauchau, just three miles from Aucone. Agents of the Nines betrayed him. Haaken led the survivors westward.

Weeks passed. Late summer came. Though Badalamen drew heavily on transfers, most of his supplies and replacements came through the Gap. Again Ragnarson fought for time, trying to survive till winter isolated Badalamen.

The born general gathered boats and exchanged stares with Ragnarson. His Vorhangs expedition hammered Haaken back toward his brother.

The holocaust had come. Badalamen's auxiliaries erased towns, villages, crops. Winter's hunger would decimate the survivors.

Then Varthlókkur and Mist came to Ragnarson.

He stared guiltily across the broad Scarlotti, repeating, "This's my fault."

"Marshall, we've made a breakthrough. The biggest since Radeachar."

Bragi could imagine nothing capable of brightening the future. "You've compelled Itaskia to move?" Itaskia's noninvolvement stance was a bitter draught.

Varthlokkur chuckled. "No. We've found a way to scramble the transfer stream. We can intercede whenever they send."

"Oh? How long before they figure out how to stop you?"

"When they create their own Winterstorm."

"Maybe tomorrow, then. They're working on it. Because of the Unborn."

Varthlokkur smiled dourly. "He has orders to obliterate anybody researching it."

"Do whatever you want. Got to play every angle." Bragi turned, stared across the gleaming brown back of the river. How long till winter closed the Gap, giving him a chance to regain the initiative?

The Battle for the Scarlotti Crossing began with a massive, surprise thaumaturgic attack at midnight. The western army got badly mauled before Ragnarson's wizards reestablished the sorcerous stalemate.

By then legionnaires had landed. That, too, was a surprise. Bragi had anticipated Badalamen shifting his emphasis toward Haaken. Comimg straight into his strength seemed suicidal.

It was. For a time. But superior training, superior skills, gradually told. Earthen ramparts grew around the beachheads. Ragnarson's counterattacks, hampered by a haphazard command structure and language barriers, fell short.

Haaken, just four leagues upriver, reported himself under heavy pressure. Several legions had crossed above him, marching into Kuratel.

Daylight exposed the grim truth. The frontal attack was a feint. Badalamen's main force had moved upriver.

Ragnarson saw the trap. The bridgeheads. They were weak enough to destroy, but strong enough to last days. If he yielded to the bait, a pocket would close behind him.

He had been outgeneraled again.

He offered his resignation. His allies and associates just laughed. Hawkwind suggested he get moving before Badalamen reaped the fruit of his maneuver.

Badalamen hadn't wanted to attack. Not here. The old man

had been adamant. Failure of the transfers had made quick victory imperative. Winter was a foe he could neither manipulate nor coerce.

Bragi took command. He set Hawkwind and Lauder to confine the bridgeheads. He sent help to Haaken to secure his flank, and flung his remaining horsemen after the spearhead plunging into Kuratel. His vast, confused mass of infantry he led in retreat again, up the Auszura Littoral, out of the pocket.

He adopted the Fabian strategy again. The Porthune crossings he cleared and abandoned without contest. Itaskia became his goal, winter his weapon of choice.

Legions caught him near Octylya. In the absence of Badalamen, Ragnarson proved he had *some* talent. He sucked them into a trap, beneath his bows, and annihilated twenty-five thousand legionnaires. But he didn't grow heady. He persevered in his strategy.

In early October he crossed the Great Bridge into Itaskia the City, where he, Mocker, and Haroun had spent much of their earlier lives.

Reskird Kildragon had problems. Some of the Rebsamen faculty were agitating for accomodation with Shinsan. It surpassed him.

Hellin Daimiel had withstood years of siege during the El Murid Wars. Those defenders had never lost spirit. And that enemy hadn't planned to obliterate them.

Kildragon couldn't convince the dons that Badalamen was truly destroying everything and everyone outside.

Chance had separated Prataxis from Ragnarson at Dichiara. Now he was Kildragon's assistant. He came to Reskird one autumn evening, pale as old sin.

"I've found the answer. Our own people. . . ."

"What?" The inevitability of failure had eroded Reskird's patience, making him a small, mean man, all snarl and bite.

"A Nines conspiracy. Here. At the Rebsamen. I stumbled on it. . . . I was on my way to see my antiquarian friend, Lajos Kudjar, about the Tear of Mimizan. I overheard an argument in the Library, in the east wing, where they keep. . . ."

"Skip the travelogue. Who? Where? How do we nail them?"

"In time, my dear man. This has to be handled properly. They have to be exposed carefully, every one identified. Else we risk turning Hellin Daimiel against us."

Kildragon stifled his temper and impatience. Survival

instinct reminded him that a politically satisfactory outcome was critical.

A perilous month passed. Three times traitors opened the city gates. One quarter was irrevocably lost.

Then the member of the Pracchia, tricked with false directives, made his misstep. Prataxis made certain the right people were witnesses.

The mob destroyed the Rebsamen Nine.

Searching at Ragnarson's insistence, Radeachar uncovered a conspiracy in Itaskia.

The Greyfells group, an opposition party, had used treason as a political tool since the El Murid Wars. Radeachar destroyed every conspirator.

Itaskia's semineutral stance ended instantly.

Political victories, tactical defeats.

The big battle loomed. The bent man gathered his might on the south bank of the Silverbind. The contest, if he won, would shatter the west. Heads bent together. Famous men, old enemies from smaller wars, shared the map tables.

They dared not lose.

Yet winning would prove nothing. Not against Badalamen, armed with Shinsan's resources.

THIRTY-THREE: Itaskia

"When?" Ragnarson asked Visigodred. He and the lean Itaskian watched Badalamen's army from the Southtown wall. Southtown, a fortified bridgehead of Itaskia the City, stood on the south bank of the Silverbind. It was the last western bastion below the river, excepting Hellin Daimiel and High Crag. Simballawein, Dunno Scuttari, Libiannin, and even Itaskian Portsmouth, had fallen during the winter.

The wizard shrugged. "When they're ready."

For months the armies had stared at one another, waiting. Bragi didn't like it. If Badalamen didn't move soon, Ragnarson's last hope of victory would perish. Each day the opening of the Savernake Gap drew closer. Marco said hordes of reinforcements were gathering at Gog-Ahlan. Shinsan's new masters were stripping their vastly expanded empire of every soldier.

Ragnarson also feared an early thrust through Hammad al Nakir. There were good passes near Throyes. The route was but a few hundred miles longer, though through desert. Megelin couldn't thwart the maneuver.

Megelin had taken Al Rhemish and declared himself King. But El Murid had escaped to the south desert, round Sebil el Sebil, where his movement had originated. He would keep making mischief. Yasmid remained in his hands.

"We've got to get him going," Ragnarson growled, kicking a merlon.

Visigodred laid a gentle hand on his arm. "Easy, my friend. You're killing yourself with caring. And the augeries. Consider the augeries."

The wizards spent hours over divinations and could produce nothing definite. Their predictions sounded like the child's game of knife, paper, and rock. Knife cuts paper, paper wraps rock,

rock beats knife. Every interpretation caused heated, inconclusive arguments among the diviners. Identical arguments raged amongst the Tervola.

Factions in each command insisted any attack would, like rock, knife, or paper, encounter its overpowering counter.

Drums throbbed. Their basso profundo was so old it bothered no one any longer. Several legions left Badalamen's encampment, making their daily maneuver toward Southtown.

It had been the coldest and snowiest winter in memory. Neither side had accomplished much. Each had weathered it. Shinsan had the force to seize supplies from the conquered peoples. Ragnarson's army had Itaskia's wealth and food reserves behind it. Badalamen had tried two desultory thrusts up the Silverbind, toward fords which would permit him to cross and attack toward Itaskia the City from the northeast. Lord Harteobben, his knights, and the armies of Prost Kamenets, Dvar, and Iwa Skolovda, had crushed those threats.

Itaskia's fate would be decided before her capital, by whether or not Badalamen could seize the Great Bridge.

The structure was one of the architectural wonders of the world. It spanned three hundred yards of deep river, arching to permit passage of ships to Itaskia's naval yards, established upriver long before bridge construction began. Construction had taken eighty-eight years, and had cost eleven hundred lives, mostly workmen drowned in collapsed caissons. Engineers and architects had declared the task impossible beforehand. Only the obsession of Mad King Lynntel, who had ruled Itaskia during the first fifty-three construction years, had kept the project going till it had looked completable.

Despite a barbarian upbringing, Ragnarson cringed when he thought he might have to destroy the wonder.

The possibility had stirred bitter arguments for months, dwarfing the debate over supreme command. *That* had ceased when Varthlokkur had declared Ragnarson generalissimo. Nobody had argued with the slayer of Ilkazar.

The Great Bridge touched every Itaskian's life. Its economic value was incalculable.

Economics weren't Bragi's forte. He admired the bridge for its grandeur, beauty, and because it represented the concretization of the dream of The Mad Builder and his generation.

There were few sins in Bragi's world-view. He felt destroying the Great Bridge would be one.

His had been a lonely winter. He had seen little of his friends.
Even Ragnar had been away most of the time, dogging,
hero-worshiping, Hakes Blittschau. Haaken Bragi seldom saw,
though his brother roomed just two blocks away. Gjerdrum
came more than most, often slighting his duties. Michael, Aral,
Valther, and Mist had disappeared, pursuing some mysterious
mission at Varthlokkur's behest. Few others had survived.

Bragi spent his time with the Itaskian General Staff,
aristocrats who considered him down a yard of nose. They
acquiesced to his command only because it was King Tennys'
will.

They were above petty obstructionism, for which Bragi was
grateful. They were professionals meeting a crisis. They devoted
their energies to overcoming it. Their cooperation, though
grudging, was worth battalions.

Varthlokkur sensed Bragi's alienation. A wizard, usually
Visigodred, accompanied him everywhere, always providing a
sympathetic ear. Ragnarson and Visigodred grew closer. Even
pyrotechnic Marco acknowledged their relationship by according Bragi a grudging respect.

"Damn, I wish it would start," Bragi murmured. It was an
oft-expressed sentiment. Even action leading to defeat seemed
preferable to waiting. Plans and contingency plans had been
carried to their limits. There was nothing more to occupy a
lonely mind—except bitter memories.

His emotional lows outnumbered highs, and had since his
return from Argon. Without Elana he couldn't be positive.
Nothing could jack his spirits, get his emotions blazing.

Too, his children, and Ragnar's wife, were still in Kavelin. He
couldn't stop brooding about that. They were hostages to
Fate. . . .

Badalamen he found puzzling. On the Scarlotti the man had
kept several threats looming. Here he seemed to be doing
nothing—and the Brotherhood watched closely.

"He's not loafing," Ragnarson declared. "But what's he up
to?"

Again he wondered about his children. He had had no news.
Were they alive? Had they been captured? Would they be used
against him?

His Kaveliner soldiers had had no news either. They were a
glum, brooding lot.

Radeachar and Marco seldom brought pleasant tidings from

the south, save that Reskird and High Crag remained
unvanquished. Reskird couldn't be reached because of patrol-
ling dragons.

Winter had been hard in the occupied kingdoms. . . .

A roar jerked his attention to the wall a quarter-mile
eastward. "What the . . . ?" A huge cloud of dust reached for the
sun.

Another roar rose behind him. He spun, saw a section of wall
collapsing, flinging into shallow snow.

"Miners!" he gasped. "Trumpets! Alert! Visigodred. . . ."

The thin old wizard was in full career already. Bragi's shouts
were drowned by a change in the song of the drums. More
sections collapsed. Friendly horns screamed, "To arms!"

There were no civilians in Southtown. Its quickly busy streets
contained only soldiers.

The maneuvering legions rushed toward the fortress.

Ragnarson's face turned grim. Badalamen had surprised him
again. But what sane man would have sapped tunnels that long?
How could he believe it would go undetected? How *had* he
managed it?

Sections of wall kept crumbling.

"Too many breeches," Bragi muttered. More legions
double-timed toward Southtown. A glow grew over Shinsan's
camp. Bragi smiled. Sorcery. He had a surprise for Badalamen
too.

The first legionnaires hit the rubbled gaps. Arrows flew. The
world's best soldiers were in for a fight this time. They were
about to meet the soul of Itaskia's army, bowmen who bragged
that they could nail gnats on the wing at two hundred yards. In
the streets they would face the Iwa Skolovdan pikes who had
dismayed El Murid's riders during those wars, and a host of
crazy killers from Ragnarson's Trolledyngjan homeland,
overpowering in their fearlessness and barbarian strength. They
were Tennys's praetorians, selected for size, skill, and berserker
battle style.

Bragi smiled tightly. His defense was reacting calmly and
well. Rooftop bowmen made deathtraps of the gaps in the wall.

Yet he was about to be cut off.

A sound like the moan of a world dying rose from the enemy
camp. The glow became blinding. Bragi ran.

Something whined overhead. He glimpsed the Unborn
whipping southward.

He saw little after that. The invaders forced a band of defenders back upon him. He escaped that pocket only to become trapped in a bigger one.

Badalamen's sappers hadn't ended their tunnels at the wall. They had driven on into deep basements.

"Treason," Ragnarson muttered. "Can't ever root it out." Somebody had done the surveying. . . .

Southtown decayed into chaos. Ragnarson just couldn't reach his headquarters. His rage grew. He *knew* his absence meant defeat.

The southern skyline flared, darkened. Thunders rolled. *Things* rocketed into view and away again. The Tervola were putting on one hell of a show. Varthlokkur's surprise must have fizzled.

He encountered Ragnar near the Barbican, the final fortification defending the Great Bridge.

"Father! You all right?"

"I'll make it." He was an ambulatory blood clot. A lot was his. "What's happening?"

"Covering the evacuation."

"What? Bring in. . . ."

"Too late. Southtown's lost. You're about the last we'll save. They ran two tunnels under the river. They've closed the bridge twice. We reopened it, and closed one tunnel."

"Drown the sons of bitches." He turned. Southtown was burning. Fighting was waning. A ragged band of Trolledyngjans hurried their way, grim of visage. They had been stunned by their enemies. No soldiers should be that good.

"Save what you can. Don't let them take the Barbican." He started for the city. Two soldiers helped. He had lost a lot of blood.

He paused at the bridge's center. The Silverbind was alive with warships, each loaded with Marines. "What now?"

It was the first thing Haaken explained. "They've launched a fleet from Portsmouth, across the Estuary."

"Damn. That bastard don't miss a shot."

Ragnarson quickly counterattacked through the underriver tunnels. Zindahjira and Visigodred spearheaded. Badalamen's assault on the Barbican petered out.

"Your spook-pushers are whipping theirs," observed Lord Hartteoben, recently appointed Itaskian Chief of Staff. "That Unborn. . . . It won't let the Tervola direct their legions."

"We've got to hurt them while we can," Ragnarson averred. His wounds were worse than he would admit. Willpower couldn't keep him going. He collapsed.

Blackfang took charge, stubbornly pursued prepared plans.

The woman wore black. He couldn't see her clearly. She seemed ill-defined, haloed.

"Death," he sighed as she bent. The Dark Lady bringing her fatal kiss.

Her lips moved. "Marshall?" It tumbled down a long, cold tunnel littered with the bones of heroes.

The equalizer, the great leveler, had turned her gaze his way at last. The last narrow escape lay behind him, not ahead. . . .

She wiped his face with a cold, wet cloth.

He saw more clearly.

This was no Angel of Death. She wore the habit of a lay helper of the Sisters of Mercy. The halo came of window light teasing through wild golden hair.

She had to be the daughter of an Itaskian nobleman. No common woman had the resources to so faithfully maintain her youth, to dress richly even in nursing habit.

He guessed her to be thirty. . . . Then realized he was nude, and tendering a half-hearted male salute.

"The battle. . . ." he babbled. "How long have I?"

"Four days." Her glance flicked downward, amused. "The fighting continues. Your Blackfang is too stubborn to lose." She bathed him, enjoying his embarrassment.

"The situation, woman, the situation," he demanded weakly.

She bubbled. "Admiral Stonecipher caught their fleet two days ago. They were seasick. He forced them onto the rocks at Cape Blood. The Coast Watch finished them. A historic victory, Father says. Greater than the Battle of the Isles."

"Ah." He smiled. "That'll warm Badalamen's heart." The fleet from Portsmouth had counted every seaworthy vessel captured along the western littoral. Tens of thousands of easterners must have drowned. "What about Southtown?"

She pushed him down. He was too weak to resist.

"The enemy who crossed over are cut off in Wharf Street South, west of the Bridge. . . ."

"Crossed? To the city?" He tried to rise.

She pushed. "Father says it's still bloody in Southtown, but going our way. When Lord Harteobben attacked from the Fens. . . ."

Bragi's head swam. He hadn't planned any operation from upriver.

"...and half the Tervola are dead. The Power went away for a while. It didn't save them." She made a sign against evil. "That thing.... The Unborn.... They say it melts their bones.... The Power is back. Really, I don't know who'll win. I just know I'm not getting much sleep. The wounded.... It's sickening. So many...."

"We're winning," he whispered, awed. "If Haaken's grabbed the initiative...."

Her fingertips brushed his stomach. Perhaps it was accidental. But Itaskian women, when their menfolks weren't looking, could be damned bold. And he was a celebrity. He had had some interesting offers, offers he wasn't emotionally ready to accept.

He was too weak this time. He drifted off cursing a missed opportunity.

There had been a change. A psyche as well as a body had begun healing.

Her name was Inger. He thought that a delicious irony. His first love had worn that name.

They had been pledged till Trolledyngjan politics had led to conflict between their parents. Inger's father had slain his. And now, so quickly, he was getting involved with a family he had fought from his arrival in Itaskia following the El Murid Wars.

She was a Greyfells, of a branch that had remained neutral in the Dukes of Greyfells's periodic assays at seizing the Itaskian throne. One of those Ragnarson himself had thwarted through the expedient of assassination. His arranging the murder had sent him flying to Kavelin....

That Duke had been Inger's father's eldest brother.

It's a bloody strange world, he thought, lying beside her, concern about the war briefly forgotten.

Possibly there was a more efficacious therapy, but neither Wachtel, Visigodred, nor Varthlokkur could name it. A week of Inger wrought miracles.

Ragnarson even stopped suffering from the wounds Mocker had dealt him. He left that hospital renewed, with plans, with a destination, a goal for after-the-war.

He had broken another resolve. Another woman had penetrated his soul.

Only Inger updated him during his convalescence. No one

came for his advice. His pride was bruised—till he heard that Varthlokkur had ordered his isolation. He had, like an athlete, been off his form. The wizard, selfishly, wanted to give him time to find himself.

Haaken managed well enough, both at battering Badalamen and cowing aspirants to supreme command. Adopting Haroun's style, he jabbed from every direction, avoiding haymakers, fading when the enemy turned to fight. In Southtown he succeeded on stubbornness, knowledge of his men, and devotion to Bragi's planning. He, like Bragi, respected the Itaskian bow. Plied from housetops, it gave him mastery of the streets. He used them as killing zones, letting Badalamen commit ever more men to Southtown's capture. He buried the pavement in corpses.

Now, Bragi saw from the Great Bridge, Southtown was so grim even the vultures shied away.

Visigodred's and Zindahjira's tunnel attacks had taken them to the heart of Shinsan's camp. They had started a few fires, then had withdrawn. The damage was more moral than physical.

Attacked from every direction, mundanely and magically, the Tervola were in disarray. Blittschau and Lord Harteobben harried all but the largest foraging parties. They made occasional forays against the main encampment.

The dismay of the Tervola communicated itself to the Pracchia. Badalamen argued that victory couldn't be attained in present circumstances. Soon his superior force would be leagued up in its own camp. Forcing the Great Bridge was plainly impossible. Attempts to outflank it had failed. He urged a staged retreat calculated to draw Ragnarson into the open. There, hopefully, he could be lured into pitched battle and obliterated. Magden Norath backed him.

The bent old man was impatient. He wanted the holocaust now. He demanded another try at the river. Or, if Badalamen had to move, he should take the entire army up the Silverbind, to Prost Kamenets, Dvar, and Iwa Skolovda, depriving Itaskia of her allies, returning south after fording the river's upper reaches.

The Tervola refused. They wanted to escape Varthlokkur's fury long enough to develop a counter to the Unborn. And Norath wanted to rearm with his own special weapons.

"It's good, Haaken," Ragnarson kept saying. "The only sane course."

"You'd think so. You did the planning."

"The trouble with nibbling is we have to finish before the Gap opens."

"How?" Ragnar demanded. "He'll treat us like a stepchild if we try to take him heads up."

Despite Badalamen's severe losses recently, that remained immutable. Shinsan couldn't be beaten on the battlefield.

Quiet, gentle, loving Visigodred offered an answer.

It was disgusting. It turned Bragi's stomach.

Visigodred said, "Remember when Duke Greyfells brought the plague from Hellin Daimiel? With the ships filled with rats?"

Ragnarson remembered. He, Haroun, and Mocker had foiled that cunning play for Itaskia's throne and had won the eternal gratitude and indulgence of the Itaskian War Ministry.

Volunteers returned to the fetor and horror of Southtown, trapping rats. Radeachar scattered them through the enemy camp.

The inconclusive fighting continued. Bragi applied more pressure, trying to keep the legions crowded so plague would spread swiftly if it got started.

Only sorcery could stop the disease.

Could Varthlokkur protect his allies? Plague ignored artificialities like national allegiance. Itaskia, packed with refugees and soldiers, made fertile disease ground.

The wizard didn't know.

Days passed. Then Badalamen suddenly came alive. He narrowly missed luring Lord Harteobben to his destruction near Driscol Fens. Later the same day Hakes Blittschau rode into an ambush Marco had missed seeing from above. While they licked their wounds, Badalamen moved.

Nighttime. Ragnarson galloped across the Great Bridge, answering Visigodred's summons. The wizard was directing the cleansing of Southtown.

He showed Bragi a southern horizon aflame.

Badalamen had won his argument with the bent man.

"What's happening?" Ragnarson demanded.

"They're pulling out. He summoned his dragons at dusk, fired everything."

"Marco. Radeachar. Where are they?"

"Staying alive."

The dragons had rehearsed handling the two. Marco was impotent against their ganging tactics. He remained grounded. The Unborn could go up, but under pressure could accomplish nothing.

Dawn came. Still the fires raged. Forests, fields, Shinsan's camp. The dragons kept them burning.

A lone masked horseman waited near the empty camp. The bones of burned corpses lay heaped behind him. He bore a herald's pennon.

"Looks like plague got some," Ragnarson observed. "Who is he?"

"Ko Feng," Varthlokkur replied. Jeweled eyes tracked them coldly. "Easy. He won't try anything under the pennon."

"A message?" Ragnarson asked.

"Doubtlessly."

Feng said nothing. He dipped his pennon staff till it pointed at Bragi's heart. Ragnarson removed the note. Feng rode stiffly into a narrow avenue through the flames.

"What is it, Father?" Ragnar asked.

"Personal message from Badalamen." Gaze distant, he tucked it inside his shirt.

Another meeting. A reckoning. An end. Softly, gentlemanly, dreadfully, Badalamen promised. Kings on the chessboard, Badalamen said. Played like pawns. Endgame approaching.

"Beyond the fire...." Ragnarson murmured, looking southward. Then he turned and hurried toward the city.

An army had to march.

Even in retreating Badalamen had surprised him. He would get a week's lead from this....

It would be a bittersweet week, he thought, filled with impassioned good-byes.

His thing with Inger was getting serious.

THIRTY-FOUR: Road to Palmisano

"Goddamnit, lemme alone!" Kildragon snarled. He pulled his blanket over his head.

The cold, thin fingers kept shaking him.

"Prataxis, I'm gonna cut you."

"Sir?"

Reskird surrendered, sat up. His head spun. His gut tried to empty itself again. It had been a hard night. A lot of wine had gone down. He fumbled with his clothing. "I said don't bother me for anything but the end of the world."

"It's not that." But it was earth-shaking.

"They *are* pulling out," Reskird whispered, awed. He hadn't believed Derel. The sun hadn't yet risen and already the besiegers were moving. Engines and siegeworks burned behind them. A rearguard awaited the inevitable reconnaissance-in-force.

"Got to be a trick," Kildragon muttered. That Shinsan should give up, and liberate him from the interminable political hassle of this walled Hell, seemed too good to be true.

A dragon glided lazily overhead. It was a reminder that Shinsan wasn't departing in defeat.

"Something happened up north," Prataxis reasoned.

"What was your first clue?"

There had been no communication with Itaskia since the fall of Portsmouth. Marco had, occasionally, tried to, and had failed to, penetrate the dragon screen. The Unborn, apparently, wasn't doing courier duty.

"We better get moving," Kildragon sighed. "Bragi will need us. Tell the Regents they can join us—if they'll stop fussing about money long enough to give the orders."

Kildragon had spent eons listening to complaints about the
cost of defending the city.

Ragnarson sent a few companies across the Scarlotti. They
met no resistance. Light horse scouts followed.

"I don't understand him," he told Haaken. "Why didn't he try
to stop us here?"

Badalamen served the Pracchia. And the Pracchia were
divided. Receiving conflicting orders from the old man and
Norath, Badalamen could do nothing adequately. Each failure
deepened the split between his masters.

The once invincible army of Shinsan now twitched and
jerked like a beheaded man.

"Palmisano," Ragnarson mused, finger on a map. There was
a fateful feel to the name. It sent chills down his spine.

The Pracchia closed ranks temporarily. Badalamen turned to
fight.

Palmisano, in Cardine, lay close to the Scarlotti. The
survivors of thirty legions waited there, an ebony blanket on a
rolling countryside. Tens of thousands of steppe riders,
Argonese, and Throyens guarded river-girdled flanks.

"We have to go to him this time," Ragnarson muttered. He
had scouted the region. The prospects didn't look favorable.

He didn't need Badalamen's letter to tell him this would be
their last meeting. He didn't need the prophecies of Varthlokkur
and his cohorts. He knew it in his bones. The winner-take-all
was coming. This would be the *götterdämmerung* for Bragi
Ragnarson or the born general. One war chieftain wouldn't
leave this stage....

He had little hope for himself.

Just when he had found new reason to live.

Each morning the armies stared at one another across the
ruins of Palmisano. The captains, generals, and kings with
Ragnarson howled at the delay. Badalamen's incoming
occupation forces swelled his army. The snows in the Savernake
Gap were melting.

Two quieter voices counseled delay. Varthlokkur and
Visigodred had something up their sleeves.

News came that Reskird was approaching. His ragtag army
had skirmished its way up from Hellin Daimiel, preventing
several thousand foemen from rejoining Badalamen. Ragnarson
and Blackfang rode to meet their friend.

When they returned, next day, the sorcerers were abuzz. Visigodred and Varthlokkur were ready.

Valther, Mist, Trebilcock and Dantice had reappeared.

The council was a convention of Kings and Champions. Twenty-seven monarchs attended. Hawkwind, Lauder and Liakopulos attended. Harteobben and Blittschau, Moor and Berloy, Lo Pinto, Piek, Slaski, Tantamagora, Alacran, Krisco, Selenov.... The list of renowned fighters ran to a hundred names. The old companions, wizards' and Ragnarson's, were all there too. And his son, and Derel Prataxis with the inevitable writing box. And near Iwa Skolovda's King Wieslaw, an esquire, unknown and untried, whose name had puzzled wizards for years.

Varthlokkur announced, "Valther and Mist have returned." He indicated Dantice and Trebilcock. "Protected by these men, they visited the Place of the Thousand Iron Statues."

"Nobody ever got out alive," Zindahjira protested. "I used to send adventurers there. They never came back. The Star Rider himself animated the killer statues."

"The Star Rider came and went at will," Varthlokkur replied.

"Armed with a Pole of Power."

"As were my friends." Varthlokkur smiled gently. "The Monitor of Escalon wasn't lying." He held up the Tear of Mimizan, so bright no one could gaze upon it. His fellows babbled questions.

"It was the supreme test. And now we know. We go into battle perfectly armed."

Ragnarson held his peace. Point, he thought. Do you know how to use it? No. Point. The old man over there does.

Getting him, too, had become an intense personal goal. The man had shaped his life too long. He wanted to settle up on the one-to-one.

"The Tervola who remain," Varthlokkur continued, "can be rendered Powerless. My friends accomplished that. They exceeded the Monitor. We control the thaumaturgic game. But let them tell it."

Michael Trebilcock did the talking. He didn't emblish. They had crossed Shara, the Black Forest, the Mountains of M'Hand, and had hurried to The Place of the Thousand Iron Statues. They had penetrated it, had learned to manipulate the Tear and living statues, had discovered secrets concerning the Star Rider's involvement in the past, then had reversed their course, reaching

Itaskia soon after Ragnarson had begun pursuing Badalamen. Michael skipped dangers, ambushes, perils that would have become an epic on another's tongue. His stage fright compelled brevity. He communicated his belief that they now possessed the ultimate weapon.

Ragnarson shook his head. Softly, "Fools."

The crowd demanded action. They were tired of war. They weren't accustomed to prolonged, year-round campaigns, dragging ever on. The exiles were eager to return home and resume interrupted lives.

Varthlokkur, too, was eager. He had left Nepanthe in Kavelin.

"Not yet," he shouted. "Tomorrow, maybe. We have to plan, to check the augeries. Those legions won't roll over."

Ragnarson nodded grimly. The Tear *might* disarm the Tervola. But soldiers had to be beaten by soldiers. What Power remained to Varthlokkur and the Unborn, through the Winterstorm, would be devoted to the creatures of Magden Norath.

Badalamen had anchored his flanks on a tributary of the Scarlotti and the great river itself, footing a triangle. He couldn't withdraw easily, but neither could he be attacked from behind. Refusing to initiate battle himself, he had repeatedly demonstrated his ability to concentrate superior force at any point Bragi attacked.

Ragnarson knew there would be no finesse in it. The terrain didn't permit that. The armies would slaughter one another till one lost heart.

He and Badalamen were sure which would break. And that, with the pressures received from his masters, was why Badalamen had opted for this battle.

Why he had chosen the imperfect ground of Palmisano remained a mystery, though.

Ragnarson attacked at every point, his probes having revealed no weaknesses. His front ranks were the stolid pikemen of Iwa Skolovda, Dvar, and Prost Kamenets. Behind them were Itaskian bowmen who darkened the sky with their arrows. While the legions crouched beneath shields, suffering few casualties, otherwise unemployed westerners scuttled between pikemen to fill the trench preventing Ragnarson from using his knights. Badalamen's men countered with javelins. It was an innovation. Shinsan seldom used missiles.

Here, there, Badalamen had integrated Argonese and Throyen arbalesters....

Ragnarson's men crossed the ditch several times, and were hurled back.

That was the first day. A draw. Casualties about even. Ultimate point to Badalamen. He was a day nearer the moment when the Savernake Gap opened.

The witch-war was Varthlokkur's. His coven gathered over the Tear and round the Winterstorm, and taught the Tervola new fear.

The bent old man could have countered with his own Pole. He didn't. His situation wasn't so desperate that he was willing to reveal, undeniably, his true identity.

The night was Shinsan's. *Savan dalage* in scores stalked the darkness, trying to reach the Inner Circle and Bragi's commanders. Captains and a wizard died....

Now Bragi knew why Badalamen had chosen Palmisano.

A half-ruined Empire-era fortress crowned a low hill beside the eastern camp. Within it, after coming west, Magden Norath had established new laboratories. From it, now, poured horrors which ripped at the guts of the western army.

The second day was like the first. Men died. Ragnarson probed across both rivers, had both thrusts annihilated. His men filled more of Badalamen's ditch.

Again the night belonged to the *savan dalage*, though Varthlokkur and his circle concentrated on Norath's stronghold instead of the Tervola.

Marco predicted the Gap would be open in eleven days.

The third day Ragnarson sent up mangonels, trebuchets, and ballistae to knock holes in the legion ranks so Itaskian arrows could penetrate the shieldwalls. His sappers and porters finished filling the ditch.

That night the *savan dalage* remained quiet. Ragnarson should have been suspicious.

Next morning he stared across the filled ditch at lines of new cheveaux-de-frise. There could be no cavalry charge into those.

The fringe battles picked up. The bent man threw in his surviving dragons. Norath's creatures, excepting the light-shunning *savan dalage*, swarmed over the cheveaux and hurled themselves against the northern pikes.

"The tenor is changing," Bragi told Haaken. "Tempo's picking up."

Haaken's wild dark hair fluttered in the breeze. "Starting to realize the way the wind's blowing. Their day is over. Them spook-pushers are finally doing some good."

It looked that way. Once Norath's monsters disappeared, Varthlokkur could concentrate on Shinsan's army....

Ragnarson's heavy weapons bombarded the cheveaux with fire bombs. Behind the western lines, esquires and sergeants prepared the war-horses. Above, Radeachar and Marco swooped and weaved in a deadly dance with dragons.

Bragi waved.

"What?"

"There." Ragnarson pointed. Badalamen, too, was observing the action. He waved back.

"Arrogant bastard," Haaken growled.

Bragi chuckled. "Aren't we all?"

Ragnar galloped up. "We'll be ready to charge at about four." He had spent a lot of time, lately, with Hakes Blittschau, enthralled by the life of a knight.

"Too late," Bragi replied. "Not enough light left. Tell them tomorrow morning. But keep up the show."

Badalamen didn't respond. He recognized the possible and impossible.

That night he launched his own attack.

Savan dalage led. As always, panic surrounded their advance. Radeachar swept to the attack. Above, Marco tried to intimidate the remaining dragons. Following the *savan dalage*, unnoticed in the panic, came a column of Shinsan's best.

As Haaken had observed, Badalamen had sniffed the wind. This move was calculated to disrupt Ragnarson's growing advantages.

The attack drove relentlessly toward the hill where the captains and kings maintained their pavilions, and where the war-horses were kept.

Kildragon and Prataxis woke Ragnarson, Reskird shouting, "Night attack! Come on! They're headed this way."

The uproar approached swiftly. Norath had committed everything he had left. Panic rolled across the low hill.

Ragnarson surveyed the night. "Get some torches burning. Fires. More light. We've got to see." And light would turn the *savan dalage*.

Ragnar, Blittschau, and several knights ran past, half-armored, trying to reach the horses. If the enemy scattered those....

"Haaken?" Bragi called. "Where the hell's my brother?"

He looked and looked, couldn't find Haaken anywhere.

Blackfang hadn't been able to sleep. For a time he had watched Varthlokkur work, marveling both at the Winterstorm and Mist, who manipulated some symbols from within the construct. He shook his head sadly. He had never had a woman of his own, just chance-met ladies for a night or a week, their names quickly forgotten. No doubt his own had slipped their minds as quickly.

He had begun feeling the weight of time upon him, his lack of a past. His life he had devoted to helping Bragi build Bragi's dreams. Now he realized he had never spun a dream of his own.

The noise from the front was different tonight. Badalamen was up to something. He rushed toward the clamor, torch in one hand, sword in the other. He didn't fear the *savan dalage*. He had met them before. A torch could hold them at bay till Radeachar arrived.

Badalamen drove through the juncture of Iwa Skolovdan forces with those of Dvar, into the Itaskians behind. Men of all three countries shrieked questions, got no intelligible answers. Some fought one another in their confusion.

A solid, single black column poured through.

Blackfang, through sheer lungpower, assembled company commanders, calmed panic, gave orders, led the counterattack.

Pikemen and arrows. A deadly storm tore at the legions, opening gaps. The Iwa Skolovdans insinuated themselves, broke the unity of the column. Blackfang, howling, brought more men to bear. That part of Shinsan's advance devolved into melee. Haaken, with a woodcutter's axe, inspired those near enough to see. Always, when not shouting other orders, he called for torches and fires.

Forty-five minutes later the gap was gone. The line was secure. He turned his attention to the thousands who had broken through.

The headquarters hill was aflame. It looked bad for its defenders.

Though near exhaustion, Blackfang ran to help his brother.

The *savan dalage* caught him halfway. There were three of

them. He couldn't swing his torch fast enough. He went down cursing his killers.

The dwarf kicked the roc into a screaming, sliding dive. Fear and exhilaration contested for his soul. One dragon side-slipped winging over, the air rippling its wings. They fluttered and cracked like loose tent canvas in a high wind. The monster vanished in the darkness.

"One away," Marco crowed. "Come on, you bastards."

The other two held the turn and took the dive, wingtip to wingtip, precisely, their serpentine necks outthrust like the indicting fingers of doom. They were old and cunning, those two.

The fire and fury of the battlefield expanded swiftly, rocking and spinning as the roc maneuvered. To Marco it seemed someone had hurled him at a living painting of the floor of Hell. The roar swelled. His heart hammered. This was his last chance. A do or die game of chicken. *They* had to pull up first. . . .

They were old and wise and knew every molecule of the wind. They stayed with him. Their wings beat like brazen gongs when they broke their fall.

Marco glimpsed startled faces turned suddenly upward. Screams. A dragon shriek when one pursuer's wingtip dipped too low and snagged a tent top.

"Eee-yah!" Marco screamed over his shoulder. "Let's go, you scaly whoreson. You and me. We got a horse race now." One on one he could outfly the granddaddy dragon of them all.

He didn't see the winged horse quartering in. He didn't see the spear of light.

He felt pain, and an instant of surprise when he realized there was nothing but air beneath him.

The stars tumbled and went out.

Six columns of two thousand men each followed scattered trails, captained by old killers named Rahman, El Senoussi, Beloul. A seventh's path defined their base course.

It was tired, deserted country they rode. The few survivors vanished at the sound of hooves.

The young King had led his tired, grumbling old terrorists through night-march after night-march till, now, they saw dragons scorching the northern sky.

"It's begun," Megelin sighed. He planted his standard and waited for his commanders.

He fell asleep wondering if his gesture had merit, if his father's ghost would approve.

The night stalkers pursued the creature calling himself the Silent, who for centuries had been anything but. He hated light almost as much as they, but in his terror spelled anything to keep them at bay. Balls of flame floated overhead. He flailed about with swords of fire.

The long span of his arrogant bluster was scheduled to end. The Norns had scribbled-in Palmisano as the destination that ended his life-road.

The nearness of *savan dalage* stampeded a herd of war-horses. In the fractional second while they distracted him, Zindahjira died.

The stampeding mounts battered Ragnar. He scuttled beneath a haywagon. It nearly capsized in the equine tide.

The smell of *savan dalage* overrode that of horse fear and manure. Sweat soaked Ragnar's clothing. He had no torch. "Hakes!" He heard Blittschau bellowing, but the Altean didn't hear him. The clang of metal on metal rose against the drumming of hooves.

Shinsan's men had reached the horses.

The last screaming, lathered stallion hurtled past....

Ragnar rose slowly, his palm cold and moist on his sword hilt. A tiger-masked Tervola and three dark soldiers advanced with scarlet swords.

The wagon frame ground into his back....

The western line bent, bowed, withdrew a hundred yards under Badalamen's predawn general attack. But he committed auxiliaries and allies, spending their lives to tire and weaken his foes. They didn't break through. The panic of the night hadn't gotten out of hand.

Ragnarson, having shed his tears, rose from beside his dead. He shook off Reskird's sympathetic hand. "I'm all right." His voice was cold and calm. He glanced at the crown of the hill where, till last night, his headquarters had stood. The surviving attackers were heightening their earthworks.

They had completed their mission. Now they would await relief from their commander.

Visigodred departed the tent concealing the remains of his oldest and dearest antagonist. Mist held him momentarily, whispering. Radeachar had just found Marco.

Like scenes were occurring everywhere. A dozen national ensigns flew with hastily stitched black borders. Death had shown few favorites during her midnight rampage.

Bragi glimpsed a winged horse settling into the remains of the Imperial fortress. He growled, "We begin."

Trumpet voices filed the air. Drums responded. The knights advanced. Their pennons waved bright and bold. Their spirits were high. King Wieslaw of Iwa Skolovda had made a speech to stir the souls of veterans as old as and cynical as Tantamagora and Alacran.

This would be their finest hour, the battle remembered a thousand years. The greatest charge in history.

An infantryman walked at each stirrup. Some were the knights' men. Most were doughty fighters Ragnarson had assigned: Trolledygnjans, Kaveliners, Guildsmen, veteran swordsmen who had been withheld from the front. They were rested and ready.

Aisles opened through the pikes and bows. Arrows darkened the air. Mangonels and trebuchets released.

The Iwa Skolovdan battle pennon dipped, signaling the charge.

How bright their crests and pennons! How bold the gleam of their armor! How brilliant their countless shields! The earth groaned beneath their hooves. The sun itself seemed to quake as the army shouted with a hundred thousand throats.

The drums changed voice as Wieslaw spurred his charger. Lockstep, the men in black marched backward.

Not many pits appeared, but enough to blunt the charge.

"Damn!" Ragnarson growled, watching the gleaming tide break on the black wall, slow, and swirl like paints mixing.

The knights abandoned their lances, flailed with swords or maces. The men who had run at their stirrups guarded the horses.

The bowmen, unable to ply their weapons without killing friends, grabbed swords, axes, hammers, mauls, rushed into the melee.

Bragi had kept no reserve but the pickets round last night's raiders, and the pikemen, who would screen any withdrawal.

From river to river the slaughter stretched, awesome in scale.

"Even the Fall of Tatarian wasn't this bloody," Valther murmured.

Derel Prataxis, without glancing up from his tablet, observed, "Half a million men. The biggest battle ever."

He was wrong, of course, but could be pardoned ignorance of the Nawami Crusades.

"Need to fall back and charge again," Ragnarson grumbled. But there was no way to order it. He could only hope his captains didn't let their enthusiasm override their sense.

Not that time. Wieslaw, Harteobben, and Blittschau extricated themselves, returned to their original lines. The easterners pressed the pikemen hard till the Itaskians again hid the sun behind arrows. Then the knights and stirrup men charged again.

Ragnarson and his party talked little. Grimly, Bragi watched Harteobben and Blittschau, on the wings, begin to be devoured. Only Wieslaw's echelon maintained momentum.

Ragnarson considered fleeing to Dunno Scuttari. He could take ship to Freyland and rally the survivors there. . . . No. Inger wouldn't be there. He had left too many dear ones behind already. His role in this war had been to leave a trail of his beloved. There had to be an end. He would share the fate of his army. He would fulfill the letter of Badalamen's message.

He saw to his weapons. His companions watched nervously, then did likewise. Prataxis rode through camp collecting cooks, mule-skinners, grooms, and the walking wounded.

THIRTY-FIVE: Palmisano: The Guttering

Flame

It seemed he had been chopping at black armor for days. He had trained and trained, but his instructors hadn't told him how arduous it would be. Here, unlike the practice field, he couldn't rest.

"Almost through!" Wieslaw screamed, gesturing with his bloody sword. Only a thin line screened the open ground beyond Shinsan's front.

The esquire glanced back. The hundreds who had followed Wieslaw now numbered but dozens.

The youth redoubled his attack.

The line broke. They were through. Wieslaw cavorted as though the battle itself had been won. His standard bearer galloped to his side. More knights surged through the gap, rallied round, congratulated one another weakly.

The respite lasted but moments. Then a band of steppe riders attacked. While the westerners turned that threat their bolt hole closed behind them.

"Badalamen," said Wieslaw. "We have to plant a sword in the dragon's brain."

The esquire stared across the quarter-mile separating them from the born general. Badalamen's bodyguards had sprung from the sorcerous wombs of the laboratories of Ehelebe. And crowds of Throyens masked them.

Wieslaw assembled his people to charge.

The Throyens put up little fight. In minutes the knights reached the tall, expressionless guards surrounding Badalamen.

Ragnarson cursed as his mount screamed and stumbled. Her hamstrings had been cut. He threw himself clear, smashed a black helmet with his war axe while leaping. He continued hacking with wild, two-handed swings, past pain, rage, and frustration, exploding in a berserk effort to destroy Shinsan single-handedly.

He knew no hope anymore. He just wanted to hurt and hurt until Badalamen couldn't profit from winning.

His companions felt the change. Morning's optimism was becoming afternoon's despair. The invincible legions were, again, meeting their reputation. Soldiers began glancing backward, picking directions to run.

Varthlokkur, too, despaired. He had recognized his antagonist at last. Shinsan, Tervola, Pracchia, Ehelebe, all were smokescreens. Behind them lurked the Old Meddler, the Star Rider. He knew, now, because someone was negating his manipulation of the Tear. Only the other Pole's master could manage that.

The devil had come into the open. He needed anonymity no more.

It seemed but a matter of time till the tide turned and the Power became Shinsan's faithful servant once more. Not even Radeachar, frantically buzzing the old fortress, would help. The Tervola had learned to neutralize the Unborn.

How long? Two hours? Four? No more, certainly.

Varthlokkur watched Mist and longed for Nepanthe.

Four still lived. The esquire. Wieslaw. His standard-bearer. A baronet of Dvar. Bodies carpeted the slope.

Badalamen fought on, alone, surrounded.

The born soldier struck. The esquire fell, a deep wound burning his side. Hooves churned the earth about him. He staggered to his feet. The baronet fell. The standard-bearer cried out, followed. The esquire seized the toppling standard, murmuring, "It can't fall before His Majesty."

Badalamen seemed to strike in slow motion. The youth's thrust with the banner spear seemed even slower.

Wieslaw collapsed. Badalamen, speartip between his ribs, followed. The esquire, Odessa Khomer, fell across both.

A mystery long pursued by sorcerers of both sides consisted of a youth with makeshift weapon. Thus the Fates play tricks when revealing slivers of tomorrow.

Megelin whipped his horse, surged out of the river. Fighting greeted him, but Beloul quickly routed the Argonese pickets. Megelin surveyed the battleground. Nothing barred him from reaching the main contest. Shinsan's encampment appeared undefended. Only the few pickets weren't in the battle line.

He gathered his captains, gave his orders. Wet horsemen, tired-eyed, formed their companies.

"Three hours, Beloul," the young King remarked, glancing at the westering sun.   •

Beloul didn't reply. But he followed. His mind had stretched enough to see the national interest in a defeat of Shinsan.

Their charge swept through the eastern camp and round the hill where the old fortress stood. Megelin and a handful of followers invaded the stronghold. They found nothing, though in a courtyard they so startled a winged horse that it took flight and vanished into the east. Puzzled, Megelin left, led his men against the enemy rear. He swept past the drama of Badalamen and Odessa Khomer only minutes after its completion, and never learned what had happened there.

A centurion informed the Tervola.

Only a dozen survived. Each had pledged himself to Ehelebe in times gone by. The Star Rider had saved each from the Unborn. But command was devolving on unready Aspirants and noncoms.

They repudiated their oaths, reelected Ko Feng commander.

"That's all. We're done here," Feng said. "Though the cause isn't necessarily lost, I propose we withdraw."

The Tervola agreed. Shinsan's destiny could no longer be pursued through the fantasy of Ehelebe. Nor could it without legions which, pushed to win today, might be pushed too far. The army's skeleton had to be salvaged so Shinsan could rebuild against tomorrow.

The bloody mind-fog lifted. For a moment Ragnarson stood amidst the carnage, shield high, axe dragging, puzzled. The pressure had eased. His men had stopped backing up. An army tottering at the brink, already disintegrating, had stiffened unexpectedly. . . .

Or had it?

He caught a hobbling, distraught horse, mounted for the instant needed to discover that Shinsan was disengaging. As always, in good order, evacuating the wounded first, still attacking along a narrow aisle to relieve the force waiting on the hilltop.

Desert-garbed men flew about behind them. The easterners ignored them, having already taught them the cost of getting too close.

The sun was nearing the horizon. In an hour it would be too dark to see....

Bragi swore, shouted, cajoled. His men leaned on their weapons, staring with eyes that had seen too much bloodshed. They didn't care if the foe were vulnerable. He was going. That was enough.

Bragi caught another horse, raged around looking for men who would fight on.

He glimpsed movement near the fortress. Someone with white hair scuttled toward a band of legionnaires. Megelin's riders chased him back inside.

A wild, evil glee captured Bragi's soul. He walked his mount toward the battered stronghold.

He passed the remains of Badalamen and hardly noticed. A mad little laugh kept bubbling up from deep in his guts.

The bent man watched the barbaric rider cross that field of death as implacably as a glacier. He studied Feng, a mile eastward, directing assembly of the pontoons Badalamen had prepared. He searched the sky. Nowhere did he see his winged steed.

He spat. A potent tool, the Windmjirnerhorn, the Horn of the Star Rider, from which he could conjure almost anything, remained strapped to the beast's back. He was naked to his enemies, defenseless—except for cunning and foresight.

And his Pole.

The rider loomed huge now, subjectively growing larger than life as their confrontation approached.

He scuttled into the fortress's cluttered recesses, through the shambles of Magden Norath's laboratories. What had happened to the Escalonian? The first rat to desert the ship, he thought. No guts. Lived his dreams and fantasies through his creations.

The Fadema, though, remained where he had left her, sitting with his ancient, mindless accomplice.

"Is it over?" she asked.

"Not yet, my lady. But nearly." He smiled, stepped past her to a cluttered shelf, selected one of Norath's scalpels.

"Good. I'm tired of it all."

"You'll rest well." He yanked her head back, cut her throat.

The Old Man frowned.

"The Fates have intervened, old friend. Our holocaust becomes a country fair. Hold this." The Old Man accepted the scalpel. The Star Rider began extinguishing lamps. When one remained he produced his golden token, placed it over his "third eye."

"The Tervola have decided to cut their losses. I should have known. Their first loyalty will always be to Shinsan. A foul habit. Ah! I can hear *Them*. *They*'re laughing. My predicament amuses *Them*."

He pocketed the medallion. "That'll scare hell out of somebody." He cocked his head, listening. The measured tread of boots echoed from a darkened passage.

"He comes." He selected an unconsecrated kill-dagger from the shelf. "The final scene, old friend."

Varthlokkur, Visigodred, and Mist, only survivors of the Inner Circle, sat, exhausted, watching the Winterstorm. Outside, dull-witted, disarmed, weary, the Unborn bobbed on the breeze, abiding Varthlokkur's command.

Valther burst in. "We've done it!" He was blood-filthy. A battered sword trailed from his hand.

They didn't respond.

He planted himself before them. "Didn't you hear? We've won! They're retreating...."

The Winterstorm exploded.

Valther shrieked once as flames consumed him.

Mist wept quietly, too drained to move.

Visigodred held her, softly observed, "If he hadn't been there...."

"We'd have burned," Varthlokkur said. "It was time. He had been redeemed. The Fates. They weave a mad tapestry.... He was the last Storm King. They had no further use for him." He didn't seem surprised that his enemy, suddenly, was able to overpower his creation.

Ragnarson paused. There was a wrongness about the dimly lighted chamber. Yet the entire fortress had that taint. The evil of Ehelebe?

He entered, knelt by the corpse. "Fadema. Thus he rewarded you." Blood still oozed from her ruined throat. She stared up with startled dead eyes.

Sensing something, Bragi whirled.

The blade slashed his already ruined shirt, turned on his mail. He drove hard with his sword. The old man groaned, clutched his belly, hurtled toward the remaining lamp as if yanked by puppet strings. It broke. In seconds the room was ablaze.

"Burn forever, you bastard." One of those mad chuckles escaped him. "You've hurt me for the last time."

A bone-weary Treblicock met him beside his mount. "Valther's dead," Michael said. "We thought you should know." He described the circumstances.

"So. He got in one last shot. Where's your shadow?"

"Aral? Him and Kildragon went around the sides. In case you came out over there. Why?"

"I think I might need somebody to carry me back."

"Mike!" Dantice's shout penetrated the remaining clamor of the battlefield. "Hurry up!"

They found Dantice kneeling beside a dying man.

"Reskird!" Bragi swore. "Not now. Not here."

"Bragi?" Kildragon gasped.

"I'm here. What happened?"

"My boy. Look out for my boy."

Reskird had a son who was a fledgling Guildsman. Bragi hadn't seen him in years.

"I will, Reskird." He held his friend's hand. "Who was it? What happened?"

The silver dagger had missed Kildragon's heart, but not by much. It had severed the aorta. Reskird gulped something unintelligible, shuddered, went limp in Bragi's arms.

He wept. And, finally, rose to assume command of the fields that were now his. Later Varthlokkur would suggest that Madgen Norath, unaccounted for, owed them a life.

"He was the last," Bragi mused. "None of us are left but me." And, after a while, "Why am I still alive?"

THIRTY-SIX: Home

Feng didn't go peacefully or quietly, with his tail between his legs. He went in his own fashion, in his own time, underscoring the fact that he was leaving by choice, not compulsion. He wouldn't be pushed. In Altea, when the Itaskian became too eager, he gave Lord Harteobben a drubbing that almost panicked the western army. In Kavelin, with Vorgreberg in sight, Feng whirled and dealt the overzealous pursuit ten thousand casualties they need not have suffered.

Ragnarson got the message that time. His captains, though, had trouble digesting it.

Feng was going home. But he could change his mind.

The Gap was open. Bragi put his commanders on short leash. Feng was no Badalamen, but he was Tervola, bitter, unpredictable, and proud. He could still summon that vast army at Gog-Ahlan.

The west had no new armies. Feng had to be let go with his dignity intact.

"Nothing's changed," Prataxis sighed their first night back in Kavelin's capital. "In fact, they've shown a net gain. Everything east of the mountains."

"Uhm," Ragnarson grunted. He had other problems, like learning if his children had survived.

Vorgreberg had been deserted. But as Feng withdrew beyond the eastern boundary of the Siege, people began drifting in. Sad, haggard, emaciated, they came and looked at their homes like visitors to a foreign city. They had no cheers for their liberators, just dull-eyed acceptance of luck that might change again. They were a shattered people.

There were, too, the problems of putting the prostrate nation

318

onto its feet, and of driving Feng *through* the Savernake Gap.

The first faced every nation south of the Silverband.

The latter task Ragnarson surrendered to Lord Harteobben. Derel, he hoped, would manage the economic miracle....

And a miracle it would be. Shinsan now bestrode the trade route which, traditionally, was Kavelin's major economic resource.

It was too much. "I'm going walking, Derel."

Prataxis nodded his understanding. "Later, then."

Bragi had never seen Vorgreberg so barren, so quiet. It remained a ghost city. Dull-eyed returnees flittered about like spooks. How many would come home? How many had survived?

The war had been terrible. Derel guessed five million had lost their lives. Varthlokkur deemed him a screaming optimist. At least that many had been murdered by Badalamen's auxiliaries. The small villages round which western agriculture revolved had been obliterated. Few crops had been sown this spring. The coming winter would be no happier than the past.

"There'll be survivors," Bragi muttered. He kicked a scrap of paper. The wind tumbled it down the street.

From the city wall he stared eastward. Distantly, dragon flames still arced across the night.

He lived.

What would he do with his life? There was Inger, if their hospital romance hadn't died. But what else?

Kavelin.

Still. Always.

He stalked through the lightless city, to the palace, saddled a horse. A sliver of moon rose as he neared the cemetery gate.

He visited the mausoleum first.

Nothing had changed. The Tervola hadn't let their allies loot the dead. He found an old torch, after several tries got it sputtering half-heartedly.

Fiana looked no different. Varthlokkur's art had preserved her perfectly. She still seemed to be asleep, ready to rise if Bragi spoke the right words. He knelt there a long time, whispering, then rose, assured his service to Kavelin hadn't ended.

He would persist. Even if it cost him Inger.

He almost skipped visiting Elana's grave. The pain was greater than ever, for he had failed abominably at the one thing she would have demanded: that he care for the children.

The torch struggled to survive the eastern wind. It was, he thought, like the west itself. If the wind picked up....

He almost missed them in the weak light.

The flowers on Elana's grave were, perhaps, four days old. Just old enough to have been placed there as Feng came over the horizon.

"Ha!" he screamed into the wind. "Goddamned! Ha-ha!" He hurled the torch into the air, watched it spin lazily and plunge to earth, refusing to die despite dwindling to a single spark. He grabbed it up and, laughing, jogged to his horse. Like a madman, by moonlight, torch overhead, he galloped toward Vorgreberg.

They arrived two days later. Gerda Haas, Nepanthe, Ragnar's wife, and all his little ones. They had been through Hell. They looked it. But they had grown. Gerda told him, "The Marena Dimura were with us. Even the Tervola couldn't find us."

Ragnarson bowed to the chieftain who had brought them, an old ally from civil war days. "I'm forever in your debt," he told the man in Marena Dimura. "What's mine is yours." He spoke the language poorly, but his attempt impressed the old man.

"It is I who am honored, Lord," he replied. In Wesson. "I have been permitted to guard the Marshall's hearth."

There was much in the exchange that went unspoken. Their use of unfamiliar tongues reaffirmed the bond of the forest people to the throne, a loyalty adopted during the civil war.

"No. No honor. The imposition of a man unable to care for his own."

"Nay, Lord. The Marshall has many children, of the peoples. It was no dishonor needing help with the few when he cared for so many."

Bragi peered at Prataxis. Had Derel staged this?

The Marena Dimura's remarks were a taste of things to come. Despite Bragi's conviction of his incompetent conduct of the war, he became a hero. Those he considered the real architects of victory went unheralded. People and wizards alike preferred it that way.

The real surprise arrived ten days after Vorgreberg's liberation.

He was at home in Lieneke Lane, busting his tail helping clean the place, wondering how Inger would respond to his message. Yes? No? Gjerdrum brought a summons from the

Thing. Bragi hugged his children, and grandson (whom his daughter-in-law Kristen had named Bragi), and went.

Kristen had soared in his regard. It was she who had maintained her husband's family graves. She, Nepanthe said, had been strong for all of them, optimistic in the darkest moments. She had lost her husband and parents and still could smile at her father-in-law as he departed.

He met Prataxis outside the warehouse parliament. "Damned Nordmen trying to pull something already?" he snarled. "I'll kick the crap out of the whole damned Estates right now." The noble party had begun calling itself The Estates during the exile.

"Not yet." Prataxis gave Gjerdrum a secretive smile. "I think it's news from the Gap."

"Aha! Harteobben grabbed Maisak. Good! Good!" He strode inside, took a seat on the rostrum.

The Thing was a raggedy-assed comic imitation of a parliament now. Only thirty-six delegates were on hand. Most of those were self-appointed veterans. But it would do till some structure could be created for Kavelin's remains.

Assuming the chair, Derel immediately recognized Baron Hardle of Sendentin.

Ragnarson loathed Sendentin. He had a big mouth, and had been involved in every attempt to weaken the Crown since the civil war. Yet Bragi grudgingly respected him. He had served uncomplainingly against Badalamen, and had been a doughty fighter. In the crunch he had stuck to Kavelin's traditions and had closed ranks against the common enemy.

"News has come from Maisak," the Baron announced. "The Dread Empire has abandoned the stronghold. Not one enemy occupies one square foot of the Fatherland. The war is over."

Ragnarson wanted to protest. The conflict could never end while the Tervola existed. But he held his peace. Hardle's remarks had drawn unanimous applause.

Hardle continued, "I suggest we return to the task we faced before the invasion. We need a King. A man able to make decisions and stick to them. The near future will be harrowing. All parties, all classes, all interests, *must* repudiate the politics of divisiveness. Or perish. We need a leader who understands us, our strength and our weakness. He must be fair, patient, and intolerant of threats to Kavelin's survival."

Bragi whispered, "Derel, they wanted me to hear self-serving

Nordmen campaign speeches?" Hardle, when wound up, could talk interminably.

Hardle spent an hour describing Kavelin's future King. Then, "The Estates enter a consensus proposition: that the Regency be declared void and the Regent proclaimed King."

Bragi's dumbfoundment persisted while the Wesson party seconded the proposal.

"Hold it!" he bellowed. He realized that all this had been orchestrated. "Derel.... Gjerdrum...."

Both feigned surprise. "Don't look at me," said Prataxis. "It's their idea."

"How much help did they have coming up with it?" He glared at Varthlokkur, who lurked in the shadows, smiling smugly.

The Siluro and Marena Dimura minorities accepted the proposal too.

"I don't want the aggravation!" Bragi shouted an hour later, having exhausted argument. "With no war to keep you out of mischief you'd drive me crazy in a month."

He now suspected the motives of The Estates. A King was more constrained by law and custom than a Regent.

They out-stubborned him. They were planning the coronation before he yielded. His election, Derel insisted, would be lent legitimacy by the attendance of the Kings with the western army.

"You know," he told Prataxis, "Haaken never wanted to come south. He wanted to fight the Pretender. If I'd known leaving would lead to this, I would've stayed."

Prataxis grinned. "I doubt it. Kavelin was always your destiny."

Kavelin. Always Kavelin. Damnable, demanding little Kavelin.

A sweating courier rushed in. He bore Inger's response. Bragi read it, said, "All right. You've got me. Gods help us all."

In his rags, with sores disfiguring his hands and face, the bent man didn't stand out. He was but one of tattered thousands lining the avenue. The King's Own Horse Guards pranced past, followed by Gjerdrum Eanredson, the new Marshall, then the Vorgrebergers.

The King and his wife approached. The Royal carriage wasn't much. Fiana's hearse converted. Kavelin had few resources to waste.

The old man hobbled away on feet tortured by hundreds of

miles. He stared at the flagstones, hoped he wouldn't catch
Varthlokkur's eye.

He squeezed the Tear shape in his pocket.

The wizard had been singularly careless, leaving it unat-
tended.

But that was the nature of the Poles. To be forgotten. His
own was the same.

Varthlokkur might not check on it for years.

He hobbled eastward, gripping the Tear with one hand,
tumbling his gold medallion with the other. An hour outside
Vorgreberg he began humming. He had had setbacks before.
This one hadn't been so terrible after all. The Nawami Crusades
had gone worse.

There were countless tomorrows in his sentence without end.

Fantasy from Ace fanciful and fantastic!